UNDAUNTED

UNDAUNTED

KAT FALLS

SCHOLASTIC PRESS

NEW YORK

Library of Congress Cataloging-in-Publication Data available

ISBN 978-0-545-37102-5

10 9 8 7 6 5 4 3 2 1   19 20 21 22 23

Printed in the U.S.A.   23
First edition, April 2019

Book design by Christopher Stengel

*For the readers who
waited — thank you!*

· ONE ·

"Everyone lies. Everyone. The people in charge. The teachers and historians. They've been lying to you for years. But I'm going to tell you the truth. Even better, I'm going to show you . . . now. With this video.

"We all know that a new virus broke out on the east coast of America twenty years ago — the Ferae Naturae virus. And we all know that it killed millions of people within weeks, and then the healthy people abandoned the sick. Utterly and completely. The healthy fled to the west and turned the Mississippi River into one long quarantine line. Then came the wall — the Titan wall — built by the very corporation that created the virus. Titan's CEO called the wall 'an act of reparation.' Whatever you call it, the wall gets the job done. It cuts us off so completely, we forget that half our country even exists — the eastern half. Most people try to, anyway. But not me . . .

"I always wanted to know what lay beyond the wall in the area we now call the Feral Zone. And then, six months ago, I found out — I learned the truth. Last fall, I crossed the quarantine line and spent three days in the Feral Zone. I wasn't supposed to be there, let alone record what I saw, but I did. And I edited that footage into a video — the one you're watching now.

"You see, the Ferae virus didn't wipe out everyone in the east like we were told. They lied to us. The government. The Titan Corporation. Everyone in a position to know . . . lied. The truth is that, over time, the virus adapted so that it didn't kill its human host anymore. Now the Ferae virus does exactly what it was created to do: transfer DNA from one species into another. Animal DNA. So now, when you get infected with Ferae, you don't die. No, you just mutate into a horrifying human-animal mash-up. And that is what is living just beyond the Titan wall — these hybrids that the Titan Corporation calls manimals. Lots and lots of manimals. And here's the truly terrifying part: They all go feral . . . eventually.

"That's the truth, plain and simple. And now you've seen it with your own eyes. I kept this video short so you can download it fast, watch it fast, and forward it to everyone you know — fast — before the truth disappears from view . . . again."

When the video ended and the music faded out, my best friend, Anna, pried her hand from her mouth — she'd clapped it there thirty seconds in — and looked up from my computer tablet. "I hate you!"

I blinked. She actually sounded like she meant it, and Anna wasn't the dramatic type. "Why? You've seen my footage before," I said.

"Not edited!" She flung the tablet onto my mattress and glared. "I've been sleeping with a kitchen knife under my pillow for months now because of your stupid footage. And then you go and turn it into a *story*? What's wrong with you?"

"So, seeing what's over there . . . that makes you mad?"

"No, Lane," she seethed, turning my name into an accusation. "I'm mad at *you* for showing me that real-life monsters live right. Over. There." She jabbed a finger at my bedroom window with its view of the looming monstrosity that was the Titan wall. "And those poor characters —"

"They're not cha —"

"Shut *up!*" She rose from the bed. "I don't want to hear that those people are real, because then all the awful things that happened to them *actually* happened. I don't want to know that. Who wants to know that?"

I got where she was coming from. Editing my footage had forced me to relive my time in the Feral Zone, and that had come at a cost — headaches, anxiety, nightmares, and a general inability to fit into my previous life. Once my dad had recovered from his many leg surgeries, he'd taken me to a therapist with the warning that I couldn't be totally honest about where I'd been and what had happened to me. Crossing the quarantine line was illegal. Very, very illegal — as in, a death-sentence offense. So, I'd let the therapist assume that the manimals in my story were human. The main predator in my story became a stalker, though I was still the prey. Big surprise, her diagnosis was that I was suffering from PTSD, something I'd already suspected. But my dad agreed that I couldn't continue to see her. Eventually I would've slipped up and said *feral* instead of *man-eating psycho killer*, and then she'd have thought I was really going off the deep end.

So I found my own way to deal with what I'd experienced. I began to edit my footage. Sometimes editing seemed to make my symptoms worse, but eventually it didn't matter. I had a new goal and I'd been willing to take the jangled nerves and nightmares if my video told the truth about what lay beyond the wall. I knew the final version affected me like a punch in the gut, but then, I'd lived it. I'd been desperate to know if it had the same emotional impact on someone who hadn't been there. And now I had my answer.

I grinned. "Thank you!"

Anna's dark eyes narrowed. "I just said I hate you."

"I know." My smile grew exponentially. "That means I got you to care about the manimals."

"*One.* You got me to care about *one* manimal. That little ape. The rest are horrifying." Her spring-loaded curls quivered as she feigned a shudder. Or maybe her shudder wasn't so feigned. "You can't post this, Lane," she said, turning dead serious. "You know that, right?"

"I know I *shouldn't* post it."

"Do you have a death wish?" she demanded. "The biohaz agents aren't going to care that you're only seventeen."

She lurched for the computer tablet, but I got there first. Jumpy nerves had their perks. Clasping the tablet to my chest, I scrambled across the bare mattress. My bedding had been put into storage, along with everything else in our apartment. For now, according to my dad; forever, according to me.

Anna rounded the foot of the bed. "If you post that video, the jumpsuits will put you in front of a firing squad!"

"Only if they catch me — and they won't. Biohaz agents can't go where I'm going."

"But then you can't come back. Ever." She pointed at the window again. "You'll be stuck over there with those monsters. You'll be stuck with . . . with . . ." Leaning into me, she scrolled back through the video until she found the image she wanted. "*Him.*"

4

With a tap, she enlarged the frame. A feline face filled the screen and hollowed out my chest.

Copper eyes glowed up at me, hot and hungry. Black lips pulled back to reveal fangs as thick as my finger. Half human, half beast, all nightmare. *Chorda*. The tiger-king of Chicago, who'd wanted to rip out my heart and eat it because he'd believed it would make him human again. Sometimes seeing a clip of him would make my heart thrash like a wounded bird trying to take flight. But not now. I brought in a slow breath. I was past this now. Editing the scenes with Chorda had been unbelievably awful. For weeks, my dad had worried about me, but I couldn't explain why I was such a wreck — couldn't tell him how I stayed up late at night, working on my video, because I couldn't tell him about my video at all. He never would've let me risk arrest and execution for "compromising national security." Heck, he wouldn't have let me risk my mental health. And editing Chorda's footage had made me crazy; even I had to admit it.

"He's dead," I whispered, more for myself than for Anna. She didn't need to be convinced of that fact, but I did. Every night after waking from yet another dream about being eaten alive.

"There are others like him," she argued.

"Not like *him*."

"Right," she conceded. "They could be worse."

Not possible. On the screen, Chorda's fangs glistened with saliva — saliva that teemed with the Ferae virus. My fingers went numb at the thought without so much as a prickle of warning. Again. The tablet slipped from my hands into my lap.

Anna didn't notice. Her eyes were on my face. "Please don't post it."

"I have to. It's not okay."

"There's a lot here that's not okay." She circled her palm over the screen. "Starting with '*tiger-man.*'"

"I mean the lies." I shook the feeling back into my hands and scrolled past Chorda's starved glare. "The Titan Corporation says there's nothing over there but infected wildlife, and the government just goes along with it. People need to know the truth."

"Forget people. I care about *you*." Anna stilled my fingers with a touch. "You don't have to go just because your dad took a job over there. Stay here with me. My parents love you."

Her words warmed me the way they did every time she made the offer — which had been every day this month — but my answer stayed the same: Thanks, but no.

Chairman Prejean had agreed to set my dad up in Moline, on the other side of the wall, and provide us with monthly supplies — including the inhibitor that slowed the rate of mutation in those infected with Ferae — if Dad fetched blood samples from people infected with the missing virus strains. The Titan scientists needed samples of all fifty in order to create a vaccine. And I'd do anything I could to help that vaccine become a reality.

Last fall, I'd come back to my safe indoor life in Davenport, Iowa, only to discover that my nerves had gotten calibrated for the Feral Zone, and nothing I did seemed to lower the setting. I simply didn't feel at home in the West anymore. As scared as I'd been in the zone, at least I'd felt alive in a way that wasn't possible on this side of the wall, with our virtual schools and adult population of germaphobic plague survivors.

But my own discomfort wasn't the main reason I wanted to return east. I'd powered through my online classes and taken my GED months ahead of schedule because I needed to get back to *him*. Rafe. I needed to know that he was okay after all that had happened. Hearing it secondhand wouldn't reassure me. Rafe was too good a liar. He'd tell anyone who asked that he was fine. He'd even convince himself of it. But one look into his eyes and I'd know the truth. Maybe then he'd stop showing up in my dreams. Stop reminding me of my promise — the one I wished I hadn't made.

Anna entwined her fingers with mine. "We'll never see each other again."

"Of course we will. The quarantine won't last forever."

"Says who?"

"Me," I said lightly. "And if it does, I'll just have to sneak back for a visit."

She smiled halfheartedly.

"I need to get going. The patrol 'copter is waiting for us on the roof." I zipped my duffel bag. Stuffed as it was, it still felt as if I hadn't brought enough. There were so many things that I'd have to learn to live without, starting with my pets. I'd found good homes for every one of them, but my heart still felt like I'd dropped it down a disposal. "Promise you'll give Gulliver lots of love?"

"Please," she scoffed. "I didn't learn how to give that cat an insulin shot for nothing."

"I'm going to miss you more than anything," I admitted softly.

"More than iced lattes?"

"More than hand sanitizer." I hugged her tightly, and she squeezed back just as hard.

"I hate this," she said into my hair. "Now I'll have to enlist in the line patrol just to see you."

I laughed as I let her go. "You'd make such a great line guard. I can just see you stomping along the river bank, hunting down quarantine breakers . . ."

"Forget it," she said with a grimace. "Now that I know those quarantine breakers have fur and fangs, I'm moving to Seattle first chance I get. As far from the wall as possible."

My smile fell away. "Are you sorry I told you about the zone?"

"No! Well, you could've left out that chimpacabras are real. But otherwise, I'm glad you told me." She paused, realizing what she'd just admitted, and heaved a sigh. "Okay. You're right. People do need to know what's over there." She plucked my tablet from the bed. "Go ahead. Put it out there for the world to see." She pushed the computer into my hands and headed for the door. "I'll distract your dad."

Good idea. If my father knew what I was about to do, he'd have an aneurism.

With a shaky breath, I signed onto a social media site, one used mostly by teens. It was after midnight, so hopefully my video would fly under the radar. Maybe get a couple dozen hits before morning and maybe get reposted on other sites before the authorities caught on and scrubbed it from the Web forever.

I'd unpinned a grenade by making this video. Now all I had to do was throw it. I gritted my teeth and hit post. Maybe my video would explode onto the Web and then set off a ripple of aftershocks. Or maybe my so-called grenade would have no impact at all. Either way, I'd never know, because after tonight, I would be beyond reach.

Beyond the wall.

· TWO ·

The hovercopter surged into the air, and my stomach plummeted — and not just because we were gaining altitude quickly to clear the seven-hundred-foot monolith that was the Titan wall. My need to post the video had been an itch that I'd finally scratched — thoroughly — though I probably shouldn't have.

As if he felt my growing unease, my dad shifted to face me, the shrinking lights of Davenport reflected in his glasses. He spoke into the mic of his headset. "We can still go back."

No, actually, we couldn't. Not unless I wanted to be arrested for compromising national security. Now was probably the moment to tell him about the video, but I couldn't. He was so excited to see Hagen, his girlfriend, who lived in Moline. I couldn't ruin this for him. I shook my head and reached out to tug his fingers the way I had when I was little.

I said into my mic, "I know too much to live in the West." And it was true. Anna was the only person I'd confided in about my time in the zone. She'd caught me on a bad night and refused to take *I'm fine* as an answer when I clearly wasn't and hadn't been for weeks. I'd been the opposite of fine — anxious and irritable and exhausted from watching every word I uttered. I couldn't mention what I'd seen or even hint at why I was such a jittery mess — Director Spurling had made that clear the day she'd come to my dad's hospital room. He'd been knocked out on painkillers, but I'd gotten her message loud and clear.

My dad looked past me, out the hovercopter window, and sighed. He clearly felt guilty about bringing me with him, but he would have felt just as guilty leaving me behind. Last year when I'd first met Dr. Solis, he'd told me about his own father, how his father's guilt for leaving Cuba had become his own. I wasn't about to let that happen to me. What was driving me back to the zone wasn't my father's guilt but my own.

"And I have to find Rafe," I added.

My dad nodded, his expression reflecting my worry.

A moment from my footage played in my head on a loop: Rafe leaping off the carousel canopy into the darkness and chaos of Chicago as the manimals took over the city. I should've hooked my arm through his before he could jump, or dodged the lionesses and tried harder to follow him. Logic told me I never would have found him, and yet these failures had worn a raw place in my heart that logic couldn't touch. Dr. Solis had said, "Reason doesn't do much for heartbreak," and now I knew exactly what he meant.

The hovercopter finally rose over the lip of the Titan wall, and the pilot hung there, waiting for the go-ahead from the guards on the ramparts. Then we were gliding over the gun turnstiles and spotlights and dropping toward the bright patch that was a fortified base camp, smack in the middle of the Mississippi River. The Titan base on Arsenal Island was a sprawling complex of mixed architecture: concrete bunkers beside century-old stone buildings; a gleaming high-tech lab surrounded by troops.

Beyond the lights of the island, on the far bank, lay a darkness unimaginable to people in the West. A darkness that hid the people and manimals who populated the zone. Of course the darkness was also crawling with mongrels and ferals . . . I suppressed a shudder.

"It won't be easy," my dad said, "but I think you're going to love living in Moline."

His eyes lit with excitement, and I felt a little less guilty about posting the video. Despite the dangers, my dad felt at home in the zone. *More alive* were his exact words. I should've guessed years ago that he was more than just an art dealer. His weathered skin and the random cuts and bruises should have been enough of a clue. Who looked like they'd wrestled a rabid dog after visiting art galleries? No one. Except when *gallery* stood for *abandoned museum in the Feral Zone.* But who would've guessed he was being literal when he'd said his associates were practically animals?

As the 'copter set down and deposited us on the landing pad outside the base, I scanned the face of each male line guard under the brim of his cap, but none was the wall of a boy I was looking for. Would Everson be here to catch us up to speed on distributing the inhibitor and collecting the missing blood strains? As far as I knew, he was still stationed on Arsenal. I'd had zero communication with him since last fall. No calls and no email, thanks to the patrol's signal-jamming efforts. I could've written him the old-fashioned way, on paper, but he wouldn't have been able to write back. The line guards stationed on this side of the wall were not allowed to contact civilians. Now, after months of silence between us, our friendship seemed like someone else's memory.

A line guard in a jeep took us across the bridge to the base, where Dr. Solis was waiting. Despite his smile, the doctor looked tired and drawn and even thinner than before. He and my dad hugged, and then Dr. Solis marveled over my dad's leg and that he was on his feet again. The last time he'd seen us, my dad had been laid out on a gurney, and it was unclear whether he'd live, much less walk again.

Dr. Solis then turned to me. Deep grooves darkened the skin beneath his eyes. "Delaney," he said with a fleeting smile. "I knew you'd be back." His gaze had a dreamy cast. Apparently he still needed a hit from a Lull inhaler to wind down at the end of the day.

"What progress have you made on the vaccine?" my dad asked. "Have the guards collected any new strains?"

I tried to focus on what they were saying, but distant yelling had hijacked my attention. The noise was nothing like barked-out drill sergeant commands. No, this was angry yelling, and I spotted the source with a single glance across the drill yard where a red-faced guard was busy dressing down a little girl. Here I was, east of the wall less than ten minutes, and already, I was feeling feral. Not literally, of course. But then, I didn't need a virus to dump animal DNA into my system in order to go wild.

Neither my dad nor Dr. Solis nor the guards loading our gear into another jeep paid any attention to the hollering guard. Not that we could actually hear exactly what the guy was saying over the whirr of the departing hovercopter, but the patrol base was lit up brighter than a stadium. Even at night, anyone with working eyeballs could interpret the guy's flapping mouth and jabbing gestures. When he thrust a pair of boots at the kid hard enough to knock her back a step, I was done being a bystander. I tossed my duffel and backpack into the jeep and stalked across the gravel.

The girl was young — ten at most — with snarled black hair. Going by her dirty adult-sized fatigues, she was probably one of the orphans who lived on base. A kid whose parents had died or gone feral and, having nowhere else to go, had shown up at the gate. She was one of the lucky ones. The guards didn't have to take in refugees — the government contracted the line patrol to secure the quarantine line, not run a day care. Still, that didn't give this guard the right to bully her.

"Do you even know what the word *polished* means?" he yelled, his back to me. "Or are you a grupped-up freak like your mother?"

As she glared up at him, I stumbled in surprise. It was Jia — the girl who'd saved my dad's life last fall. He'd come upon her mother circling Jia like she was prey. *Her own child.* My dad had thrown himself between them and gotten off a killing shot, but not before the woman slashed up his leg. He would've bled to death if Jia hadn't loaded him into a wagon and hauled him across the bridge to the base.

My eyes swept over all the guards in the vicinity again. I didn't see Everson, but I wished he was here. He'd taken care of Jia that night, when she was so terrified. But even then she hadn't been helpless, and she was far from helpless now.

"I asked you a question, stray," the guard snapped.

"If I was grupped, Guardsman Bhatt," the girl hissed, "I'd polish your boots with extra spit."

"What was that?" His hand shot out, and he grabbed a fistful of her hair.

I broke into a sprint. "Let her go!"

Jia thrashed in his grip, kicking and contorting like a mongoose. And Guardsman Bhatt's response? To tighten his hold and yank her up onto her tiptoes, which, of course, sent Jia into screeching, clawing insanity. He may as well have grabbed a stray cat by the tail. He actually looked surprised when Jia sank her teeth into his forearm, and then shocked when she didn't stop at a warning snap, and finally he bellowed as she broke skin . . .

I winced at the spit-plus-wound combo. Like every kid in the West, I'd grown up obeying the golden rule: No biting. As in never! An infected bite couldn't be taken back or undone because Ferae had no cure. Not then. Not now.

Bhatt shook her off. He looked from his bloody forearm to Jia, and his fingers curled. I got there just as he pulled back his fist. Snatching the riot baton off his belt, I slipped between them.

He dropped his fist, looking guilty, and then got an eyeful of me. His confusion lasted a split second before turning into scorn. "Which Disney princess are you?"

"The Beast."

"Funny. Give it back," he ordered, and made a grab for the baton.

I danced back. "So you can hit her with it?"

"No, I . . . You're crazy," he sputtered. "I don't hit kids."

"Right. You were going to pet her with your fist." I pointed the baton at his face. "I don't care if the patrol took her in. You don't get to grab her or yell at her or *ever* make her feel like she's not a person!"

"Lane!" a voice shouted from behind me. My dad. I pivoted and winced at the sight of him loping for me, cane in hand, face pale and glistening with sweat.

"Dad, stop!" I dropped the baton. "Your leg!" Moving that fast had to be sending stabbing pain through his right thigh. The doctors might have stitched up the mauled muscles and flesh, but his leg was far from healed.

He slowed to a hitched jog and then his eyes narrowed. "Don't even think about it!"

I jerked around to see the baton gripped in Guardsman Bhatt's meaty fist.

The urge to flee electrified my limbs, but I raised my chin and silently dared the fuming guard to hit me with it. It would be worth taking the blow just to see him get dragged off to patrol jail. There had to be a cell somewhere on this island — maybe even a torture room, considering the line patrol was a private paramilitary security force.

Bhatt's fingers tightened on the baton, but before he could make up his mind, my dad shoved between us.

"Get away from her," he snarled. *"Now."*

Bhatt must have heard the threat in my dad's tone, which made leaving seem like the better option. Guess even a jerk knew that military training didn't stack up against an angry father.

"Try to act human," I shouted at his back, then saw that my dad had paused to lean heavily on his cane. "Oh! How bad does it hurt?"

"How bad does what hurt?" he quipped, though strands of his dark hair clung to his sweat-beaded forehead. He was obviously in pain but as usual refused to show it. He nodded at the retreating guard. "What was that about?"

I shrugged, despite my racing heart. "He thought it was okay to bully a kid. I disagreed."

My dad's glasses gleamed under the stadium lights as he studied me. "Are you all right?"

"Yeah. Fine." I wiped my damp palms down my new canvas pants — tough material for what would be my new, tougher life. Something Jia would know a lot about. I glanced around, but there was no sign of the little girl. She must have escaped the second she got the chance. Smart kid. Unfortunately, as awful as the line guards were, she was still better off living on base. At least here she got three meals a day and didn't have to worry about being attacked by feral animals . . . or feral people.

"McEvoy!" Captain Hyrax stood like an aging rodeo star at the edge of the drill yard, chest puffed out, thumbs hooked on his belt. "You want an escort to Moline? You go now or you go alone."

"Be right there, Captain," my dad returned, and then glanced back at me. "Are you sure you're ready for this?"

No. But that wasn't going to stop me. "As I'll ever be."

My dad's smile deepened the crinkles by his eyes. He slung an arm over my shoulders, and we headed back to the waiting jeeps. Now that we were facing west, we had an unobstructed view of the Titan wall. Was building a seven-hundred-foot-tall barricade punishment enough for unleashing a viral pandemic on the nation?

Not in my book.

Before the plague, Titan had operated Imaginariums, which were enormous labyrinths, fifty stories tall and hundreds of acres wide. My dad, like the rest of America, had loved the Titan theme parks. He said he'd wasted many a weekend getting lost in them. You started at the ground level and tried to make your way to the roof by completing challenges to win clues for the maze on each floor. People came back over and over, picking up where they'd left off. Only a handful ever made it to the glass-enclosed paradise on the roof. Not only did the challenges get harder, but also there were wondrous things to see and experience on every floor, according to my dad. Apparently, each Imaginarium contained thrill rides, circus spectacles, haunted houses, water parks, and genetically modified animals — all under one roof.

It was no surprise that the Titan Corporation had had the construction resources to build the wall that marked the quarantine line — and the security force to guard it. But reparation should mean *repairing* the damage the Titan scientists had caused, not just slapping on a humongous Band-Aid to hide the injury. A covered wound left unchecked didn't heal — it festered.

Dr. Solis was waiting for us in the backseat of the jeep.

"How are things in Moline?" my dad asked Dr. Solis as we joined him there.

The doctor's languid expression turned grim. "Not good," he admitted. "The inhibitor stopped working. The protein that encased the infected cells dissolved. After being forced into dormancy for so long, the virus . . ." He looked like he was going to be sick. "It multiplied at an incredible rate. Everyone who took the inhibitor went feral within days of one another."

The night air thickened, making it hard to draw in a breath. Faces floated up in my mind. Sid, Moline's gate-keeper, infected with boar; Ed, the walrus-man whose wife stayed by his side even though she didn't have the disease; and all the other infected people who'd lived peacefully inside the compound. They'd been allowed to stay, so long as they remained sane.

"All of them?" my dad asked, sounding hoarse.

"Only those who took it," Dr. Solis said apologetically. "Apparently many of them didn't trust medicine that came from a Titan lab."

My dad just nodded, still looking shocked.

I was past shock. The inhibitor was the main reason I'd encouraged my dad to take this job. Chairman Prejean had promised to send cases of the inhibitor to Moline every month instead of the small box my father had been taking there — enough for the whole compound, including Rafe. Without the inhibitor, the virus would eventually destroy much of Rafe's brain. And now I had no way to stop it.

"What happened when the place went feral?" my dad asked. "Was Hagen hurt?"

I flinched, my control beginning to splinter. Besides being my dad's significant other, Hagen was the mayor of the Moline compound and wouldn't have taken cover during a crisis. She would've put herself in the vanguard.

"No," Dr. Solis said quickly. "And I heard she's the reason the situation didn't turn into a complete bloodbath. Though there were casualties."

I crossed my arms to hide my trembling hands and asked, "Is Rafe all right?"

"I wish I could say." Dr. Solis rubbed his forehead as if fighting off a headache. "No one has seen him in months."

A cold feeling crept over my skin. "How many months?"

"Not since the two of you were in Moline."

No one had seen him since I'd left the zone? Was my worst fear true? Had I left him there in Chicago to die alone?

My dad shifted uneasily beside me. "Have any of the hacks come across him in the zone?"

Dr. Solis shook his head. "The guard asked on every visit. I knew you'd want to know."

"You mean Everson?" I asked. "He was the one taking the inhibitor to Moline, right?"

Captain Hyrax dropped into the front passenger seat with a snort. "That's the Titan prince you're talking about. You really thought Chairman Prejean was going to let her precious son rub shoulders with grups?"

Grup, as in "genetically corrupted," wasn't a medical condition; it was an insult.

"Go," Hyrax barked at the driver, then took off his beret and rubbed a palm over his bald head.

The jeep pulled onto the paved road that crossed the southern tip of the island. Nothing had changed on base since my last visit, except the weather, which now held the soggy chill of early spring. I'd changed, however. And so had Everson and Rafe. They'd started our venture as different as could be. Guard vs. thief. Civilized vs. crude. Selfless vs. selfish . . . Yeah. Very different. Though not as much by the end. They'd rubbed off on each other — even started to like each other. And both had rubbed off on me.

So where were they now? And more important, *how* were they?

Why hadn't anyone seen Rafe in six months? Whenever I thought about him, which was often, I pictured him alone and suffering, which was stupid. If anyone could survive among the beast-men, he could. More than survive, Rafe *thrived* on the wild side of the wall. But that had been before he'd gotten infected. Maybe he'd gone feral fast. He'd said that usually happened when a person got infected with reptile DNA, but ultimately, there was no telling how the virus would affect someone. And that fact ate at me. Wondering if he'd gone feral — worrying that he was so crazed he couldn't take care of himself — was keeping me up at night as much as my nightmares. I wasn't going to rest easy until I knew for sure that Rafe was okay. Well, as okay as an infected person could be.

Our jeep stopped at the massive electric gate that blocked the only bridge across the Mississippi River. At Hyrax's nod, the guard in the sentry booth pushed a button, and the gate creaked open. Last fall, the bridge had been shrouded in darkness, but now every rusty nail and rickety plank was visible.

"Why did the patrol put lights on the bridge?" I asked Dr. Solis, speaking loudly so as to be heard over the rushing water below.

He glanced up as if only now noticing the change. "Perhaps because the patrol expanded the base."

Squished together as we were, I felt my dad stiffen. "What do you mean?"

Captain Hyrax glanced back, a smirk perched on his thick lips. "Chairman Prejean didn't tell you? Welcome to Gateway Station." He extended his hand toward the end of the bridge like a game-show host revealing a prize.

When I'd sprinted across the bridge last time, I'd exited through a narrow opening in an ancient blockade, but now the corrugated steel was gone. We drove straight onto a fenced construction site that took up over half the meadow. And like the fence around Arsenal Island, this twenty-footer had "Danger! 10,000 Volts!" signs and ominous-looking electrical posts every twenty feet. Between those and the elevated sentry boxes, the area could have passed as a prison yard. But I knew better. That state-of-the-art barrier wasn't here to keep people in but to keep them *out*.

"The area is a work in progress," Captain Hyrax said, gesturing to a single squat building surrounded by construction equipment. "We still need to double the fence and add trip wires and an enclosed checkpoint. Maybe change out the wooden guard towers for concrete and add a few observation bunkers. It'll be a thing of beauty when we're done. We've already trained more dogs in feral eradication — track and attack," he crowed. "We plan to push those grups back, mile by mile, till they fall into the Atlantic. We'll have this country back in one piece within a decade."

"Is that why there are more guards on base?" my dad asked, his voice taking on an edge. "So you can 'track and attack' sick people?"

I hadn't noticed the increase in guards, but then, I'd only come east one time, while my dad had spent years sneaking through the base to get to the Feral Zone.

Hyrax's dark gaze narrowed on my father. "Let's see how much sympathy you have for those 'sick people' when you're living with them." Abruptly, Hyrax shushed my dad and touched the listening device in his ear. After a moment, he said, "Yes, without incident." His gaze tracked back to a mega-sized white RV trailer parked by the bridge entrance. A shadow hovered behind its tinted window. "Yes," he clipped. "They're good to go . . . father and daughter."

Our jeep maneuvered between bulldozers and a backhoe while my dad eyed the guards patrolling the perimeter.

"The patrol is giving out food, medicine. In exchange,

the manimals let us take a sample of their blood," Dr. Solis explained, his tone oddly flat. "It's a one-time deal."

"The point of Gateway Station isn't to give the grups handouts." Hyrax sent Dr. Solis a sharp look. "The point is to find carriers of the missing strains. And it's working. We've collected two out of three of them. You should thank us, fetch. We made your job a whole lot easier."

We pulled up to another gate — only this one had a tent standing in for the usual sentry box.

"This is where the doctor and I leave you." With a jerk of his chin, Hyrax ordered Dr. Solis out. "Don't worry," he assured us with a fake smile, "we'll know if you run into any trouble out there." He pointed at a small camera mounted on the dashboard.

A guard climbed over the back of the jeep, shoving muddy boots between me and my dad to settle on top of the seat.

I looked up with surprise and then smiled. "Bear Lake."

"Bearly," she replied, laying her assault rifle across her knees. With her hair shaved within an inch of her scalp and iron-spike posture, she was intimidating, but I was thrilled to have her along. Unlike the other line guards, Bearly had set foot inside Moline's walls — the day she'd accompanied Everson to retrieve me from the compound. But then I'd hijacked their jeep and left her surrounded by manimals. If she was still mad at me or nervous about going back, she didn't let on. She had her guard face screwed on tight.

"They'll drop you at the compound and leave," Hyrax told my dad. "Then you can get started on your *mission*."

What was his problem? The chairman herself had offered my dad the job.

"Get into position," Hyrax barked at the guards patrolling inside the fence.

I moved to the front seat so my dad could stretch out his bad leg.

"I'm Frank," the driver said as soon as I settled into the passenger seat.

"Nice to meet you. I'm Lane," I said, though my eyes were on the gate as it rolled open.

The night hung heavy and dark over the meadow and smothered the woods beyond it. I took a steadying breath and forced my gaze away from the shifting shadows. Behind us, Arsenal was an island of light in the middle of the river — an oasis in the darkness, throbbing with human activity. Unlike the very dark, very chaotic world of the Feral Zone.

"Are you okay?" My dad's voice broke through my very dark, very chaotic thoughts.

"Fine." I glanced back and gave him what I hoped was a reassuring smile. My dad did not look reassured. "I just forgot how dark it gets without electricity." I upped my smile and added, "I'm good."

As if anyone would ever use the word *good* to describe a criminal on the run. Oh well. I'd be safely out of reach soon enough. Safe in the Feral Zone, ironic as that was. Biohazard agents couldn't cross the quarantine line to arrest me. I couldn't go home again, true, but that didn't matter so long as my video convinced the West that people still lived in the East — both healthy people and infected — and that they needed our help.

I glanced at Bearly, whose gaze flicked between my dad and me. No doubt every word we spoke would make it into her report, which she'd probably have typed up and turned in before sunup.

"Drop them at the gate," Captain Hyrax told Bearly and Frank. "You don't set foot inside the compound. Not one step. You unload the gear and come straight back to base."

They both snapped out a "Yes, Captain" followed by a salute. And then, just as the driver took his foot off the brake, a hideous howl echoed through the night — part human, part who-knew-what. Every warm drop of blood drained from my body. Surprisingly, no one else seemed affected. A guard in the tent sipped his coffee. Another wiped down a monitor screen.

I tightened my ponytail and crossed my fingers, my fight-or-flight instincts on red alert, as our jeep rolled into the meadow. I was back in the Feral Zone — birthplace of my nightmares.

· THREE ·

As we left the sweeping spotlights of Gateway Station behind, the darkness closed in around us. The jeep's headlights lit up the windswept prairie grass like a lighthouse beam stretching over a turbulent sea. Perched on top of the backseat, Bearly switched on the flashlight mounted to her assault rifle and scanned the darkness on either side of us.

"Watch out for those monkey holes," she told Frank.

"Chimpacabra," I corrected hoarsely. "They're chimpacabra warrens."

"Right," she scoffed. "Because that sounds much more reasonable."

There was nothing reasonable about falling into a chimpacabra's larder. In fact, just thinking about my time underground with Rafe, surrounded by paralyzed animals of all sizes, glassy eyed and terrified as they waited for the chimpacabra to come back and eat them alive, had me feeling very unreasonable indeed. But I wouldn't think of that now. Couldn't. Not if I wanted to stay sane.

We bumped over the patches of asphalt until we crossed into the woods, where the trees seemed to have crept closer to the road since my last visit. These were the woods of my father's bedtime stories. Only now, at midnight, the setting seemed more horror movie than fairy tale. Especially since I couldn't see the glow from Arsenal Island anymore because the road had veered inland, though I could still hear the rush of the river.

"Turn here," Bearly told Frank, and he veered the jeep onto what was left of Route 92.

The two-lane highway wasn't nearly as overgrown as the road through the woods; however, we didn't even get half a mile before Frank had to pull up short. An enormous tree lay across the broken asphalt like a ship run aground. He shifted into park and rose in his seat to look around. "We can get through there." He gestured to the overgrown meridian strip with its tangle of trees.

My dad leaned between the front seats, shaking his head. "The brush is too thick. The jeep won't make it through."

I heard the tension in his voice. I twisted around in my seat, wanting more than anything for him to reassure me, but his eyes were ticking over the fallen tree and the over-grown vegetation on either side of the road. Did he feel it too — that creeping sensation of being stalked? Hopefully it was just mongrels peering out from between the trees and not something more . . . intentional. Chorda stepping from the woods flashed through my mind, and I went cold all over. My fingertips prickled with tiny aftershocks of pain.

Bearly shouldered her assault rifle and hopped out of the jeep to walk the length of the fallen tree. "We've got boulders on this end," she called when she reached the unearthed roots. "Then a steep drop to the river."

Cursing under his breath, Frank hefted his gun and climbed out to join her. I slid a six-inch serrated knife from its sheath, which instantly brought to mind how Rafe had strapped a blade to his leg every morning the way other people put on socks.

Something about the fallen tree felt wrong. I rose halfway in the front seat and squinted past the headlights. The moss on the trunk was torn up, same with the shelf mushrooms, as if the tree fell someplace else and was dragged to this particular —

"It's a trap!" I shouted to the guards just as my dad yelled, "Get back in the jeep!"

As I scrambled into the driver's seat, Frank went down with a shout and some invisible force dragged him into the thigh-high scrub. He twisted onto his back to fire blindly at whatever had hold of him, but when he vanished into the darkness, the gun fell silent.

Bearly charged after him, swerving her rifle, looking for a target, when a tawny-skinned woman appeared above her, balanced on the fallen tree trunk. She was larger than life — a spiky-haired Amazon whose muscles gleamed in the glare of the headlights. I gasped with recognition. She'd traded her frayed evening gown for cargo pants and combat boots, but Deepnita had lost none of her rock-star glamour. Maybe it came from being infected with lion, or maybe she'd honed her regal air as Chorda's queen years ago, but her fierce beauty still had a mesmerizing effect. Bearly whipped around, gun trained on the lioness, only to blink in surprise, which was all the time Deepnita needed to pounce.

"Lane, get —" My dad's shout became a muffled cry as he was jerked backward.

I twisted to help him just as something heavy slammed onto the jeep's hood. I reeled back to see auburn curls spill over the steering wheel. Above me, another one of Chorda's discarded queens leaned over the windshield, the furriest of them — the most mutated. Charmaine. The limbs of the other lionesses had been dusted with golden hair, while Charmaine had a pelt. Her wild eyes — Chorda's eyes — narrowed as she reached for me.

Pain exploded between my brows. I shoved back in the seat to escape her even as my vision flickered from the pain. I knew this ache. It was too precise to ever forget. It came whenever I'd stared too long or too hard at my computer screen. But I wasn't editing Feral Zone footage now, just focusing on a living, breathing manimal. I closed my eyes and knuckled the throb with my knife hand, only to have the blade slip from my grip as my hands went numb. I forced my eyes open and kicked at the gearshift to pop it out of park. Once. Twice. But before my boot could connect a third time, the lioness hauled me up by the wrist, forcing me onto my feet.

Her eyes were wilder now than back in Chicago, and Charmaine had not been all that sane back then. She wrenched my arm higher to peer into my face. Recognition sharpened her gaze, and then she took in my T-shirt and canvas pants with a hiss. "You could have been a lion . . . But you became one of them?" She flicked her free hand at Bearly, who was flailing within Deepnita's crushing embrace.

"I'm not —" I clenched my teeth against the white-hot ache in my arm socket. "I'm not a guard." I tried to twist in her grip to get a glimpse of my dad, but she just hiked my wrist higher, forcing me onto my tiptoes. Pain blazed through my shoulder as the joint began to dislocate.

"I freed you," I gasped.

"Because you needed us," she spat back. "If you could've saved your friend without us, you would've left us there to rot."

She was right. I probably wouldn't have unlocked their cage if I'd had another option. I'd realized by the time I reached Chicago that helping Chorda get free of Rafe's snare had been a terrible mistake. The worst of my life. And with their long ivory fangs, gleaming eyes, and big-cat grace, the lionesses had reminded me much too much of the insane tiger-king. I would've been too scared to free them, though they'd all suffered at Chorda's hands.

I writhed in Charmaine's grip. If I could get enough leverage to throw myself backward, she'd tumble face-first over the windshield. She put a foot on the glass as if anticipating my move and leaned down, her breath hot on my face. "What have you done with my sister?"

"Wh-what?"

"Mahari!" she roared. "Where" — she shook my arm, wrenching a shriek out of me — "is she?"

Another shake, another shriek, and then she tossed me out of the jeep like a cat flinging aside a dead mouse. I hit the ground hard, the impact knocking the air from my lungs. I forced my eyes open even though I couldn't rise yet. Nearby, Bearly had gone still in Deepnita's hold, though she was alert. And radiating fury.

I craned my neck but didn't see my dad in the back of the jeep — probably because he was underneath the lioness who was lounging there. A teen with snarled blond hair, surfer-girl beauty, and muscles worthy of the entire Olympic beach volleyball team — Neve. She broke into a toothy smile and waved at me, which made her seem demented, not friendly.

Charmaine leapt off the hood and landed in a crouch. She had the body of a marathon runner, roped with muscle, which she showed off in low-slung red track pants and a cropped tank. She stalked toward me with the fury of a goddess.

I rolled onto my knees, blinking against the throb between my eyes. "I don't know where your sister is."

"You took her," she hissed.

"No! I —"

"Humans like you. Guards." She loomed over me. "They caught her outside Moline and threw her into a truck. I'm going to kill a human for every day she's gone. That's twelve days so far."

"I don't know where she is. My dad and I . . . We just came east tonight." I held up my hands to ward her off. We were going to die for something the patrol had done. For all I knew, Frank and my dad were already dead. "We drove through the base — didn't stop. We're going to live over here. In Moline," I panted. "We're not here to hurt you. I don't know why the patrol took Mahari." I met Charmaine's glare and hardened my expression. My terror would only excite the predator in her, and she already seemed more feral than sane.

"You run to your island, little rabbit, and you tell whoever's in charge that they can have these two back" — she swept a hand from Bearly to the jeep — "when they return our sister."

"No!" I pushed to my feet and stumbled toward the jeep. Charmaine stepped into my path. Even with her blocking my way, I could see my father's legs hanging off the backseat.

"Dad!" I tried to dodge past the lioness, but with a single swipe, she knocked me flat.

"He's good," Neve called. Then she lifted my father's arm and waved with it. His hand flopped limply as she said in a deep voice, "Hi, honey. I'm fine."

I shoved up to face her. "Please let me check him."

"You're not listening," Charmaine warned softly.

"Your plan won't work," I sputtered. "If you take a guard hostage" — I hooked a thumb at Bearly, who stood rigidly and showed no fear — "the line patrol will storm into these woods with Uzis. They will maim and kill every manimal they see until they get her back."

Charmaine growled. "You're lying."

"You're diseased animals to them, and the guards are just itching for an excuse to put you down." If I could just make her see that I was closer to them than the guards. "I came here to find my friend Rafe. Remember him? Chorda caged Rafe just like he caged —"

Bearly's shout cut me off. I whirled to see her flying through the air away from us. She arced impossibly high before hitting the ground in the distance. I gasped. Her spine had to have snapped in two with that landing. But before I could run to her, she flipped over and glared at Deepnita, who must have thrown her.

The largest lioness pointed at Bearly. "Stay," she ordered, then strolled over to us, scooping up Bearly's assault rifle on the way. "So, Lane . . ." she said with a languid smile.

She remembered my name! I clenched my jaw shut to keep from gaping at her.

"You being so smart and all," Deepnita went on in her

rumble of a voice, "tell us, what would you do if the patrol took one of your family?"

Charmaine sent her a furious look, but Deepnita shrugged a shoulder. "She knows the layout of the base. She can help us. After all" — this time her smile included a flash of fang — "if she came here to find *him*, she'll want to know where to look."

Hope pushed up from my gut, sudden and raw. "You mean Rafe?"

"That's not his name anymore," Neve called as she propped her filthy Converse sneakers on the driver's seat headrest. "He's called Wraith now."

"Wraith? What — why?"

She tipped her head, considering. "It's scary?"

I drew a slow breath but couldn't keep my questions from bubbling over. "Is he all right? Where is he living? Did you talk to him?"

"We'll tell you everything. Where he is. How he is." Deepnita's dark amber eyes gleamed as she angled closer, her voice pitched low. "When you bring us Mahari."

In other words, find out where the guards had stashed the lioness, break her out, and then escape from a high-security base. I was seventeen and had zero military training. Piece of cake. The only thing I had going for me was the burning desire to know that Rafe was okay.

Deepnita began to say more but then cocked her head. In the beat of silence, I heard the rumble of jeeps closing in fast. I caught Bearly's eye over the lioness's shoulder.

"Camera," she called with a nod toward the pinprick of red, glowing on the jeep's windshield.

Neve sprang up. "Fleeing," she sang out over the whip of jeeps tearing through prairie grass, then ran off.

"We'll be watching from the tree line. Come at night." Deepnita threw the assault rifle into the tall grass a good distance away from Bearly. "And come alone, except for Mahari."

"Unless you want to see how predators bring down prey," Charmaine added. Then, with inhuman speed, the two women whirled and bounded over the tree trunk.

Bearly sprinted in the direction Deepnita had thrown her assault rifle while I ran to my father. He lay on the backseat of the jeep, blinking as a small line of blood trickled down his temple. He gripped the front seat.

"Maybe you should stay down," I said.

Ignoring my suggestion, he hoisted himself upright and assessed me. "Did they hurt you?"

I shook my head, deciding to keep quiet about my nearly dislocated arm.

"I shouldn't have brought you," he muttered, lightly touching his bloody temple. He frowned at the fist-sized rock on the ground, and I knew I had to diffuse his anger before he decided we'd be better off returning to the West.

"They're mad because the guards kidnapped one of their pride." I took a seat beside him, speaking softly in case Bearly was listening. "They know where Rafe is."

"Where?"

"They wouldn't tell me," I said as four jeeps plowed to wet stops around us. A dozen armed guards leapt out, guns raised.

On a gesture from Captain Hyrax, the guards fanned

out. "I want them alive," he ordered. His gaze cut to Bearly, who rejoined us, having recovered her gun. "Which strain?"

"Lion, sir. I think. I can't say for sure," she replied in a military clip. "McEvoy knows them."

My dad didn't know anything about Chorda's ex-queens except what I'd told him. But then Hyrax locked hard eyes on me, and I straightened. Oh. She meant me.

"Could one of them be infected with something else?" he demanded.

I was coming off the rush and beginning to shake, but I considered his question. "I don't think so. They call themselves sisters because they're all part lion."

Hyrax's lips thinned with displeasure. "You've got no way of knowing for sure what they are."

"I know that they were bitten by the same feral — just not at the same time." Under Chorda's rule, infection was grounds for instant divorce. That way, when he grew tired of a wife, he could end the marriage fast. He'd forced each out-of-favor queen into a tiny space between two caged ferals. Given the choice between a bite laced with lion DNA and a bite laced with baboon DNA, no surprise, all four had picked lion.

"Maybe they lied," Hyrax sneered. "Want to know what doesn't lie? A blood test."

Two guards crashed through the brush — Frank with his arm slung over the other man's shoulders. "Frankfort, how are you, son?" Hyrax called.

Frank gave the captain a shaky salute, and I sagged under the weight of my damp, sweaty shirt, so thankful the lionesses hadn't killed him.

"Take him to the infirmary. Tell Solis to scan him for open wounds," Hyrax told the guard bearing Frank's weight and then shifted his attention to my dad. "We'll get this tree moved and have you on your way in no time."

"No." My dad hefted himself out of the jeep. "I'm not taking my daughter into Moline until I see what's going on there."

"Dad, no." He couldn't be thinking of sending me back to the West. I'd be in far more danger there than at the compound.

"She can stay on base tonight," Hyrax allowed. "But that's it. One night. The government isn't paying us to baby-sit civilians. She can sleep in the infirmary."

"That's fine," my dad told him, then turned to me. "I'll come to Arsenal tomorrow and let you know if it's safe."

"And if it's not?"

He wrapped an arm around my shoulders. "Then we go home."

"The West isn't my home. Not anymore."

He surprised me by nodding. Then again, he'd probably felt that way for years but had stayed in the West for me. "I know it's been hard, knowing what you know," he said quietly. "But, sweetheart, I'd rather see you struggle to keep a secret than struggle to stay alive," he finished. "If things have changed in Moline, if the situation is too dangerous, we're going back." He held up a silencing finger before I even got my mouth open. "No debate."

Great. He was using *that* tone. The one that said, "My back is up, my ears are deaf, and nothing — not logic, not guilt, not even a high-drama fit — is going to change my mind." I clamped my lips shut. For now, all I could do was hope that all was well in Moline, because if the situation had turned bad there, I'd have to tell him the real reason I couldn't go home, and I didn't want to think about how that would go over.

"Back in the jeep, McEvoy," Hyrax ordered. "Those grups are probably giving their pals a big heads-up that you're coming. Every minute you waste here gives them more time to round up a pack. I'm not having my people ambushed because you took too long fussing over a scared little girl."

"I don't see *you* agreeing to live in Moline," my dad said dryly.

"Either you go now or you go without guards. Your choice, fetch."

"He'll go now." I grabbed my backpack and two-ton duffel from the jeep and dropped them on the wet ground to hug my dad. "Be careful."

"Back at you," he returned.

I didn't go straight to the infirmary as Hyrax had ordered. Instead, I waited in the muddy construction site that was Gateway Station until Captain Hyrax's convoy of jeeps returned an hour later. If chaos had broken out in Moline, my dad wasn't going to let me live there, and I'd more than burned the bridge back to the West — I'd nuked it into oblivion. So where did that leave me?

On Arsenal Island.

All things considered, it wasn't a bad fallback plan. If I was living on base, I'd have a shot at finding out where the patrol had taken Mahari. And if I could free her, I'd find out about Rafe. No reason not to dream big. The first step was easy enough: get official permission to stay.

To that end, I sidled up to Captain Hyrax as he climbed out of a jeep. "No luck finding the lionesses?"

He held up a silencing finger, covering one ear with his

other hand. A transparent wire coiled from his ear to a radio on his shoulder. "We lost the trail, and then ran into some trouble with another bunch of grups." He paused to listen. "A few cuts and scrapes. Nothing that could lead to infection." Pause. "Understood."

He waved over a guard. "Tell Solis to send over some medics to patch up your team." He finally turned his reptilian gaze on me.

"Captain, if I need to stay on base for more than one —"

"No," he said. "When your father shows up tomorrow, you're out of here. East, West, I don't care where you go as long as you're gone." His face could have been carved from granite.

I thought of that big RV sitting by the bridge. I had a sneaking suspicion about who was lurking behind those dark windows. It was time for step two: go over Hyrax's head.

· FOUR ·

I sprinted across Gateway Station toward the enormous RV, shouting, "Chairman Prejean, can I talk to you?"

No response.

"Please." I rapped on the tinted window. "It's really important!"

A guard spilled out of the front passenger seat, fingers to his earpiece, listening intently. "Yes, ma'am. I'll tell her." His eyes cut to me. "Go," he said, motioning toward the back of the trailer.

Another guard stood by an open door at the back, but when I started for it, he dropped an arm in my way. "When you're inside, wash your hands and then stand directly under the blower for two minutes."

I noticed the air system embedded in the trailer's ceiling just inside the back door. Beyond that was a dividing wall of plastic.

The guard handed me plastic shoe coverings. "Put them on after the dry bath."

I hoisted myself into the sterile antechamber, washed my hands with a chemical solution at a built-in sink while the air system whisked the germs off me. All these precautions would have comforted me six months ago; now they seemed like overkill.

Once I was bootied up, I slipped through a slit in the divider and into a plastic bubble of a room that was kept inflated by filtered air. The interior resembled a comfortable living room, though every surface was seamless and slick. Easily wiped down. And I had no doubt it was — on the hour, every hour. Was this what Everson's childhood had been like? He'd mentioned air filters and plastic sheeting and said that all his mother's employees, including his tutors, had been required to change into sanitized clothing.

"No, no. Don't move," Chairman Prejean said from where she was curled up on a window seat, her back to me. "Wait for the air to settle." With her lean body wrapped in a long white jacket and her hair shaved down to stubble, she reminded me of the cancer patients who'd wandered the hospitals halls when my mother was dying.

I stayed by the slit of a door. Originally, Chairman Prejean had been Titan's chief executive officer. But when the company — *her* company — got out of the labyrinth theme park business and put Titan's considerable resources toward building the reparation wall, Ms. Prejean gave herself a new title: chairman — a title so bland, it didn't go at all with the paramilitary force that Titan had become. But then, that was probably why she chose it.

Chairman Prejean unclipped her earpiece and placed it on the windowsill — perfectly aligned with the edge. "I'm not usually quite this cautious, but being so close to the quarantine line . . ." She rose to face me and sighed. "Well, it's a trigger."

I didn't flinch at her flattened features. Chairman Prejean's transparent surgical mask was as much her trade-mark as her stubbled head. Thankfully my germaphobia had never gotten that bad. She looked worse than creepy — pale and hairless as she was — and sounded like a speech therapist with a headache. Voice soft, words precise — probably to make up for the mask's muffling effect.

She beckoned me closer with a latex-gloved hand. "We should be fine now. The filters will have sucked up whatever came in with you. One can hope, anyway." Her spine curved like a snake's as she settled onto the corner of her desk.

I swallowed against the tightness in my throat. "I'm Delaney. Mack's daughter."

A crease appeared in her forehead, indicating that she had arched her plucked-to-nothing eyebrows. "I know who you are, Lane. We met last fall, albeit briefly. It's not every day that I overlook quarantine breaking."

I nodded. She was reminding me that she had already done favors — lifesaving favors — for my dad and me. As if I didn't already realize the power she had over me.

"In fact," she continued, "I know quite a bit about you, between Ev's report and the background check we did when I hired your father." She clasped her gloved hands, entwining red-tipped fingers.

"You're bleeding!" I gasped before I'd fully processed what I was seeing.

"It's nothing." She splayed her bloody fingertips as if flashing a new manicure. "I cut my nails below the quick to keep debris from collecting."

Debris. Another synonym for germs. The Inuits with their fifty words for snow had nothing on the germaphobes in the West. I adjusted my attitude and changed the topic. "Chairman, I'd like to stay on Arsenal." This got me another invisible brow arch. "After the lion-women attacked us tonight, my dad went ahead to Moline without me. To check out the compound. If he doesn't think it's safe —"

"Of course it isn't safe," she said simply. "It's on the wrong side of the quarantine line."

"Yes, and we knew the risks, and I signed the waiver. But if Moline has changed since last fall — if my dad thinks it's gotten too dangerous, he won't let me live there."

She frowned. At least that's what it looked like. I couldn't be certain with the transparent mask distorting her nose and mouth.

I hurried on with my idea. "But that doesn't mean he can't do the job. If I could stay here on the base . . . he'd be okay with that. He could still live in Moline and fetch the missing strain for you."

She smoothed a gloved hand over her stubbled head as she considered my request. "He *will* have a problem with Moline. It's a hotbed of violence and only getting worse."

"I'm willing to enlist," I blurted out before she could say no.

"Enlist?" She blinked at me from her perch on the desk. "As a guard?"

I nodded. If my life wasn't on the line, I'd scrub toilets before enlisting in the patrol. Actually, being a new recruit probably meant lots of toilet scrubbing. Didn't matter. Right now, I'd do whatever it took to stay on this side of the wall.

"I see." Clasping her blood-tipped hands, she rested them on her knee. "Do you know what a line guard does, Lane?"

Was that a trick question? "Guard the quarantine line."

"Why?"

"To make sure that we don't have an outbreak of the Ferae Naturae virus in the West."

"That's the simple answer. The *accurate* answer is: The patrol is responsible for keeping the humans in the West safe from genetic contamination."

I straightened. "I can do that."

She studied me intently, like she was checking my DNA for weak links. "If you see someone infected with Ferae," she proposed, "say, a young woman infected with colobus monkey on the west bank of the river. She landed there in a small rowboat. What would you do?"

"Arrest her."

"No, Lane. We don't have jails for infected people. We don't hold trials for them. There is only one correct answer."

Shoot her! Shoot her in the head with the cold determination of a psychopath. That's what Chairman Prejean needed to hear, but I couldn't get those words past my lips. Yes, I'd killed Chorda with a machete. Standing back and pulling a trigger *had* to be easier than that . . . But I was hung up on the cold-blooded part, the not-in-self-defense part. "I'd convince her to cross back to the east bank," I said finally.

Chairman Prejean's smooshed features betrayed nothing. "Have you ever thought that certain animalistic mutations can make a person seem *more* appealing, not less?"

Another gimme question. So easy a baboon could guess what she wanted to hear. But Chorda's ex-queens were even more beautiful — and terrifying — because of their powerful muscles. "That depends on what you mean by appealing."

"Well, you've certainly made this easy." She pressed her hands to her knees and stood. "The answer is no. You're no line guard. You haven't got it in you to put the safety of every man, woman, and child in the West first."

"No. I do. I —"

"You don't," she said flatly. "You're too sensitive, and that makes you reactive — reckless, even."

"I'm not reckless," I protested.

"Really?" She leaned toward a screen on her desk and turned it on with a touch. On it, a fight broke out. Two people with white blind eyes that came from shooting with a night-vision camera. That was me! Me, stealing a baton from the guard who'd been yelling at Jia. Guardsman Bhatt. The Chairman's gaze slid from the monitor to me. "You were saying?"

I gritted my teeth. "He was bullying her."

"And that bothered you, proving you're too sensitive. The last thing the patrol needs is a sensitive guard."

She paused the recording just as I dropped the baton. Jia stood off to a side, slightly hunched, with her teeth bared and her fingers curled as if clawed. Every inch of her revealed her wild child years in the Feral Zone. Had Rafe been that savage when my dad left him in the orphan camp all those years ago? If so, who'd tamed him? Not that Rafe was all that tame now, but at least he had the basics of social interaction down.

On the screen, Jia looked as friendly as a snarling pit bull. Worry nipped at me. It wouldn't matter that Jia had 100 percent human DNA; if she couldn't act human, she'd never be accepted into a compound like Moline. All the orphans were too wild to mix in with civilized people. At least, that was the explanation the patrol gave for why the orphans couldn't immigrate to the West. Really, the Titan Corporation didn't want anyone confirming the rumors about what existed beyond the wall.

And then it hit me.

"Let me take care of the orphans," I said in a rush. We were all misfits, stuck between two worlds. Why not be misfits together? At least we'd understand one another.

Chairman Prejean did a slow blink. "The strays?" She flicked a blood-tipped finger at Jia's image on the screen. "They may as well have Ferae. They watched their infected parents get wilder by the day. Parents with misshapen mouths and overlarge teeth who mangled language until they forgot how to talk altogether. You really think you can undo years of living with beast-people with what — good intentions?"

"I can try," I said firmly. "If you'll let me stay."

"No."

She began to rise as if to dismiss me, and I had to clench my fists against the flailing desperation invading my limbs. But then the chairman paused, and her pale predator's gaze turned me into prey. Maybe the lionesses had been right. Maybe I was a rabbit.

"Unless . . ." she said.

"What is it? I'll do it," I blurted, just as she wanted me to.

She sank back onto the desk and crossed her latex-encased forearms. "If I do agree to employ you on Arsenal to civilize the strays, you'll have to agree to a stipulation that won't be written into your contract but will be binding nonetheless."

"What stipulation?"

"Stay away from my son."

So Everson was still on Arsenal.

"Your recklessness puts others in danger," she went on. "Namely the people you drag along on your adventures. They get hurt. People like . . . Rafe."

I inhaled sharply. "That wasn't my —"

"Fault?" She pretended to consider it. "Maybe not. Yet you came out of it just fine while he clearly didn't."

I shook my head. Not in denial but to keep her words from putting down roots in my brain. I couldn't deny it. Rafe had accompanied me to Chicago, and he'd gotten more than hurt: He'd gotten *infected*.

But how did Chairman Prejean know about it?

From Everson, obviously, and I resented it. He had no right to tell her about things that had happened to me or to Rafe — especially when he hadn't even been there. Personal, private, heartbreaking things.

"I suppose I should be grateful that my son came back with just a few scars," the chairman went on.

And with that, my resentment evaporated.

"Five scars on his perfect face. But he's the lucky one." She hefted her words like rocks, piling them on my shoulders, waiting for me to collapse under the weight. "So what if people wince when they look at him? At least he's alive. Not like that little ape-boy . . . What was his name?"

"I'll stay away from Everson." I couldn't spit the promise out fast enough. Anything to get her to stop talking. Thinking about Rafe was painful enough — if she poked at my memories of Cosmo, the little ape-boy, if she forced me to remember his murder and small unmarked grave, I'd shatter. And I wasn't going to give her that satisfaction. Not when she was the person responsible for the virus that caused Cosmo's messed-up DNA in the first place. Because of her, he'd been treated as less than human every day of his short life.

"I'm protecting my son, Lane. Face the facts. You're a loose cannon."

I bristled. I'd gone into the zone because my dad's life was at stake. I hadn't asked Everson to come with me. But I wasn't going to waste my breath explaining that to her. "I'm going to run into him. This island isn't that big and we're friends. He —"

"*Were*. Past tense. Make sure he knows it."

How? Brush him off without explanation? Everson had shown up in Moline — *unasked* — out of concern for me. And when I couldn't find my dad and decided to do Director Spurling's fetch for him, Everson had insisted on coming along even though it meant traveling deep into the Feral Zone. He'd said he wanted to hunt for the missing strains of the virus, and he had, but Everson also had my back. He didn't deserve to be scraped off like old gum now.

"He's going to ask why," I pointed out.

"Lie to him. Unless you have a problem with that?" she asked softly.

No, but *she* should. She'd lied to him his entire child-hood, including telling him he had an autoimmune disease to keep him from ever leaving their home. Given her honesty scale, what she was asking of me was nothing. Besides, I'd gotten good at lying over the past six months. The threat of arrest had been an amazing motivator. "Nope. No problem at all. I'll think of something to put him off."

"I'm sure you will." She straightened with an undula-tion, the way a python unfurled to swallow its prey. "But if you tell him that I've interfered in his life, if you even hint at it, I'll have a hovercopter dump you on the roof of the biohazard department with 'quarantine breaker' stamped on your forehead. That would certainly make Director Spurling happy. She's not your biggest fan, as I'm sure you know."

"I won't go near Everson," I vowed. "And I won't tell him the order came from you."

She peered at my face for a moment, and then her posture became languid once more. "When it comes to the strays, you have no idea what you're asking for." She glanced at the frozen image of Jia on the monitor.

I shrugged. "I'm reckless like that."

She chuckled, which surprised me. Her germ obsession had me thinking she was humorless. Or maybe it was the fact she'd destroyed the earth's biosphere. A toss-up.

"All right, Lane," she said. "You may stay and try to socialize the little beasts. I'll pay you what we pay a new recruit, though you won't have the status of even the lowest guard."

I straightened to keep from sagging with relief. Chairman Prejean had no idea just how life-or-death my request had been, and I wasn't about to clue her in. As I considered what it was going to be like staying on Arsenal, the lionesses sprang into my thoughts. If the patrol had Mahari locked away somewhere, this woman would know. The odds that she'd tell me? Not-in-this-lifetime to zip.

"Thank you," I said with all the sincerity I could muster. Completely sincere sincerity.

She extended her bloodstained fingers. Suppressing a shudder, I took her proffered hand and then had to suppress another shudder when she didn't shake my hand. She squeezed it.

Her transparent mask tightened over her forced smile. "Welcome to the line patrol, Lane."

I left the van with a new job and a new certainty: Chairman Prejean was not someone I ever wanted to cross. I scoured the muddy ground for my bags before spotting them outside the sentry tent near the gate. The tent flap was open.

"So you killed them all?" someone inside the tent demanded, his voice tight with disgust.

Inside, a guard slouched in a chair, one leg outstretched. "You bet we did!" he bragged to the medic who was unlacing his boot. "Put those grups down like the mutts they are. I wish more had come at — ow! Hey. That hurts."

"You want me to check your ankle, the boot had to go," the medic said, setting the boot aside.

I stiffened, recognizing the sharp, clear voice. Crouched that way, he looked like the ultimate line guard with his dark hair cut ruthlessly short and his gray shirt stretched tight over a body that, even from the back, hinted at extreme military training.

Oh no, no! I wasn't ready to go face-to-face with him yet. I didn't have a good excuse for giving him the cold shoulder, and I could feel the chairman watching me through her tinted window. What was I supposed to do?

Not talk to him. That's what.

But suddenly, with him less than ten feet away, I wasn't okay with that at all. Now I wanted to wrap my arms tight around him and lean into his warmth and hear his heart beating strong and steady. I wanted to tell him about my awful dreams and how they always ended with Chorda clawing out my heart. And I wanted to hear about his — every terrifying detail — because he had to be having nightmares too, right?

Did he wake up from his own shouting? Did the most random, stupid things make him cry? Did he think about our time in the Feral Zone every waking moment of every day and make himself sick and crazy by listing all the things he should have done differently?

Or was that just me?

Everson manipulated the guard's ankle. The guard gripped the edge of his chair with a hiss of pain. "I don't think it's broken," Everson told him. "You twisted it?"

The guard nodded. "Chasing down the last couple of 'em. Man, we fixed them good," he gloated.

"A vaccine is a fix. You made things worse." Everson let go of the guard's ankle abruptly. The guard flinched as his foot touched the ground. "Think anyone infected with Ferae is going to come near this place after your shoot-out tonight?" he asked in a deceptively calm tone. "If they don't come to us, we lose all chance of finding that last strain. Yeah, you really fixed things."

"Get bit." The guard jerked upright in his chair. "I'm paid to follow orders. I'm not some rich jerk here slumming for kicks."

Everson rose to his full height — as in, well over six feet tall. "Your ankle is sprained. Ice it, keep it elevated and wrapped tight." He snapped off his latex gloves and turned. "Stay off it for —" The words died on his lips as he caught sight of me outside the tent. His eyes, gray as the Titan wall, widened as they met mine, and he inhaled sharply.

It was too late to duck out of sight. Too late to run.

"Hi," I said softly, my throat raw.

His dark brows snapped together, and he frowned. No, not frowned. He *scowled* at me. "What are you doing here?"

· FIVE ·

Everson was not happy to see me — not at all — which made no sense because we'd parted on good terms.

He stalked out of the tent, his gloves in one large fist. "Tell me Mack isn't taking you to Moline with him."

"Um . . ." My thoughts scattered at the full force of him under the floodlights. His features seemed sharper than I remembered. His eyes, harder. But none of it detracted from the impact of seeing him again. Not his obvious irritation, not even the pale, raised scars that slashed down his cheekbones to the corners of his firm mouth. Two on the left, three on the right. Thank goodness the feral who'd clawed open Everson's cheeks had missed his left eye — but only after Everson had smashed the feral's head against the wall of Chorda's castle again and again. I wondered if Everson relived those moments like I relived killing Chorda.

He closed the distance between us, his gaze sliding over me, seeming to take in every detail. "Lane, answer me." He was even bigger than I remembered — so tall and broad he blocked out the stars.

"Uh . . ." I was uncomfortably aware of the white RV parked on the other side of the meadow. When Ilsa Prejean told me to keep away from her son, she probably meant by more than twelve inches. I sidled back a couple of steps and recaptured the reins of my runaway thoughts. "Dr. Solis said you knew about my dad's mission."

"*His* mission. Not yours." Everson tossed his gloves through the open tent flap. The gloves narrowly missed the guard who'd limped out to watch us, his face alight with curiosity. Everson ignored him and stood, hands on hips in perfect symmetry, glaring down at me. "Your dad should've left you in the West. What was he thinking?"

I frowned. "That I can handle it."

"You're sixteen," he said, like that explained everything.

"Seventeen," I corrected. "My birthday was last month." The ego on him! He was only eighteen. Or nineteen. Maybe giving him the cold shoulder wouldn't be so hard after all.

The guard with the sprained ankle looked me over. "I'm glad your dad didn't leave you behind." He grinned. "So, your name's Lane?"

"Don't you have somewhere to be?" Everson asked, irritated.

The guy didn't take his eyes off me. "Nope."

"What are you doing here, Cruz?" Captain Hyrax demanded as he stalked toward us. It seemed to be the question of the night.

The guard hopped out of the line of fire, leaving us to face the captain. Everson straightened and snapped off a salute. "Dr. Solis put out a call for all medics, sir."

Hyrax wheeled on Dr. Solis, who was watching the exchange from the tent. "I told you to keep Cruz in the lab tonight."

Because I was going to be on base tonight?

Everson's scars whitened as his lips pressed tight. Guess that was news to him, and he didn't like it. Not one bit.

"Yes, Captain, you did." The doctor strolled closer, tall and elegant, even with his lab coat fluttering in the breeze. "But when I called for medics, it didn't occur to me to specify who *shouldn't* respond. Next time, I'll be sure to keep my priorities straight."

Hyrax glared at him, but Dr. Solis returned his look with the serenity of a Buddhist monk.

Everson turned to me. "Where's Mack now?"

"He's already gone on to Moline. It'll be our home base."

He cut a look at the captain. "Where some rando grups rammed through the gate last week?"

"Her father is scoping out the situation," Captain Hyrax informed him. "Won't surprise me if we're hovering the two of them back over the wall come tomorrow."

"Won't happen," I said coolly. "My dad will stay in Moline and do the job. If he thinks it's too rough for me, Chairman Prejean said I can stay on the base and take care of the orphans."

Everson stiffened as if touched by a live wire. "Lane, those kids will chew off your hand faster than —"

"She got the okay, Cruz," Hyrax cut in with a smirk. "From the *chairman*."

"My mother's never set foot in the orphan camp," Everson replied, seeming to forget whom he was talking to. Or maybe he hadn't. Maybe his guard act was just that — an act. One that he could drop at will because, ultimately, Everson was Chairman Prejean's son and sole heir, and someday Captain Hyrax would report to him. "She has —"

"The final say," Hyrax snapped, ending the discussion. "Get her bunked with the brats and report back. Don't turn it into a slumber party. You've got ten minutes."

Everson's jaw went hard, but his reply was pure patrol. "Yes, Captain."

I hesitated as he strode toward an ATV parked by the fence. Any second now Hyrax's radio was going to squawk to life as Chairman Prejean unloaded a mountain of protest.

"What are you waiting for?" Hyrax snapped. "That's your ride. Unless you want to hike a mile across the island."

"No. I'm going." I shot an apologetic look at the RV, hefted the duffel bag across my back, hung the nylon backpack off my other shoulder, and hurried over to where Everson was revving the ATV.

He raised a brow at my duffel. "That's all you brought?"

"I'm traveling light." There was no point in bringing things that I would run out of like body wash and deodorant. Eventually I'd have to get used to the off-grid equivalents. Might as well start now. Hopefully the soap and shampoo they made in bulk in Moline wouldn't turn my skin into rawhide and my hair to straw.

I climbed onto the ATV behind Everson and hesitantly looped an arm around his waist.

"You're going to have to hold on tighter than that," he called over his shoulder.

When the vehicle lurched forward, I snaked both arms around him. If this ride was going to get me booted off the island, at least I could take some comfort from the warm, solid feel of Everson's back. However, when we peeled past the RV, I loosened my hold. Chairman Prejean might tolerate me getting a ride, but clinging? Why push my luck? In fact, if I was going to be smart about this, I'd put more than just a few inches of distance between Everson and me.

Starting . . . now.

Back on the island, we pulled up at a large tent on top of a wooden platform, tucked into what had to be the only dark corner on base. As soon as Everson cut the engine, I clambered off so fast, I nearly landed face-first in the mud. Luckily, my bag acted as a counterbalance. I shrugged it off and onto the first step up to the platform.

"The orphans used to have their own barracks," Everson explained as he swung a long leg over the ATV and joined me by the wooden steps. "But with all the new recruits, the patrol needed the space." He frowned up at the tent. "You'd be better off sleeping in the infirmary. No one stays with these kids overnight."

Well, that sounded ominous. I'd endured scratches and a couple of bites while volunteering at the Davenport animal shelter — not fun. Stray children had teeth, nails, *and* imaginations. Guess sleeping with both eyes closed wasn't in my future. "Your mother hired me to take care of them, so that's what I'm going to do. Even if I had to talk her into it."

Everson snorted. "So you think. No one can talk her into anything. No one. She doesn't listen," he said bitterly. "Her own scientists told her using a virus to drop DNA into animals was a crap idea, but she wanted a Minotaur for her labyrinth. End of discussion." He directed a finger at me. "If she's letting you stay on base, she has a reason."

I swatted his hand away. "Like what?"

"Rafe."

Something shifted in my chest at the regret in his voice. Regret that I shared ten times over. "What about him?"

"She knows about his history with Mack — that Rafe

would do anything for him . . ." Everson paused, looking faintly uncomfortable. "And you."

"You told her?"

"During my debriefing, yeah."

I let out a harsh breath. Everson might be the one line guard I trusted, but he was still a line guard whose mission it was to stop the virus. Nothing came before that with him. Not friendship, not flirtation, not even a promise. He'd proved that the night he'd promised to help me rescue Rafe from Chorda's human zoo, then reneged in order to bring twenty-nine missing virus strains to Dr. Solis. "What does Rafe have to do with letting me stay on base?"

"She probably thinks he'll come looking for you."

A prickle of unease slid down my spine. "What does your mother want with Rafe?"

Everson cleared his throat and unfolded his arms. "We need his blood."

I stared at him, trying to breathe, trying to think, until finally I stupidly asked the obvious: "The missing strain is tiger?"

"No one told you?" he asked with surprise.

"Tiger," I repeated and closed my eyes. "Of course."

Chorda would never have allowed his queen to take his blood for her collection of genetic mash-ups — animal and human — that she infected and crossbred. Chorda would never have let *anyone* take his blood. He denied that he was even infected, despite his fur and fangs. And now Dr. Solis needed Chorda's blood to create a vaccine, but Chorda was dead . . . thanks to me. I had plenty of regrets from my time in the Feral Zone — more than I wanted to remember. But even after hearing this, I still didn't regret killing that heart-eating lunatic.

"Can you get a blood sample from a corpse?" I asked, though I had no idea what the people in Chicago had done with Chorda's body. Ripped it to pieces and flung them over the fence for the ferals to eat? That would have been my choice.

"No. The sample has to come from a living host. That's why Rafe is on the patrol's most wanted list."

I didn't like the sound of that. At all. The line guards had hated Rafe long before our jaunt through the Feral Zone. He'd been stealing supplies from the base for years, and none of the guards had ever managed to catch him, although the cook's assistant had come close and had gotten stabbed in the gut for his trouble. The bad history between Rafe and the line patrol meant the guards wouldn't care how they got a blood sample out of him. In fact, they'd probably skip the hypodermic needle altogether and simply take a bowie knife to his arm.

"You haven't heard of anyone else infected with tiger?" I asked.

Everson shook his head.

Unlike other ferals, Chorda hadn't been compelled to bite his victims; instead, he ripped out their hearts, leaving no survivors. As far as I knew, Chorda hadn't told anyone where he'd been when the feral had infected him.

Everson glanced away from me. "They sleep under there," he said, tipping his chin toward the shadowy space underneath the platform. "The strays."

"Don't call them that," I hissed, then bent to see several small figures scuttle deeper into the shadows. I straightened, heart racing, and sent Everson a questioning look.

"They're not used to beds," he explained. "On the upside, you get the tent to yourself and all the blankets you want. They're stored in the footlocker."

I took a long breath, stowed my panic, and crouched. A cluster of children watched me with suspicion. Jia broke from the huddle and crawled forward, as quick on her hands and knees as I was on my feet. "You," she rasped.

Was she glad to see me? "Yep, me. I'm Lane," I said loudly enough to address all of them, and then pointed to the platform above. "I'm going to stay up there for a while. That okay with you?"

Growls erupted from the huddle, but Jia just narrowed her eyes, considering me. I rose and faced Everson. It felt risky to turn my back on them, but I refused to show fear.

"You sure you don't want to stay in the infirmary?" Everson lowered his voice. "There's no predicting them. Sometimes they act human. Sometimes . . . not."

"I'm fine." That was fast becoming my mantra, though it was more hope than fact.

"I could stay with you," he offered.

"No! I mean, thanks, but no," I said quickly. "Since the kids don't trust guards . . . So they'll give me a chance." He seemed about to argue, so I said, "You should go. It's been ten minutes."

"At least," he agreed, glancing away, but not before I'd caught a glimpse of what looked like regret in his eyes. He probably thought I was mad because he'd told his mother and Hyrax about my friendship with Rafe. Actually, I *was* mad about that. How many times did he have to prove to me that he was a line guard first before I believed it?

Maybe what Everson said was true — maybe the

chairman was using my presence at Arsenal to draw out Rafe. But I didn't want to press my luck with her. I'd steer clear of Everson as she ordered. Besides, if Mahari was hidden away on base somewhere, I wasn't going to find her with him on my heels.

He climbed back onto the ATV and started the engine. "Let me know if you need anything."

"Okay."

I couldn't say something to soften my rejection. Could not. If I did, he'd approach me another day and I'd have to shut him down again. Now he felt bad and I felt worse — on top of being worried for Rafe and terrified that biohaz agents were probably tearing apart our empty apartment right now, all because I thought the West deserved to know the truth about the Feral Zone. Hours ago, posting my video had felt urgent and important. Now it seemed like the stupidest, most reckless thing I'd ever done in my probably short life.

Suddenly a cool feeling crept along my neck as I heard scuffling under the platform. A small figure darted out. I took two steps back before recognizing Jia. Hunched and wary, she curled her fingers as if she had claws. The other orphans followed, surrounding me — not close enough to touch, but close enough that their odor brought a sour taste to the back of my throat. Their faces were savage, some bared their teeth, others growled and grunted. My skin slickened with sweat, and my muscles tensed, but they came no closer.

"Okay," Jia said, her voice a rasp. "You can stay . . . but maybe don't close your eyes when you sleep."

The other kids snorted and giggled at her not-so-subtle threat.

"No problem," I said, hefting up my duffel bag and turning toward the wooden stairs. "I'm not much of a sleeper. Too many nightmares." I glanced back at the cluster of dirty kids, who'd suddenly fallen silent. "You ever have nightmares?"

Not a single one answered. They just regarded me with wary eyes and lips pursed tight to hold in any embarrassing admissions.

"No?" I asked. "Lucky you. Well, I'll be up here if you need me."

"We don't need anyone," Jia snapped.

"I'll bet you don't. You all look pretty fierce," I said, trying for a light tone. "But if you *want* me, I'm here."

"For now," she said sourly.

"For now," I agreed, and headed up the stairs. Halfway up, I paused and turned back toward them. "And if you want to hear a story, I know some good ones."

"Huh," Jia said doubtfully. "What kind of stories?"

I could feel all the kids leaning toward me. I wondered how the stories my dad had told me differed from the stories he'd told Rafe. We'd never had a chance to compare notes. Would the stories he'd told me be too tame for these kids? Maybe I should spice things up.

"There's one about a girl who fell down a hole and got trapped in a chimpacabra den," I said casually. "Actually, that one might be too scary." I studied my fingernails nonchalantly. It was probably the last day I would have clean fingernails — maybe forever. I thought of Chairman Prejean's fingernails and suppressed a shudder.

"I like scary," insisted the tallest boy.

"What happens to the girl?" another orphan asked. She

was younger than Jia and wore a belt cinched tightly over at least three layers of shirts.

"Come up into the tent, and I'll tell you."

Every single kid looked at Jia to see what she thought of my offer. With a shrug, I turned and climbed the rest of the stairs and disappeared into the tent. I chose the only single cot among the sets of metal bunk beds, conveniently located farthest from the doorway, and set my backpack and duffel bag down next to it. When I turned around, the orphans were huddled together just inside the tent flaps.

Jia stepped forward. "We'll stay for one story," she said. "Then we're out of here."

Someone behind her growled nervously.

"Agreed." I found the footlocker wedged between two bunk beds and started pulling out wool blankets. "Make yourselves comfortable." I tossed the blankets toward them, and they settled in on the floor, well out of arm's reach.

"But first, tell me your names. I know you're Jia," I said with a nod toward her.

She didn't seem the slightest bit surprised that I knew her name. Did she remember me from the night she'd come to the gate with my dad in tow? Or maybe she was just used to being infamous around here. That was more likely.

She introduced the kids, pointing them out as she rattled off, "Dusty, Tasha, Sage, Trader, Rose, Fixit."

"Okay, then." I settled cross-legged on my cot. "Once upon a time . . ." The kids grew still, all eyes on me. "There was a little girl who lived in a glass tower on the other side of a wall that was tall as the sky. Her father collected things for people, fetched them from the wild and dangerous land on the other side of the wall."

"That's here, right?" Dusty said. "We're in the wild and dangerous land."

Jia nodded.

"One day the girl found out that her father had disappeared and that he might be in danger. So she went to the other side of the wall to find him . . ."

My eyes blinked open, but it was as if I'd gone blind. I should have brought a flashlight to bed with me. Or left the battery-powered lantern on dim. But I hadn't and now the darkness pressed in around me, heavy and smothering, like something to run from. Why was I even awake at this hour? Had I heard something? Something like the scritch of claws on the tent's plank floor. No, not claws. The orphans didn't have claws. Did they?

I swallowed the bitter taste on my tongue and forced myself to lift my head a couple of inches. After the story, the orphans had fallen asleep on the floor, curled together in their blankets. But now they were gone, probably back underneath the platform. That's what woke me. The sound of them slipping past tent flaps and down the steps. Nothing to freak out over. Nothing to —

Someone drew in a breath and released it on a sigh.

A scream lodged in my throat when two golden eyes appeared in the dark. I bolted upright and came face-to-face with Rafe sitting on the edge of my bed. I flinched and then drew in a shuddering breath. He lounged, half in shadow, looking as gorgeous as he had when I'd first met him in the supply closet last fall. Sun-streaked hair and tanned chest on full display. His eyes were brilliant blue, not golden as I'd first thought. The chairman had been right — Rafe had come to the base to find me. I sagged with relief. He showed no signs of infection. Not so much as a whisker.

"How did you get past the gate?" I asked.

"Trade secret," he said softly, his voice strangely cold.

"But if the guards find you —"

He pressed a finger to my lips. "You remember your promise?"

I cringed back into my pillows. His narrowed glare burned like dry ice on skin. During our time in the Feral Zone, I'd exasperated and frustrated him, but the one time I'd witnessed his rage, there'd been nothing cold about it.

"Say you remember," he hissed.

My body felt bloodless, and yet I managed to whisper, "I remember."

"Good." He rose, aqua eyes glittering like jewels. "I'm waiting for you."

"No, it's not time." I threw my legs over the side of my bed. "You're not a danger to anyone yet."

His eyes grew as luminous as any nighttime predator's. "Guess again."

As he turned away, something whipped across my arm. A tail! Long and hairless like a rat's. My lungs spasmed, locking in my scream. Fur glimmered across Rafe's shoulders; stripes darkened his back like marks from a lash. I clapped my hand over my mouth to keep from keening at the sight.

"It's time to put me down, Lane," he said, sounding gentle for the first time.

I shook my head so hard my hair clung to my cheeks. "Dr. Solis is working on a cure. When he finds one, I'll bring it to you."

"Too late. The tiger is already here . . ." He held up a hand, fingernails ripped and dangling where his emerging claws had broken through. "You promised."

"I know! Wait," I cried as he turned away. "Don't go."

"I can't stay here. I'm not human," he said without looking back, and pushed through the door.

I scrambled out of my tangled blanket and staggered after him. But Rafe was already, impossibly, at the far end of the dimly lit hall — just a dark silhouette, disappearing around a corner.

My bare feet slapped the cold linoleum as I tore down the tunneling corridor. Finally I reached the corner and slid around it, only to slam into three handlers in leather aprons, dog whips in hand. They grabbed me before I could sprint away. I bucked and punched, but they forced me down, pinning me to the floor as soft footsteps padded toward us . . .

Chorda, the tiger-king, paused over me, his auburn eyes burning like embers in the darkness.

I clawed my way from under the handlers, but my bare feet slipped on the slick tile. From where I knelt I stared up at the velvet-robed tiger. Three-inch claws sprang from his nail beds, and I lost all semblance of courage. With a sob, I crab-scuttled backward, only to bang into a wall, trapping myself as Chorda reached for me, claws extended, long and curved. My hands went numb. I couldn't push myself up, so I floundered on the floor, silent and helpless as Chorda plunged his claws into my chest.

But it wasn't Chorda. It was Rafe. Horribly mutated now — fangs bulging past his split upper lip, yellow eyes gleaming with insanity. "I told you to put me down. Now it's too late." As he tore my heart from my body, a scream finally ripped loose of my throat.

I snapped upright on my cot, my hands burning with the pricks of a thousand needles as I pressed them over my heart, protecting it from . . . nothing. There wasn't a single deranged tiger-man in sight. Chorda was dead, and Rafe was on the other side of the river. Not here and — oh, please, please — not feral. Not yet.

· SIX ·

My breath came out in small bursts as I focused on the empty bunk beds around me. I'd been on Arsenal Island for more than two weeks, and yet I was still jolting awake from the nightmare that had tortured me in the West. I'd thought somehow things would be different on this side of the wall, that I'd be different. No and no. Rafe was as relentless in my dreams as he was that night in the zoo when he'd made me promise to kill him if and when he went feral. If I could just see that he was okay, maybe then the nightmares would stop.

I got up, shivering from head to toe. I was done sleeping for the night. Even without the nightmare lingering at the edge of my brain, I wouldn't be able to drift off again. There was nothing comfortable about the orphans' platform tent with its planked wood floor and metal-framed bunk beds. The morning was cold enough that I didn't take off the long underwear that I'd slept in. I just added more layers — regulation fatigues and a very un-regulation hot-pink hoodie. Officially, I wasn't a guard, so why limit my color choices to gray and speckled gray? I pulled my un-regulation-length hair into a ponytail and woke up my brain by tightening the rubber band until my scalp hurt.

Maybe when my dad came to the fence to visit me tomorrow night, he'd take me back to Moline with him. Right.

And maybe the orphans would stop digging through the dumpsters for food scraps to stash away "in case."

It had taken a week of nightly bedtime stories to get the kids used to drifting off inside the tent. They didn't always stay inside all night, and none were into the bed concept. Instead, they piled together like puppies in a nest of blankets on the floor. I was just thankful that they didn't expect me to pile in with them. For one thing, I wouldn't be able to sleep smashed between seven wriggling, snoring kids. For another, they might get used to it — or I might get used to it, and I already missed my pets crowding my bed. Missing a person was so much worse. I'd learned that when my mother died. As orphans, these kids had learned it too.

There was a whimper by my knees. I bent to find Dusty asleep on my duffel bag, a grimy fist tucked under his chin. When I smoothed back his dark curls, my fingers came away wet. The first time it happened, I'd panicked, thinking he was in the first stage of Ferae — incubation — which brought on a high fever. Now I knew that Dusty broke out in a night sweat every time he fell asleep, and the cause wasn't fever. His dreams were even worse than mine, going by his cries and what I knew of his past. For three days, he'd huddled inside a broken oven as his father, newly feral, had torn apart the abandoned house they'd been living in, searching for him.

I stroked Dusty's back. "*Shh*, you're safe," I whispered, using the magic word. It soothed the orphans like nothing else. Being safe was all they cared about, and it was all the more precious because they knew it was temporary. Once they showed signs of puberty, they'd be returned to the Feral Zone. Dr. Solis said teenagers didn't do well on base. Their hormones made them rebellious. At eight, Dusty didn't have to worry about that yet. He rolled over to blink up at me in confusion.

"You're safe," I repeated — as if saying it often enough would make it true. "It was just a nightmare, and now it's over." As if any nightmare was *just* anything. I wanted to gather him up and hold him tight, but he'd just thrash free. The orphans didn't tolerate hugs or any touch that felt like restraint.

"Wake the others," I said, and tousled his curls. A small touch. Nothing alarming and nothing he'd miss later. "And we'll get breakfast."

As I waited for the kids to pull on cleanish clothes, I stood at the edge of the raised platform with my face tipped up to a sky so overcast there was no sunrise, only a brighter strip of gray along the horizon. Our tent didn't have indoor plumbing. No surprise there. But at least we lived apart from the barracks.

Interacting with the guards at mealtimes was hard enough. It turned out my first impression of the orphans as innocent victims was not quite accurate. In fact, they liked nothing better than to rile up the guards. I did what I could to keep them in line, since staying on base was my best chance of finding out what had happened to Mahari. Also, apparently the melting pot society of the Moline compound was not functioning as well as it once had. According to Dad, it was the Wild West over there. As the mayor, my dad's girlfriend, Hagen, supposedly had authority to enforce rules, but she had little backup. Until the Moline compound settled down, my father felt it was too dangerous for me to live there — which was all the more reason he didn't want me taking risks on base. He'd asked me not to search the island for Mahari, but he'd had no luck tracking down Rafe.

What Dr. Solis had said on our first night back was true: No one in Moline had seen Rafe in the past six months, nor had the hacks who traveled between the compounds heard anything. It was as if Rafe had disappeared from the zone. The only ones who might know something — the lionesses — weren't talking. Sometimes I'd catch glimpses of them at dusk, slinking along the tree line, waiting for me to bring them Mahari. Despite my dad's explicit orders to leave it alone, I'd tried to find her, only to hit a dead end with every person I'd questioned and every building I'd searched. The only building I hadn't been able to scour was the virology lab, where Everson spent his days. I had put it off, knowing that Chairman Prejean's ever-present cameras would record my visit and that she'd assume I was there to see Everson. A small obstacle. And now that I'd searched the rest of the base, it was time to find a way around that problem.

A squad jogged past the orphan tent with inhuman syncopation. A childish part of me hoped one of the guards would trip, so the others would trip one after the other like a ten-car pileup. No one missed a step, of course, and not a single guard acknowledged me, though they had to have spotted me up here, lounging eight feet above them. They'd taken on Captain Hyrax's opinion of me, which was that I had no place in the patrol hierarchy and, therefore, no business being on base at all. But I didn't care.

Well, except in one case.

With Everson living on the south end of the island and me on the north, I rarely saw him. We'd exchanged greetings in the mess hall, but anytime he'd tried to say more, I'd found a reason to excuse myself. Luckily, the orphans provided me with endless excuses, and I'd hustle off to put a stop to whatever trouble they were getting into. But now it was time to risk talking to him. Who knew if he could help me? It was time to get him alone and at least ask if he knew what the guards had done with Mahari.

"Get back here, you brat!"

Nice. It was barely dawn and already a guard was hollering at an orphan. Jia raced up the platform's wooden steps and flew into the tent with a flushed-faced guard three steps behind her. I ducked into the tent in time to see her scramble under my itchy patrol-issue blanket.

The guy was older than the average recruit. Probably a career guard with a cushy staff position, meaning he didn't go out on patrol to scour the riverbank for quarantine breakers — human or manimal. I inserted myself between him and Jia, a move I'd perfected thanks to all the practice I was getting. "You can't just barge in here."

"She stole something from the mailroom!"

I poked the girl-sized lump under my blanket. "Hand it over."

A hand appeared and offered up a candy bar. I took it and tossed it to the guard. "Your blood sugar must have flatlined if you ran halfway across the island for this."

He threw the candy against the tent's canvas wall. Two of the orphans scrambled under a bunk to find it. "She took a package," he snarled.

"Did not!" Jia thrust aside the blanket and held up her empty hands.

"It's under the covers!" the guard shouted.

The other kids watched this exchange with wide eyes. Jia's indignant act didn't fool me, but I'd confront her when we were alone. "You need to leave. *Now*," I told the guard. "This is our tent."

His expression turned a darker shade of truculent, and he crossed his arms over his chest. Good tactic. The orphans always responded so well to intimidation.

"If I find any stolen items, I will bring them back to the mailroom myself," I told him.

"Like I believe that," he scoffed. "You're not even a guard."

"Nope," I agreed.

"What is brass thinking? Letting you stay here, taking up valuable space?"

"Someone needs to keep jerks from bullying little kids."

He snorted. "They're not kids."

One by one the other orphans angled closer, some hunched, others crouching, but all glaring with narrowed eyes and parted lips. I sighed.

"They're animals," he went on, getting sweatier with the vehemence he put into each word. "Just like their grupped-up parents."

The growling started then, of course, along with some low-pitched yammering. The guard's eyes bulged in his head. At the first snarl, he fumbled for the tent flap but then paused long enough to toss one more comment my way. "Do us all a favor: Dump that litter of freaks across the river where they belong."

The snarling got louder, and Rose, whose brother had been infected with rhino, heaved out great snorts of air. At that the guard hauled his bulk out of the tent. The orphans quieted only after his heavy boots pounded down the platform steps and squelched into the mud below. I faced Jia, who was now lounging cross-legged on my cot. "Don't make enemies," I scolded. "I won't always be here to stick up for you."

"We can stick up for ourselves," she scoffed.

"Yeah, but the way you guys do it just gets you in more trouble." I leveled a look at the others. "What did I say about using words?"

Out of the seven of them, five dropped their eyes and two started growling again — Sage and Trader, the oldest boys, though both were under twelve. "Act human," I snapped. "Or you two can eat with the patrol dogs while we go to the mess hall." Sage's growl turned into a whine. Trader fell silent, though he continued to glare. That, I'd accept. Humans glared.

Tasha rose from her crouch but held herself stiffly. "When're you gonna leave?"

"I don't know. But when I do, I might not be able to say good-bye."

Jia snorted. "You already told us that."

"Did I tell you that it makes me sad?"

She shrugged, while the others watched me with big eyes.

"I don't want you to go!" Dusty said suddenly.

Don't make another promise you might not be able to keep, I told myself firmly. "I'll stay for as long as I can."

None of them looked happy at that. But what could I do? I was living on borrowed time. Every day I waited for biohazard agents to clamp their hands on me and announce that I was under arrest. Every night I went to bed shocked and relieved that it hadn't happened yet. And that was the key word — *yet*.

I dropped my open palm under Jia's nose. "Hand it over."

She pouted, but when my palm continued to hover, she sighed and dug a large envelope from under the covers. "It's for Ev," she said, clutching the padded envelope to her chest. She'd adored him ever since the night she arrived at Arsenal's gate, towing an injured man in a wagon — my dad, as it turned out. Everson had looked out for her that night and gotten her into the orphan camp when the other guards would have forced her back into the Feral Zone alone. Considering that she followed him around base like a starstruck groupie, I was surprised that she'd steal his mail.

"Why'd you take it?" I asked.

"Because they weren't going to give it to him. And they opened it!"

"The mail staff opens all the packages. That's their job." I plucked the envelope from her grasp. It was addressed to *Everson, Arsenal Island, Mississippi River,* with a curly flourish. Girly writing. And what was up with the missing last name? The thought that came to mind wasn't flattering to the girl who sent it or to Everson. Not that it was any of my business.

"Why were you even in the mail office?" I asked Jia. The orphans didn't get mail. No one in the West knew they existed, and no one in the East cared, which was how they'd ended up on base.

"She takes the food sent to the guards," Dusty piped in. Jia shot him a warning look.

"They always get cookies and stuff," said Trader. "If you go early, before the postmaster logs it in, nobody misses it."

"Nice." I leveled her with a hard look. "A guard's family sends a care package, and you steal it?"

"They'll send more." Jia flung a hand toward the West. "They eat brownies and cookies every day over there and never run out."

Okay, she wasn't completely wrong about that.

"And the guards don't share," she added angrily.

Time to drop the morality issue. Trying to convince a kid with nothing that it's wrong to steal from an adult with plenty was beyond my pay scale. Still, she had to stop. "If you get caught stealing mail, they'll send you back to the Feral Zone."

The kids fell silent at that, even tough little Jia. After all the stories I'd heard about their hardscrabble lives in the zone, I knew they never wanted to go back. And they knew my warning was dead-on.

"But they were the ones stealing!" Jia burst out, fists clenched. "I heard the postmaster say, 'Anything for Everson Cruz goes in the incineration bin.' They were going to burn it!"

Yes, the patrol checked all incoming packages for contraband, but they weren't supposed to destroy the guards' mail. "Are you sure that's what he said?"

Jia nodded adamantly. I glanced down at the envelope. From the weight of it, it contained more than a letter. One edge had been sliced open, tempting me to peek inside, but I resisted. What kind of example would I be setting for the orphans? Still, I wondered what was so problematic it had to be destroyed. Even more mysterious, it sounded like this wasn't the first time — not if the postmaster had a system in place for dealing with Everson's mail.

Jia reached for the envelope. "I want to give it to Ev."

I jerked it out of her reach. "I'll give it to him."

"I'm the one who took it," she protested.

"Which is why you can't be seen with it." Plus, she'd just handed me the perfect excuse to approach him.

She pouted and then dropped her hand with a sigh. "Tell him I was the one who stole it for him."

"Sure. He'll be so proud." I shot her a smile. "Wasn't it just yesterday he threatened to put you in the brig for throwing things at the electric fence?"

She grinned, completely unrepentant. "Potatoes make the biggest sparks."

"Ev said it's dangerous," Tasha said reproachfully. "He said you could hurt your heart."

"He's right. And, even worse" — I tugged Jia up from my bed — "you were wasting food."

I sent the orphans outside and slid Everson's envelope under the thin mattress of my cot, planning to tell him at breakfast that I had it. Maybe I could work in some questions about Mahari on the walk from the mess hall back to the tent. But Everson wasn't in the mess hall when we got there, and he wasn't there for lunch either, which wasn't that surprising since he practically lived in the lab on the other side of the island. The guy wasn't just devoted to Dr. Solis; he took his work as seriously as a quest for the Holy Grail. He wanted to undo the damage his mother had done.

He wanted to fix the world.

That morning, the orphans and I worked on reading, using the few children's books my dad had managed to bring me on his last visit. Then we swept the barracks and hung the blankets on the clothesline to air out in the cool spring breeze.

In the afternoon, we worked on a group project, planning a trip from Arsenal to Moline using an old map I'd found in one of the footlockers. The least I could do for these kids was help them get somewhere relatively safe when they were kicked off the base.

We stopped an hour or so before dinnertime.

"Let's take a break," I said. "You can watch the recruits if you want to." They responded with gleeful whoops. "Just don't get in anybody's way." Hah. The orphans had sprinted for the ropes course before I'd even finished speaking.

Jia, now wearing my pink hoodie, which hung to her knees, scrambled up a hanging rope at twice the speed of the guard next to her. The recruits glared at me. Their commanding officer seemed less irritated and immediately used Jia's dexterity as one more way to humiliate the newbies. I sent them a shrug of apology and called to the orphans, "Meet me at the tent in an hour." Only Dusty acknowledged that he'd heard me with a thumbs-up. The rest of them high-stepped their way through the lanes of crisscrossing ropes. Who was I kidding? These kids didn't come when called. Most of them didn't even know how to use a fork and knife. Not as eating utensils, anyway.

I retrieved the envelope addressed to Everson and slid it under my T-shirt. As I hurried toward the lab along the paved road that bisected the base, I tamped down the flutter in my belly. This was not about getting to see Everson. This was about delivering a package and finding out about Mahari. Period.

The wind picked up as the recruits suffered through belly-busters, atomic sit-ups, and the sadistic reverse push-ups. Team captains roamed among them, snarling instructions and kicking recruits into the proper positions. The guards on laundry duty glared at me as I hustled past.

"Sorry I ruined your sweet deal on child labor," I called. A jerk move, but so what? I was proud that I'd gotten the patrol to stop forcing the orphans to work from dawn till dusk. Captain Hyrax still scowled at me over it every time we crossed paths. Guess his boots didn't shine quite as brightly when not polished with orphan sweat. As much as I didn't trust Chairman Prejean's intentions, she'd backed me on that. Now the orphans had to keep their own clothes, tent, and latrine clean, but not the guards' too, which meant they had time to learn and play. I hoped it would last — that Captain Hyrax wouldn't turn them back into indentured servants the moment I left.

I pushed open the door to the virology lab, which was the tallest and most modern-looking building on the island. It was also the most fortified, and I had to pass through a laser decontamination booth before guards let me enter the main area on the first floor, which looked like a hotel lobby with its comfy couches and coffee tables.

None of the guards at the doors or by the elevators asked why I was there, but then, this building was filled with scientists who worked in the Titan labs. The top floors were their living quarters, which included private suites, a dining room, and a recreation room. I'd overheard some guards complaining that Everson also had rooms on the top floor but that he rarely used them. He lived in the barracks and ate in the mess hall with all the other grunts, even though he worked in the lab. The guards didn't like him any better for it. No matter where Everson slept or how hard he worked, he'd always be the chairman's son, and most of them would always resent him.

If the guards' resentment bothered Everson, he never showed it or made an effort to tone down his bossiness. Maybe he didn't know how. He'd grown up inside an old Titan labyrinth theme park, surrounded by tutors and Titan employees. Since he wasn't allowed to leave or interact with anyone but staff, he'd thrown himself into studying. He started taking online college science classes when he was in his early teens. He'd earned his place on Dr. Solis's research team.

Once inside the elevator, I pushed the button for the third floor while noting that the basement didn't have a button, just a thumbprint screen.

The elevator door slid open, and I strode out, only to slow my pace as I took in the series of photographs along the opposite wall. The photos represented a trip through history, starting with the outbreak. The lurid colors attacked my eyes while the subject matter hijacked my brain. Figures in jumpsuits swung body bags into flaming burial pits; slavering dogs chased a man struggling to carry two children; a crazed woman lunged at the lens, bloody teeth bared to bite; a family threw aside their suitcases to flee as firebombs fell from the sky; the terrified refugees crowded onto the last bridge across the Mississippi River, hoping to be allowed into the West.

By the time I passed the last photograph, I was hyperventilating, which was stupid. I should have been immune to these kinds of images by now, considering that I'd been raised on all things plague: facts, images, personal accounts, analysis, and opinion. People over thirty were obsessed with the topic. *Obsessed*. Still, it was weird to see these pictures on display in a Titan lab.

I turned the corner and found a group of people blocking my way. Everson's husky voice filled the corridor as the group shuffled forward. "The lab was built fifteen years ago, when Titan began funding drug research." Standing a head taller than the rest of the group, he was easy enough to spot. Plus, he was walking backward to face them.

I couldn't interrupt him while he was giving a tour, so I tagged along to wait for my chance.

The group was an equal split of men and women and a wide range of ages. Scientists, going by their questions. Definitely new Titan employees. But unlike new guards, their welcome-to-base orientation didn't include getting dropped from hovercopters into the river.

"As you all know, when the plague first hit, the course of the disease was short," Everson continued. With his ramrod posture, cropped dark hair, and gray pullover with shoulder patches, he looked every inch the line guard, but he sure didn't sound like one. He sounded like a science geek. "Infection meant insanity and death within days," he went on. "Since then, the Ferae virus has adapted so that it's no longer lethal to humans. Now the virus acts as a mutagen — changing the host's DNA, exactly as it was designed to."

The scientists hung on his every word. Like most people from the West, they probably believed that the only humans living in the East were criminals banished from our side of the wall. They wouldn't get the whole truth until they'd signed a confidentiality contract with the Titan Corporation. Now they were so wound up with anticipation they were practically thrumming when Everson paused in front of the door to the virology lab, where he spent his days and many nights.

Instead of a handle, the steel door had a control pad, to which Everson pressed a finger, and the door swung open. Excited whispers passed through the group. Before coming to Arsenal Island, none of these scientists would have seen a hybrid animal other than in photographs. It was no wonder that they stampeded into the lab the moment the door thunked open.

I hesitated in front of the open door. I didn't have the clearance for this. I should wait for another time to approach him. Sometime when he was alone. That would be the smart thing to do. The safe thing.

Except . . . I'd been playing it safe the past two weeks — staying far away from Everson — and had gotten nowhere. I was no closer to finding Mahari than when the lionesses had scared all sense out of me. So maybe it was time to step off the safe path. Or take an all-out leap . . .

I hurried into the virology lab just as the door closed behind me.

· SEVEN ·

Head ducked, I joined the scientists in a vestibule furnished with leather club chairs, a wall screen to the left, and swinging doors on the right. What had everyone staring, however, was the glass wall before us and the multilevel space beyond it. Workstations lined the platforms, accessed by curving metal ramps. Researchers in protective jumpsuits and goggles maneuvered carts between the vault-sized refrigerators on the first level. And just when I thought it couldn't get any more sci-fi, a tower of glass-fronted cubes rose out of the floor, each containing a hybrid animal. The scientists surged toward the glass wall for a glimpse of the different animal mash-ups, and I hurried to stay hidden in the group.

As the tower topped out at ten cubes high, a researcher rotated the whole thing with a swipe of his finger and then stopped it with a touch when he reached a specific animal. He tapped the glass twice and red text appeared, floating across the front of the cube. Assured that he had the correct animal, the researcher pressed a button and the cube filled with blue gas.

"Lull," Everson said in response to the group's murmurs. "It's a quick and painless way to sedate the animal . . . Or put it down. Depending on the dose."

So, which was it — asleep or dead? There was no way to tell when the researcher opened the cube and lifted out the limp fuzzy body.

"Those animals are infected, right? What if one gets loose?" someone asked Everson.

"Chances of that are slim. We keep the animals in a restricted area one level down and bring them up as needed."

The scientists spread out along the glass wall, vying for views of specific workstations. I kept plenty of people between Everson and me. If he saw me now, he might kick me out for not having the right clearance. I edged closer to the swinging doors on my right in case I needed a quick exit option, but then a low growl snapped my attention to a wood crate shoved into the corner on our side of the glass.

I wasn't the only one who'd heard it. A scientist shoved past me in his hurry to crouch and peer through the slats. Within seconds, the others rushed over. I scooted around the group to put more bodies between Everson and me.

"Not too close," he warned. "The patrol caught it on the riverbank an hour ago, and it hasn't been tested."

"It's a GMO." The man sounded like a kid at the circus.

Genetically modified organism. Animals and people usually got infected from being viciously attacked by a feral. Then came a raging fever and painful physical mutation, followed by insanity. *Modified* wasn't quite the right word to describe that transformation.

"What's the DNA mix?" the man asked.

"I won't know until I do a blood test," Everson said with a shrug. "But if I had to guess . . . a lynx that caught a bad case of lizard."

Between the slats, yellowish eyes darted from side to side, scanning us with such malice, goose bumps broke out across my skin. It might not be feral, but it was furious. The creature yowled, and the crate shuddered under the force of scrabbling claws. The scientists leapt back in a perfect splash pattern.

Everson remained relaxed against the chair, his arms crossed. "It might not even be infectious."

"Not infectious?" one man scoffed. "It's a hybrid. Just look at its skin."

"It could have had an infected parent," Everson explained. "Parents pass down their messed-up DNA but not the virus itself. In fact, the offspring are immune to Ferae, which means we can't use them in our research."

If they couldn't use the animal in tests, would they set the scaly lynx thing free? Not a chance. They'd just kill it, and it wouldn't even have died for a worthwhile cause. Clearly, I wasn't cut out to work in a lab.

"This can't be safe," someone complained, "leaving it out here."

"Nothing on this side of the wall is safe," said a cool voice from the doorway.

Unlike the rest of the group, I didn't turn to see who'd spoken. I knew that voice, with its mashed words and muffled tone and silky ability to raise all the hairs on my body. I slipped behind two tall scientists just as Chairman Prejean strolled into the antechamber.

Dr. Solis was by her side and two guards were at her back. "Welcome to Arsenal Island." She pivoted to take in the group, a study in contrasts. Intimidating in silky white scrubs and transparent surgical mask. Very sickly chic. I didn't want to see her move past intimidating into scary, which would happen if she spotted me here.

"I hope you all found your living quarters acceptable," she went on. That got a chorus of positive replies, and the chairman's lips pulled into a smile under the skintight latex. "You've all met Vincent." She gestured to where Dr. Solis stood, sleepy-eyed and elegant as always. "He'll be taking over now as your tour guide."

He gave the group a warm smile. "Let's head up to the labs on the fourth floor, where you'll be working."

Before anyone could take a step, the creature in the crate let loose with a piercing yowl. The chairman's eyes flashed above her surgical mask at the tufts of brindled fur poking from between the slats. "What is that thing doing in here?"

"The river patrol just brought it in," Everson replied evenly. "I don't want to expose it to the research animals until I've tested it for Ferae and other diseases."

"You're going to take that thing's blood? *You?*" She didn't wait for his response before turning to Dr. Solis. "I said he could work here as long as you kept him away from anything dangerous."

The scientists glanced from her to Everson, clearly confused.

Everson's mouth hardened into a tight line. "I take every precaution."

He had to be embarrassed at being treated like a child in front of the scientists, but he continued to give a good guard face. Unlike his mother, whose latex-covered jaw was clenched in a grimace.

"You want to stay and play with test tubes? Then you follow my rules. Brooklyn." She snapped her fingers at a guard. "Kill that thing and destroy the carcass. Boil it, burn it; I don't care. Douse it with acid if you have to. Just make sure every germ in its flea-ridden body is dead."

The guard scrambled to unholster his gun.

She glanced upward as if praying for patience. "*After* we leave."

He dropped his gun hand. "Yes, Chairman."

"Dr. Solis," the chairman said serenely, "please clear the room. I'd like a word with my son."

The scientists hurried for the door, thinning the group. In a matter of seconds, I'd end up exposed to her sharp eyes. The swinging doors were behind me, and I backed toward them as the group scurried past Everson, stealing looks at him as they passed. His expression remained stony.

I backed through one of the swinging doors, caught it, and closed it smoothly. Something hissed behind me — a soft, threatening sound. I whirled to face row upon row of steel cubbies, stacked seven feet tall, with cage doors — not glass-fronted like those in the lab, though these also contained animals. Infected animals. Their scratching and scrabbling echoed off the hard surfaces, which were probably hosed down hourly given the overwhelming antiseptic smell.

I slunk down the middle of the farthest aisle, keeping well out of reach of the cages with my gaze front and center. No reason to make eye contact and set off a crazed animal even if it couldn't sink its teeth into me.

A gunshot blasted in the other room, and my heart leapt. I wasn't the only one to startle. A cacophony of yips and chittering broke out around me. The guard must have had less-than-stellar aim, because the lynx-lizard thing screeched out its torment and the crate rattled so loudly I expected to hear it explode into splinters. Another shot, and the mongrel's scream cut off as fast and completely as a knife slash.

"What are you keeping back there?" I heard the chairman demand. I needed to get out of sight before she barged in, but even as big as the room was, there was nowhere to hide. There wasn't so much as a gap between the steel cages.

"Test animals," Everson replied dryly. "If you want Brooklyn to kill them too, he's going to need more ammo."

She grated a reply too low for me to catch. My only option was to hide on top of the cages. I hated, *hated* that choice but hated the thought of being sent back to the West and executed even more. Up it was.

I jammed my boot toe under a knee-high cage door and prayed that I didn't pull the whole row down on top of me. Not that that was the worst thing that could happen. No, that would be infection. The beaver in the eye-level cage cowered in a corner. Above him, a raccoon paced. They didn't look feral. Actually, they didn't even look like hybrids. But then, they wouldn't if they'd been infected recently. The only way to do this was fast. With a hop, I clambered up six rows of cubbies like a sugar-high monkey — so fast that nothing sank its teeth into my grasping fingers. At the top, I hoisted myself up and rolled out of sight just as the swinging doors whooshed open.

· EIGHT ·

Only one set of footsteps crossed the room.

"Lane?"

Everson. And yet, I stayed pressed to the steel-topped cages on the off chance his mother was hovering by the door.

"Lane, I know you're here. I saw you duck in." He strode down the next aisle. "Tell me you're not hiding in a cage."

I risked a peek over the edge of the row. He was alone, crouching to check the big cages on the bottom. I pushed up and sat cross-legged. Not because I was feeling so relaxed, but I didn't want to dangle my legs and test my patrol-issued camo pants against teeth. "Is she gone?" I whispered.

When he straightened and our eyes met, a tingle went down my skin.

"How'd you get — never mind." He stalked down the aisle, not keeping his voice down. "What are you doing in here?"

"I didn't want to run into your mother."

He stopped below me and let out a breath. "A lot of people feel that way," he said. "But they usually stick to hiding behind doors." When I didn't move, he sighed. "She left. I told her this area is covered in germs."

I snatched my hands off the metal-topped cage. "Is it?"

He raised a brow. "Well, this *is* the virology lab . . ."

I furiously rubbed my palms on my camo pants. Why had I worked to break my hand sanitizer addiction? Why had I thought that was a smart, healthy thing to do? Carrying hand sanitizer, *that* was the smart move. Self-respect didn't kill germs; chemicals did.

"Of course, we keep the infected animals in a secure area. These" — Everson lifted a hand toward the cages — "are the control group. But you knew that, right? You knew they weren't infected before you climbed up there?"

His eyes dared me to admit the truth — that I'd been incredibly reckless. I took a deep breath and yanked my ponytail very tight to keep my brain alert. "Of course I did," I lied.

"Uh-huh," he said with so much irony, he might as well have rolled his eyes. Instead, he held up his arms. "All right. Scoot out and jump."

I stared at him. "Jump?"

"I'll catch you."

"I'm not four. You can't catch me."

"Lane. Jump." His tone made it clear he was done arguing. "Now."

Right. Bossy. I kept forgetting that about him. "I'm not jumping," I snapped. "I'll squash you. Isn't there a step stool around here?"

"Lane, if I go down, I'm going down with an armful of girl. I'm okay with that."

Okay, first off, I was a lot more than an armful, but I wasn't going to point that out. And second off, was he flirting? Hard to tell. The words were nice, but he still looked impatient.

"Lane." He lifted his hands higher.

Yep, impatient.

"Oh, all right," I huffed, and scooted to the edge of the metal-topped cages. I dropped my feet to prop my heels on the top row. Whatever was inside that particular cage took a swipe at my calf. Its claws didn't rip through my pants, but it was enough incentive to hurl myself at Everson.

I slammed into him, and his arms closed around my hips. He let me slide slowly down the long, hard line of his body until my feet touched the ground. I exhaled on a shaky breath as animals paced in their cages on either side of us. I craned my head back to look into his storm-cloud eyes, which were intent on me.

Even if he had been flirting, that wasn't why I'd come to see him, risking his mother's wrath in the process. And possibly my life. I stepped back to put a little space between us since he hadn't. "Does the patrol have infected humans locked away somewhere?"

Everson tensed and let his hands slip from my hips, as if I'd dumped a bucket of cold water on him. The crease between his brows deepened. "What?"

"Guards kidnapped a manimal out of the zone — Mahari. They took her away in a truck."

"Where'd you — never mind, I can guess. You heard this from the grups who attacked your jeep the night you got here?"

I nodded. "Does the patrol have her?"

"No. That's why we put up electric fences everywhere. To keep the infected humans *out*."

"Maybe they took her to another base," I pressed.

"The rest are just field camps. Prefab buildings. No labs

or scientists — and no bridge to the Feral Zone. You said they took her away in a truck."

"That's what the lionesses said." And I believed them. All three of them couldn't have imagined it. "Maybe the patrol has humans stashed away, and you don't know about it."

"I'd know."

"Maybe —"

"Lane, I'd know." His words were casual, but I could hear the underlying steel in his tone.

I gave up. If Everson didn't know where Mahari was, bugging him wasn't going to change it. But that meant I'd hit another dead end.

He propped a shoulder against the row of cages. "Now can I ask you something?"

I nodded as I studied the random assortment of animals curled up in their cages behind him: raccoons, skunks, cats, and a fox. It wasn't hard to picture Mahari locked in a human-sized version.

"Why have you been avoiding me?"

My eyes snapped to his. "I haven't," I said quickly. Too quickly. He'd caught me off guard just as he'd intended.

"Yeah, you have," he said like it was no big deal. "My mother told you to stay away from me, didn't she?"

"No." I edged back up the aisle.

Everson's gaze dropped to the space I'd just put between us and then back to me. "Did she give you an ultimatum?"

Was he kidding me with this nonchalant act? The night Rafe locked us in a supply closet, Everson himself told me that he'd joined the patrol to fight Ferae on the front line *and* get away from his mother. If he found out that she was still interfering in his life, his anger would redline. Even if he promised not to tell that I'd outed her, he'd give it away somehow with body language or a cool undertone. I wasn't going to risk my life on his acting abilities. "If she'd said something to me, would I be here now?"

He studied me. "Then why?"

"Why?"

"Every time I get near you, you can't get away fast enough."

"I —" Had no answer for that.

"Look, I know I was a jerk when I first saw you again. I just couldn't believe your dad would bring —" He cut himself off and then let out a long sigh. "I'm sorry."

My skin burned. Not just on my face but across my body like a brush fire. I wanted to break into a hundred apologies for shunning him and explain that his mother hadn't given me a choice. "It's not that," I muttered. "It's just — I'm not going to be on base for very long, and it seemed like it would be better if we didn't, you know . . . spend time together."

He shot me an exasperated look. "Better?"

"Yes." As I said it, I realized I wasn't lying. "You didn't spend last month saying good-bye to people and pets you love. I did, and it sucks."

Everson watched me as if my thoughts were scrolling across my face. "You know," he said quietly, "for as long as I can remember, my mother has played fast and loose with the truth. Told me I had an autoimmune disorder to keep me at home. Didn't tell me that she'd started the plague. Big lies, right?"

I nodded. That he spoke to her at all was shocking.

"But I know that everyone isn't like her," he went on. "I know you're not. And after what we went through, I hope you know I'm not like that. I've got your back, Lane. You can trust me."

I did trust him. He was the only person on the island I trusted. He wouldn't rat me out to his mother. I knew that in my gut. So then, why not give him the honesty he deserved? I cleared my throat. "She might have mentioned something about not fraternizing with you . . ."

He didn't look surprised to hear it, though a muscle in his jaw twitched. "Why?"

"I'm a bad influence."

"Right. The girl who lives on a base so she can take care of orphans. You're the worst."

I shook my head. I couldn't let him put a shiny polish on my actions. "I'm here because my dad won't let me live in Moline."

"Okay," Everson said, stepping closer. "You're here. You shouldn't be, but you are. And while you're on Arsenal, I'm going to get as close as you'll let me — because my mother doesn't decide who I fraternize with. I do."

His gaze was so intense my face felt scorched by it. I backed up. I wanted no part of his pushback against his mother. He wasn't the one who'd get booted off the island. Why had I put myself in this situation?! For Mahari. For Rafe. Oh, and the letter.

I reached down the front of my shirt and fished out the envelope. Everson arched a dark brow when I offered it to him. "It's for you," I explained.

"You switched to mail duty?" he asked dryly.

"No, I — Jia stole it . . . because — Just take it." I thrust it toward him.

When he took it from me, something slithered out of the open end. I scooped up the knitted scarf from the floor. It was emblazoned with "My hero" in red yarn. Ew.

"Uh . . . Here." I offered it to him.

He eyed it and then looked back at me with a silent "What the heck?" "No return address," he said, glancing at the envelope.

"They probably cut it off in the mailroom."

"Probably," he agreed, shaking out a piece of pink paper. He flipped it over and read: "*Your future wife, Nola.*"

Whoa. He had a future wife named Nola? I tried to keep the shock off my face as I asked, "Your girlfriend?"

He shot me a bemused look. "I don't know anyone named Nola."

"Someone you don't know knit you a scarf?"

"That bother you?"

"No. I —" Was still holding the scarf. I offered it to him again, but he'd gone back to the letter. "I'm going to leave it here, okay?" I hung the scarf on the latch of the nearest cage and headed for the swinging door.

Behind me, he read aloud. "*Dear Everson, the next time you have a taste for something wild, you don't have to go all the way to Chicago — come back to the West. I promise I've had all my shots . . .*"

I spun back to see him looking as disconcerted as I felt. Making up something like this wasn't Everson's style. Dirty jokes, lewd come-ons — that was more Rafe's thing. "Some guard is messing with you," I guessed.

"No guard knows I went as far as Chicago. That

information is classified," he said, and shifted his gaze back to the letter. "*I want to see you in that leather apron again — but this time, just the apron.*"

"I didn't write that!" The words burst from my lips, sounding incredibly defensive, which was exactly how I felt since I was the only person on this side of the river who'd seen him in a handler's apron.

"I know." He crumpled the letter and shoved it into his pocket. "But the only people present when I was debriefed were Hyrax and my mother."

"I really hope neither of them wrote that."

Everson snatched the scarf off the cage and tossed it into the bin labeled "Medical Waste." "C'mon," he said, steering me toward the door.

We entered the warehouse-sized building that housed the commissary, gym, and mailroom, the door to which stood wide open. The only guard in the place was in the back, stuffing mail into slots as fast as he stuffed cookies into his mouth, taken from an open tin perched on his rolling cart. Every so often, he'd chuck a letter or package into a fat drawstring sack on the floor.

I started for the counter, ready to demand answers, but Everson hooked my elbow. I followed his stunned gaze to the opposite wall. The floor-to-ceiling collage of photos didn't stun me. It was just . . . Ugh. Okay, I was a little surprised that the patrol allowed the mailroom workers to put up pictures of half-naked women in a public area. Maybe on this side of the wall, everyone got less civilized, not just the infected.

"Classy," I muttered.

Everson dipped his head, putting his lips by my ear.

"Those weren't there a week ago. And they shouldn't be there now." He surveyed the mail office, eyes narrowed. "What's with this place?"

What was he talking about? The mailroom was messy, true, but not in a dirty, germy way. It looked more like organized chaos along the lines of Santa's workshop. Stuffed-to-bursting canvas bags lay in heaps across the floor while packages covered the counter in teetering stacks. A lot of those packages had been cut open, but that was protocol.

The guard in the back pulled the drawstring sack closed and hefted it over his shoulder. As soon as he disappeared into a back corridor, Everson headed to the wall for a closer look. I didn't think this was the time to be eyeing girly pics, but whatever. I closed in on the counter. The opened parcels contained snacks and baked goods and most were half empty. Eating other people's care packages was crappy, but hardly evidence of a conspiracy.

Everson fell back a step from the wall of photos, both hands resting on top of his head.

"What is it?" I joined him.

"You tell me," he said, gesturing to the pictures. "We fell into another dimension, right? That's the only way this makes sense."

I saw now that the glossy pictures weren't magazine centerfolds but real photos from real girls, signed with x's, o's, and/or hearts. But the shocking part — really shocking — was that most of the scribbles began with some variation of "To Everson."

"There must be another guard with my name," he said, though he didn't sound like he believed it.

"Maybe . . ." I pivoted to take a longer, closer look at the mailroom — at the open care packages and the overstuffed canvas bags. "Is this more mail than usual?"

"A lot more," he confirmed.

I squatted by a canvas sack, tugged open the drawstring, and let the letters spill out. Every single one was addressed to "Everson on Arsenal Island."

Given the pastel shades of the stationery, most of these letters were from teens and maybe even tweens, going by the doodles and stickers. I snatched an envelope from the pile and ripped it open. The letter began with "Dear Everson," written in big, rounded letters.

He crouched beside me. "She turned the V into a heart," he groaned. "Please let there be another Everson."

"*I think what you're doing is so great,*" I read aloud, pitching my voice higher, since the writer had to be a kid. "*I wish I could come to the Feral Zone and help you take care of the manimals . . .*"

Everson brought in a sharp breath. "Manimals? She used that word?"

I lowered the letter before he noticed that my hand was trembling. "Yeah."

He snatched up a red envelope and tore it open while I scanned the rest of the girl's letter. There was nothing in it to confirm my growing suspicion. I reached for another envelope and saw Everson's eyes widen.

"I really hope a kid didn't write this one." Face flushed, he tossed that letter aside.

I opened a card with a picture of a puppy on the front. Within one line, I sat down hard. "Oh no . . ."

"If it's too graphic, don't read it," Everson said.

"I did this," I whispered. "This is all my fault."

· NINE ·

"What do you mean *your* fault?" Everson demanded in a hoarse whisper.

I scanned the mailroom, but the guard had yet to return. Lifting the puppy card, I read aloud: "*Dear Everson, If it weren't for that video, I wouldn't know what's happening on the other side of the wall or about you . . .*"

"Video? Your dial — the things you recorded when we were over there —"

I continued to read. "*What you did was so brave. I hope you get a medal someday for risking your life like that. I've watched the video at least a hundred times and —*"

"Lane," he said, his tone sharp, "did you use my name?"

"No! I don't know how — well, I suppose they can guess you're stationed on Arsenal. The last bridge is here. But I never used your name or —" My voice had grown steadily louder as my mind spun with the implications of what had happened.

Everson gestured for me to be quiet. He rose and tipped his head to the door.

I followed him outside, feeling more panicked by the second. No one could have matched Everson's face in my video to a photo of him because there were none. Not online anyway. I'd checked. So many people still hated Ilsa Prejean for starting the plague that she lived in terror of someone hurting her only child as payback. She'd kept Everson's image off the Web and threatened to arrest anyone who posted a candid shot of him. The fact he'd never set foot outside the fortress that was their home, an old Titan Imaginarium, had made it impossible for the paparazzi to snap a shot.

We slipped between the enormous stone buildings as the wind picked up. "What were you *thinking*?" he demanded.

I bristled at his tone despite my growing anxiety. "You let me keep my dial. You knew I'd been recording the whole time."

"Yeah, and I knew you'd turn it into a video. What I don't get is what you're doing *here*. On Arsenal." Everson raked a hand through his hair. "Right where the biohaz agents can find you. Did you see all those mailbags? If that many people wrote me —"

"Girls," I corrected. "If that many *girls* wrote you."

He waved that off. "Those are just the ones who wrote — as in, the tip of the iceberg."

I felt cold, bloodless. "Your mother? Do you think she knows about the video?"

"She has to," he said grimly. "When do you see your dad again?"

"He's meeting me at the gate tomorrow."

"Good. He can take you back to Moline with him."

Where the biohaz agents couldn't go. But leaving base meant I'd never find Mahari.

Everson frowned at my hesitation. "Lane, you recorded illegal images — images that compromise national security. You know what the punishment is?"

I nodded because I couldn't get the word past the knot in my throat.

"Execution," he said for me.

"I have to stay."

"No, you —"

"No one in the zone knows where Rafe is or even if he's okay," I explained.

"What does that have to do with you getting arrested?"

"The lionesses said they know where he is."

Everson's lips parted with surprise, though he recovered quickly enough and jammed his hands into his pockets. "They're probably —"

"Lying," I said, cutting him off. "Maybe. But the hacks passing through Moline have no news about Rafe — no one has seen him. And since my dad has nothing to go on, all I can do is hope the lionesses know where he is. The problem is, they'll only tell me if I bring them Mahari."

The crease between Everson's brows deepened. "Got it."

"I need to get back to the kids," I said suddenly. It wasn't even a ploy to get away from his penetrating look. I'd left the orphans alone for too long, which always meant at least one of them getting yelled at, if not manhandled.

Everson reached for me. "Lane —"

I waited for him to say more, but he dropped his hand without ever touching me. "Nothing."

With a nod, I pivoted and jogged toward the north end of the island.

At the orphan tent, I stumbled to a stop. A jeep had pulled up right next to the wooden steps of the platform. This could not be good. Only the top brass got carted around the island. I approached the jeep warily. What had the orphans done this time, and would I be blamed? Probably, since I'd all but deserted my post.

I stiffened my spine and approached the guard in the driver's seat. "What's going on?"

"You've got a visitor."

My skin prickled at this alarming news. No one was allowed to just drop by the base. Even my dad had to talk to me through the fence at Gateway Station during our every-other-evening meet-ups. "Who?"

The guard raised a brow and gave me a "Really?" look.

Right. Even if this guy knew that Hyrax had come by to break my legs, he wouldn't give me a heads-up; he'd follow orders.

He jerked his chin toward the tent. "Get up there."

And there was another not-so-lovely trait — the barked commands. Considering that I was already in hot water, I did not point out that I wasn't a guard, cross my arms, and wait stubbornly for him to tack on a *please*. No, I hurried up the steps to the platform, ducked into the tent, and spotted my "visitor."

The orphans were sprawled across the floor, listening intently as a woman read aloud from a book of fairy tales. The book blocked my view of her face, but I knew she wasn't line patrol — not in a snug black pantsuit and patent leather pumps.

"*So off Little Red Riding Hood went, taking the basket to her grandmother,*" the woman read from her perch on my cot. Her crisp inflection and spiky gray hair turned my blood into slush.

"It's not a basket; it's a letter," Jia corrected.

The book dipped as the woman shot the little girl a silencing look, confirming my fear. I hadn't seen her in months, but Director Taryn Spurling wasn't someone I'd ever forget.

I hovered by the tent flap as sweat plastered my T-shirt to my skin. The director of Biohazard Defense was here. Now. And the only reason that made any sense was that she'd come to arrest me for posting the video. But then, would she really hang around, reading to the orphans until I showed up? Strange. Even stranger that she was being nice at all. In my few encounters with the pixie-sized witch, her personality had been as prickly as her hair.

"*As she strolled along the wooded path, a voice called out, 'Hello, little girl.'*" Spurling made her voice gruff, getting into the part, which just baffled me even more. "*Little Red Riding Hood looked over, and there, sitting among the flowers, was a very large, very hairy . . .*"

"Tiger-man!" all the children shouted.

"Ah, no." Spurling lowered the book with a puzzled frown. "A wolf."

"No, a big, hairy tiger-man," Jia said crossly.

A smart fugitive would slip out of the tent now, before anyone spotted her, and find somewhere to hide. But unless Director Spurling had other proof that I'd posted that video, she couldn't arrest me simply because I was the most likely suspect. Not without explaining that she'd sent me across the quarantine line six months ago to find my dad.

I folded my arms and stayed put. Maybe she had other evidence linking me to the video, but until I knew for sure, I was going to brazen this out.

"With diamond studs in his ears and gold rings on his fat, hairy fingers," Jia finished.

"Clearly you've heard a different version of this story." Spurling closed the book. "Tell it to me. Does the tiger-man trick Little Red?"

"Yes," Jia said, sitting up straighter. "And he finds out where her grandma's house is in Chicago and he —"

"Burns it down?" With her manicured fingers loosely entwined on top of the book, Spurling leaned toward the kids. To them, she simply seemed curious, but I detected the tinge of bitterness in her tone.

The day after my dad and I returned to the West, Spurling had hustled into his hospital room to find out if he'd gotten what she'd needed him to retrieve from the East: a photo of her daughter. He hadn't, and neither had I. When I couldn't find my dad on the other side of the wall, I'd made the trek to Chicago to do the fetch myself and failed. Chorda had burned Spurling's abandoned home and everything in it to keep me from completing the job and returning home. Upon hearing this, all the color had drained from Spurling's face, and without another word, she'd clipped from his hospital room with surprising poise considering her spike heels and clear devastation. In trying to thwart me, Chorda had forever destroyed her chance of recovering a picture of her little girl. I didn't blame her for being bitter.

"No," Jia said as if Spurling's guess bordered on insane. "The tiger-man *eats* the grandma. Then he puts on the grandma's nightgown and gets into her bed."

"Silly me," Spurling said dryly. "So, what happens next? Does Little Red show up and say, 'Grandma, what big eyes you have'?"

"'What *golden* eyes you have,'" the orphans corrected in unison. They then played out the rest of the scene, hamming it up as they asked the singsong questions about night-vision eyes, hairy ears, and big, sharp canine teeth. "The better to eat you with!" they shrieked, which made Spurling flinch.

"And then the tiger-man chased Li'l Red out of the house," Jia said, taking over the narrative again. "Through the empty streets all the way to the zoo!"

Spurling's blue gaze sharpened with interest. "Is this where the hunter comes in to save her?"

"No." Jia's tone was the verbal equivalent of an eye roll. "He's locked up in the lion cage, and he's hurt. He can't help Li'l Red. No one can. She has to save herself because she knows that you can't count on a hunter being around when you need him."

"Or your mom or dad," Dusty added.

"Or anyone," Sage said softly.

Jia growled to shush them, which worked as it always did. She had an insanely scary growl. Then she went on, "So Li'l Red takes her dad's machete out of the messenger bag and sneaks up behind the tiger-man and —"

"Chops off his head!" the other kids yelled with delight.

"Did she cut him open and get her grandmother back?" Spurling asked.

The orphans fell silent, including Jia. Their expressions ranged from disbelief to . . . pity.

"The tiger-man *ate* her." Tasha put a gentle hand on Spurling's arm. "The grandma's dead. She's not coming back."

"Not ever." Dusty hugged his knees and began to rock.

"So, Li'l Red killed the tiger-man and never ever went near a feral again," Jia said quickly. "The end."

"A useful lesson," Spurling murmured.

"It is," I blurted, not caring that her gaze narrowed upon

seeing me. "It's something they'll need to know later, when they're sent back to the Feral Zone. A beast doesn't turn into a prince no matter how much you love him."

Jia nodded gravely. "He just gets wilder . . ."

"And wilder and wilder," the children chanted while lifting their hands in unison, extending imaginary claws. Poised to strike. "Until he bites you!" Their hands clamped together like jaws snapping shut — just as I'd taught them.

Spurling shot to her feet. "I think I've had my fill of stories today." Her tone was deceptively pleasant as she dropped the book onto the cot and scooped up a metallic satchel, which coordinated perfectly with her silver-tipped nails.

Jia hurried over to me and asked, "Did you give Ev the letter?"

I kept my eyes on Spurling. "Yep."

"Did you tell him it was me who swiped it?" Jia demanded. When I nodded, she beamed.

Spurling's heels clicked across the uneven wood planks. "If you two are done catching up," the edge in her voice could have drawn blood, "I'd like a word with you, Delaney."

I tilted my head. Reluctantly Jia settled onto a bottom bunk, where she not only glared at Director Spurling but also began growling, low, steady. Spurling stopped short at the tent flap, expression wary as she looked to me for an explanation.

I shrugged. "Jia's mom got infected with panther when she was two. She picked up a few habits."

"I see," Spurling said lightly, as if she heard such things every day. Hah. I'd bet a bottle of bug spray that the orphans were the first people from the Feral Zone she'd ever seen in person.

"What are you doing here?" I asked, trying to sound calm.

"I came to see the base and heard you were still here. I wanted to see what you were up to. Must be something important."

"It *is* important."

She followed my look to the orphans, who were watching us with keen eyes. To my surprise, Spurling's expression softened. "Yes, it is," she agreed, and then jammed her hands in her suit jacket pockets and seemed to shake off what must have been a foreign feeling for her tiny, spiky self: empathy. "Well, Delaney, if you're done wasting my time, let's get a move on." She thrust aside the tent flap and waited for me to precede her. When I didn't budge, she smirked. "Why so nervous?"

A few more kids joined in with Jia's rumbling threat. "I'll be right back," I told them.

"No, you won't," Spurling corrected. "We're taking a ride."

· TEN ·

I stared stupidly at Director Spurling as every pulse point in my body began to thrum. Was she banishing me to the zone without a trial? "Into the zone?"

"Please. Do I look suicidal?" Clearly tired of holding the tent flap open for me, she ducked out first. "You're taking me to the landing pad." She clattered down the platform steps.

"But —" I hurried after her. "You have a guard to take you."

"Had." Spurling paused by the jeep to glare at the ogre-sized guard behind the wheel, then her gaze cut to me. "Can you drive this?"

I nodded, though I was still feeling iffy about going anywhere with her.

She directed a silver-tipped nail at the guard. "Out."

He straightened in his seat. "Ma'am, I've been assigned to —"

"Did I sound like I was asking?"

I struggled to keep my smirk in check as the seething goon faced off with the sharp-tongued witch. And then the guard ruined everything by not giving me material for a new bedtime story. He just climbed out of the jeep and tapped his shoulder mic. No face-off. No epic battle. Just guardspeak.

"Inform Captain Hyrax that there's been a change of plan," he said into the mic while glaring at Spurling.

She turned her manicured jab on me. "Hop in. I'd like to get back to civilization before it collapses."

That she was less of a jerk to me than the guard was a point in her favor. I slid behind the wheel, and she dropped into the passenger seat. As I pulled onto the paved road that ran down the center of the island, she lifted a palm-sized disc from under her shirt.

A dial!

I missed mine so much, my chest felt odd without the familiar weight resting there. Not that most of its functions would work over here anyway. The line patrol jammed the signals. Spurling checked the time on her dial and then tucked it out of sight.

"Have you noticed more guards on base lately?" she asked, sounding oh-so-casual as we passed the squat barracks where the guards lived.

"New recruits have been showing up every couple of days."

She dug sunglasses out of her satchel and slid them on. "How many new recruits?"

I shrugged. "A lot. There are new scientists too."

As if she was lounging on a rooftop, cold drink in hand, she leaned back in her seat and lifted her face to the sun. "You can thank a certain five-minute video for that."

And there it was — the bomb she'd been waiting to drop. The reason she was here. Every part of me flinched. A nearsighted mole couldn't have missed my reaction. And Spurling? She'd tilted her glasses my way and waited for it.

I played dumb anyway. "What are you talking about?"

She snorted, and I didn't blame her. My acting skills sucked.

"A video was posted on a social media site two weeks ago," she said, her tone droll as she indulged my pretend innocence. "It went viral overnight. The speed, the damage — it was like the plague all over again . . . without the drooling and biting and death."

I struggled to keep from nicking the corner of a barracks as I turned the wheel. All I wanted to do was slam on the brakes and beg her to tell me everything.

"Some people think the video is a hoax," she went on casually. "Others — the conspiracy nuts — they've taken it apart frame by frame looking for clues. It's amazing how they can blow up a fuzzy long shot — a flash frame even — and clean it up enough to make out a name on a guard's dog tag." She sent me a sidelong look. "The first name, anyway."

A sick feeling bloomed in my stomach. Well, I now knew how the fangirls got Everson's name. After that, figuring out where he was stationed was easy. Just one base guarded the last bridge into the Feral Zone.

"So, what was the point, Delaney?" Spurling's tone turned acidic. "To terrify people? Show them that monsters are real? Or worse, that the monsters are the very people they've been grieving?"

People deserved to know the truth. I still believed that, though my reasons hadn't been completely unselfish. If the public knew about the infected humans, there'd be more demand to find a cure. At least, that's what I'd hoped would happen. Someone needed to come up with a cure. And once a cure existed, I'd get a dose to Rafe. No matter how long I had to search for him, no matter how far into the zone I had to go. Because putting him down or even hiring someone to do it wasn't an option. Screw my promise.

Spurling heaved a sigh. "You can drop the ignorant act. I'm not here to arrest you."

I cut her a look. "And I'm supposed to believe you why?"

"I haven't lied to you yet," she said all matter-of-fact.

"Maybe not, but you did send me over here six months ago — *alone*."

"So?"

I didn't expect an apology, but smugness? That was too much. "I could have gotten infected!"

She cocked a brow. "Did you?"

"That's not the —"

"Of course it's the point."

Now I actually hit the brakes and gave her my best death glare. She worked for the government, not the line patrol. She couldn't have me thrown off Arsenal for disrespect.

"Give me some credit," she said, though not with her usual prickliness. "My instincts are dead-on when it comes to judging people's motives and abilities. You wanted to save your dad, and you were up to the task. You just went too far with that video."

"What video?"

"Oh, come on, Delaney. The tunnel, the crawling through rubble to get to Arsenal Island. Like I don't know who made that journey with a dial around her neck."

"What does that prove? Anyway, you're the one who let me keep my dial when you sent me over here."

"Yes, I did. Did you think that was an accident? Letting a budding filmmaker keep her recording device? I even made certain it was fully charged."

That took me aback. It was something I hadn't considered before. "Why?"

"I wanted to see what was going on here." She flicked her hand at the squads of drilling guards. "I didn't expect you to go all the way to the Feral Zone."

"What's so interesting about Arsenal?" This island looked like any old patrol base to me.

"Drive and maybe I'll tell you."

She wouldn't give me the truth, or at least not the whole truth, but whatever. I hit the gas. "I'm listening."

"First, let's jump to the part where I tell you the effect your little video has had over there." She jabbed a finger at the wall, the monstrosity that loomed over the west bank.

I thought of the mailroom's bags of love letters for Everson and winced. "I have some idea."

"Then you know you set off a firestorm of panic?"

Ah, no. I didn't know that. That certainly hadn't been my intention.

As we passed the ancient stone clock tower, Spurling twisted in her seat to face me. "What did you expect would happen when you shared images of those mutated humans? A big outpouring of compassion?"

"Uh . . ." Yeah, I had. Well, I'd hoped anyway.

Spurling saw my expression and made a noise of disgust. "Spare me your good intentions. I'd like to keep my lunch in my stomach."

"I was trying to get people to care about the manimals!"

"Your video didn't make people care about the manimals.

It whipped them into a frenzy of fear, which is why no one objected yesterday when the president pledged to triple the line patrol's budget in his State of the Union address. As if employing more mercenaries will make us safer," she scoffed.

I shrugged. What did I care if the line patrol had three times as many guards marching along the top of the wall?

"Use that creative brain of yours and try to imagine it," Spurling ordered. "The danger we're heading for with arms wide open."

"What danger?"

"In the wake of your video, Ilsa Prejean asked for and received the authority to do whatever is necessary to safeguard the West against those creatures and the virus they carry. Well done, Delaney. I hope she gave you a bonus for your help. As soon as the president signs that executive order, her private army will outnumber and outgun what's left of our national armed forces."

Well, that explained why the chairman hadn't ordered me off the base. My video had boosted her bottom line.

"The line patrol isn't an army," I pointed out. "It's a security force."

"A *paramilitary* security force owned by the Titan Corporation, which is wholly owned and controlled by Ilsa Prejean. I'd say 'private army' fits the bill."

As we neared the southwest tip of the island, I could feel Spurling's gaze on me, sparking with curiosity. "Tell me something," she said. "The guard who went to Chicago with you —"

"Everson," I supplied.

"As in Everson Cruz?"

I gave a quick nod. Why lie?

"Ah, that's why he got the hero edit." She smirked at me.

I hadn't edited the video to make Everson look heroic. He just was.

"Everson and I are friends." I stopped the jeep just short of the bridge, where a guard stood before the locked gate. "That's all."

"Of course you are," Spurling conceded with obvious amusement as the guard unlocked the gate and waved us through. "Why would Everson Cruz limit his options when a million girls are ready to throw themselves at his feet?" She sent a smirk my way. "Bet you didn't see that coming when you hit post."

A million fangirls — that's what I'd risked execution for? Yes, Everson was all over my video — start to finish. Rafe, less so. I'd given the manimals the starring roles because they were supposed to be the takeaway message.

I eased the jeep onto the ancient bridge. On the far bank, Spurling's white hovercopter, emblazoned with a black bio-hazard symbol, waited on the landing pad.

At least Everson didn't seem to mind too much about the bags of letters, even if a few of them teetered on obscene. Okay, probably more than a few, and probably more than teetered. But so what? Fan mail had to be better than the mountain of death threats he and his mother were still getting twenty years after the outbreak. Besides, what guy would mind being adored by thousands upon thousands of strangers?

Guilt punched me in the gut. Everson, that's who. The last thing he wanted was more attention. That's why he lived in the barracks and ate in the mess hall instead of using his private suite in the research building or its fancy dining room. He had serious goals he was trying to accomplish and hated being known as "the prince" on base. I knew because I'd watched him bloody another guard's nose after the guy had shouted it across the mess hall. So, if being "the prince" bugged him, how much more would he hate being known as a teen heartthrob? For once I was really glad the patrol blocked internet access on this side of the wall.

"He's a strapping young man, I'll give you that," Spurling said over the rush of the river. "Attractive, if you can forget for one minute who his mother is, which I can't. But putting all that aside, Delaney, you can't trust anyone who works for a private militia. They don't stick to the same codes of conduct as real military, which is precisely why the government hires them."

I waved off her concern. "Everson isn't like the other guards."

"I'll say."

"No. I mean he doesn't think like them. He hasn't had the empathy drilled out of him. He's the one person on this island I trust."

She shrugged as if I was beyond help. "Personally, I was rooting for the other one. Rafe. Now, *he* was fun. He —" Her words cut off with a gasp. "What are they doing?"

We'd reached the end of the creaking bridge, but that wasn't what had her gasping. No, that honor belonged to the gray Titan hovercopters, circling overhead. As soon as one cleared the bridge, guards began dropping out, one after the other, to crash into the churning river below.

"New recruits," I yelled to be heard over the hiss of the hovercopter fans. "That's how they get to base. It's a test."

When the guards surfaced, spitting out water through chattering teeth, they inflated their vests, secured their weapons on top of their waterproof rucksacks, and held up an arm for pickup. No easy feat. Several struggled to stay upright; others kicked frantically to catch up with gear that had been swept away by the strong currents.

"Secure your weapon first!" boomed a squad leader via a bullhorn from where he crouched in the prow of a rubberized speedboat. More boats skimmed the river, staying just out of the floundering guards' reach.

As we waited for a sentry to unlock the gate at this end of the bridge, another hovercopter swooped overhead. "This is so much worse than I thought," Spurling said darkly.

I drove through the gate onto the island of pure black asphalt that served as the patrol's landing strip. "What do you mean?"

"If the president signs an executive order to increase Titan's budget, this drizzle" — she waved at the plummeting recruits — "will turn into a typhoon. Thanks to you."

I navigated between the patrol hovercopters, black and multibladed, that surrounded the biohaz 'copter like drones around a queen. "Okay. I messed up. Made my video too scary because I wasn't over what had happened. They're not all bad — the manimals."

"Nobody cares about the manimals," she snapped. "That's not why I'm here. I came because I learned something from your video, Delaney."

My eyebrows hiked.

"Drop the face," she ordered without heat. "I never said I knew everything about the Feral Zone. Titan limits our intel, even at the highest levels. For example, I had no idea there were so many *un*infected people still living in the East."

"You didn't know about Moline and the other compounds?"

"I knew about Moline, but I thought the other compounds had been abandoned or overrun by the infected. It seems that isn't the case. Now," Spurling said as if getting down to business, "this is where you come in."

My internal warning system powered on, red lights flashing. I threw the jeep into park, a hundred feet from her hovercopter, and twisted in my seat to face her. "What do you want?"

"Same thing as last time, Delaney." A corner of her mouth quirked up. "You're going to give your father a message for me."

Right, 'cause last time worked out so well.

"I want the name of every healthy person living in the zone," Spurling went on. "Starting with Moline. And I want Mack to get those names for me."

Questions exploded in my mind like timed fireworks, one after another, but all I got out was, "Why?"

"Let's call it a census."

"Are you going to let them immigrate to the West?" I asked, remembering how Hagen had wanted to do exactly that years ago. Did she still want to leave the zone?

Spurling held up a hand. "One step at a time, Delaney. Let's get people over there" — she hooked a thumb at the wall looming over us — "to put down the pitchforks first."

A census was a good idea — a step in the right direction — except for the part about my father being the one to fetch the names. "My dad can't do it. He's still spending all his time looking for a certain strain of the virus. And his leg isn't —"

"So he'll delegate. He must know someone who can handle a job like this."

The answer came to me in a flash. "Hacks!" At her nonreaction, I explained, "Path hackers. They're like jungle guides, only they guide people from compound to compound and kill ferals along the way. They can get you names."

"Hacks," she said as if tasting the word and finding it acceptable. "That'll do. Take care of it." She plucked up her satchel and swung her legs out of the jeep.

"What?" I scrambled onto the asphalt and rounded the jeep, blocking her path to the hovercopter. "What do you mean 'take care of it'?"

"You said Mack is too busy for the job," she said, as if stating the obvious. "So you do it."

My jaw went slack. She was joking. She *had* to be joking. Why didn't she look like she was joking?!

"You started this," she went on. "You fix it."

"I didn't start the plague!"

"No," she agreed. "You agitated the public with your video. Do you want to see Titan's budget tripled? No? Then help me fix this, Delaney. Not by playing on people's fears or throwing up a wall to hide the problem. We need to remind them" — she jabbed a finger toward the West again — "of what we left behind — of *who* we left behind."

"Okay," I said slowly, though my mind was racing. "But if you really want to fight that" — I nodded toward the swarm of speedboats scooping recruits out of the river — "you're going to need more than just a list of names."

She arched a thin brow. "What do you suggest?"

"Give me your dial. I'll go to Moline and record the healthy people living there. I'll get you a lot more than names. I'll get you their faces and voices. Their stories."

Spurling lifted her sunglasses to study me. "You'll humanize them."

I shrugged. Who cared what she called it? I just knew what worked from volunteering at the Davenport animal shelter. To get people to care about the abandoned animals, they needed to *see* the animals. Every time I'd posted a video showcasing the shelter's available dogs and cats, introducing them by name, we'd get a spike in adoptions and donations. Every time. Without fail.

"All right, Delaney. You want a do-over, you got it." Spurling unfastened the silver chain around her neck and held out her dial. I met her eyes. She knew that Titan didn't allow its employees to have dials on this side of the wall, and that included everyone: guards, scientists, staff . . . me.

I stared at the steel-and-glass disc dangling from her fingertips. It was all that I could do to take the dial calmly. "How will I get you the recording when I'm done?"

"Oh, you'll be hearing from me again." She headed for the hovercopter, her spiked heels clacking on the asphalt. "Count on it."

I left the jeep on the landing pad and walked back across the bridge to the island. As I neared the gate, I fastened the dial's chain at the back of my neck and dropped the palm-sized disc down the front of my shirt. If a guard saw it, he'd confiscate it and throw me in a cell. Maybe the one next to Mahari's . . .

As soon as I stepped off the bridge onto the base, a voice shouted, "Lane!" from across the drill yard.

I looked up to see Bearly jogging toward me. "Hey. What's up?"

As Bearly closed in on me, her dark skin gleamed with sweat. She touched the speaker-mic clipped to her shoulder. "Got her. Tell the captain we're heading over now." She let go of the button and looked at me. "Let's go."

"Where?"

"The lab."

I glanced past the guard securing the gate that I'd just come through to the landing pad on the riverbank. Was it too late to make a break for Spurling's hovercopter?

Stupid thought. Who knew why Hyrax wanted me? Maybe it was for something minor. I fell into step beside Bearly and asked, "What'd they do?"

"Who?" she asked without slowing her pace.

"The orphans. Are they in trouble?"

"No idea." She gave me a sidelong glance. "Good visit with Director Spurling?"

Is that what Hyrax wanted? To debrief me about my talk with Spurling? Or maybe Bearly was asking for someone higher on the food chain.

"We were just catching up," I said.

She eyed me for a moment as if looking for a chink in my armor. "I hope you enjoyed it. She isn't allowed back on base. Chairman's orders."

Yep. Top of the food chain. "Titan can block the director of the Biohazard Defense?"

"No one is above the quarantine," she said in a tone that sounded like a warning.

After seeing the video in Chairman Prejean's van of me fighting with the guard, I shouldn't have been surprised to learn that she had eyes everywhere — mechanical and human. Still, it stung to think Bearly had probably been joining me at the orphans' table at dinner because she'd been told to. But then, why was I hurt? I'd learned this lesson already — many times over. Everyone lied. Big lies and little fibs. Even the people who loved you lied.

My dad had wanted me to pass the lie detector test if I was ever interrogated about his illegal profession as a fetch. Every time he'd gone away, he told me he was doing business with art galleries when really he was fetching art from abandoned museums in the Feral Zone. I understood his reasoning. I'd probably do the same to protect someone I loved. But good intentions didn't change the fact that my dad *had* lied. At least I could still count on Everson to be honest with me.

Everson and Captain Hyrax were waiting for me in a lounge on the main floor of the building. Everson was dressed in all black instead of the usual Titan gray, from his tactical jacket to his combat pants and spit-shined boots. Before I could ask why, I noticed Chairman Prejean looming behind them on the giant wall screen.

"Hello, Lane," she said in a voice like dry ice. She must have been calling from somewhere incredibly clean because it was the first time I'd seen her without gloves or a surgical mask. She still looked like a corpse — hairless and pale — but she was wearing lipstick. Bloodred. No doubt hypoallergenic. Probably tested on animals.

"You're here," she went on, "because my son believes we can help each other. After all, we both want the same thing."

"Which is?" I asked while shooting a suspicious glance at Everson.

"To catch a tiger," Captain Hyrax replied, sounding as smug as ever.

"To find your friend Rafe," the chairman cut in. "Lane, you do understand that the only way to truly protect people from Ferae is to vaccinate them?" she asked with feigned patience. "To do that, we need the last strain of the virus — the strain carrying tiger DNA. Your friend Rafe is the only person we know of infected with it." Her cool gray gaze strayed to Everson. "My son seems to think you'll be able to get Rafe's location out of the lion-woman."

"The lion-woman?" I echoed. They'd caught one? How? The answer hit me like a Taser strike. The guards hadn't just captured a lioness. They'd had one all along. "You have Mahari."

"Yes," the chairman confirmed.

My blood went hot, and my gaze whipped to Everson. "You knew the whole time?"

He said nothing, which was answer enough. I gritted my teeth against my rising temper. Who cared if he'd lied to my face? It didn't matter. I'd been stupid to think he was the exception.

I turned back to the mother of the liar. "What makes you think she knows where Rafe is?"

The chairman raised her nonexistent brows. "If the other lion-women know, I'd say chances are good this one does too."

"Will you free her if she tells me?" I asked.

"That's a big no-go." Hyrax hooked his thumbs into his waistband as he regarded me. "The grup's got a serious hate on for humans. She tore out a guard's tongue. With her *claws*. Tore it right out. He nearly died from shock and blood loss."

"Why was his tongue anywhere near her?" I demanded.

"Irrelevant," Chairman Prejean said smoothly. "We don't need to release the lion-woman. We just need to find out Rafe's location. As soon as she tells you, Captain Hyrax will send out a strike team to retrieve him."

"Don't you mean *hunt*?" I snapped.

She waved a hand so raw, it looked as if she'd soaked it in bleach. Actually, she probably had.

"Don't be so dramatic," she said. "We need one small vial of his blood, that's all. If he cooperates, it'll take less than a minute."

If he cooperates. That was a big *if*. Rafe hated line guards. They hadn't exactly been kind when he'd lived in the orphan camp. Even if the guards explained that they needed his blood to create a vaccine, Rafe might not cooperate. At this point, a vaccine wouldn't help him. He wasn't as selfish as I'd first thought, but I didn't see him letting himself get caught by the patrol for the greater good. Not even if the guards asked nicely — which they wouldn't.

"You should know, Lane," Chairman Prejean said, breaking into my downward spiral, "we have more efficient ways to extract the information. I'm only offering you this opportunity because my son asked me to."

I glanced at him, but he was still in guard mode, giving away nothing.

"Ev thinks the lion-woman might give you Rafe's location willingly . . ."

She paused, giving me time to figure out the alternative. For a moment, we just stared at each other as a knot tightened in my gut. It tightened and tightened, hard and cold, until it was all I felt.

"And if she doesn't, you'll torture her?" I asked quietly.

"Nothing in the Geneva Conventions prohibits using interrogation techniques on an animal," Hyrax drawled.

I glared at him. "Mahari isn't an animal, and we're not at war."

"We *are*," the chairman corrected. When I started to protest, she held up a blood-crusted finger. "Not with the infected. They're the casualties. We're at war with the virus, and it's winning."

"Then maybe you shouldn't have created it," I said under my breath, though not softly enough, going by the warning look Everson shot me.

"Captain Hyrax, have the strike team ready to deploy," the chairman said, clearly dismissing him. She waited until he'd left the room before adding, "You'll make sure no animal gets hurt, won't you, Lane? After all, you did work at a no-kill shelter."

The gall of her, calling Mahari an animal when she was the reason Mahari had gotten infected with lion DNA in the first place. Her twitch of smile was my breaking point. "Chairman, why *did* you invent Ferae?"

Everson swore under his breath, using words so obscene that, any other time, I would have gaped at him. Instead, I watched every muscle in Chairman Prejean's body go rigid and the color drain from her already-pale face.

"Because human ingenuity needs to be encouraged," she finally ground out.

I shook my head to signal my confusion.

"People were getting so lazy," she explained with an impatient huff. "The world was a mess — environmentally, politically — and yet, people wanted easy answers, expected easy solutions. They didn't value tenacity and outside-the-box thinking anymore, not even in others. So I created the Titan Imaginariums and filled them with mazes and puzzles and other challenges — to encourage human ingenuity. After spending the day experiencing wonder, people left with the sense that the world is filled with possibilities just waiting to be unlocked."

"Some possibilities shouldn't be unlocked," I said acidly.

"Who's to say which those are?" she countered. She clasped her throat with raw, reddened fingers. "We can fix this. We can. I still believe in human ingenuity." Her tone had regained its usual coating of freezer burn. "But it won't happen if we're not human."

I held in my "Give me a break" and settled for, "I'll talk to Mahari."

Chairman Prejean closed her eyes. "Good."

"And *when*" — *if* wasn't an option — "she tells me where Rafe is, I'm going with the strike team. Rafe won't show for a bunch of guards, but he'll show for me." At least, I hoped so.

"Of course," the chairman agreed without hesitation. Seeing my surprise, she smiled faintly. "Ev said you'd insist on it."

Everson handed me a black nylon backpack and a flak jacket. Not just a jacket, I realized, feeling its heft. Body armor.

ELEVEN

Anger settled like a spiked ball in my stomach as we took the elevator to the basement level. Everson, however, acted as if he did this every day — went to work in a silent, scary basement. Oh, wait, he did.

Would anyone tell the orphans where I'd gone? Probably not. And making it worse, I'd left without saying good-bye. At least I'd never promised them that I would. I'd always known that chances were good I'd leave this island unexpectedly. I should count myself lucky that I wasn't leaving in handcuffs.

Still ignoring Everson, I opened the nylon backpack, aka a bug-out bag, and found energy bars, bottled water, first aid supplies, a lighter, compass, flashlight, and Swiss army knife. I stuffed the flak jacket in as well.

Everson frowned. "You should put that on."

I shot him a dagger of a look. "You're using Mahari in medical tests, aren't you?"

"Yes." For once he sounded as stiff as Rafe had always made him out to be. "An antigen."

"I don't know what that is."

"It's a kind of cure."

"For Ferae?"

"What else?"

"Don't you have to test it on animals first?" I asked accusingly.

"We are." His scars stretched flat over his cheekbones as he spoke. "Do you know how America *legally* defines who's human? Simple: one hundred percent human DNA. Less than that, you don't cross the quarantine line, you're not a citizen, and you have no rights because you're *not* human. In other words, manimals don't qualify."

"If you really believed they're not human, you wouldn't hide them in a basement. You'd put them in your lab with the other mongrels and give tours."

The elevator door slid open, revealing a brightly lit corridor. Neither one of us moved.

"Did you want us to hold off on humans until the antigen goes through six rounds of animal testing? That'll take a decade at least," he said, the rasp in his voice even more pronounced. "And by then, anyone who's infected now will be feral. As in, mutated and insane. That includes Rafe. Think he cares how we define him so long as we're testing the cure on manimals now?"

Rafe, mutated and insane — I could picture it. *Had* pictured it many times awake and asleep. But still. "You could've asked for volunteers. Infected people would've lined up from here to Moline for a possible cure."

"We tried it, but they didn't come back for follow-up testing. Just took the dose and disappeared into the zone. And we learned nothing. We don't know if the antigen has side effects or if it stopped working. Maybe that's why none of the *volunteers* came back — 'cause they went feral fast, like with the inhibitor. So we made a choice. A hard choice.

No one on Dr. Solis's team feels good about it. But this way has gotten us a lot closer to a cure."

They could have found another solution if they'd tried, but they took the quick, easy way: defined infected people as animals and took away their rights. And there was no one to stop them on this side of the wall. It was revolting. Everson had lied to me and that was the least of it. He was imprisoning people to use as test subjects. Yes, they were infected with animal DNA, but they were still people. And yet, some small part of me — some horrible, selfish part — was glad Dr. Solis's team had moved forward so fast. For Rafe's sake.

I swallowed the acid burn of my own double standards and asked the billion-dollar question: "Does it work?"

Everson shot me a knowing look, clearly aware of the moral contortions I'd just performed to ask about the end result.

"We're calling them functionally cured," he threw over his shoulder as he strode out of the elevator.

"What does that mean?" I followed him down the corridor.

"It means we can remove the virus from the subject's system, but not the animal DNA. That's why my mother refuses to call it a cure. She thinks the infected are a lost cause."

My stomach clenched. "What?"

"That's why she goes on record saying 'Everyone in the East is dead.' To her, they are."

"So she can forget what she did," I growled.

"Yeah," he said like I'd stated the obvious.

"Do they have to keep taking it?" And more important, could I get a dose to Rafe?

"It's a single-dose serum. It interferes with an enzyme that Ferae needs to multiply. After a week, there's not a trace of the virus in their blood." Everson paused before a steel door with a mesh-wire porthole. "They can't infect anyone, and they don't have to worry about going feral. Isn't that worth pursuing? Finding a way for manimals to hang on to their humanity?"

Definitely worth pursuing. "I want a dose for Rafe."

Everson put his back to the mesh porthole, blocking it, and took what looked like a small yellow toothpaste tube from his pocket. "I figured as much." He dropped the tube into my outstretched hand. "You have to take his blood first. The blood sample won't do us any good after he takes this."

I tested that the cap was tight and then tucked the tube into the pocket on my cargos with a Velcro seal. "How does he take it?"

"He squeezes it out under his upper lip. But before that, you need to tell him we don't know the long-term effects. It's an untested drug. If he wants to take it, the risk is on him."

I gave a curt nod. It was Rafe's body. His health. His choice. Of course I'd tell him the risks. I wasn't the one going around kidnapping people to use as test subjects.

Everson pressed his index finger to a control pad by the door. A green light flashed, and the door clunked ajar. Beyond it, a big, impassive guard sat before an enormous control console watching camera feeds — row upon row of them. The guard nodded at Everson as we entered.

"We call this the skybox." Everson pointed to the console. "We can run the whole installation from here. It's the same setup that was used in the Titan theme parks."

I drew closer to the wall screen displaying the multiple camera feeds. Shadowy figures flickered on the tiny screens. "Are those people?"

"People?" the guard echoed with a snort.

Everson gave the man a sharp look.

There were so many screens. So many pacing figures. I felt sick through and through. "Who took them from the Feral Zone?" The correct word was *kidnapped*.

"The strike team," Everson said in a flat voice. "They were trained to infiltrate hostile territory. Now their job includes recovering ferals infected with the different strains."

"Mahari isn't feral."

"Mahari?" the guard asked.

"Subject 2666," Everson told him.

"Not feral?" The guard raised a brow. "Could've fooled me."

His fingers flew across the keyboard and enlarged one of the screens. The feed from the holding cell was set to night vision, which turned the occupant's eyes an eerie white as she paced. Though a tangled mane of hair hid much of her face, it had to be Mahari. She had a lion's prowl and the heft of an Amazon. Going by her darting glares at the cameras, the floating bots irritated her immensely. Maybe because they were rotating to follow her moves, or maybe she just hated being watched as she paced. With shocking speed, she snatched up a tray and whipped it at one of the cameras. As the bot swerved, she leapt into the air and caught it, but the camera bot didn't so much as dip under her considerable weight.

The guard gave a low whistle. "Those are set to hover at ten feet. Heck of a jump." He flipped the view on-screen to the second camera. In a tank top and hospital pants, Mahari dangled from the hovering bot, her body swinging as she tried to disembowel the camera with her claws.

The guard twisted in his chair to face me, all smug humor gone. "Still think she isn't feral?"

"She's mad because you've caged her." I glared at Everson. "Like Chorda caged her. You made her like this."

"She's been like that from the moment she woke up from the tranquilizer." Everson sighed. "But you're right, that's not feral behavior."

"Are you kidding? She tries to bite anyone who gets close," the guard protested.

"That's intentional, not virus driven," Everson said. "If she was feral, she'd be drooling and acting more animal."

"How many people do you have down here?"

Everson jabbed another button and Mahari's image disappeared as the giant screen became a window, which overlooked darkness broken only by pinpricks of light forming lines. I moved closer to the glass, trying to make sense of what I was seeing. The guard station was perched high above a vast maze, its many twisting avenues illuminated by tiny footlights.

"A labyrinth," I breathed, awed by the beauty of its pattern even knowing that manimals were imprisoned within those curving walls.

"One of my mother's designs," Everson explained.

"The patrol added it?"

"No. It was in the original building design. The patrol planned to keep ferals on base to study the progression of the disease, but we only began doing it four months ago."

I frowned at that news.

"Light up 2666's cell," he told the guard.

"Mahari," I corrected. Was it easier to mistreat her if she remained nameless? Probably: A number dehumanized her, but I wasn't going to let it slide.

Deep within the labyrinth, a square of light flicked on.

"And the path," Everson said over his shoulder as he opened a door onto a steel catwalk outside the skybox, three stories above the maze.

I joined Everson in time to see a glowing path cut its way through the twists and turns of corridors to end at Mahari's cell.

"Why do you keep this place so dark?" I repositioned my bug-out bag to cross my chest.

"They stay calmer this way."

"How did you get them all down here without anyone noticing?"

"Through a retrieval tunnel at the back of the maze. It accesses the river's lock-and-dam system. Come on. I'll take you down to the start of the path." He beckoned me to the metal stairs that spiraled into the darkness below.

My fingers prickled again, now verging on numb. "You're not coming into the maze with me?"

"I'd just stir them up. They hate guards."

"Can't imagine why."

"You'll be fine." Everson tapped an impatient fist against the railing. "They're behind weapons-grade glass. Just go fast and touch nothing."

I managed to nod before following him down the metal steps, my heart pounding louder than my feet.

Three stories down, we stepped into a holding pen of sorts. Tucked under the skybox was yet another lab behind glass. Technicians in hygienic jumpsuits paused in their work to stare at us. One sharp gesture from Everson and all gazes dropped. Such was the power of the Titan prince. I was feeling distinctly uncharitable toward him, even with a dose of the cure in my pocket.

I turned my back on the lab with its grisly goings-on to face an enormous door with a line of clockwork gears embedded between layers of glass. Everson turned the silver disc centered on the door, and it slid open silently.

"I know how this looks," he muttered. "Bad. Cruel. But we're curing them."

My skin grew clammy as I eyed the cell doors staggered along the corridors. "Are you going to dissect them to make sure?"

"Of course not. But we need to keep them here to see the long-term effects."

Before me, four corridors branched off, all dark except the single path of light, the second on the left. I entered the maze, following the glowing floor tiles. The smell of bleach, sharp in my nose, reminded me of the animal shelter where I used to volunteer. The virus was passed via a bite or open cut. I couldn't catch Ferae just by breathing the same air as infected people. And anyway, the cells must have been sealed up tight, since the maze was as silent as an airless room. The walls gleamed in the darkness, cleaner than clean, which gave me some comfort. Clean was good.

With my back to Everson, I drew my dial from under my shirt. He wouldn't like me recording his secret lab, but too bad. I tapped the dial's screen and turned on the camera.

"Are you sure the glass will hold?" I called over my

shoulder, knowing it was a stupid question, but needing the reassurance.

"A bullet couldn't pierce it," he said, still in the open doorway, arms crossed like a sentry. "It's made from the stuff they used to use on space shuttles."

Before the country took a giant step backward, thanks to his mother.

"But what if a lock breaks?" The last thing I wanted was a showdown with a slavering feral in a dark maze.

"Won't happen. But if it does, steel barriers will shoot up from the floor and seal off the corridor. Then the guard up in the skybox will fill the hot zone with sleeping gas."

"Lull?" I asked, spotting the blue levers mounted to the right of every door.

"Exactly," Everson said. "We put the subjects to sleep when we need to enter their cells."

Okay. All that sounded good. But just the same, I snatched the bite-proof flak jacket out of my backpack and put it on. Only then did I slink past the first door. Movement within caught my eye. I paused to peer past my reflection into the shadowy cell beyond, only to jolt back with a shriek when a man launched into the glass. A jagged row of thorny growths bisected his scalp like a scaly Mohawk.

I pressed against the opposite wall, staring at him, trying to make myself believe that he couldn't get to me as he slammed himself into the glass again and again. With every hit, writing exploded across the door's surface: numbers and dates.

"Stay in the middle of the path." Everson strode toward me, stopping just before the first cell, though I didn't know why he bothered. How much more stirred up could a feral get?

I eyed the creature and repressed a shudder. "I thought you said the cure is working."

"It is. He's not infectious."

"He's not sane!" I slid farther down the passage, my back to the wall.

"We can't fix brain damage that's already happened. The serum only deals with the virus."

I had to get the cure to Rafe before the virus made its way into his brain. *Before* he went feral.

"Lane . . ." Everson warned just as I sensed a presence.

I whirled and came face-to-face with a grinning madman, saliva dripping, baring unnaturally large and crooked teeth. My body forgot there was unbreakable glass between us, and my brain didn't believe it anyhow. When he leaned in and dragged his tongue up the glass as if licking my face, I'd had enough. I bolted, racing through the corridors while following the light trail around curves and corners. I made myself glance into the dark cells as I tore past.

Most of them had to be in stage three of the disease — the last stage: psychosis. They flung themselves at the walls and ripped apart bedding, their mouths open and foamy — all without a sound. Only my pounding feet broke the silence. But those occupants weren't the ones who rekindled my anger at Everson. It was the ones who were clearly sane. Some rapped at the glass, trying to get my attention as I jogged by. Others gestured frantically while silently pleading for help. And then there were those cloaked in a sadness so profound they did nothing more than follow me with their eyes as I passed. I couldn't help them — at least, not now.

I skidded to a stop where the glowing path ended. Light spilled through the glass door into the corridor. I tried to slow my breathing as I faced the cell and its occupant. The three interior walls were made of metal, which put Mahari and the few pieces of furniture on stark display. I saw why the guard in the skybox thought she was feral. She stalked past the glass like the caged lion that she was — agitated, ferocious. Bones littered the floor, picked clean. I really hoped they were chicken bones.

I spotted several switches to the left of the door and, with my heart beating like a hummingbird's, flipped the switch labeled "Mic." Before I could even choke out a word, Mahari noticed me, her eyes glowing like jewels in the dim light. She peeled back her black lips and lunged, ivory fangs jutting. I jerked back with a cry as she slammed into the glass so hard it vibrated. Writing scrolled across the surface: "Viral Load — 0%."

Mahari's claws raked the transparent barrier but didn't leave a scratch. Spitting and snarling, which unfortunately I could now hear, she tried to claw her way out. Maybe she *had* gone feral.

"Mahari." It came out choked, so I cleared my throat and tried again. "Mahari, I'm Lane. Do you remember me?"

She froze, hands still raised, claws extended as if she might pounce again, but now her gaze bore into me.

When she said nothing, I went on. "I was in Chicago." I moved closer to the door, into the light. "I opened your cage."

She cocked her head, spilling her dark tangled hair over her shoulder. "The little rabbit."

"Yes. Listen . . ." I pressed both palms to the glass. "They think you're feral. Are you?"

Her golden eyes glowed in the dim light, which sent a shiver down my spine. Her gaze, unblinking and intense, was too much like Chorda's. "Angry isn't feral," she said in a low rasp.

"It looks the same to them."

She dragged her fingers through her wild dark hair, pushing it off her face, and shook out her shoulders. "You want calm?" She stretched her arms wide, claws retracted into the nail beds. "I'm a kitten. Dangle a string and watch me play."

"Now you're overdoing it."

Her black lips parted as she chuffed out air. "What do you want, Lane? My sisters?" She flicked a hand toward the camera bots with barely contained rage. "You think I'd tell you anything with the humans listening?" Her eyes narrowed. "Guard," she hissed.

"What? No. I'm not —"

Then I heard it too and recognized the long-legged stride, the echo of his heavy combat boots. Everson rounded the corner and paused, just out of Mahari's sight line. Didn't matter, she'd heard his approach. She slammed her fists against the glass, her irises gone black with fury. "I hear your weasel's heart scampering. You're right to fear me, guard!"

I glared at Everson. He'd just ruined any chance I'd had at getting information out of her without trickery or force.

"Hyrax called in the interrogation team." He came up beside me, expression grim. "They'll be here in ten minutes."

Maybe if he'd said ten hours, I would've had a chance of getting Mahari to talk. But upon seeing him, she was even wilder than before. With a roar, she body-slammed the door, trying to get at Everson.

"It's *you* who's making her crazy. What did you do to her?" I demanded as suspicions sprouted in my mind.

"Nothing," he said firmly.

Mahari shrieked with rage, her tendons knotting as she scrabbled at the glass. I snapped off the mic before she blew out my eardrums. "What did you do?" I repeated.

"It's the uniform. We all look the same to her," he said above her muffled pounding.

Mahari's fury seemed more personal than that. I tightened my lips and waited for a better explanation.

"Oh, for — I take her blood," he snapped. "She hates being gassed."

Yesterday I would have believed anything he told me, but not now. Not when he'd played so fast and loose with the definition of *human* that he'd ended up treating people worse than animals. Not after knowing that he could lie so well and so easily.

Mahari leaned against the glass, panting, as her eyes darted between us.

"You see why we can't let her go?" Everson demanded. "She'll kill the first human she sees."

"She's angry because you locked her up. She spent years in a cage and now you've put her back in one."

"The why doesn't matter. We can't set *that*" — he gestured sharply at Mahari — "free." At that moment, he saw my dial, glowing faintly, recording. He growled low in his throat. "Are you trying to get yourself executed?"

Mahari straightened and pointed at the mic by the door. I adjusted the dial to get the best shot and flipped the switch.

"I won't hurt him," Mahari rasped. "Let me out."

"Nice pivot. I think we can trust her," he said sarcastically, and then glanced at me.

"I don't trust anyone anymore." I gave him a pointed look, and he had the grace to wince.

She wasn't going to talk unless I let her out, and even then, she might not tell me anything. I could explain that her alternative was torture, but no. I wasn't going to do that. I'd made a deal with the lionesses. Maybe I wouldn't have unlocked their cage in Chicago if I'd had another option. But this cage? This one, I *would* unlock.

I couldn't trust Everson to choose me or Rafe over advancing the greater good. But maybe I could trust him to do the right thing right now.

I faced Mahari. "Promise you won't attack him if I free you."

"That better be a joke," Everson told me while letting his fingertips brush the ever-present tranq gun holstered on his thigh.

Mahari's eyes gleamed in the shadows. "You have my word, little sister. I won't spill his blood in here . . . In this place."

That was the best assurance I was going to get out of her and probably the most honest. I nodded.

Everson planted himself in front of the door. "Don't even think about it."

I darted right. Chairman Prejean had called me reckless. Fine. Sure. But it was a calculated kind of reckless. I yanked the blue lever mounted by the door.

Everson cursed as coils of blue fog filled the cell.

"How long till she's out?" I demanded, holding down the lever. I didn't want to give her too much and kill her. The twilight-colored fog blanketed the cell.

"It'll shut off automatically," Everson growled.

Mahari pounded on the glass, wild to escape, but the Lull slipped around her, catching her in a soft embrace. Her chest stopped heaving and her expression softened as the gas worked its magic on her system. With one clawed hand still pressed to the door, she slipped down the glass until she puddled on the ground — all soft curves and silken limbs. Her face was so peaceful, she looked almost human. And then with a jerk of surprise, I realized she couldn't be more than a year or two older than me.

"Will she be okay?" I asked.

"She's fine," Everson said coldly as the scene inside the cell seemed to play in reverse. The fog bank separated into blue streams and slithered back into the ceiling holes. "So what did that get you? She'll be out for the next thirty minutes at least."

"Good. I'm keeping my deal with the lionesses. I'm trading Mahari for Rafe's location."

"Trading her," he echoed, brow furrowed.

"I'll take her out through the tunnel — the way she came in."

"Yeah? How much are you bench-pressing lately? 'Cause with the muscle she's packing, she's up in my weight class."

"Oh, you're right. Guess I'll have to leave her here for a bunch of guards to work over. What do you think they'll do first — pull out her fingernails?"

His jaw clenched so hard, his scars paled. "She doesn't have fingernails," he ground out. "She has claws."

I ducked around him. One hard twist of the disc and the strip of gears embedded in the glass began to whir and spin. A second later, the door slid open soundlessly. The second after that, a shrieking alarm blew out my eardrums. "What the —"

"This is a high-security facility," he shouted to be heard over the alarm. "Think you can just open a cell without punching in a clearance code?"

"How was I to know?" I said defensively.

"You could've asked me!"

I hurried into the cell. The pulsing alarm wasn't nearly as loud in here, and yet I hesitated, worried that Mahari would spring up and attack. She didn't move. In fact, only the rise and fall of her chest proved she was even alive.

"Put in the code," Everson shouted into the mic on his shoulder, his eyes on the skybox.

The guard stepped onto the catwalk to peer down at us. "Why'd you open her cell?" The guy's irritation came through Everson's radio loud and clear.

"She's gassed. It's fine," Everson snapped. "Enter the code."

"Not until you shut the cell with 2666 in it. I don't care which side of the door you're on."

Everson yanked his fingers from his mic. "Move! Quarantine protocol's about to kick in." He hunkered by Mahari. "They'll seal off the maze and send in a team to secure this level."

He hefted Mahari over his shoulder and rose with a grunt. He might've lied to me, but I was right when I'd guessed that he wouldn't be okay with torture. Another calculated risk.

As I followed him out of the cell, the alarm faded into silence. "Is that good?"

"No. Countdown's on. Keep up!" He veered left — not the way we'd come — and broke into a sprint.

· TWELVE ·

As we ran down the corridor, crashing booms sounded in quick succession from all around us.

"Metal shutters," Everson shouted over his shoulder. "They're sealing off the cells."

I followed him into an open circular area — a hub for eight corridors. The floor was tiled with glassy squares in every color imaginable. "Is this the middle of the maze?" I asked.

Everson grunted what I took to be a yes as bigger booms echoed down the corridors. Eight in total — one after the other — resounding like cannon blasts.

"Those were the bulkheads closing off the corridors. The tunnel's the only way out now." Everson halted at the room's center, where a brass disc the size of a kiddie pool had been embedded into the floor. Four letters were carved into the disc's outer edge: *E*, *W*, *N*, and *S*.

"Don't step off the circle," Everson ordered as he hefted the deadweight that was Mahari higher on his shoulder. "See the knob there?" He lifted his chin at a raised bump in the center of the circle. "Yank it up and let it drop like you would to spin a top."

I did as he directed, and suddenly our island of brass began to slowly rotate while the floor around us spun in the opposite direction, picking up speed until the colored tiles blurred into an image — a panoramic vision of a circus. I let out a faint "Ooh" of appreciation.

Everson shot me a droll look.

"It's cool," I said defensively. Because, well, it was. Not that it made up for testing an experimental drug on unwilling humans.

"The compass moves every half hour," Everson explained as the brass disc slowed to a stop. "The knob resets it to point north."

As soon as the tiled floor stopped spinning as well, Everson stood on the *S*, facing one of the corridors. "*S* for *start*," he explained.

"Not *south*?"

"That too." He banded an arm across Mahari's thighs and took off for the S corridor with me right on his heels. We stopped again when the hall divided into two. "Round and round the labyrinth goes the grizzly bear . . ." Everson muttered in the tempo of a children's rhyme. "Two right, two left, tickle him under there."

He ignored my raised brows. "This way," he said, taking the corridor on the right. He jogged right at the next intersection as well and then took two lefts. Metal shutters covered the cell doors, for which I was grateful. I'd seen enough ferals for one day.

I followed the back of Mahari's head, watching her dark hair swing with every turn and curve. When Everson stopped short, I peered around him. The corridor dead-ended at a darkened glass door — a cell door — the only one left unshuttered.

He took another step, and a light inside the cell snapped on to reveal a man hunkered over of a slab of raw meat. The dark fur covering his body bristled at the sudden glare, and he careened around. Everything about his face seemed bloody, from his bloodshot eyes to the reddish foam dripping from his lips and inhuman teeth. With a silent roar, he barreled for us, slamming into the glass so hard the door vibrated.

"He's the grizzly!" I gasped. "In the rhyme."

"If he was real, yeah. But it's a projection." Everson backed against the corridor wall, giving me a better view. "Run your fingers across the door, three inches from the bottom. You'll find a button. Press it."

"A projection?" That was hard to believe with the door vibrating from another grizzly body slam.

"To scare off anyone without clearance. *Lane*," Everson added with obvious irritation as his right arm twitched under Mahari's weight.

"On it." I wiggled past him and dropped to my knees, tracing my fingers along the glass until I did indeed find a button. One push and the feral disappeared. In his place was a glass door with more embedded gears than any I'd seen so far. I scrambled up as the door slid open — not onto a rampaging feral, thank goodness, but another corridor. A short hall this time, without a single cell or metal shutter.

I headed for the double glass doors at the end marked "Restricted" and tried pushing them open. No-go. Not a surprise, really. If you were going to kidnap people to use in evil science experiments, of course you'd keep your creepy underground lab locked up.

Everson adjusted his hold on Mahari and touched a control panel on the wall. The doors opened with a pop and hiss, as if they'd been vacuum packed, and we entered a room filled with massive gears grinding away, bathed in crimson light.

"The patrol added the doors a couple of months ago. They're built to withstand a flood if the door to the drainage tunnel ever fails." Everson lifted his chin toward a steel door at the other end of the chamber.

"Drainage tunnel?" I asked.

"The tunnel under the lock that the water drains into." Still carrying Mahari over his shoulder, Everson made his way around the huge gear works. "When they were building Gateway Station, they needed to bring the construction equipment in on barges, so Titan reactivated the river's lock and dam system."

He approached a row of glowing meters that looked a lot like the gas meters in the basement of my apartment building back in Davenport. He tapped the largest one. "The tunnel is filled with water right now. When it's empty again, we can unseal the door. We'll have ten minutes to get to the other end before it starts filling again."

I sucked in a breath through my teeth, not liking the sound of that at all.

Everson laid Mahari on the floor and pressed two fingers to her throat. She never even cracked an eyelid. After nodding to himself, he glanced over. "Rafe used to sneak onto base using this tunnel."

"How do you know?"

"We found guns and gear planted in here. The patrol had sealed off this room and forgotten about the drainage tunnel under the lock. They found the entrance when they were digging up the meadow."

He opened a locker to reveal an impressive array of supplies and weaponry inside. I moved in for a closer look. "Why do you have guns down here?"

"The strike team uses this tunnel to cross into the zone."

He snagged a slim flashlight and several glow sticks and pocketed all but two of the sticks, which he cracked. I blinked at the sudden burst of light. These were nothing like the glow sticks I'd waved around as a kid. He tucked one into an elastic loop on my flak jacket, took the other for himself, and then dug back into the locker. He shoved a magazine into the barrel of some kind of big-as-heck gun, which accepted it with a faint electronic sizzle, and then thrust the thing into my arms.

"I don't know how to use this," I sputtered.

"I don't expect you to." He stuffed more magazines into the pouch pockets on his jacket and sealed them. "Just carry it while I carry her." Squatting, he tugged Mahari into a sitting position. "Get ready. When I say go, throw open the door."

Suddenly the massive gears around us engaged, and the walls began to tremble. The needle on the biggest meter swung into the green. "Now!" he ordered while hefting Mahari over his shoulder once more.

With the crank of a wheel, I opened the steel reinforced door onto a dank, dark tunnel and got hit with a foul smell.

Everson grunted as he rose. I braced the door as he splashed into the tunnel. I took a deep breath and followed, slinging his gun over my shoulder. When the heavy door slammed shut behind me, Everson broke into a jog before my eyes even had time to adjust to the dim light of the glow stick. Not that I really wanted to see the puddles of slimy water that smelled like rotted sewage. I hurried after him, hating the way our footsteps echoed off the curved metal walls.

The tunnel was wide enough to jog side by side, though it was far from comfortable between the darkness and the dripping. I traced my fingertips against the wall to stay oriented and felt a tremor in the cold metal. When we passed through a giant valve, that tremor turned into an all-out vibration.

"We're under the river now," Everson explained. "I don't know how Rafe did this, coming from the other side, without the meters telling him when the tunnel was empty."

"Where does it come out?"

"In the meadow."

"Inside Gateway Station?"

"Outside the fence."

"Good," I said. "The lionesses told me to bring Mahari to the tree line if I found her."

"If we get Rafe's location from them, I'll take you to Captain Hyrax. The strike team will keep you safe when you're in the zone."

"What about Rafe?"

"They'll take a blood sample, that's all."

"*If* he cooperates," I said skeptically. "If he doesn't, they'll kill him."

By the light of the glow stick, I saw Everson's expression turn grim. "That's why you're going on the mission — to convince Rafe to give up his blood willingly."

Hopefully, that wouldn't be too hard, since I was bringing him the cure.

"I saw the video," Everson said abruptly. "Your video."

"How? The internet's blocked."

"Not in my mother's RV. I watched it this afternoon after you left. I'm all over it —"

"I never identified you by name," I said defensively.

"I know." He remained serious. "And you barely show Rafe. He's in a couple of the clips with Cosmo, but you cut him out of the rest. Why?"

What was putting the edge in his tone? Everson came off really well in my video. The piles of mail for him should have proved that much. What did he care if Rafe ended up on the proverbial cutting room floor? "Whatever shots I had of him must not have added to the story."

"Rafe getting infected didn't add to the story?"

"I put that in," I protested. I'd cut around Rafe because he was the color that refused to blend in. I'd wanted to show the truth about life in the East, but when Rafe was on camera, everything else just faded into the background. Everson was doing guard face again, which bugged me. "What?"

"At the end, just before he jumps off the carousel, he says, 'When I said I lied to Omar and the queen — *that* was the lie.' What's he talking about?"

I brushed aside his question with an impatient flick of my hand. "It doesn't matter what Rafe said then. He's infected *now*. These questions you're asking — Why did I cut Rafe out of the video? What did he say at the end? — they're pointless. What you want to know is if there's something between him and me and the answer is *yes*. A promise. One I'd give anything to break."

"What promise?"

We'd reached the other end of the tunnel.

"To put him down when he goes feral." I glanced at Mahari, hanging over Everson's shoulder, still unconscious.

"I still think it was wrong for you test the cure on her without her consent — on all of them — but I do want to save Rafe."

"So do I," Everson said softly.

"Oh, I get it." I arched a brow at him. "*You're* in love with Rafe."

At Everson's look of surprise, I almost laughed. He relaxed then. "Nah. He's too cocky for me."

I gave him a faint smile, glad that we'd somehow made it past a bump I had no name for. Deep down, I was still angry with him for treating the manimals so callously — so cruelly — but I couldn't deal with it right now. I needed a friend on this side of the wall, even one I didn't totally trust.

Everson pointed to a ladder bolted into the cement. "Up you go. Let's finish this mission."

"I'm not a guard," I said over my shoulder as I climbed the icy metal rungs.

"Really? Would not have guessed."

Upon reaching the hatch, I twisted the recessed metal handle and shoved. The heavy metal lifted, and I sucked in a lungful of the cold pine-scented air.

THIRTEEN

We exited the tunnel through what looked like a storm door in the ground, surrounded by mud and dead prairie grass. Everson carried Mahari across the moonlit meadow to the tree line. Crouching, he laid her by a pine tree where dead needles covered the dirt. "You're sure this is where we're supposed to meet them?"

"I think so. The guards wouldn't have scared them off tonight, would they? Hyrax would've told them not to, right?"

"Captain Hyrax wants that vaccine as much as my mother does. Maybe more. He's itching to dose up the whole patrol. He doesn't want to lose any more guards to infection."

Because once they got infected, they were nothing to Hyrax. Last fall, he'd shot an infected guard like he was putting down a rabid dog and showed no remorse as he did it.

Something shifted among the trees. Or someone. Then three figures pushed through the branches — the lionesses. Dangerous even if they weren't feral. There was no turning back now. Reckless or not, this was happening.

Charmaine bounded for us, a growl in her throat. "What did you do?"

"She's tranqed, that's all," I assured her.

She dropped to a knee next to Mahari. "Why . . ." she snarled low. "Why . . . believe you?"

Was she losing her words? Oh, this wasn't good.

"Don't," Everson said with a shrug. "She'll wake up soon enough, and you'll see for yourself."

Charmaine lifted her glittering gaze to him, and I took a step back. She was even wilder than she had seemed two weeks ago. Her every breath hummed as her gaze shifted between us and Mahari, as if she was working to process what we were telling her. Deepnita and Neve crouched beside her. No one would call them well groomed, but their faces weren't streaked with mud, their clothes weren't torn, and their hair wasn't tangled with twigs and dead leaves. However, after one close look at Mahari, they sprang to their feet looking nearly as savage as Charmaine.

"She's cured," I said quickly to head off the explosion.

Neve gave a slow blink. "Of what?'

Really? *The flu*, I wanted to say. Did any other disease matter where they were concerned? "Ferae."

"We *think* she's cured," Everson corrected. "Her viral load is down to an undetectable level."

"We don't speak science," Deepnita warned in a low rasp.

"It wipes the virus from her system," he explained.

Neve's lips parted with surprise. "It's all gone?"

Swinging her head between us and them, Charmaine growled. Probably more to cover her confusion than as a threat.

Deepnita crossed her arms, lightly furred and roped with muscle, over her chest. "Prove it."

"How?" Everson, her match in breadth and height, looked perfectly calm as he hooked a thumb through his belt loop. "You want me to get her medical charts and show you?"

"No," Deepnita snarled. "You're going to prove it in a way we'll believe."

Charmaine rose. "I won't believe."

Deepnita's broad nose wrinkled as she smiled at the other lionesses and then turned that now-evil smile onto Everson. "Kiss her."

Neve and I gasped in unison, and then I stammered out a "No!" as Neve growled, "She'll kill you."

"Touch her . . ." Charmaine growled, hands curling. Probably meaning "Don't touch her."

Deepnita pulled Charmaine to her, away from Mahari, and draped a staying arm around her shoulders. "It's for science," she said with a smirk.

Instead of springing away as I expected, Charmaine relaxed and turned into the hug, mewling softly.

"All right," Everson said without a trace of concern.

"No!" I grabbed a handful of his jacket. "You can't."

With his eyes pinned to Deepnita, Everson dropped to one knee beside Mahari. He slipped a hand under her head and lifted it as he lowered his face to hers. He kissed her softly, letting his mouth drift over her lips until her eyes fluttered open. Her golden gaze focused instantly, and with a snarl, she heaved him aside. Her incredible strength sent Everson sprawling. With an earsplitting roar, she threw herself on him, batting aside his hands to grab his throat.

I scrambled over to them. "She told him to!" I shoved against Mahari, but I may as well have thrown my weight against a brick wall. "She told him to kiss you!"

Her left hand hovered over Everson's eyes, claws extended, while her right tightened on his windpipe. He pulled at her wrist, frantically trying to loosen her hold. Mahari lifted blazing eyes to me. "Who?"

"Deepnita." I pointed at the lioness.

The biggest lioness shrugged. "I didn't think he'd be stupid enough to do it."

Mahari rose, looking even more furious. "You told a human to touch me?"

Everson struggled to sit up, but she shoved him back down with a bare foot pressed to his chest.

"To prove that you're cured," I said hurriedly, before she could impale him with her clawed toes.

Mahari's lush lips parted with surprise, revealing two-inch fangs. "Cured . . ." With a cat's yowl, she leapt aside.

"Ticklish?" Everson rose and dusted off his pants.

Mahari glared at him and angled closer, a wild look in her eye. Not how I expected a cured person to act. "Am I cured?"

"The serum neutralizes the virus, that's all. But you're not infectious, and if it works the way we intend it to, you shouldn't mutate any further."

"So . . . I'm cured?" she demanded.

"We're not calling it cured. Not yet. Viruses can hide — sometimes for years — in the lymph nodes, the spleen. There's a lot we don't know." He tensed as Mahari closed in. "I don't have to kiss you again, do I?"

"Only if you want your lips torn off your face," she purred, and then cupped his cheeks. "If I find out you're lying" — her thumbs traced the scars on his cheekbones — "and that I'm still infected, I will hunt you until the day I turn."

Everson exhaled softly. "Or you could say thank you."

Thank you for kidnapping her? I thought. *And injecting her with an untested drug?*

Mahari let go of his face and turned to the other lionesses. "Do I look different?"

They shook their heads.

"The serum can't remove the lion DNA. It can't make you human again," Everson said, sounding steadier with each sentence. "It can't fix what's already —"

"Fix?" Mahari snarled. "I'm not broken, human."

"You have corrupted DNA."

"You say corrupted. I say enhanced. And now that I know I'll never go feral, I'd say I'm just about perfect."

The other three lionesses stared at him, all ferocity gone. "She'll never go feral?" Deepnita asked softly, as if not daring to hope that it was true.

"Theoretically, there's no virus left in her to invade her brain," Everson explained.

"Will I stay fast and strong?" Mahari demanded, sounding excited despite herself. "Keep all this?" She ran her hand against the downy fur that gilded her sinuous arm muscles and then extended her claws.

"Uh . . . yeah. As far as we know," Everson confirmed, and then shot me a questioning look. I shrugged and clicked off my dial to conserve the power.

With a squeal, Neve launched herself at Everson. "I want it!" She jammed a hand into his pants pocket. "Give it to me! Give it!" Finding nothing, she patted down the rest of him impatiently like a child searching him for hidden candy. A very strong child whose pats equaled thumps.

Everson put up his hands like he was being mugged, which he kind of was. By a teenage lion, no less. A beautiful one. One with long honey-colored hair. Tangled, yes, and her fingers were disgustingly grubby, but Everson wasn't complaining as she pushed up his shirt. In fact, he looked as if he was holding back a laugh.

I rolled my eyes. "He doesn't have it on him. He didn't know he'd be coming out here with me."

Neve released him with a put-out chuff. "Go get it," she ordered, giving him a shove that sent him stumbling back a step.

Whoa. Everson was big — as in well over six feet tall and strapped with muscle, because despite putting in long hours in the lab, he still trained daily with his squad. Pushing him off balance was no easy thing, and Neve had done it without even trying. Forget her savage beauty; I was jealous of her strength.

"No," I said firmly. "We had a deal. I bring you Mahari, and you tell me where Rafe is."

"We don't know where, exactly," Deepnita admitted. "Just that he sticks close to the place where the two rivers meet."

"Which two rivers?" Everson demanded. "The Mississippi and what? The Illinois?"

She shrugged. "I don't know what you guards call them."

"We call them the big rivers," Neve said helpfully. "They're very big."

"Anyway, your friend is always there — in those woods. We saw him there three weeks ago," Deepnita said in her lazy rumble of a voice. "Well, Neve didn't."

"I was chasing a rabbit," Neve said dreamily. It must have been a good memory.

"He sticks close to one compound," Mahari put in. "It's called Heartland."

"Rafe lives in a compound?" Everson asked with surprise.

"Are you being funny?" she asked, eyes narrowed. "He's feral."

"*What*? No." My heart went jackrabbit on me. "You don't mean . . . all the way feral?"

Deepnita's look of sympathy was answer enough.

"No! It's too soon," I protested. "He only got infected six months ago."

Everson's look was grim. "It's possible. We don't know why some of them go insane sooner. Genetics, maybe, the particular strain or location of the bite."

I hugged myself tight, refusing to let the monstrous lie take root inside me. I glared at the lionesses. "You can't know for sure."

"Sure we can," Mahari said coldly. "We get close and he attacks like a rabid dog . . . or should I say, rabid tiger?"

"Physically, he's mutated?" Everson asked.

Mahari scowled. "I don't like that word." She glanced at Charmaine, who sniffed the air while scanning the dark meadow with a predator's eyes. Was she going to take off after a rabbit?

As if sharing my concern, Deepnita tucked Charmaine closer into her side. "Not much," Deepnita said, answering Everson. "But that doesn't mean anything. Some ferals look almost human."

"Till they start drooling," Mahari added, shooting another worried glance at Charmaine.

"Gateway? Cruz," Everson said into his lapel mic. "Relay is, I got the target's location."

The tiny radio crackled to life. "Solid copy. Hold your position."

"He really is feral," Neve told me softly, and then turned to the others. "He bit that hunter, remember?"

Mahari flicked a dismissive hand. "A human."

"What hunter?" I worked to keep my voice steady.

"From the compound," Deepnita explained. "There were four of them outside the fence. They don't come out very often. They were bowhunting. We saw Rafe stalking them and stayed back. The human didn't even know he was there till it was too late."

My stomach did a flip. "Rafe killed him?"

"No," she assured me. "Bit him." She touched the nape of her neck. "Here."

"You mean, he *infected* him," Everson said with disgust.

"The boy's feral," Mahari said with a shrug. "It's what they do. They bite. They're driven to it."

"He's *craaaazy*. In the bad way," Neve put in. "That's why they call him Wraith. He pulled that hunter down and bit him. Just like a ghost."

"Ghosts don't bite people," Deepnita said.

"Yes, they do," Neve said firmly. "That's how they eat. They suck out your blood. They live inside their coffins and come out at —"

"Stop it," I hissed. "Just stop."

"Is there anything else we need to know to find him?" Everson asked.

Deepnita shrugged. "Wraith stays in the woods, out of —"

"Rafe," I corrected.

Deepnita continued as if she hadn't heard me. " — sight. But he's always there, casing the compound."

"Why?" I asked before I could stop myself.

"Why does a predator sniff out prey?" Charmaine asked softly, suddenly back in the land of the sane.

I flinched as her eyes sought me out and she inhaled deeply. When a slow smile curled over her mouth, I wanted to run back to the hatch.

"Cruz!" Captain Hyrax's voice barked out of Everson's radio. "What did you think you were doing, letting that animal out of its cage?"

Charmaine snarled, but Mahari hooked her by an arm and drew her aside. She beckoned the others over as well and then spoke to them in a low voice. Too low for me to hear, though I tried.

"I'll brief you later," Everson told the captain in a flat tone. "I got the intel on the target's location. I'll drop McEvoy on the beach south of Gateway. Send the strike team in a Zodiac."

"Where's the target?" Hyrax demanded.

"Downriver, in central Illinois."

Why wasn't he telling Hyrax about the rivers merging? That had to be a very distinct location. Especially if the lionesses were talking about where the Illinois River joined the Mississippi. Not a place you could miss. And he wasn't saying anything about the compound either. Heartland. Maybe to give me some leverage with the guards? A bargaining chip to keep Rafe safe? I couldn't read Everson's expression, and he wasn't meeting my eyes as he finished his recap.

I glanced to where the lionesses had been huddled, but they were gone. No thank-you, no good-bye. But then, we were just humans.

Everson switched off the radio and said, "You don't have to go with the strike team. They can handle it."

I scowled. "By handle it, you mean take Rafe's blood, then shoot him."

"You promised to put him down when he turned feral," Everson said gently. "Sounds like he's there."

The thought of it made my chest ache, as if my heart might shatter into pieces. I didn't want to see him foaming at the mouth or snapping like a rabid dog. I wanted to remember him the way he'd been — the wild boy from my dad's stories — handsome and rude and funny and fast and vulnerable in ways he'd never admit. I should let the guards handle it. Rafe hadn't asked me to shoot him, only to see that it got done when the time came. If the lionesses were right, that time was now. But no matter how much I wanted to hand the whole painful mess over to the patrol, I couldn't. "I need to see him with my own eyes."

"And if he's feral?"

"Are you sure the cure can't bring him back?"

"If the virus has damaged parts of his brain, there's no undoing it."

"Then I'll keep my promise."

Everson raised his brows. "To put him down?"

I nodded despite the prickle behind my eyes.

· FOURTEEN ·

As we cut through the meadow for the riverbank, Everson handed me a cigar-sized metal cylinder. "A collection vial," he explained as he flicked on a slim flashlight. "Touch that end to Rafe's forearm." He trained the light beam on the wide end of the cylinder. "Over his vein, then push the button. It'll draw his blood without any effort from you. Just hold it steady for thirty seconds."

I slipped the metal cylinder into a zipped pocket on my jacket above the glow stick, which was beginning to dim. My legs felt shaky, but still, I wanted to meet up with the strike team and head into the zone. I couldn't let another minute slip by in case the virus had wormed its way into Rafe's brain. Every minute I wasted could be another brain cell destroyed.

"Remember to take his blood before you give him the —" Everson inhaled sharply, his attention on the river's edge. "What the —" He sprinted for the bank.

The riverbank looked fine to me from where I stood — dark and rocky — but I followed the bouncing flashlight beam and saw the problem soon enough. The strike team lay scattered across the beach like logs of driftwood. Dead or unconscious? I slowed my steps, hesitant to get any closer until I knew —

"What did you do to them?" Everson slammed to a stop in front of the black speedboat pulled up on the rocks.

And there were the lionesses, looking supremely pleased with themselves as they lounged on the boat's rubber hull — all except Neve. She sat cross-legged on the rocky shore, humming to the unconscious man she had cradled on her lap.

"What did you do to them?" Everson asked again. There was fury in every line of his body.

"Nothing. Hit them." Neve rubbed her cheek over the unconscious guard's blond buzz cut. "He smells nice."

"You hit all of them?" I crouched by one of the downed guards but saw no hint of blood. "Are they alive?"

"As alive as they'll ever be," Deepnita said with a chuckle. "They are human after all."

With a bouncing leap off the boat's prow, Mahari landed within feet of me. "If a pack of guards can't defend a boat, how're they going to keep you safe, little sister?"

With a bared foot, she flipped the guard at my feet onto his back. He groaned but didn't crack an eyelid. If he was awake, he wasn't admitting to it. Not that I blamed him. If a wild-haired Amazon of a woman was huffing over me, I'd play possum too.

Mahari hooked a toe-claw under the neck of his shirt. "We got within striking distance — *upwind* — and they still didn't know we were here. You think they can track down Rafe for you? Think again. He'll smell them from a mile away. Hear them crashing through the woods like the stinking, stumbling humans they are. You need us, so we've decided to help you."

Everson locked hard eyes on her. "For a price."

She smirked. "You're smart for a human."

"You want the cure," I guessed. Did I want them to come with me? Guards or the pride: Which would be worse for my health?

"Three doses," Mahari confirmed.

All the patrol cared about was getting Rafe's blood in a vial. They wouldn't chance getting close to him if he was a threat — feral or not. Why risk their health when they could just shoot him from afar and take his blood as he lay dying? The lionesses, on the other hand, wouldn't be afraid of Rafe's bite since they were already infected. Plus, they would be the better trackers and not just because of their lion DNA but because they knew the zone. It was their home after all. And as for protecting me? Well, I didn't matter to either group, but the lionesses might actually look out for me considering that I'd helped them twice now.

"Okay," I confirmed.

"Okay, with conditions," Everson corrected, his gaze pinned to Mahari. "First, you help us find Rafe and then get us back to the base unharmed. Only then do you get your three doses."

"Us?" I demanded.

Mahari cocked her head, amused. "You don't trust me?"

"You're smart for a mongrel," he said dryly.

Claws slipped from her nail beds and her lips pulled back, but I jumped between them before it went farther. "There's no *us*. You're not coming," I said firmly. "Your mother would skin me alive," I added in a whisper.

He waved aside my words as if I was exaggerating, which I wasn't.

"I'm not letting you go alone with them," he said.

"I didn't ask for your permission," I snapped.

He nodded past me to Mahari. "She hates humans. Got real poetic about it back in the lab — her plans to slaughter every human she could get her claws on and bathe in our blood."

"Lane doesn't count as human." Mahari flicked a hand toward me. "She set me free."

"Twice" was on the tip of my tongue, but I settled for "Thanks." Faint gratitude was still gratitude.

"Lane gets a pass, but you . . ." Her voice hummed with warning. "You should stay here."

Her glittering gaze reminded me so much of Chorda's that an electric current shot through me and fried my peace of mind. Not that I'd had much to start with.

Everson hooked a thumb at the boat — a Zodiac. "So one of you knows how to drive that, huh?"

Boats were not in my skill set, and going by the abrupt crease in Mahari's brow, they weren't in hers either.

"No?" Everson crossed his arms, unfazed. "Guess you'll be walking, then."

"Fine," I said quickly. "You can come." Chairman Prejean's wrath was the least of my worries right now. I had to find Rafe, somehow get a vial of his blood, and then give him the cure . . . or kill him. Yep, Everson's mom — low on my stressor list.

Mahari didn't look happy, but she didn't argue. Good. Because we were out of time. Hyrax was going to check in with the strike team any minute now.

"Grab their weapons," Everson ordered as he crouched by a downed guard. "Everything. We'll sort through it on the boat." As we all bent to the task of tossing guns and

Tasers into the Zodiac, Everson whispered to me, "We don't have the gear for this. It's reckless."

"I've got a few things in my back — what?" I asked when he snapped to his full height.

"This isn't going to work. There are patrol boats up and down this river. One look at them" — he jabbed a finger at the lionesses — "and we'll be blown out of the water."

He was right. Manimals on a boat were exactly what the guards were patrolling for. Infected people near the quarantine line — aka the Mississippi River — were shot on sight. "It's dark. We'll be in a patrol boat. Anyone looking will assume we're guards," I said, talking fast. "If they put on fatigues . . ."

"Like they'll pass," he scoffed.

"People see what they expect to," I argued. "The guards on river patrol won't look twice at a bunch of uniforms in a Zodiac."

"We can act human if we have to," Deepnita said, then glanced at Charmaine. "For a little while, anyway."

"Strip them." Mahari swept a hand at the fallen guards.

"Yay!" Neve clapped like a kid on Christmas.

Charmaine crinkled her nose. "And stink of human?"

"This one's mine." Neve gathered her guard in a tight hug and dropped kisses on his head.

"You're taking the uniform, not the man," Deepnita reminded her, then stepped over the limp form of a female guard to divest the biggest man of his jacket.

"Toss the radios, or the patrol will use 'em to track us." Everson unclipped the radio from his lapel and chucked it into the prairie grass. The lionesses did the same, except

Neve, who was still crooning to her guard. Mahari crouched beside her, unclipped his radio, and tossed it into the river. Then she put her fist under the man's nose like she was letting a dog sniff her.

"He's breathing," Neve said defensively.

"He is," Mahari confirmed as she rose and brushed off her drawstring pants. "And his heartbeat is steady."

"How do you know?" I asked.

"I can hear it."

"Oh." I exchanged a glance with Everson, who looked equally surprised.

Mahari pointed a commanding finger at Neve. "Drop the human and take his clothes."

Instead of obeying, Neve cradled the limp guard closer and rose without so much as a huff of exertion — and the guy was not small. She lifted her chin. "I'm keeping him."

Mahari and Everson sputtered in unison, but he found his voice first. "His name is Stanton. And in no way are you *keeping* him."

Charmaine rolled her eyes skyward. "Not again."

"You play too rough, little girl," Deepnita said, not unkindly. "He'll just run away like the others."

Others?! How many men had Neve tried to keep? And had they gone along willingly? As beautiful as she was with her leonine features, she wasn't exactly tame . . .

"I'll be really careful this time," she promised. "I won't wrestle with him or play Catch the Prey or —"

"This isn't a discussion," Everson snapped.

"I'll feed him!" she shouted. The other lionesses hurried to shush her. But she ignored them, her expression fierce. "He's mine."

"He's not a pet," Everson snapped. "You don't get to just *take* him."

"You took me," Mahari pointed out. Despite her purring tone, she looked less like a contented cat and more like one about to disembowel a chipmunk. That got a frown from Everson, but he didn't slap back a retort. Because he realized she had a point? I could hope.

Neve's clutch on her guard only got tighter. "He wants to come!"

I opened my mouth to argue that unconscious people tended not to have opinions, but Deepnita sent a head shake my way. More like a head shift, but I got the message: Don't bother using logic.

"Drop him," Everson ordered.

When he got in Neve's face, the Klaxon horn in my head put my nerves on red alert.

"Now," he warned. "Or you don't get in the boat."

A rumble rose in her throat, but he didn't back up or back down. I tensed, waiting for the claw lash that would tear open his throat, but it didn't come. Instead — while scowling so hard her face must've hurt — Neve opened her arms and dropped her guard. He hit the ground hard. Wincing, I started forward, only to get shoved back as Neve plowed past me and hopped into the boat.

Mahari and Deepnita exchanged a look, brows hiked with surprise.

Everson crouched beside Stanton. After a quick check, he rose and met Neve's lethal stare. "Out. We have to push it into the river first. And quit it with the growling."

She didn't quit it with the growling, but she did leap out and drag the boat to the water's edge. Beside me, Charmaine began to growl as well. Her eyes were pinned to Everson, and if she'd had a tail, it would've swished.

"Get his uniform, sister," Mahari told Neve as she strolled over to Charmaine, nonchalantly putting herself between Everson and the enraged lioness.

"Breathe, kitty," Deepnita crooned into Charmaine's ear. "There's no trouble here. Everything's good. The human is helping us."

Heart hammering in my ears, I eased back into the prairie grass. As the other lionesses coaxed Charmaine into the boat, Everson joined me. I rolled onto tiptoes and put my mouth to his ear. "Maybe you should go back to the lab and get —" I began, but he shook his head before I could finish.

"It's too late," he said, his voice no more than a breath. "The virus is in her brain."

"But —"

"We've tried. It won't work. She's too far gone."

"Then maybe we shouldn't be getting in a boat with her."

"We shouldn't," he agreed. "It's a stupid idea. Suicidal."

"Without us, human," Mahari snapped, "you won't find Rafe."

"Wraith," Neve corrected.

They stood a good twenty feet away by the water. Obviously, their hearing was as inhuman as their strength — something we'd do well to remember.

"So find your courage and get in the boat," Mahari commanded, sounding exactly like the queen she'd been.

"We're coming." I pulled my ponytail tight, dropped the dial down the inside of my shirt, and zipped my flak jacket. Then I tugged Everson over to the Zodiac and climbed in, keeping sharp eyes on Charmaine.

She seemed calmer . . . for now. Sane. Serene, even, as she gazed at the choppy waves that lapped at the sides of the rubber speedboat. Mahari leapt aboard with a bundled uniform in her arms, including boots. As the others settled along the Zodiac's inflated sides, I took a seat on a padded box in back that was bolted to the floor. Oars were lashed to the grip bar on either side of the outboard motor.

Once Everson dropped onto the chest behind the wheel, our combined weights had the boat sitting low in the water — a fact that especially bothered me when he warned us not to fall out. "The water's near freezing, so you'll go into a cold shock response. Staying afloat will be hard, and that's if we can grab you before you're whipped downriver."

He selected a rifle from the pile of weapons and slung it across his back by the strap. Following his lead, I took a handgun and put it into my backpack. He threw the Zodiac into reverse and maneuvered it out of the lock and under the bridge, where the river ran deep and slow. The lionesses rode in silence, gripping the rope handles, watching the base with wary eyes until we rounded a bend in the river and Arsenal Island was just a glowing spot above the trees.

"Stop sulking," Mahari told Neve. "You would've gotten bored with him. You always do."

Deepnita slid to the bottom of the boat and stretched her long legs. "Humans make terrible pets."

Neve rounded on her. "I like them."

"They don't like you," Charmaine snarled. "You're a beast to them."

"Stop talking," Everson ordered in a low voice. "Voices carry over water, and you don't sound like line guards."

The lionesses didn't seem offended by this pronounce-ment as they pulled on their stolen uniforms over their clothes — except Mahari, who shimmied out of her scrub pants without standing up. She didn't seem to care at all about letting us know that she was going commando. Everson cared, though, going by the way his spine snapped straight. From where I was sitting at the back of the boat, I couldn't see if he was uptight or annoyed. Probably both.

The moonlight slanted in through gaps in the cloud cover and cast ominous shadows along the riverbank. It had been only twenty years since the exodus, and yet nature had swallowed most of the signs of civilization. The rem-nants of razed buildings lined both sides of the river, though the Titan wall overshadowed the ruins on the west bank.

Everson glanced back at me, his expression grim. "I can't use the spotlight," he said quietly. "Move up front and watch for debris, floating and submerged."

I ignored his domineering tone — this time — and scooched past the steering wheel console, which was chock-full of equipment, including a large radio. I tucked myself into the front of the boat in the nick of time. A concrete pil-lar jutted a foot above the water directly in front of us — all that remained of a bridge that once crossed the Mississippi. "Turn, turn, turn," I shout-whispered.

Everson swerved in time, which spilled the lionesses onto the floor. Mahari sent him an implied death threat. "Your driving leaves much to be desired, boy."

"How old are you?" he demanded.

She shrugged and stretched out like a lounging cat which, of course, was exactly what she was. "What does it matter?"

"'Cause I only need to look at you to know I'm older. Don't call me boy."

She gave him a long, slow blink. "Have you been married?"

"No," he said. "I've never been married."

"I have. To a tyrant. A violent, insane tyrant. I was crowned his queen and ruled the Chicago Compound alongside him. A man I hated with every cell in my body. I dispensed justice and brought back electricity. Don't talk to me about years, boy."

Everson ground his jaw and probably a retort.

"Everson's royalty too," I said. "The other guards call him 'the prince.'"

Mahari sat up, interest piqued.

"Not to my face." He shot me a warning look.

He needn't have bothered. I wasn't going to tell her who his mother was. I wasn't stupid. And watching Mahari rip out his throat wasn't going to get me any closer to Rafe. She slid her golden gaze onto me, no longer languid.

Her muscles bunched as she brought her legs under her. Easier to pounce with leverage. "Why do they call him the prince?" she asked.

I gave a deliberate shrug. "He's bossy."

Neve gave a joyful shout. "Presents!" she cried, tossing a rolled sleeping bag over her shoulder. She'd lifted the lid on the metal box in back and was digging through the contents.

"Leave it all in there," Everson ordered. "We might need it."

I caught Mahari's eye. "Like I said — bossy."

Everson scowled as Neve ignored him, piling things on the floor of the boat beside her: tins of crackers, a bottle of iodine, matches, and a tarp. Then, with a happy cry, she snatched up a pack of jerky and settled on the boat's wet floor. "Can I drive?" she chirped.

"No!" Everson and Mahari said in unison.

With a harrumph, Neve ripped open the jerky with her teeth. She looked so put out, I had to bite my lips to hold back a laugh.

The other lionesses made themselves comfortable, stretching out their Glamazon limbs. At least they'd be able to hold their own against any attacking feral.

Key words being *their own.*

By the time we were miles downriver, the clouds had covered the moon completely, and I couldn't see much beyond the bow, not even upcoming bends until we were yards from the shoreline. Despite this, Everson never lost control of the boat or swamped it while swerving to avoid mud banks, floating trees, and bridge wreckage.

We passed only one patrol boat, which paid us no mind once Everson flicked a green light on the console on and off three times. Good thing he'd insisted on coming along, though his mother would never let me back on Arsenal after this little adventure. So what? I wanted to live with my dad anyway. And I was taking the orphans with me.

When it started to rain, Mahari told Charmaine to take over lookout duty. "We see better than you in the dark," she explained. "And Charmaine sees best of all."

I wanted to ask, "Because she's been infected the longest?" But I didn't, not being up-to-date on manimal etiquette.

Clinging to the handhold rope, I made my way past Mahari and stepped over Neve to resume my seat on the metal box in the back. Something large thudded against the side of the boat and then crashed back into the murky water. I wasn't the only one to yelp.

Deepnita peered over the side. "A fish . . . I think."

"Let's hope so," I said, quietly grateful that fish couldn't catch Ferae. I'd have hated to run into a catfish infected with lion or any strain that would give it teeth.

"Once most of the humans died off, the birds and fish came back like crazy," Neve said, and then noticed my surprise. "What? My dad told me."

"What else did he say?" Everson asked.

"That the predators came back fast after that. Wolves and bobcats first, later the bears and cougars. Now they're everywhere."

"There're bears and cougars everywhere?" I asked, only to wish I hadn't when I got three nods in answer.

"Don't worry," Mahari crooned. "One whiff of us and they steer clear."

"Okay." Which meant I'd be sticking close to them. Well, not Charmaine. The way she kept rolling her head on her shoulders and cracking her jaw did not give me a sense of security. She caught me looking at her and growled. I quickly turned back to Neve. "Where's your father now?"

"Dead," she said simply. "You killed him."

"What? No!" The denial burst out of me, which was stupid because Neve obviously got things wrong — a lot of things. She'd just named me because . . .

Then I remembered. She'd been there, that night in the zoo —

I forced the name past the tightness in my throat. "Chorda?"

At her nod, I just stared because I couldn't have killed someone's *father*. "You look nothing like him," I said finally. A lame argument, but it was true. She was blond and fair, and he'd been, well, orange. "Nothing," I insisted.

She waved aside my words. "He adopted me when I was little — when he was married to 'Nita."

I exhaled a shaky breath. An apology was out — I wasn't sorry for killing Chorda — but to say nothing? Murdering psychopath or not, he was her father. "I had to, uh, to defend myself. He — Chorda . . . He was going to eat my heart."

She blinked and then gave me a smile that was one part surfer girl and two parts shark. "Don't worry. I'm not mad. Daddy needed to be killed."

Okay. Creepy. But . . . true.

"He was crazy," she added.

"Like Wraith," Charmaine added.

"Are you ready for that?" Mahari asked me. "You're going to have to kill Wraith to get his blood."

"I know. That's why I'm here. I promised to put him down if he's feral."

They seemed unsurprised by this and just nodded. "When you find him, don't hesitate," Deepnita said. "Just shoot. He won't know you, and trying to make him remember will just get you killed."

"Don't hesitate," I said under my breath.

An hour later, the rain launched an attack, pounding down on us until we were soaked and beaten. Everson squinted to see, his free hand shielding his eyes as he slowed the boat until we barely cut through the choppy water. "We need to stop," he shouted over the downpour.

Nobody put up an argument — not even me. There was no point in trying to find Rafe when all trace of him would be washed away. However, there was no good place to pull ashore and wait out the storm. Abandoned industrial sites dotted the Missouri side of the river, which Everson said was exactly where guards on patrol would go to lie low. "We'd be safer on the Illinois side," he explained.

Safer in the Feral Zone? Now, that was a thought. But there was no good place to pull up the boat. The river clashed against limestone cliffs and rock formations that looked like they belonged in the Old West.

"Ahead! Turn!" Charmaine screeched as a hard turn in the river rushed into view. Everson spun the wheel — too late. His eyes went wide. The river had undercut the shore, leaving a deep ledge of rock hanging over the water, which we zoomed under, ducking as we went.

Once we were clear of the ledge, Mahari twisted to look back. "We're almost there!" She pointed past me to a giant pine tree growing at the edge of the overhang. "Close to where the rivers merge. Keep going."

So, we kept going, despite the rain, and finally the bank widened along the bottom of the ridge, until suddenly a rickety pier jutted into the current, directly in front of us. A welcome sight. The rain had even eased up. I hefted on the backpack Everson had given me in the lab. But just as he sidled us up to the pier, something burst through the brush on the riverbank, rolling and snarling. No, *two* somethings — animals — entangled, flailing. It was impossible to get a good look at them from the water, but the sounds were enough to get Everson to lay on the speed. As we took off, the thrashing gave way to a goose-bump-raising screech, followed by bone crunching. I couldn't help but look back, as did the others. Going by Everson's grimace, he was as thankful as I was for the dark.

Another growl cut through the night — so much closer this time. So close the boat had to be inches from the shore. I started to turn when hands grabbed me from behind and yanked me right off the metal box. I hit the floor of the boat with a landing that was as soft as falling backward into bed, but my relief was short lived. My eyes widened as I stared up into the face of a growling . . . Charmaine.

How had she moved back here so fast?

With my backpack wedged under me, putting an arch in my spine, I couldn't roll aside fast enough. She swung one leg over both of mine and pinned me into place. Her hands dug into my shoulders as she pressed me down, her ferocious face inches from mine. Inches! And she was drooling! Pure terror flooded me. I whipped my face aside — terrified her saliva would get in my eye — and clamped my mouth shut, forcing back a scream.

"Get off her!" Everson shouted.

A growl rumbled low in Charmaine's throat. I sensed movement all around me but didn't dare make a sound other than my thundering heart. If it pounded any harder, it would crack a rib.

"Don't!" Mahari growled at someone. "She'll bite."

Bite? She looked ready to tear out my trachea.

"Hey, kitty," Deepnita crooned from my right. Her knees dropped into my sight line.

Charmaine's rage-filled glare shifted from me to Deepnita, though she didn't lift her head. Her eyes narrowed to slits as the growl deepened inside her throat to a vicious snarl.

The boat rocked as someone sprang up. "Char!" Neve shouted. "Let her go!"

Charmaine's grip on my shoulders eased, but she didn't let go. She moved back a bit, though — no longer hovering all the way over me. Her lips pressed together to hide her canine teeth, and she took deep breaths through her nose.

"Come sit with me, Char," Neve demanded. "I need you."

Charmaine's grip loosened, and she pushed up and away me from me as if touching me burned her. Then she spun around and shoved the other lionesses out of her way. My mouth opened, but nothing came out. I lay unable to move until Everson touched my leg. Suddenly the boat rocked wildly.

"No!" Deepnita sprang to her feet.

I sat up to see Charmaine balanced on the inflated edge of the boat. One curl of her clawed toes and — *pop*! The rubber began to hiss. She glanced back, eyes no longer wild, her expression stricken.

"Sister, no!" Mahari cried as Deepnita lunged for Charmaine, but with one hard bounce, the lioness dove into the churning water. And then the boat flipped and sent us tumbling in after her.

· FIFTEEN ·

By the time I kicked my way to the surface and burst into the air, spitting out water through chattering teeth, the icy current had bulldozed me a long way downriver. I struggled to stay upright as the overturned boat careened past me. Gone in a blink. Dark figures thrashed against the current as they swept by. Then someone crashed into my back and stuck there, clinging to my backpack, legs entwining with mine, dragging me under. I kicked, trying to stay afloat, only to bury my boot in muck. The riverbed was right there! All I had to do was straighten my legs.

I dug my feet into the sediment and stood. The river was only shoulder-high. I shrugged off one strap, and Neve flipped around to my front, still clinging to my backpack, though her legs had whipped free. She flutter-kicked like a kid learning to swim. I coughed up enough water to gurgle, "Stand up," into her face. With the current pounding on my back, I'd topple if she didn't let go. Eyes squeezed shut, she shook her head and mewled. I grabbed two fistfuls of her jacket and yanked as much of her as I could below the surface. Her kicks nearly unbalanced me, but she must have also touched ground, because her eyes popped open. Neve blinked and then straightened. The water only came up to her chest.

We managed to drag ourselves over to the steep bank and claw our way out of the water — all while shivering uncontrollably. Gasping, I rocked onto my side and curled around my sodden backpack.

"Can you see the others?" I sounded drunk, mumbling and slurring.

Neve sat up with a groan and squinted into the darkness. "No."

My heart sped up again, and I got to my feet, the backpack clutched to my chest.

"But I can hear them." She pointed downriver. "There."

As I staggered forward, the mud sucked at my boots, making me work for every step. The moon was out again by the time we stumbled upon the glow that was Everson. Flashlight in hand, he hunkered beside someone on the riverbank. "Is it Charmaine?" I asked.

"She's gone." Deepnita's rasp came from the shadows at the base of a bluff where slabs of rock formed plateaus. Everson directed the flashlight to where she sat, her head down, her knees akimbo.

"She didn't even try to swim. And wouldn't let me help. I caught her arm." Deepnita looked up, her amber eyes twin embers in the dark. She held up a bloody fist. "She made me let go."

Neve dropped onto the rock and wrapped her arms around Deepnita, as if she could absorb the other lioness's despair. Mahari lay on a rocky tier above them, still as a corpse, staring at the night sky. She said nothing.

My throat clenched around the words of sympathy that I wanted to pour out like a balm, like that would lessen their pain even a little. I forced myself to breathe and said, "I'm so sorry."

If they heard me, they were beyond responding. Neve comforted Deepnita without words, hugging her so fiercely, her claws tore at Deepnita's shirt. The light shifted away, and the shadows reclaimed them.

"Lane," Everson said, urging me to come to him.

He crouched at the water's edge, where a boy lay half in the water. He was a young teen, with skin so pale and rubbery-looking, he could've been a film prop. But he wasn't. Not with the way Everson was inching the flashlight beam over every limb. I wrung out my wet hair as I made my way over to him, my steps shaky. By the time I dropped my sodden backpack in the mud, I was shivering uncontrollably. So was Everson.

"We're lucky," he said. "The river isn't as cold in the shallows."

I didn't feel lucky as I sank to my knees beside him, only to see the unconscious boy had been even less lucky. His torn sleeve revealed a semicircle of gouged skin.

"Something bit him," I croaked.

"Yeah," Everson agreed. "And we're going to assume that something was a feral until this kid gets tested for Ferae."

"It doesn't look like a human's bite," I pointed out. "Or even a tiger's."

"You're an expert?" Everson asked dryly.

"No . . ." I pointed to the puncture wounds. "But look, the tooth marks are slits, like what a knife tip would make. A tiger's fangs would punch holes in his skin."

"Can we worry about this later?" Everson grabbed hold of the boy's boot. "We have to get him out of the water."

The river stunk like rusty metal and algae, but now the scent held a trace of blood as well. I took hold of the kid's other boot and, between us, we pulled him onto the grass at the foot of the bluff. I carefully laid the back of my hand on the unbroken skin of the boy's brow. He was cool to the touch. I glanced at Everson. "No fever."

"Doesn't mean anything. He probably has hypothermia."

I remembered the symptoms of hypothermia — one of the few facts that stuck with me from the survival skills classes my dad made me take. Why hadn't I paid attention in those classes? But no, I'd sat there like a lump, resentful over what I'd considered a waste of my time. Still, I remembered that the "umbles" were signs of early hypothermia: stumbles, mumbles, fumbles, and grumbles. The symptom for advanced hypothermia was even easier to spot: death.

I met eyes with Everson. I didn't want to give Rafe's dose to anyone but Rafe, but if it could save this boy, then I'd have a hard decision to make. "Should we give him . . ." I asked, silently mouthing: "the cure."

"Let's see if he lives," Everson muttered. "Who knows how long he was in the water."

"We need to get him warm and dry if he's going to have a chance."

"Yeah, but first I need to check his wounds. See how bad they are before we move him."

I nodded, but neither of us moved. Blood drenched what was left of the boy's long-sleeved shirt. Without gloves and face masks, how could we do anything for him?

"Hey," Everson called to the lionesses. "You can touch him. You can't get infected twice."

When they didn't reply, he aimed his flashlight at the rocky tiers. They were gone! Everson swept the light along the endless cliff face that edged the narrow beach. Not a trace of them anywhere.

"Maybe they're looking for Charmaine," I suggested. Or her body.

"Maybe," he said grimly.

Or maybe they just needed time alone. They'd just lost one of their own. If they didn't come back for days, I wouldn't be surprised, though the thought terrified me.

"You don't have any gloves in your pack by any chance?" he asked.

Dragging the backpack to me, I rummaged through it and pulled out a ziplock bag that contained a few first aid supplies. "You can use the bag," I suggested.

He nodded. "And the bandage. Don't get it dirty."

The boy's eyes blinked open — dull brown and seemingly human. And then he saw us, and his expression turned to one of alarm, though he didn't move. Or maybe he couldn't.

"You're safe," Everson told him. "You were in the river; that's why you're cold. Can you feel your fingers?"

The boy parted cracked lips, trying to say something, but his words came out as a wheeze.

I put out a comforting hand but snatched it back at Everson's hiss of warning. "What's your name?" I asked softly.

He licked his lips and tried again. "Aaron." It was little more than a croak.

"We'll get you back to your compound soon," I promised him.

He shook his head. "I didn't know . . ." Tears welled up in his eyes, and he turned away from me. "Now I'm the ghost."

"No," I soothed. "You're not a ghost. You're going to be fine." I glanced at Everson for confirmation, but his expression promised nothing.

"Do you know what bit you?" he asked.

When the boy didn't reply, I leaned over him to see that his eyes were closed and his features had gone slack. "He's out."

On a nod, Everson dug through my pack for my water bottle; then he emptied the ziplock bag, taking only the Bactine and the rolled bandage. After sliding his hand into the empty bag, he dropped to a knee beside Aaron. He poured the water over the bleeding teeth marks and then took hold of Aaron's wrist with his bag-protected hand, before torturing him with the Bactine spray. Aaron's eyes popped open at the sting. Everson held on tightly as the kid flailed.

"Almost done," Everson assured him.

Aaron shivered silently, uncontrollably, and then closed his eyes as Everson tore off a piece of the rolled bandage and wrapped up his arm. When he was done, Everson peeled aside Aaron's torn shirt. Crisscrossed scratches marred his chest, but thankfully, they didn't look deep. "This probably happened yesterday. The blood is caked and dry. While the bite" — Everson pointed to where Aaron's bandaged arm lay across his stomach — "is still bleeding. Maybe he was attacked twice."

"Or maybe . . ." said a voice from behind us. "The bite is infected." Mahari stood, flanked by the two remaining lionesses. All were pale and dry-eyed. "Tigers do have dirty mouths."

"No," I sputtered. "It wasn't Rafe. Not with all those scratches."

"What? Tigers don't scratch?"

"He's feral," Deepnita said, though at least she sounded sympathetic. "He's thinking like an animal, so he attacks like one."

"But those are claw marks," I said, pointing out the obvious. "He couldn't have grown claws that fast!"

Mahari held up a hand, claws extended. "My fingernails fell out within weeks, along with half my teeth. Don't tell me how this works, human. I lived it."

I shut my mouth, not daring to offer sympathy. She liked the final result of her mutation, but I couldn't imagine the horror of living through it. Of having your muscles grow and your bones shift. Losing hair or else having it sprout over every inch of skin, inhuman in color and texture. Or growing horns or scales. But none of that compared to the terror of knowing the virus was invading your brain, stealing your humanity, the part that made you *you* — your soul.

"There are a lot of ferals in these woods," Deepnita said, essentially throwing me a bone. "Might not have been Rafe."

"Wraith," Neve corrected. "That's what the hunters call him."

There was no way to know until Aaron was awake. Then, hopefully, he could tell us who or what had attacked him.

"That doesn't matter right now," Everson cut in. "If this

kid's going to have a chance, we need to get him out of the elements."

On my last venture into the zone, we'd had our pick of decrepit buildings to bunk down in — office buildings, malls, entire cities. Places that had bustled with people twenty years earlier. Those buildings were husks, covered in vegetation, their windows long since blown away. Death waited inside many of them, and it was impossible to tell which from the outside. Ferals didn't decorate.

"Where can we find an abandoned house?" I asked the lionesses.

Mahari smirked. "You don't know where you are, do you?"

"On the Mississippi," I replied. "Somewhere south of Moline."

"Way south."

Was that supposed to mean something to me? Everson closed his eyes and tipped back his head. Guess it meant something to him. "There are no houses," he said with a groan. "We're in Pere Marquette State Park."

My stomach dropped. "So . . . there are no buildings at all? Nothing? Just woods?"

Neve tilted her head in thought. "There are caves."

No. No way was I getting trapped in a cave with no back door. "Where'd he come from?" I asked, pointing at the boy.

The lionesses exchanged wary looks. "Heartland, probably," Deepnita said.

"The compound Rafe stays near?" I asked.

"Yeah."

"Fine," Everson said. "We'll take the kid there."

"No," Mahari hissed. "We steer clear of that place. They're hunters."

"They won't let him in anyway." Deepnita padded closer, her eyes on the boy. "Not if he's infected."

"If he's one of theirs, maybe they'll see him through the fever," Everson said.

Mahari pulled off her soaked patrol shirt. "They'll shoot before you even get to the gate," she said as she wrung out the river water.

"They always shoot," Neve said, joining our group. "Even the young ones." She nudged the boy with the tip of her muddy sneaker.

"If we don't help him, he'll die," I snapped.

Standing there in her clinging tank, streaked with mud, Mahari looked semi-feral. "One less human in the zone means one less hunter trying to kill us."

"You don't know that he's a hunter," I said. Though, going by the boy's woodsy camo shirt, she was probably right.

"All humans are manimal killers," Mahari snapped, "with or without guns. Here, in the zone, they force the infected from their compounds, leaving us to starve in the wilds or get eaten. They don't care what happens to us."

"Not in Moline."

"Maybe not, but everywhere else." She jabbed an accusing finger at the boy. "We're not human to them."

I rounded on her. "But *you* know you're human, so act like one."

"Oh, no . . ." she said softly. "That much they have right. We're not human. We're so much *more*. And it scares them to the marrow." She directed her gaze at Everson.

"Guess again, Princess," he said, sounding completely unfazed.

"Queen," she hissed, and then shifted her attention back to me. "Humans put up the walls, the fences, the razor wire . . . They hunt us. Lock us up and inject their drugs into us —"

"*Cure* you." Everson crossed his arms over his chest.

She ignored him. "I don't help an enemy get back on his feet when he'll use that foot to crush my neck the first chance he gets."

She was hurting over Charmaine — beyond logic and without empathy to spare — but still I had to say it: "Not every human is your enemy."

She curled her black lips, revealing sharp fangs. "You want something from us, Lane, and we want something from you. That doesn't make us friends." It shouldn't have stung, but it did. "So don't ask us to help one of yours."

"He's infected," Everson said, his temper starting to fray. "Doesn't that make him one of *yours*?"

"Not yet," she said coldly. "He has to live through the fever."

"Fine." Everson snatched her wet shirt out of her hand. "Just tell me where the compound is, I'll take him myself."

"They shoot from the trees," Neve whispered. "And the trees are everywhere."

"Snipers," Deepnita explained. "Mahari's right. Go at night and they'll shoot before you get a word out. If you're going to have a chance, you'll have to go during the day so they can see you're totally human."

"Okay." He glanced back at the boy on the ground. "Get us as close as you can to the compound, and let's hope he lives through the night." Everson wrapped one hand in Mahari's shirt and yanked down his sleeve to cover the other. "I'll have to carry him without —"

Mahari cut him off with a scoff and tipped her head to Deepnita. The largest lioness sighed and scooped up the boy like he weighed nothing.

As she bounded up the rocky tiers toward the top of the bluff, I shouted, "Careful! You'll hurt him!".

"He's already hurt," she replied without looking back.

Mahari and Neve sprang after her, leaping from one rock slab to the next without a sound. Everson and I followed at a more cautious pace. Had it been daytime, the view from the top would've been panoramic. But even under the half-moon, we saw that we'd clearly left the flat plains of the Midwest far behind. A wide gorge sliced between the rocky, tree-covered cliffs. Everson ended my gawking with a nudge, and we followed the lionesses through the woods. None of us wanted to attract attention — human or feral — which also meant no flashlights, though Everson did crack two more glow sticks. Without them, I would've ended up at the bottom of a ravine. Every ten minutes or so, the lionesses stopped to scan the terrain. Warily. They weren't checking our route, I realized with a shiver. They were checking for ferals.

The area must have been hit hard in the winter. There were branches down everywhere and even whole trees. We crossed only one road. More accurately, what had once been a road. We weaved through the ancient gridlock of rusted cars, and weirdly, I felt a rush of relief once we were surrounded by trees again. The woods felt natural, even if the going was tough. Walking through the frozen-in-time traffic felt like cutting across a graveyard.

The lionesses paused at the top of the next bluff while I leapt from one boulder to the next slowly, planning and executing each jump. Once Everson and I caught up to them, we looked around. "What is it?" I asked, seeing nothing but a dark ravine before us.

"This is a bad place," Neve whispered.

Deepnita shifted Aaron onto her other shoulder. "Something down there is dead." She inhaled deeply. "Lots of somethings."

"I don't smell anything," Everson said.

"Most have been dead a long time," Deepnita said, stepping back from the edge. "They smell like dried-up meat. But there are a few that are —"

"Rotten meat." Neve wrinkled her nose.

"Recent kills," Deepnita finished.

I worked to suppress my panic. One misstep and I'd be down there too. "Were they human?" I asked through my sleeve, which I'd pressed to my nose and mouth to keep the decomposing body germs out of my lungs.

"Who knows? Dead prey is dead prey," Mahari said, her tone fierce; however, her darting gaze gave her away. She was spooked. "We'll find another way to cross." She took off at a brisk pace with Deepnita smack on her heels.

"That'll take too long," Everson called after them.

"Shhh." Neve pressed a finger to his lips. "Don't wake it up."

"Wake what up?" I asked in a whisper.

"The hungry thing that lives down there."

"You don't know what it is?"

"No, and I don't want to," she said, and hurried after the others.

Everson and I exchanged a look and then followed as fast as we could. If it scared the pride, one glance at it would probably shut down my higher brain functions.

· SIXTEEN ·

An hour and a dozen steep climbs later, the lionesses finally announced that we were as close to the compound as we dared get.

"See that drop-off?" Mahari pointed toward a distant corridor between two cliffs that seemed to end at the stars. "The compound is in the valley below. The humans hide behind their fence at night, so they shouldn't stumble on us up here."

For a second, I felt better about being within shouting distance of a human compound, but then I remembered that these humans liked to hide in trees and shoot people.

We settled under a low rock ledge with the cliff at our backs. In many ways, this spot was better than an abandoned house. There was no creepy element. No tattered curtains, cobwebs, mildewed walls, or smell of dust. It was almost like camping, but without a tent or sleeping bag or change of clothes. Instead, we were still wet, cold, and muddy. I was, anyway. The lionesses just looked muddy.

Deepnita gently rolled the boy onto the ground, where he writhed and thrashed, muttering. "He's hot," she informed us. "Really hot."

Aaron gasped as the lionesses surrounded him, his expression one of reeling terror and incomprehension.

When he struggled to rise, I crouched beside him. "They won't hurt you."

"Wraith . . ." he cried. "He'll find me."

My breath came thick in my throat. "What?"

"Told you," Mahari said in a flat voice.

Aaron's eyes rolled, showing the whites, as he tried to take us all in. "He'll follow the blood."

"Did Rafe — Wraith," I amended, "did he bite you?" I had to know.

With a choked cry, Aaron curled on his side, arms crossed protectively over his head. When his shivers turned into shudders, Everson pulled a lighter from his sealed pocket and tossed it to Mahari. "Go make a fire."

Her eyes narrowed, but before she could snarl a response, I asked, "Won't that attract ferals?"

Deepnita tugged on Mahari's arm, leading her away. "No, most of 'em are terrified of fire."

As soon as they were out of sight, Everson began tearing what was left of the bandage into long strips. I dug into my bag until I found a packet of instant ice. I paused and exchanged a look with Everson. At his nod, I squashed the packet between my palms to start the chemical reaction. It wouldn't do much, but it couldn't hurt.

"Aaron," I said softly. "No one's going to hurt you. We're going to keep you safe." When he relaxed enough to look at me, I held up the cold packet. "This will feel good, but you need to lie on your back." As soon as he did, I laid the packet on his forehead. His cheeks had taken on a flush, and his eyes were glassy.

"We're going to take you to your compound in the morning," I promised.

It was the wrong thing to say. Instantly, Aaron rolled his head hard enough to send the cold pack flying. "No," he said through gritted teeth. "No. Boone said . . . he said —" In his agitation, Aaron tried to sit up, but Everson dropped to a knee and pressed him back with a hand on his shoulder, one of the few patches free of blood.

Tears welled in Aaron's eyes. "I didn't know," he told me in a tone that sounded like he was asking for forgiveness. "I didn't, I swear. I didn't know."

"You need to take it easy for a while," Everson said firmly. "You were cut up pretty bad, and I'll be mad if you start bleeding again." He looked up, his gray gaze trapping mine as he held up the strips of bandage. At my blank expression, Everson said, "Aaron, I'm sorry, but we have to do this now. It'll be too hard later," he went on. "I don't want to have to chase you down in the dark."

Everson's eyes were on me as he spoke, willing me to understand what needed to be done with those bandages. And yeah, I got it. I didn't like it, but I got it. I nodded to let him know I was on board with his plan. Looking relieved, he tossed me the makeshift bindings and quickly drew Aaron's wrists together. "We'll untie you in the morning . . . after the fever's gone. Lane, now," he growled at me.

Either Aaron had seen sick people get tied up before or he was too weak to fight. He lay there, dazed and docile, as we bound his wrists and ankles. It felt cruel, but it was necessary. On my first trip to the base, I'd seen a newly infected guard strapped to a bed in the infirmary. At the height of the fever, he'd been practically feral — a threat to himself and everyone around him. Feverish, howling, and crazed — the hallmarks of stage one of Ferae. Incubation.

I got to my feet, dismayed that there wasn't more we could do for him.

Everson pointed to my pocket. The pocket that contained the small yellow tube of serum. He leaned into me and whispered, "If he makes it through the night, we'll give it to him tomorrow."

I clapped a hand over the pocket. "This is for Rafe," I whispered back.

Everson lifted his chin toward Aaron. "He said Rafe bit —"

Aaron erupted with a scream at Rafe's name. I dropped into a crouch. "Shhh. He's not here. You're safe."

However, Aaron continued to thrash and yell, which brought Mahari running. She clamped a bare foot over his mouth, cutting him off mid-shriek. "You just rang the dinner bell," she snapped. "Ferals love a wounded animal. It's easier to catch."

I scanned the dark trees while wishing for better night vision.

"Fine." Everson thrust the last strip of bandage at Mahari. "Gag him."

The virus wouldn't get into Aaron's salivary glands until late in the disease, but I understood why Everson was asking Mahari to do it. She couldn't get infected twice. She plucked the strip from Everson's fingers and gagged Aaron with brutal efficiency.

Ten minutes later, the lionesses had a fire going, and Aaron was burning nearly as hot. We moved him farther underneath the ledge, where it was cooler, but he continued to thrash against his bindings. Everson touched my arm. "Go get warm."

I didn't argue. I was cold to the bone, even though the

hike had taken my clothes from sopping to semi-soggy, and worse, I was in agony wondering whether Rafe was the unseen monster that was terrorizing the compound. Had he really become Wraith?

Neve threw an armful of branches onto the fire, which sent a surge of smoke billowing into my face as I settled as close to the flames as I dared get. When Neve bounded off to find more wood, I smothered a cough against my sleeve and crawled even closer, drawn by the blissful warmth. The sounds, pops, and crackles over a dull roar soothed me as well. Of course, something creepy or scary was bound to happen that would yank me back to the reality of our situation — that we were stranded in the Feral Zone. But the combo of fear and adrenaline was a jittery high, and it was wearing me out, body and mind. I couldn't sustain it, not without falling apart. So I inhaled the smoke-heavy air and thawed out my freezing hands, only glancing up when Deepnita sank to her haunches a few feet away.

She nodded but said nothing as she watched the gold and amber flames dance. After a quick scan to see that no one was close by, I asked quietly, "How old is Neve?"

Her amber gaze slid to me, gauging. "Near your age."

"I'm seventeen."

"Sounds about right."

"She, uh . . . seems younger." That was about as diplomatic as I could put it.

"She had gaps on her way to seventeen."

"Gaps?"

"You'd be" — she pursed her lips with distaste — "*different* . . . if you lived a year on your own in the zone. A band of men, humans, raided Neve's compound and took their supplies. Then they lined up the residents and shot them. Neve's mother boosted her over the fence, before taking a bullet in the back. Neve was six."

"Oh." Younger than any of the orphans had been when they'd lost their parents.

"She didn't talk for years after Chorda brought her to the castle. He treated her like a princess. He was always a power-hungry tyrant, but surprisingly, he loved her. He really did. But then he got infected. I was queen then." She stared at the fire without blinking. "We all knew he was going feral — slowly — definitely sinking into that swamp a little more each day. But he wouldn't even admit he was infected, and he had the men and the guns to make sure nobody pointed it out. Then he started disappearing for weeks at a time."

On his hunting trips looking for human hearts to devour.

"Eventually he tired of me," Deepnita continued, as if it had been no big deal. "And off I went, newly infected, to live in the cage with Charmaine, his first queen. That night, he forced Mahari down the aisle. Through all of it, Neve never said a word. I figured the words had been scared out of her forever. Then Chorda disappeared for a long time. Months. We thought he was dead. We *hoped* he was dead. But the day that Mahari planned to unlock our cage, Chorda came back. And he'd . . . changed. The disease had done its work. He'd become a monster with fangs and a tail. I was in the cage, but I saw it all. How the humans in the courtyard froze in horror. Mahari too. Only one person was happy to see him . . ."

"Neve."

Deepnita nodded, her expression surprisingly vulnerable. She was the toughest lioness, which was saying a lot. The unflappable one. And yet, this memory clearly cut her to the core. "Neve threw herself into Chorda's arms, and for the first time since he'd brought her to Chicago, she spoke."

I winced. "What did she say?"

Deepnita tossed a stick into the fire. "Pretty tiger."

"He had her caged for that?!"

"He had her *infected* and caged for that. Then he broke every mirror in the castle."

I touched the small lump in the sealed pocket on my thigh. Possessing one dose of the cure was beginning to feel more like a burden than a blessing. I was tempted to push the tube into Deepnita's hands and ask her to choose who should get it. I could make a case for all of them: her, Neve, Aaron, and Rafe. But there were more tubes back in the lab. It wasn't a matter of *who* got it, but *when*. And if Rafe was already feral . . .

I clasped my hands in my lap and pushed the yellow tube and its promise to the back of my mind — at least for tonight. I didn't have to decide anything tonight.

The others joined us around the fire, though Everson kept one eye on Aaron. "We can take turns sleeping," he said. "I'll take first watch."

"Can you see in the dark?" Mahari asked with a scoff. "No? Then how will you see anything until it's already attacked?"

"Fine," Everson said evenly. "I'll stick close to the kid. He's sleeping, but with the way his fever is hiking, he'll be awake again soon."

The ground felt cold and wet, thanks to the dead grass and soggy leaves. The tarp and sleeping bag from the boat would have been a gift from the gods right now. But they'd been swept off downriver along with the boat. I zipped my jacket up to my chin and tugged my sleeves over my hands, but nothing kept out the cold. I envied the lionesses in their sleeping pile, even if technically Mahari wasn't asleep. She still looked warmer than I felt with the other two using her thighs as pillows.

I shifted onto my side, propping myself onto an elbow and then lying back. I wanted a blanket. And a pillow. Or better yet, my whole bed. No, my room. And a Skype session with Anna.

Everson took a seat between the fire and Aaron to clean his rifle. I was determined to do the same — dig the handgun out of my backpack and clear the river water out of it. But watching his fingers slide over the polished steel as he examined each component was enough to send me off to dreamland, despite the cold, despite our surroundings.

I jerked awake hours later with the pressing sense that one of the orphans needed me. An orphan was rustling around, struggling to kick his blanket aside. I lifted my chin from my . . . crossed arms? Where was my pillow?

Several yards away, Neve sat propped against a boulder, softly snoring. Within two blinks, my brain rebooted. The dunk in the river. Charmaine! The woods. Mahari waking Neve to take her turn on watch.

Again, someone flailed under his blanket. But no, we didn't have blankets. I rolled onto my side. Beyond the glowing embers of the campfire, Aaron squirmed against his bindings as he slid closer to the trees. Wait, slid? I sat up.

Aaron wasn't sliding! He was being dragged by a hunched figure of a man who had him by the boots. A hunched figure that was now within steps of the tree line. I scrambled up, a scream trapped in my throat. The intruder glanced up. I caught only a flash of unkempt hair falling across a dirty face before he threw aside Aaron's feet.

It was Rafe. The nightmare version of him. The version I'd prayed I'd never see.

· SEVENTEEN ·

Poised at the edge of the clearing, Rafe stared back at me, looking angry and wild in the faint light of the dying campfire. His once-blue shirt was muddied and rife with small tears. Dark as it was, I could still tell that he'd put on muscle, and I could've sworn his canines were longer.

My heart exploded in a thunderous pounding, and blood rushed to my ears. I opened my mouth to say something. Anything that would bring him back to himself. Turn him rational. But then his nose twitched, and he inhaled deeply. His glare turned ferocious, and his eyes . . . It had to be a reflection of the firelight. Had to be. But whatever the cause, his eyes were now lit with a golden sheen. Just like . . . Chorda's eyes.

I flinched, and my fingertips started tingling. I braced myself for the numbness that always followed. Always at the worst time! On the ground, Aaron echoed my flinch with a full-body buck, which caught Rafe's attention. His expression turned stark as he stepped over Aaron's thrashing legs and straddled him. The world slowed as I watched him drop onto the boy, and then everything stopped like a frozen slice of nightmare when Rafe raised a clawed hand high . . .

My scream tore free of my throat just as his claws slashed downward — across Aaron's face.

Mahari appeared next to me as if out of nowhere.

"Now do you believe us?" she hissed.

I nodded, unable to speak. And then Everson was there too, sliding his rifle into my hands.

Both of them existed only in my peripheral vision, because I couldn't tear my eyes away from Rafe, who was still crouched over Aaron's body and looking through his tangled hair at me.

You promised.

I raised the rifle and aimed it at him, felt for the trigger with my numb finger, gasping with the effort not to start sobbing. How could I forget what I'd promised with him reminding me every night in my dreams?

And then I did exactly what Deepnita had warned against — I hesitated. I couldn't make my finger squeeze the trigger. Something wasn't right. And it wasn't just the idea of killing a person — Rafe — in cold blood. The seconds stretched out until they felt like minutes, hours. And still he stood there looking at me as if he *wanted* me to shoot him. What feral would do that?

Then his expression turned savage, and he let loose a low snarl before pivoting and tearing off through the trees.

"Go!" Everson shouted at the lionesses. His voice startled me, pulling me from my trance.

"Find him and pin him down," Everson told them. "I'll take his blood."

On Mahari's signal, she and Deepnita and Neve fanned out and slipped into the woods with only the faintest snapping and crunching of underbrush.

Everson turned to me. "Lane —"

"Sorry," I said, holding the rifle out to him. I was grateful that he and the lionesses had given me a chance to keep my promise. "I couldn't do it."

"It's okay." He took the rifle and slung it across his back.

I unzipped my pocket and pulled out the metal cylinder — the blood-collecting device. I tossed it to Everson, who snagged it out of the air. He lit out after the lionesses while I dug in my backpack until I found the gun I'd taken off the guard on the riverbank. I didn't know how to clean it without Everson's help. Would it work if I needed it? Just holding it sent my heart into a gallop. If Rafe — *Wraith* — came back now . . . I didn't know what I'd do.

You promised.

So what?! He'd forced me into that promise. Hadn't given me a choice. But how could I leave him like this? Living like the monsters he used to hunt? I didn't want to think about it right now. I didn't have to decide anything if Rafe didn't come back. For now, I would stay here with Aaron —

Aaron!

I scanned the area, but he wasn't in sight. I rushed to the spot where Rafe had dumped him but found only a torn strip of bandage — a remnant of the ties that had bound him. Fevered out of his mind and smelling of blood, Aaron was now wandering around in the woods at night. No way would that end well. I sank onto the nearest rock to let my heart slow . . . or break. Whatever.

Everson stepped from between the trees minutes later or maybe hours, who knew? Time wasn't working right in my head. I kept getting caught in a golden gaze, unable to move, unable to scream. Frozen like a bug in amber — all while *you promised, you promised, you promised* pounded in my head like a dialed-up bass beat.

"They lost him," Everson announced. "They're going to — what's wrong?"

"Aaron's gone," I said, suddenly feeling cold to the bone. The frigid air prickled the damp skin along my forehead and down the back of my neck.

Everson did the same sweep of our campsite I'd done, looking just as upset as I felt.

"We'll never find him in the dark," he said after checking behind every boulder. "We'll stay here and wait for the others." He scanned the tree line, cylinder in one fist, rifle at the ready. "If we're lucky, Rafe'll come back."

I nodded while fervently hoping that we wouldn't be that lucky.

As agreed, Everson kept watch for two hours while I slept, and then we traded places. I got the better deal. Thirty minutes later, dawn lit up the horizon and the sky faded to a deep blue-lavender. But I let him sleep on. Why not? The lionesses hadn't returned. Were they still searching for Rafe? No doubt. They wanted the cure. They'd scour the entire Feral Zone for him if they had to. And if they never came back? Everson and I would be okay. We'd make it back to the base somehow . . . but without a sample of Rafe's blood. And without keeping my promise to him.

As the sun rose, I munched on half a protein bar while staring in awe at the trees lining the clearing. Against the dull brown of rock outcroppings, the frost-encrusted trees shimmered like ghosts. It was then I realized that I was shivering. I rubbed down my limbs to wake up my nerve endings and then rose to twist out the kinks in my spine, only to gasp at the black spiral of smoke rising just beyond the distant cliff edge.

"Wake up," I whispered, hand outstretched, but Everson was on his feet without another word from me, let alone a shake. I pointed to the smoke, and he frowned. We quickly picked up what little gear we had. I handed him the other half of the protein bar as we made our way through the upheavals of rock to the edge of a sandstone cliff.

Kneeling, I peered into the densely wooded canyon below. At the base of the cliff, a crowd of people stood huddled in a semicircle around a dying bonfire. They were all wearing long-sleeved thermal shirts and cargo pants in various earth tones, even the children.

Everson crouched beside me. "It's a pyre," he whispered. "They're burning a body."

The fire collapsed in on itself, shooting sparks skyward. I jerked back, though I was high enough that they wouldn't reach me. As I leaned over the edge again, the people began to sing. It sounded like a church hymn but not one that I knew. The lyrics expressed grief over the "lost one" and wished him a safe journey on his way to a better place. The chorus repeatedly urged the lost one not to mourn or worry about his family and friends but to move on without looking back, knowing that his memory would be cherished.

Everson kept his voice low as he said, "They're wearing woodland camo. Pre-exodus. Same as Aaron's."

They'd blend in with the environment even better come summer. Now the trees were just starting to bud, and green spikes poked through the dead prairie grass. It was a good setup for a compound. Much better than Moline's with the surrounding cliffs, which were close to vertical in places. Here and there, cascades of water spilled over the cliffs' edges, creating tiered waterfalls. They fed into a seething ribbon of water that bisected the valley.

There were also plenty of signs of human habitation. First, the clearing, scored with long, dark furrows — ready for planting — and then the sprawling building beyond that had once been a large rustic-chic hotel with a wraparound porch and stone chimneys. Bathed in the golden light of dawn, the lodge retained its pre-exodus charm. But that didn't go for the fence that encircled the whole property. I'd never seen such an ugly fence, though it was probably effective. A hodgepodge of corrugated metal sheets had been lashed onto the chain-link, two layers worth at least. And even from the top of the bluff, there was no missing the message spray painted over and over along the fence: "Heartland Lodge. No Infected!" Over the open gate hung a modified American flag — missing about half its fifty stars. Not because the flag was tattered. There wasn't a crease in it or a frayed hem. Those rows of stars had been removed on purpose. Maybe to commemorate the twenty-six states lost to the Ferae plague?

Everson touched my arm, and I followed his nod. If I hadn't known to look for them, I wouldn't have noticed the wooden perches in the tall pines within the fence. The lionesses hadn't been lying. The snipers could shoot a person before he even got anywhere near the gate.

A few of the remaining people raked the dry grass away from the fire, widening the circle of bare earth. A woman stood among them, dry-eyed and talking to no one, just standing as straight and hard as a marble column. The widow? The mother . . . Oh. Oh no.

I caught Everson's sleeve. "Could that be Aaron?"

"I was thinking that too," he said grimly.

The woman never took her eyes off the smoldering pyre. Never acknowledged the others in any way. Her steely grief was almost more than I could bear. I tore my gaze from her to the open gate and then to the hunters who solemnly stood by, guns slung across their chests. The hunters peeled off from the mourners and headed down a trail that led away from the compound.

"They could be going after Rafe — Wraith," I whispered.

"Maybe. Or maybe they're hunting for dinner."

"We should follow them. We can't just sit here and hope Mahari and the others come back. The hunters know these woods better than we do, and if they're looking for Rafe, maybe they'll find him."

He glanced back to our campsite from the night before. Still no sign of the lionesses. "Okay," he relented. "We'll follow them. But if they find Rafe, we hang back."

I frowned. "Hang back?"

"If they're going after Rafe, it's to kill him — so let them do the job for you. I can take blood from a corpse if it's still warm."

"It? You're talking about Rafe," I hissed. "And he might not even be feral."

"You believe that? Even after seeing him last night?"

"He looked at me. He looked at me like he knew me. And he wasn't drooling. And he wasn't trying to bite anyone. Maybe he's feral . . . But maybe he's not. I want to be sure."

If you hear about a grupped-up tiger gone feral, promise you'll hire a hunter to put me down. Those were Rafe's words. But had he gone feral, or was he just a manimal with a death wish? He'd always held them in contempt . . . manimals. So now that he was one, did he hate himself? Until I knew for sure, there was no promise to keep.

"If you really think there's a chance he'll talk to you," he said, sounding skeptical, "then you should hang on to this." He handed the metal collection vial back to me, and I put it in the Velcro pocket in my cargo pants with the cure. "He's more likely to let you take the sample."

He looked toward the compound again. "There's a trail down to the valley — cut into the cliff. Problem is, we'll be exposed on the way down."

My brows lifted. "How do you know there's a trail?"

He kept his eyes on the pyre below. "Mahari showed me last night."

"You snuck off with Mahari while I was asleep?" I got to my feet.

"I wouldn't put it like that." He motioned me back from the cliff edge. "You're in their sight line."

"Yeah," a voice said from behind us, accompanied by the sound of a shotgun being pumped. "You sure are."

· EIGHTEEN ·

Everson and I whirled as three men stepped from behind a rocky outcropping, guns pointed at us.

"Keep your hands out," one of the hunters ordered — a big redheaded man with a thick neck and beefy fingers, one of which he used to point at me. "I'm talking to you, girl."

They weren't particularly scary once I looked past their woodsy camo and weapons, but I still felt like I couldn't catch my breath.

Everson let his rifle dangle from its tactical sling as he spread his hands wide.

"Put your weapon on the ground," another hunter barked at him — a pinch-faced man with watery red-rimmed eyes. Everson laid his gun exactly where the red-eyed man indicated.

"Take it all, including ammo," ordered the third man — the oldest of them. Older than my dad, going by the gray in his pointed beard, and probably their leader, going by the swift way the other two obeyed him.

The redhead picked up Everson's gun while the other one moved behind me, unzipped my backpack, rummaged through it, and took out my handgun, ammo clips, and Swiss Army knife. Then he patted down Everson. I was now officially without a weapon in the Feral Zone, and the feeling unnerved me.

The leader pulled off his wraparound shades to glare at us. "Don't you idiots know it ain't safe in the woods?"

"It's not safe in the zone, period," I said, meeting his intense gaze.

There seemed to be something simmering inside him. His shoulders were tight, and when he spoke, it was in a low, angry drawl. "Then what are you doing up here spying on us?"

"We weren't — we saw the smoke."

"We're burning what's left of a dead boy," the rheumy-eyed hunter said in a flat voice.

My first thought: "What's left?" My second thought went unspoken: *Aaron?*

"What was left after some feral made a meal of him," the hunter went on.

"Enough," the leader cut in sharply, giving the hunter a censoring look. "I want to hear their story. They don't need to hear ours."

"We're with the line patrol," Everson told him.

"I got that," the man said with a nod at our flak jackets. "What I don't get is why you're so far from the river. Help me out with that." He indicated me with the barrel of his rifle. "You first." My eyes shifted between his face and the gun. His brows furrowed, but then he followed my gaze to the gun. "I'm not planning on shooting you. Not unless you give me a reason."

"I won't," I promised quickly. "My name is Lane McEvoy, and this is Everson Cruz."

Everson stiffened beside me. Apparently guards didn't hand out information like names to strangers. The leader seemed surprised as well, but then his eyes crinkled at the edges as if he was looking at me a little harder. Really seeing *me*, not the patrol-issue jacket. With a shrug, he lowered his gun and motioned for the other two to do the same. "Nice to meet you, Lane," he said with a smirk. "I'm Boone. Now go on."

Maybe he knew my dad and that's why he was letting down his guard so easily. I nodded and did as he ordered. "We came here because we found a boy on the riverbank last night. He was hurt. Badly hurt. But he told us his name — Aaron — and we guessed where he was from. It's the closest compound. So, we were going to —"

A boy about Aaron's age darted out from behind the rocks. "You found Aaron?" He looked so much like Boone he could only be the man's son.

Boone scowled. "I told you to stay back."

The boy didn't spare him a glance. "What got him?" he demanded, eyes on me.

"We don't know," Everson said — to my great relief.

Though truly, we didn't. Just because Rafe had tried to drag Aaron away last night didn't mean that he was the one who took a bite out of Aaron yesterday. And it certainly didn't mean that he'd killed the boy last night. Maybe Rafe had been trying to help him in some warped way.

"Something bit Aaron," Everson told them. "He was fevered — probably infected. We cleaned him up, but he ran away during the night. We don't know where —"

"Like I said, we found him," said the watery-eyed hunter, looking as ferocious as a feral. "In little pieces. We're burning them now." He swept a hand toward the rising smoke. "Carmen ain't never going to get over losing her boy. Never."

Grief pushed up from my gut, sudden and raw. I'd guessed the pyre was for Aaron, but knowing for sure was worse.

"The last time we saw him," Everson said, looking grim, "Aaron was fevered, but he was in one piece."

"You talked to him. Did he say what bit him?" Boone asked.

"Like I said, he was fevered." Everson remained calm — like he was simply reporting in. "He wasn't making a lot of sense —"

"Except for when he told you his name." Boone's expression hardened. He held up a silencing hand when Everson tried to explain. He nodded to the two other hunters. "You're going to take a walk with Habib and Zeke and tell 'em the truth about what you're doing in the Feral Zone." He gave the two hunters a look that I couldn't decipher. "Take him over by Rip-Rap Falls and get his story. Jacob and I will get hers. Relax," he told Everson. "We're just going to talk; then you'll come find us. If your stories match up, you're free to go. We'll even give you your guns back."

With that, the two hunters gripped Everson by the arms and escorted him back the way we'd come — past our campsite — and into the woods, with Everson looking none too happy.

Once they were gone, Boone waved over the boy and motioned for him to turn around. "This is my son, Jacob," he told me as he took a thermos from the boy's backpack.

Jacob glanced at me over his shoulder. "Aaron was my best friend," he said, expression tight with held-back emotion.

Boone poured steaming dark liquid into a tin cup and offered it to me. I wrapped both hands around the cup, hoping to warm them. "Thank you," I said — and I meant it.

He nodded and tipped back his head to pour coffee directly into his mouth from the thermos. Only then did I lift my cup to my lips. It was silly to think he was carrying around a thermos of poisoned coffee. Or maybe not silly. The bitter liquid in my mouth was definitely not coffee. As much as I wanted to spit it out, I swallowed and cleared my throat. "What is it?" I asked, sniffing the liquid.

"Chicory. It's too cold here to grow coffee outside," Boone explained. "Plus, with chicory, you can eat the whole plant — leaves to root."

"What's that?" Jacob pointed at Spurling's dial on my chest.

"A camera." I tapped the record button, and a green light on the rim flicked on. "And a phone." I held it out so Jacob could see the palm-sized screen. Another tap and his image appeared.

"Whoa! You put me in a movie — like the ones we watch at the lodge. Every week we set up a —"

"Jacob," Boone cut in. "Go tell Carmen and the others that two outsiders are coming in for a quick visit." He shifted his attention to me. "Carmen will want to meet you. You two were the last people to see Aaron alive. Tell her how you took care of him — bandaged him up and all. Tell her he wasn't alone last night. She might take some comfort from it."

"I can do that," I said, happy to do so.

"But I wanna hear what they're doing here," Jacob protested.

"And you'll find out with the rest of the compound," Boone said firmly. "Now go give 'em a heads-up."

I slipped the dial down the front of my shirt and again tapped the record button. In a moment, I'd be alone with Boone. I didn't think he was planning to hurt me, but in case I was wrong, I wanted a recording of whatever came next. If things got bad, I'd drop the dial somewhere close. Somewhere Everson might find it . . . assuming he was still alive. The thought that he might not be made my chest hollow out.

As soon as Jacob disappeared down the cliff-side trail, Boone settled back on a large, flat rock, rifle laid over his lap, and made a "Go on" gesture.

"You want to know why we're in the zone?" I asked.

"Yeah, I do — considering you're on Heartland territory and you were spying on us from the ridge."

"It wasn't like that," I assured him. "We saw the smoke in the sky. We went to the edge of the cliff to see what it was. If you check the area, you'll see we camped over there last night. Under the ledge." I pointed to the long shelf of rock.

Boone gave it a cursory glance. "Why're you camping on this side of the river?"

"We're looking for someone. The line patrol wants him."

"That explains the guard." He lifted his chin toward the woods where the hunters had taken Everson. "But not you."

"What do you mean? I'm a guard t —"

"You're no guard. Him, yeah." Boone again indicated the woods, and my worry for Everson cranked up a notch. "He's pure patrol," Boone went on. "But you? You're something I never thought I'd see again. An old-fashioned girl."

I bristled. "I'm not old-fashioned."

"Honey, I was thirty when the plague hit — that was the last time I ever saw one of your kind. No sign of hardship on you. Not on your skin, not in your expression. You got everything a kid needs — plenty of food, doctors, dentists . . . Meaning, you grew up in a place where all those good things exist. And that ain't here. Not anywhere in the zone. So, I think I'm looking at a near-mythical creature here." He pointed a finger at me. "A girl from the West."

"All the guards are from the West."

"Yeah, and they've all been put through drills so hard they're more robot than human. That ain't you."

I stared at him, taken so far aback, I could've been swimming in the Mississippi.

"Life in Heartland is good, all things considered," he went on. "But it's never completely safe. Tragedy dogs us, and we know more is coming. Like today. Losing Aaron. We're always bracing for the next blow, and it shows. Even in our toddlers. So now you know lying to me won't work." He leaned back on his rock. "Do it again, and I'll toss you in a feral pit."

I swallowed. "Okay, I'm not a line guard. What else do you want to know?"

"Why're you here?"

"I'm looking for someone. The patrol wants him too, so Everson and I came together."

Boone considered my words and then seemed to shrug them off as not his concern. "Did Aaron say what bit him?"

"He was really hot. Really sick."

"Did Aaron say what bit him?" Boone repeated slowly as if we had all the time in the world and his patience was infinite.

"No."

"Did Aaron say it was Rafe?"

I gaped at him. How . . . ? He must have overheard us — me and Everson — at the edge of the cliff. What had we said exactly? Then something hit me. "You know him. Rafe." It was the familiar way Boone had said his name.

He shot me a look of disgust. "We all know Wraith. I shoulda put a bullet in him back when he was just a joker. Now look at what I have to deal with. A feral in his prime, juiced on something powerful, something that's putting muscle on him and giving him speed. And topping it all off, he's crazy. And Rafe wasn't exactly sane back when he was just a pain in my —"

"How long have you known him?" I asked, cutting him off. Why was I surprised? Before he'd gotten infected, Rafe was a professional hunter. He went from compound to compound, trading his skill at killing ferals for food and supplies. Any compound with a rogue in the area — a feral with a grudge against humans, or worse, a taste for human meat — hired Rafe on the spot. My dad told me that Rafe had visited more compounds than anyone he knew. And knowing Rafe, it was no surprise that he'd ticked off a compound leader along the way. Probably more than one.

Boone's expression turned assessing. "I think the real mystery is, how do *you* know him?"

"I —" wasn't going to admit to this man that my dad had been telling me stories about Rafe since I was eight — about Rafe's adventures in the Feral Zone. I opted for the easiest explanation. "My dad hired him whenever he was on this side of the river."

"Whenever he was on this side?" Boone scoffed. "That wall's a quarantine line. You don't get to go back and forth."

"My dad's a fetch."

"He fetches stuff from over here?" Boone guessed.

"Exactly. For a price."

"That's gotta carry a death sentence."

"Usually, but my dad worked out a deal. Anyway, that's how I know Rafe. He was my dad's guide through the zone."

"You know he's feral?"

"I know he got infected."

"And lost his mind fast," Boone added. "We've had three people go missing. Aaron makes four. Aaron would've been an easy catch — an easy kill. The kid is only thirteen . . . was."

"Four," I echoed hoarsely. Rafe couldn't have killed four people. He couldn't have. But then, why had he been dragging Aaron away last night? "When did the first one go missing?" I asked, hoping to prove that it wasn't Rafe based on the timing.

"Five months ago," Boone replied, and my heart sank. "I know because that's when we started letting the flock leave the compound in pairs instead of in groups. Now we're going to have to return to the old ways. At least until we kill Wraith."

"Why do you call him Wraith?"

"'Cause ever since he went feral, he goes for the sneak attack. Bites, then disappears. Waits for his prey to weaken from blood loss, then comes back for the kill."

"That makes no sense. Why would he do that?"

Boone shrugged. "He's feral. Don't look for meaning in it."

"But how do you know it's Rafe?" I demanded.

"Because he tried it on me. Yeah, he bit me. Not deep, but I knew chances were good I was infected, so I took myself off. Waited for the fever, but it never came. When I got back to camp, I did a blood test. Nothing. I'm clean."

He must have been the man that the lionesses saw Rafe attack. "The virus wasn't in his salivary glands yet," I guessed.

"Too bad Aaron wasn't that lucky."

"Even if Rafe did bite Aaron, that doesn't mean he killed Aaron. It could've been another feral. Or an animal. A bear, a cougar, anything . . ." But then why had Rafe slashed at Aaron?

"You seem real invested in him not being a killer," Boone mused, "when I know he's been rotten to the core for a long time. Long before he went feral, he was stealing our meat. Taking our animals right out of their pens. Pigs, goats — and threatening anybody who tried to stop him."

As far as I knew, Rafe didn't steal from compounds. He did business with them. Yes, he stole from the base. But he had a grudge against the patrol. Maybe he had a grudge against Heartland as well . . .

"What's the patrol want with him?" Boone asked.

"A sample of his blood."

"You can have all you want." Boone spread his arms wide in a gesture of generosity. "After he's dead."

The way he'd said it sent a shiver down my back. "You can't just kill him. We need to make sure Rafe is really feral."

"Girl, I've seen him up close." He touched fingers to the back of his neck. "Real close. And I can tell you for sure he's feral. So you don't want me holding off while you go give him a once-over. He'll have his teeth in you by then."

"Does Rafe have some kind of grudge against Heartland?" I asked. "Is that why he bit you?"

Boone plucked the tin cup from my hand and shook out the last drops of chicory. He twisted it back on the thermos and shoved it in a side pocket of his coat. "He was one of ours," he said finally.

"What?"

"Born at Heartland. Grew up inside our fence. He lived with his sister, Sophie. When her husband got infected, he was forced out. Sophie went with him and took Rafe. He was young, maybe ten. He hates us for making them leave. But it was Sophie who made 'em a package deal. Her choice to throw in with a disease. We can't risk letting infected people past the fence. You never know when someone's gonna turn."

I resisted the urge to tell him about Moline, since I didn't feel like listening to the lecture I suspected would follow. Also, I wanted to know why Boone hadn't mentioned Rafe's parents. If Rafe had been born in Heartland, his parents must have lived there too. In Moline last year, Hagen had told me about Rafe's sister, but she didn't know what had happened to his parents. Apparently Rafe didn't want anyone to know. And neither did Boone.

"That's enough of that," Boone said after a moment. "Time to find your guard."

"Everson."

Without another word, we made our way to the woods. The trees looked different in daylight — not nearly so ominous. My thoughts, however, were more ominous than ever. I didn't want to be alone in the woods with a stranger, and there was a lot wrong with this picture. Rafe had come back for Aaron, just like Boone described. But maybe he had another, less obvious reason for dragging Aaron away from our camp . . . in the middle of the night . . . still gagged and bound. And even if Rafe did bite him, it didn't mean he tore Aaron into pieces. That was an image I did not want in my brain.

"Can you make it across?"

Boone's question startled me right out of my spiraling thoughts. I glanced up to see two ropes strung across a ravine, tied to trees on either side. One rope for my feet, the other at chest level for clutching for dear life. "Uh . . ." I peeked over the edge of the ravine. The drop wasn't bad, about ten feet. The problem was the raging river at the bottom.

"The stream's swollen because of the snowmelt," he explained. "And two weeks of rain."

What he was calling a stream, I would've called white-water rapids. Okay, brownish, very fast water. "Where does it end?" I asked, testing the bottom rope with my foot. It seemed taut enough to take my weight.

"Runs right off the cliff. Lotta them do. Makes for some gorgeous waterfalls every spring. Fifty-foot drops."

This stream ended with a fifty-foot fall? I backed off. The survival courses I'd taken in the West were a joke. Rock climbing and ropes courses were indoor sports and only attempted with helmets, safety lines, two spotters, and a thick mat. Because it's not protection unless it's overprotection. "Is there another way across?" I asked.

"Not to get where we're going."

"Which is where?"

"We're going to join up with your friend."

"Wait." I stepped back, away from the rope bridge. "You told your men to bring Everson back to you."

"Not that friend."

It took me a second to get what he meant. *Who* he meant . . . Rafe.

"You said you came here looking for him," Boone reminded me. "So I'm going to help you out. I'm going to take you right to his doors."

"Doors?" I said dumbly.

"Caves. We've tracked him to a cliff pocked with caves, but we don't go in, and he's never come out on my watch. But maybe he'll come out for you."

I was shaking my head before he'd even finished speaking. I wanted no part of that plan.

"You go over the ravine or you go in it. Your choice." He nudged me with his rifle, forcing me up onto the rope.

· NINETEEN ·

I slid along the bottom rope while holding the top rope with both hands. I shuffled past the edge of the ravine and over the rushing water it contained, heart wedged into my throat, hands gripping the top rope so tightly, each step forward scraped another layer of skin off my palms. Falling was not an option. I'd never be able to swim against the current or even climb out. A hundred years of erosion had polished the steep sides to a smooth finish.

"If the patrol needs Wraith's blood so bad," Boone called to me, "why'd they send only you and one guard?"

I tore my eyes from the swollen stream below to glance back at him.

He leaned against the tree that anchored the ropes. "I'm guessing it's 'cause they knew that's all it would take," he mused. "A guard to shoot him and take his blood. And you to draw him out. You're the bait — the honey to his bee."

"Pollen," I muttered, still edging along the rope. Bees went out looking for pollen, not honey. Either way, I got the gist.

"You're here," Boone went on, "because someone in the line patrol knows Rafe won't be able to stay away from you. They're betting the whole op on it. I'm not even going to ask you why. Doesn't matter. If the patrol is willing to take that bet, then so am I."

Why wasn't he following me? Because it was safer to go one at a time, of course. His weight and movement would jostle the ropes, and I was having a hard enough time staying balanced as it was. Anyway, I was almost to the far bank. Only ten more shuffles and I'd —

"Lane."

I glanced back.

"You holding on tight?"

"Yes," I said while reflexively tightening my grip.

"Good." Boone crouched by the clamp, which secured the bottom rope to the tree. "Three . . ." he warned, fingering the clamp.

"No!" I screamed.

"Two . . ."

"Please don't," I begged while swinging a foot over the upper rope.

"One and done," he shouted, then flipped the clamp open. The rope fell away just as I swung my other leg up and over, hanging off the remaining rope like a panic-stricken sloth.

"Don't look down," he called above the water's roar.

Ankles locked together and eyes closed, I hung, unable to move, unable to breathe . . . until I felt the rope shimmy in my hands. My eyes snapped open, and I twisted my head to see Boone plucking at it.

"Go on, girl. You don't want to keep Wraith waiting." He walked his fingers back to the upper clamp.

I didn't need another warning or countdown. I propelled myself forward along the rope with my nonexistent upper-body strength, expecting it to fall away at any second and spill me into the water below. Just as I crossed over the bank, the rope slackened, dropping me onto the ground, inches from the edge. The other end of the rope hit the water and whipped downstream. I rolled to my side and pushed up to face the ravine — to face Boone. But he was gone.

I rolled onto my back, pants so wet from the spray they clung to my legs. Or maybe I'd peed myself without even noticing. My heart was still trying to punch its way out of my chest. But I couldn't stay here. I shoved to my feet. Boone and Habib and Zeke could all get grupped. Stupid, uncivilized savages. What was Boone's game anyway? What good would it do him if Rafe killed me?

It seemed darker on this side of the ravine. The trees were just beginning to bud, but the branches tangled overhead, letting in only shafts of light. Where was Everson? Were they using him as bait too? Or had they just killed him outright?

I didn't know what to do or where to go. I knew the stream ended in a waterfall, so I might as well head the other way and see if there was another place to cross. If I headed back to the place where we'd spent the night, maybe the lionesses would show up. Or Everson. More likely another group of hunters would find me. I sucked in a breath through my teeth. I couldn't panic. It would only make things worse. The only way to shut down my welling anxiety would be to do *something*.

It was hard going through the dense underbrush with only filtered sunlight to see by, but I marched along, determined not to get spooked. Not even when I passed a deer, which reared up with a hiss, revealing a scaled underbelly, and then bounded away.

Despite the steadily climbing sun, the air had a distinct bite to it. I'd been walking for some time when the hair started to go up on the back of my neck, and I had the creepy feeling that someone was watching me. Probably Boone. He must have crossed the ravine another way and was now following me. Of course he was. He'd planned on using me as bait. I continued on, cautiously, listening carefully. When I heard the faint snap of another twig behind me, I paused, overcome by a feeling of dread.

Yeah. Someone or something was there. If not Boone, then probably a lynx or a fox. A feral would've attacked by now . . . right?

Like I knew.

I sped up, veering away from the ravine and stream. I had no choice — the terrain had grown too rocky, the outcroppings too steep. I scuttled between the trees, breaking through spiderwebs face-first. I rubbed my forearms over my cheeks and head but couldn't lose the feeling of spiders burrowing into my hair.

Branches cracked off to my left, and I froze, petrified by the image of something big stalking me, drawing closer with every step. I glanced around but saw only scraggly pines, still as death. And then a blur shot past me — the deer. I whipped around to see what was chasing it . . . Nothing. Worse, the forest had fallen silent. No birdcalls, no chittering squirrels, or even the snap of a twig, which I now missed because it meant, one, the animals weren't making sounds for a reason and, two, that reason was nearby.

The air was stifling and smelled like death and decay. Then, from within the trees, I heard what sounded like the most pained moan imaginable. Not a human sound. I took off, desperate to scream for help, but terrified to draw whatever it was closer to me. The roar of my pulse made it nearly impossible to hear, and my lungs burned from exertion. I ducked into a thick stand of bushy pine trees, hoping I'd lost it. Whatever *it* was. And if I hadn't, hopefully the trees would make me hard to spot. I worked to slow my breathing and listened for any hint of my pursuer. More branches cracked. The image of a drooling feral flashed through my mind and had me springing into motion once more.

I darted through the trees to the edge of a clearing filled with decomposing animal carcasses. A lot of the bones hadn't been picked clean. I veered off in disgust. I didn't dare go back the way I'd come, but I couldn't go forward either. The clearing was at the foot of a cliff — a cliff that was pocked with man-sized holes . . . Caves.

My anxiety spiked so hard my chest felt like it was cracking apart. I stumbled toward an outcropping of rock, half-hidden by pine trees. Just as I started around it, a hand snagged me by the wrist and yanked me backward into a crevice between the rocks. I struggled to free myself, but the person had one arm around my ribs while he clamped a hand hard over my mouth, cutting off my screams and air supply. I threw back an elbow, catching him in the gut hard enough to make him grunt and send an achy tremor up my arm but not hard enough to get free.

A voice rasped in my ear. "Don't fight me." The man's mouth was so close, I felt his words more than heard them. "When I take my hand away, do *not* make a sound. Get me?"

I wasn't sure how he expected me to answer when I couldn't even breathe. He growled as if trying to get my attention. Like he didn't already have it, standing so close behind me. His warm breath on the curve of my neck made the hairs all over my body rise. My survival instincts were screaming at me to get free, so I was going for a backward head butt. I'd even stay silent — just like he'd ordered. But before I could execute my plan, his hand tightened across my mouth, and with the other, he gripped the hair at my nape. Probably looking for some indication that I did in fact "get him."

I blinked as he angled my head back to make eye contact. Orbs of aqua blue returned my look. I blinked. Beautiful eyes, dark lashed and edged in black. Familiar eyes . . . except for the wide, gold starbursts around the pupils and what looked like eyeliner — but wasn't. Those familiar eyes were — were Rafe's!

· TWENTY ·

"Not. A. Sound," Rafe hissed when I would have gasped.

He could talk! And the eyeliner, the black smudges extending from his eyebrows — he hadn't painted them on. His skin was changing color. As were his eyes. The golden starbursts — those were new.

Seeing Rafe behind me was a relief — for exactly one second. Then he spoke again. "There are things out here a lot worse than me." He took his hand from my mouth and added, "At least I'm warm-blooded."

Before I could reply, heavy footsteps approached. Probably Boone. I wanted to warn Rafe but sensed his mounting tension and decided to keep my mouth shut. Good thing too, because the man who came crashing through the trees was not Boone. Not even close. He was a massive reptilian creature, more monster than human at seven feet tall — taller, even, though his legs were bowed. The bones beneath his scaly skin were swollen and distorted. He wore a filthy tattered garage jumpsuit, a name stitched above the pocket. Dry skin hung in strips off his face, chest, and arms. This thing had once been human, but now . . . now . . .

He started hacking like a cat with a hairball. He paused near our hiding place, flicking his tongue in and out. His forked yellow tongue! Was he part snake? Was he smelling us? He twisted his upper body and arced like he was warming up for workout. *Please let it have nothing to do with us. Please.* He started hacking again — no, hocking. He was hocking up something big and dripping. The football-shaped mass slid out of his gaping mouth and hit the ground at his feet — a gray bundle of hair and bone. When he was done, bloody drool unspooled from his lips like scarlet twine.

I clamped a hand over my mouth to keep from gagging or shrieking or whatever sane people did when a monster vomited up the indigestible parts of his breakfast. I clamped on a second hand as insurance when the smell hit me — an odor so foul, so rancid, my vision blurred. Finally, the horrifying man crashed away.

"What was that — that?" I rasped, unable to come up with a word big enough or horrifying enough to describe it.

"That's what's been killing people around here," Rafe whispered.

"But what is he? What's he infected with?"

"Best guess . . ." Rafe's grip tightened around my ribs. "Komodo dragon."

The branches of the pine tree weren't bushy enough to block out the steaming pile of hair and bone on the ground near our hiding spot. Bile burned the back of my throat while thoughts and questions circled my mind: Rafe wasn't the Wraith. He hadn't killed the people from the compound. Hadn't eaten them! Wasn't feral!

And yet . . . Rafe had looked right at me last night and said nothing. Why? And why had he tried to drag Aaron away?

I twisted in the cramped space between the rocks to face him. He was still half a head taller than me, and his teeth were still white and even. He had changed his shirt since last night — this one was worn but clean — and combed his sun-streaked hair. Last night, I could have sworn he'd had claws, but in the light of day I could see that his fingertips ended in fingernails just like mine — only dirtier. He could almost have passed as uninfected . . . Almost. His arms and shoulders and thighs bulged with new muscles. His eyes and the edges of his ears were rimmed in black, and faint slashes adorned his cheekbones, forehead, and collarbone like faded war paint — the start of stripes. Tiger stripes. Like Chorda's.

Pain shot through my wrists, and my hands began to tingle, and I looked away from his face, only to find myself staring at the mess that the feral — the Komodo-dragon-on-steroids thing — had vomited up.

I closed my eyes.

"Hey," Rafe said. "Are you about to — whoa." He shuffled me out of the crevice and, with a hand to my back, bent me over one second before the chicory coffee geysered up my throat, tasting twice as bitter this time.

Rafe handed me a flask from his back pocket. I pushed it away. "It's water," he explained, and then chuckled when I snatched it from his hand. "When did you become such a delicate flower?"

I didn't bother to reply until I'd rinsed out my mouth and wiped off my entire face on the inside of my shirt hem. Then I said, "You're not feral."

"Glad you noticed."

I smiled faintly at his flippant tone, but he didn't return it, just devoured me with his eyes. The intensity of his stare set my nerves buzzing, but I couldn't look away. The last time we were together, he'd basically told me he loved me, but now as we stood there staring at each other, neither one of us said or did anything to address what we'd been through together. I'd thought about him nearly constantly for the past six months; I'd been torn apart worrying about what might have happened to him. But now that we were together again, there was a barrier between us, and I didn't understand what it was.

Then it occurred to me: Rafe didn't seem feral in this moment, but months ago, he had told me that sometimes the road to feral wasn't a straight line. Sometimes it included roundabouts and backtracking and that during the manimal's sane moments, he might not remember what he'd done during those periods of insanity. What if Rafe had killed Aaron last night but didn't know it?

Without meaning to, I eased back a step away from him, and his expression closed off.

"What happened to Aaron?" I asked abruptly. "What were you doing with him?"

"He's fine," Rafe said in a flat voice.

"He's not fine. He's dead. They found —"

"They?"

"The hunters. They were burning his —"

"Did you see it?" Rafe demanded. "The kid's body. Did you see it with your own eyes?"

"No," I admitted. "But —"

"But nothing." He moved abruptly past me and swept aside the pine boughs, heading for the heap of gray-brown slime beyond the tree.

"Wait! Don't . . ." I gripped the back of his shirt. "What if that thing comes back?"

"I'll know." Rafe lifted his face and inhaled. "New and improved," he said, tapping his nose. "Right now, he's headed away from us. There's no missing his smell. Or yours."

"I don't smell," I huffed. Though I probably did after a dunk in the river and a night on the ground. I thought longingly of the hand sanitizer I used to carry everywhere. I could have used a vat of it just then. Industrial strength.

"Yeah, you do, silky," Rafe said, turning back toward me. "But your scent is sweet. And one of a kind." He stepped closer. "I knew it was you long before I saw you. I followed your scent from the riverbank."

My whole body grew warm. And that explained why he hadn't seemed surprised to see me.

"I could have — I could have killed you," I stuttered.

He shrugged and looked away, through the trees toward the clearing. "Everybody's got to go sometime."

So he did have a death wish.

"Why'd you chase the lionesses away?" I asked him. "They thought you were feral."

"I don't want them coming around here."

"Why?"

"Because wherever they go, things get ugly." He scooped up my backpack and thrust it into my hands. "What are you doing, traveling with them? They hate humans."

"So everyone keeps telling me," I muttered.

"Then maybe you better start listening. Manimals get reps like that for a reason. Usually a very bloody reason. That's how those cats like their humans — bloody."

I'd thought the lionesses were starting to warm up to me, and even to Everson. But maybe they had been putting on an act as well, one they'd drop the second they got their doses of the cure. "Humans haven't exactly been kind to them," I said in their defense.

"If that's an excuse, then every manimal in the zone would join them," he scoffed. "They've been traveling up and down the Mississippi, stirring up the outcasts. Getting them to arm themselves and attack the human compounds."

"Why?" I asked.

"Sometimes for food and supplies. But mostly, they see every fence as an insult. Which is why wherever they go turns into a battleground."

That news didn't surprise me. "I heard a group of manimals attacked Moline last month. Bashed in the gate and wrecked the compound. Were the lionesses in on that?"

"No idea. I haven't been back to Moline since I turned tiger," he said like it was no big deal. "But I'd bet yes. Maybe you noticed — one of them is thirty seconds from feral."

"Not anymore," I said softly.

"She turned, huh?"

I nodded, thinking of how Charmaine's eyes had cleared in those moments before she had thrown herself into the river. "She could have infected me, but she didn't," I said.

Thinking of Charmaine reminded me why I was there. Rafe wasn't feral, and I needed to get his blood and give him the cure.

"Rafe . . ." I ripped open the Velcro pocket in my cargo pants and found the cure and the collection cylinder.

He ignored me and instead approached the horrifying puddle of Komodo vomit, picking up a stick along the way. "Let's see what he had for supper last night."

"I don't want to know," I said queasily. "I have to tell you something."

Rafe covered his nose with a forearm and crouched. "And people say I have a dirty mouth," he muttered. Using the stick, he rolled over a slime-covered chunk. "Hip socket," he pronounced.

My stomach heaved.

He flipped over another lump. "Here we go — hoof." One last poke and he rose with a wet clump of hide dangling from the tip of the stick. "This here is a pile of digested deer. Now he's ready for breakfast."

Gagging, I whirled to face the pines.

"You really have gone soft," he mused. "You should've stayed in the West where you belong."

"I couldn't stay there," I said, my back still turned. "I promised I'd come back for you."

As I turned back toward him, Rafe's knees hit the ground, and he fell forward, revealing Boone behind him, holding his shotgun like a club.

"No!" I shouted. "He's not feral!" I stuffed the cylinder back into my pocket. How had I forgotten that Boone was using me to draw out Rafe?

"Maybe not this minute," Boone said, "but you wanna vouch for him tonight? Tomorrow?" He slammed the toe of his boot into Rafe's ribs.

Rafe didn't react — no groan, no movement. "Stop it!" I ran to him. "He isn't the one killing people!"

Boone caught my arm, keeping me from kneeling next to Rafe. "And how do you know that?"

"There's a feral out here — a man infected with Komodo dragon. He —"

"A lizard?" Boone cut in, expression incredulous. "You think a lizard is tearing people apart?"

"I saw him! I'm just lucky Rafe found me first or that" — I jabbed a finger at the pile of slimy bones — "could've been me." I jerked my arm from Boone's hold and knelt next to Rafe. He was so still. I couldn't even tell if he was breathing.

"Ever hear of a man-eating lizard?" Boone scoffed as he snatched Rafe's rifle from the holster on his back. "No. But a man-eating tiger? That sounds about right."

"You're not listening," I hissed, then shot a quick look around the clearing and wished I had Rafe's sense of smell. "I *saw* him. He's huge and far gone — probably infected for a long time. The Komodo dragon DNA is really show —"

"Nice try, girl." Boone slung Rafe's rifle over his shoulder. "But I think we would have noticed a dragon wandering around."

"Not a dragon, a Komodo dragon. He's got teeth like a shark's and claws like —"

"You think I don't know what you're doing?" Boone demanded as he crouched and ran his hands over Rafe, checking for other weapons. "You know this boy. Came here looking for him. You'll say anything to save his life." He collected two knives off Rafe, stood, and flung them into the woods, one after the other.

"You're wrong. I didn't come here to save Rafe." I rose to look Boone in the eye so he'd know I was dead serious. "I came to kill him."

Boone stiffened with surprise.

Guess I wasn't quite the old-fashioned girl he'd thought I was. "I promised Rafe I would put him down when he went feral. But it's not time yet. He's not feral. Not even a little."

Boone snorted and pulled a ball of twine from his pocket. "You're wrong, honey. It might be coming on him in spells, but he's already biting. I should know." When he reached for Rafe's wrist, Rafe suddenly shoved himself up from the ground, knocking Boone back with his head.

Even as Boone stumbled backward, he whipped his rifle around and pointed it at Rafe. "Stay right there."

"Geez, you stink." Swaying on his knees, Rafe rubbed the back of his head. "You might want to wipe off all that sweat. He'll smell it from a mile away."

Boone lifted his gun to aim at Rafe's head. "Keep talking and I'll turn that smart mouth of yours into a gaping hole."

"Boone, listen," I pleaded. "I saw it. Right here. I saw it cough up those bones. That's what killed Aaron."

"*Bit* Aaron," Rafe corrected, sitting back on his heels like he didn't have a care in the world. "The kid is still alive."

I shook my head and said softly, "They found Aaron's body this morning."

Rafe studied me and then smirked at Boone. "That what you told Carmen? What you told all of them? Did you make a big show of burning his body? Singing him off?"

I looked back and forth between the two of them.

Rafe never took his eyes from Boone. "All these years, and they still believe your lies. Gotta say, that's some serious charisma you're working."

Boone seemed unfazed by his accusations. "You're losing your mind, son. Seeing things that aren't there. Maybe your lizard-man exists, maybe not. But I know firsthand you're a threat to humans."

"It was just a love bite," Rafe said with mock reproach.

Boone's expression turned murderous. "It didn't take."

"Next time, it will," Rafe promised softly.

"Stop it," I snapped at Rafe. "Stop making things worse." I turned on Boone. "Is Aaron still alive?"

"Not that it's your business," he said levelly. "But I've led that compound for near on twenty years. Those are my people. And you can be sure I wouldn't put Carmen or any of them through that kind of pain 'less her son was truly dead."

"Unless . . ." I said, halting to let my mouth catch up with my thoughts. "Unless you thought that by lying to her you were keeping her safe." It was the reason people always gave for lying. Good people like my dad and destructive people like Chairman Prejean, who, when she'd told the public that no one had survived the outbreak, did it "for our own good." "Because she'd leave the compound if she knew Aaron was out here. Infected. Alone."

"My people are free to leave Heartland anytime they want. No one's making them stay." Boone's eyes narrowed. "If you know what's good for you, girl, you'll stop listening to this infected piece of trash. I've known him his whole life, and he's always been a liar and a thief."

Rafe scrambled to his feet. "He's coming."

"Shut up," Boone snarled.

The trees rustled off to one side. Suddenly Rafe was next to me. "Climb a pine," he urged, pushing me toward the trees. "It'll cover your scent."

I nodded, stumbling toward the nearest tree.

Boone swung his gun toward me. "Don't you move."

Just then the forest fell silent — too silent. Boone glared at us.

"You're sweating, old man." Rafe stepped between him and me, gesturing behind his back for me to head for the pines to our left. "That'll draw him as quick as blood. Smells like fried chicken to him."

"I said shut up!" Boone snarled.

"Lane, go!" Rafe ordered. "Now!"

I pivoted, only to have my guts turn to slush. Half-hidden by the towering pines stood the creature I'd tried but failed to accurately describe to Boone. It — he — was so much more terrifying than I had words for, with his bloodshot eyes and the long ribbons of dead skin hanging off his cheeks.

I edged back several steps, brushing Rafe's hand on the way, barely a warning, and yet he understood and glanced over his shoulder.

In a blur of motion, Boone jammed the gun's muzzle into Rafe's gut, forcing him closer to the feral and back onto his knees. "There you go," Boone rasped to the feral as he backed away from Rafe. "Breakfast is served. Right here. Help yourself."

When Rafe started to rise, I dropped my gaze from the horror behind him long enough to catch his eyes and gave the barest shake of my head. Obeying me, he went completely still as death hovered within three powerful leaps. Watching. Waiting. Salivating . . .

Seconds stretched into minutes as we held our bodies rigid — Rafe on his knees facing me, Boone somewhere behind me — waiting for the Komodo to attack, to roar, anything. My heart threatened to knock right through my rib cage. The Komodo-man stared at us, taking us all in with burning eyes above a distended jaw. And then his lips parted and bloody drool spilled out in ropes, accompanied by a hissing sound. It was all I could do to keep from falling into a sobbing, begging heap.

"I — I know you . . ." Boone said in a strangled voice.

The Komodo-man's hissing grew louder. It was a word. A name!

"Booone . . ."

Leaves crunched behind me as Boone reacted. I could feel him slipping back into the woods.

"Booone . . ." the feral man rasped again. His yellow tongue flicked out, and then he parted his peeling lips and slurped in air like I'd guzzle soup. Tasting us! Tasting our fear on the wind. I could've screamed over that alone.

Sticks snapped in the forest behind me as Boone picked up speed.

Rafe ducked and wrapped his arms around the back of his neck just as the horrifying Komodo-man lunged. He hurtled past Rafe and sprang for me. I whirled, crouched, arms over my head, and waited for the two-ton impact of lizard crashing into me, its bloody teeth clamping onto my neck. But the impact never came. Instead, the stench of rotting corpses whooshed past me as the lizard-dude pounded after Boone with the force of a tsunami. I squeezed my eyes tight, not wanting to see what came next.

Hard hands hauled me to my feet. And, without a word, Rafe entwined his fingers with mine and dragged me into a sprint. We raced so fast we should have broken the sound barrier, and yet, the scream caught up with us. It slammed into my back like a two-handed shove propelling me forward.

It was Boone. Dying awfully. Dying as no one should die. Not even him.

· TWENTY-ONE ·

Rafe waved me up yet another rocky slope to a narrow crack in the cliff face.

"They knew each other," I gasped, unable to catch my breath. "The Komodo said *Boone*."

"Most of the ferals around here came from Heartland," Rafe said while nudging me toward the crack. "Go! It's a cave. He can't follow us in."

Yeah, because the crack in the cliff was literally a crack, but I didn't need any further prodding. I wedged myself through the narrow opening without looking first. *Please be empty. Please*! Thankfully the crack opened up within a few feet of the entrance. Light shafted in from a gap above us. It wasn't a cave at all but a wide fissure in the rock.

"Keep going," Rafe directed. "We'll climb out after we've put some distance between us and him."

The ground was rocky and uneven, but I kept my gaze pinned to the sky above. I didn't care if I tripped. However, I'd care very much if lizard-dude jumped down twenty feet and turned me into a semi-digested lump of teeth and bone.

Rafe must have guessed that I was down to the dregs of my composure. "Hold up," he said as we reached the darkest, narrowest part of the fissure. A boulder wedged into the gap above neatly hid us from a view.

"Take a minute." He put a hand to my shoulder, encouraging me to sit. "Forget what you saw back there," he ordered.

"Sure. On it," I said, heaping on the snark. Without turning to face him, I sat down hard and dragged in a shuddering breath. But then jagged teeth, coated in blood and gristle, crowded out every other thought in my head, and sweat slicked my skin. I probably reeked, thus turning myself into a feral's dinner bell.

"You're not okay, are you?"

Rafe's voice tickled my ear as he sank to his haunches behind me. He lifted my hair and did something with it. Wrapped it around his fist, maybe. I couldn't tell, yet the slight tugging had a calming effect on me.

"I've got you, Lane," he said, his voice velvet soft. "I'll keep you safe. Always."

His words reminded me of what I said to the orphans every night. And like them, I relaxed under the soothing promise of safety. I nodded and rubbed my wrists, then shook the ice out of my fingers.

"What's the matter?" he asked.

"My hands. They feel dead sometimes."

He went still. "Dead?"

"Numb," I explained.

"Like when whiskers had your wrists duct-taped."

I glanced back, stunned. That was *exactly* right. The numbness, the prickling . . . That was the sensation I'd felt upon waking in Chorda's killing house — wrists bound, hands bloodless, looking into the face of a corpse. And what I'd felt ever since when something or someone triggered my memories of the tiger-king.

And the explosive headaches?

Those I had put down to eyestrain from editing late into the night. But now, thanks to Rafe, I knew — knew deep in my gut — the *when* of editing wasn't the cause. It was the *what*. Chorda's footage — that's what brought on those sudden, blinding headaches. Seeing his face again, hearing his roars and growled promises of vivisection, took my body back to the moment he'd pistoned his fist into my forehead to knock me out before carrying me off. How had I missed such an obvious cause-effect until now?

I wiggled around to face Rafe. Somehow the signs of infection only made him more beautiful — the black markings around his eyes made the blue more striking, and the faint dark stripes on his skin only emphasized the symmetry of his face. Even his multiple scars didn't detract from his looks — any more than a vein in the marble detracted from a statue's ability to take your breath away. I ran my fingers over the raised lines on his forearm that Chorda's claws had made — puckered and crisscrossing. As open gashes, these wounds had let the virus into his body. If I'd just lifted his forearm off the ground before Chorda's blood seeped across the floor, he might not have gotten infected . . .

It would be okay. The cure would clear the virus from his system. I covered the scars with my palm.

Rafe stiffened under my touch, but when he spoke, his tone was light. "Pretty ugly, huh?"

"You don't want smooth skin," I said, trying to match his tone. "Everyone would think you're a silky. Inexperienced. Soft . . . You'd lose your tough-guy cred." I looked into his black-rimmed eyes. "I have to tell you something."

He rotated his hand and took hold of my forearm. His fingers were rough on my skin, calloused and strong. When he gathered up my other hand as well and massaged my wrists and fingers, words left me. I closed my eyes and felt my breathing slow, along with my pounding heart.

"Better?" His tone was warm — good-natured.

Suddenly self-conscious, I opened my eyes and nodded, only to realize that the prickling sensation really was gone.

When he dropped his hands and stood, I resisted the urge to pull him back down. I wanted to tell him how good it was to see him, to know that he was alive, not feral. And I really wanted to ask him if he meant what he'd said right before he jumped off the carousel and disappeared into the night. I'd replayed that moment endlessly — on my dial and in my head. I'd picked apart the double negative, trying to shake out the truth: "Remember when I said I lied to Omar and the queen? *That* was the lie." Had he really loved me since he was ten? Before we'd even met, he'd said. Through my dad's stories.

The boy before me now did not seem like the big declaration type. In fact, he seemed to have taken our reunion in stride and moved on to business as usual. He patted down the sheaths on his belt, but Boone had taken his knives. He lifted one leg of his cargo pants and then the other and replaced the missing knives with those he had strapped to his calves.

"I have to tell you something," I said again. I rose and took the tube of antigen from my pocket, along with the collection cylinder. "Dr. Solis developed a cure for Ferae." I paused, waiting for his reaction, but he just watched me with those disconcerting eyes of his. I held out the yellow tube. "I brought you a dose."

He didn't take it, but he did step closer.

"You have to squeeze it out under your upper lip," I explained, hand still outstretched, offering him the cure. "Everson wants me to tell you that it seems to work so far, but they don't know the long-term effects yet. They've been testing it on — on manimals —" I dropped my gaze to the tube of antigen, suddenly ashamed to even offer it to him, knowing how it had been developed. But I was also desperate for him to take it. He had to stop the virus before it took him away from me forever.

"The stiff wants me to have it, huh?" he said. "Did you bring him with you?" He looked around the small space as if Everson might appear. "I'm surprised his mother let him out of her sight, after what happened last time."

"He came with me against orders."

Rafe chuckled then. The sound was low, stroking over my already inflamed nerves. "Good for him. But he should have left you back at base." He nodded at the metal cylinder in my other hand. "What's that one?"

"Before you take the cure, I need to get a blood sample from you. Everson got all those samples from Chorda's castle, but not tiger. Now your blood is the last one they need to create the vac —"

It was as if the cylinder magically migrated from my hand to his — that's how fast he grabbed it from me. And then he squeezed it until I heard the crunch of the glass vial breaking inside.

I flinched, and then snatched back my open palm and locked the antigen in my fist. "Why?" I demanded.

Rafe tossed the crushed cylinder onto the rocky ground. I had come all this way to help him and this was his response? I wanted to smack his beautiful face, but he turned away from me and pressed his hands against the stratified rock, as if he could move the entire rock formation through sheer will and tiger-amped muscles in his back and arms.

"Don't you get it, silky?" he asked, his voice almost a growl. "The sooner the patrol has a vaccine protecting the guards from infection, the sooner they'll declare war on the zone."

The anger drained out of me. The worst part of what he said was . . . I believed him. Chairman Prejean wanted to erase her mistake from the face of the earth. If she could send guards into the zone to kill every single manimal, she would.

"But a vaccine will protect everyone from infection," I said half-heartedly. "If the people in the West are vaccinated, they won't be afraid of the manimals. They won't need a quarantine wall at all."

"You really think that's how it will play out?"

No. Though I wished I could believe it. I'd come to help Dr. Solis and Everson save the world by collecting Rafe's blood, and I'd failed miserably. But Everson and I had always had different priorities, mine less noble than his.

"Then just take the cure," I said, not caring that Everson would be left with the task of finding another tiger-man, one willing to give blood. I touched Rafe's back, trying to ignore how warm his body felt against my palm. He turned to me, and I held the tube out to him, but he shoved his hands deep into his pockets.

"Maybe later," he said.

I gritted my teeth and tried to stuff the tube into his front pocket despite the fact that his hand was in the way.

"You could try putting it down the front of my pants," he suggested.

"Why," I huffed, "are you being such a jerk?"

I spent several seconds wondering how I could knock him out and force the cure on him, but then I'd be doing exactly what Everson had done to all those "test subjects." I'd have to talk him into taking it later. When we weren't hiding from a Komodo-man. Or maybe Everson could talk him into taking it . . . Everson.

I slid the tube back into my pocket and quickly told Rafe about Boone's buddies taking Everson into the woods, somewhere called . . . "Rip-Rap Falls, I think."

"They're probably using him as bait," Rafe said. "Just like Boone did with you."

I peered down the length of the fissure but couldn't see the end. "Are there a lot of ferals around here?"

"Yeah, but most won't eat him. They'll just be driven to bite."

"Biting is bad enough," I muttered. "Can you track Boone's men?"

He smirked. "Walking backward, with a bucket on my head. Let's go."

As I followed him farther along the fissure, a thought struck me. "Why'd you bite Boone? You're not feral."

"Later," he whispered. "Now we need to stay quiet . . . unless you want a dragon on our heels."

Nope. I did not. So I stopped talking and nearly stopped breathing.

Half an hour later, Rafe crouched among the trampled

weeds, studying what he'd said were footprints. "Two went that way." He pointed south. "Back to Heartland. And four of them went that way." He pointed north. "This bunch includes three people in boots, and one in track shoes."

Neve. "The lionesses. They must have taken him from the hunters." I scanned the area for bodies, surprised the lionesses had allowed the hunters to escape with their lives.

Rafe rose, looking bemused. "Why? Last I checked, the stiff was still human . . . sort of. And, like I said, they hate humans."

"Stop calling him that," I snapped.

He grinned. "Someone's touchy. Worried about a cat-girl stealing your boy?"

"No. For one thing, Everson isn't my boy," I ground out, realizing that it had been true even before I'd come back to the East. "And two, I'm just worried about him. Period. Because, you know, there's a lizard-dude running around eating people."

"Lizard-dude?" he echoed with a laugh. "Look, if the felines went to the trouble to snatch the stiff from the hunters, they'll keep him alive . . . For now. They're probably on their way to Camp Echo. It's a manimal village."

I refrained from pointing out that he too had feline DNA coursing through him. "Why would they go there?"

"Because the pride has been casing Echo off and on for months."

At least Everson was safe. Relatively safe, anyway. I followed Rafe down the rocky bluff and into a valley covered in dense brush. We had to go single file, making it difficult to talk, so I contented myself with throwing imaginary daggers at Rafe's back while simultaneously admiring his catlike grace as he navigated the deer paths and rocky rises.

We rested when we reached a ledge that ran along another swollen stream cutting through the rock, this one louder than the others — because, I soon discovered, we were right next to a waterfall. The sound of rushing water filled my head as I crouched on a flat slab of rock in the sun overlooking the falls and dug two protein bars out of my backpack. I looked at my filthy hands and then went to stand on tiptoe at the edge of the rock. I watched the wild rush of water below, which shattered into a cloud of spray in two places where jagged rock tiers interrupted its descent to a small lake. Water droplets coated my face and hair and made me long for a shower — or at least a place to wash my hands.

"Careful there, silky," Rafe said from behind me. "These rocks break away easily."

"Okay," I said, still mesmerized by the swirling water. "Do you think there's anywhere to wash my ha —" When I turned toward him, he had moved so close I could see the flecks of gold around his pupils, starbursts in the center of the vivid blue irises. I'd almost gotten used to the black markings around his eyes.

He grabbed my hand and tugged me away from the edge.

"I didn't know you cared." I smirked, giving him a taste of his own medicine.

Without taking his eyes off mine, he lifted my hand. "Dirty," he said. "But not too bad right here." He put his lips to the inside of my wrist, sending a jolt of electricity through me. "I care," he said, almost as an aside.

My cheeks grew hot, and he must have noticed, because he smiled.

"I can't kiss you . . ." He let go of my hand, his tone teasing. "But there's no risk in touching." He brushed his thumb across my cheek. "So put your hands on me — anywhere. You know you want to."

I shoved him away. But he didn't move very far.

"It's okay, Lane," he said softly, tracing his fingers along the curve of my hip. "I won't tell the stiff a thing."

I flung myself past him, hating him for playing with me and hating myself for wishing that he really did want to kiss me. "I didn't think it was possible, but you are an even bigger jerk than before you got infected."

"Not true," he scoffed. "I was just as big a jerk then. I just hid it from you 'cause I thought I had a shot. But you fell for the stiff, which I get. Actually, I'm relieved. Now I can be myself. You know, it's exhausting trying to impress a girl. You gotta watch what you say. You —"

"If that was you censoring yourself, I don't even want to . . . Forget it. And by the way, Everson and I are friends. That's it."

"Friends?" He quirked a brow in disbelief. "Well, I know he didn't ditch you, so what happened?"

"My dad was in critical condition when I got back to Arsenal after —" *After leaving you wounded and infected to suffer and possibly die alone.* "They weren't sure he'd make it."

"One of the hacks told me," Rafe said. "I'm glad he's okay."

"We came back to Arsenal two weeks ago, and now Everson and I are friendly. Mostly. When he's not dissecting things . . . or locking up manimals."

"Tell me that's not why you dropped him. For cutting up animals? Silky, out here we dissect animals every day. Then we eat them. And sometimes we skin 'em and wear —"

"I didn't drop Everson. We were never — never mind. The point is he and the patrol are treating the manimals like lab rats . . . like animals."

"Because we are," Rafe said with a shrug. He watched me as if Ferae had given him X-ray vision and he could see inside me. "You're making a mistake. He's a good guy. The kind of guy you should be with."

Why would he kiss my wrist and then say something like that? I didn't want to admit even to myself how much that hurt. I tried hard to shift my focus to why I was in the zone in the first place, but it didn't help much. I'd come for him, and this was the thanks I got. I'd come to find him because of a promise. At least that's what I'd told myself — that I was here out of guilt and loyalty. I hadn't let myself think of him as anything more than a difficult friend, because we had a seven-hundred-foot-tall wall between us. And a river. But I couldn't deny it anymore: He was more than that to me.

I dug into my pocket again for the cure. "Let's just find Everson. Maybe he can talk you into letting him take a blood sample. And then you can take the cure, and I can get out of here." I grabbed his hand and thrust the tiny yellow tube into it and squeezed his fingers closed around it.

"I'm not going to take it," he said.

"What are you not understanding? Ferae is a *disease*. And it's working its way to your brain. But if you take the cure, it'll never get there, and you won't go insane. Ever."

He backed up, arms outstretched. "But, silky . . ." he crooned while doing a slow turn. "Look at this." He lifted his shirt, revealing his ripped torso. Aside from the faint stripes on his ribs, I saw the similarities, not for the first time, between him and Michelangelo's *David*. "There's nothing in me I want to cure."

I could understand why he felt that way. I'd been mesmerized by the lionesses' ferocious beauty and muscular grace since I first saw them in their cage at the Chicago zoo. Had I been more horrified or flattered when Deepnita had said I'd make "a nice addition" to the pride? It was a toss-up. And when Mahari had said, "Let me *uncage* you," for a moment I'd longed to be as beautiful, as powerful, as unafraid as they were. But even under the spell of that temptation, I knew the price was too high.

"I'm the perfect host for Ferae," Rafe went on. "The tiger blood made itself right at home. It didn't have to do much to turn me into a predator. Just a couple of tweaks. And the final result" — he smoothed down his shirt and grinned — "is awesome."

"It's not awesome! You're turning into Chorda. It's horrible and —" I clapped my hand to my mouth. How could I have said that to him? But his smile never wavered. It remained plastered across his stupid gorgeous face as if nailgunned on. I dropped my hand. "I'm sorry. I didn't mean horrible."

"It didn't seem so horrible to you a minute ago," he said slyly, and my face blazed. "The best part of this deal is that with every little change, I become a better hunter . . . And I wasn't exactly average before. All my senses are sharper, and I'm aware of dimensions I didn't even know about before." He leaned toward me as if sharing a secret. "I can see in the dark." He took a deep breath, seeming to savor the air as he sucked it in, and I thought of Mahari reveling in her own stealth, strength, and speed.

"A few days ago, a mountain lion spotted me and figured I'd make an easy meal," Rafe went on, sounding pleased. "But I'd already spotted him from a quarter mile away, so I was ready for him. The animal in me is keeping me alive. Safe. And soon I'll smell so much like tiger, nothing will come after me."

Except humans, of course. Was he serious, arguing that Ferae was keeping him alive and safe?

"Boone snuck up on you this morning," I pointed out.

He waved off the thought. "I was distracted. You showed up outta nowhere, looking too good by half, and my nose was full up with Komodo puke. Could happen to anybody."

I shook my head, speechless. At least the lionesses had the sense to be afraid of going feral.

Rafe lifted a shoulder as if in answer — a shrug — like he'd read my mind. "When the Ferae reaches my brain, you'll hire a hunter to put me down, like you promised. Or send a guard. I won't know the difference. Until then I'm going to enjoy the perks." He spread his arms wide. "The more I beast out, the more everything works better — my eyes, my nose . . . other parts." His gaze dropped to my lips.

The fluttering in my stomach turned into a thrum, but I ignored it. Rafe was halfway to feral as it was, yet willing to ride this viral wave the whole way just for a few perks. He'd throw away the rest of his life just to be a better *hunter*. Could he really be that shortsighted? That shallow? Suddenly I regretted giving him the cure. I should have saved it for Deepnita or Neve or someone else who deserved it.

Deserved it.

A penny dropped and echoed through my skull. Rafe *thought* he didn't deserve the cure. His arrogance, that was an act. He'd hated Chorda, had spent years hunting him, was set on killing him, and now he'd turned all that hatred onto himself. Why?

He bent to pick up the protein bars I'd taken out of my backpack. "Are you sharing?" he asked, and without waiting for an answer, he threw one to me, opened the other, and began munching on it.

If he didn't think he deserved to be cured — if he really thought so little of himself — he'd never take the antigen willingly. And he'd pull every trick he could think of to make me go away so he wouldn't be tempted by its promise of sanity.

I needed to eat, but the protein bar tasted like sand, and I struggled to finish it. Rafe was still grinning, but now I saw the levers he pulled to keep it in place.

· TWENTY-TWO ·

Daylight was fading when Rafe announced we'd arrived at Camp Echo. I felt bedraggled through and through, which made sense considering I was cut, bruised, covered in dust, and soaked in sweat. Yep. Utterly bedraggled.

A loud crack had me looking up into the budding trees, but just as I did, someone dropped to the ground three feet in front of us. He bounced onto his feet as if the ten-foot drop was nothing to him. Going by his long, furry forearms and heavy brow overshadowing bright, curious eyes, I figured he was infected with simian DNA. Chimpanzee, maybe?

He held a bugle in one hand, which he pointed at Rafe. "Dude, another one?" he asked, sounding amazed.

His voice was young, and I realized then that under all the dark facial hair, his face was young too. He probably wasn't much older than me.

"Don't know what you're talking about," Rafe replied.

The guy grinned at me, revealing square, gappy teeth. "You feline too?"

"No, I'm —"

"With me," Rafe said firmly. "So toot your horn, chuckles, and let 'em know we're coming. Then get out of our way."

Instead, the guy strolled closer, eyeing me with delight. "She doesn't smell like you," he told Rafe as he circled behind me. I twisted to keep him in view. "She smells —" When he put his nose within inches of my armpit, I smacked him away. His pronounced brow ridge shot up. "Human."

"Whoa," Rafe drawled. "Can't get much past you."

I shot Rafe a dirty look and then offered the manimal a smile. "Hi. I'm Lane."

The guy's grin widened. "Nice to meet you, Lane. I'm —"

"No one she needs to know," Rafe pronounced.

"Happy," the chimp-man finished smoothly.

I blinked. "That's your name? Happy?"

"Name, aim, and avocation," he replied . . . happily.

Rafe rolled his eyes. "How 'bout making *me* happy by blowing that thing and then hiking your chimpy self back up the tree?"

Happy kept grinning and kept staring at me. "Dude, four in one day! Where are you finding these girls?"

"Four?" Rafe met my eyes, clearly coming to the same conclusion I had. The three lionesses were here. "The others were infected with lion?" Rafe asked.

"Oh, yeah. They said you sent them."

Rafe frowned, but Happy shook his head like he couldn't believe his luck. "You have my eternal gratitude, man. The other girls in camp are all too young, or too attached to someone who isn't me, or too close to feral . . . though sometimes that can be —"

"Was there a guard with them?" I cut in.

Happy's attention swung back to me. "Yeah. A human," he said dismissively, and then seemed to realize his mistake.

"Not that there's anything wrong with humans. Least not *female* humans."

"And Glenfiddich let him in camp?" Rafe asked sounding surprised.

"He wouldn't have, 'cause, well, *human*. But he didn't want to turn away the guard and have the lions leave too. One of them caught his eye."

Rafe tipped his head, considering this. "The blond?"

I felt a spark of irritation, though really I couldn't deny Neve's appeal.

"No," Happy said. "The alpha. Mahari."

Rafe made a face. "If those two get together, we'll be at war with humans before the week is out."

Happy put the bugle to his lips and blasted out three loud, harsh notes. "I'll take her from here," he told Rafe.

"You'll lose her on the way to the kitchen." Rafe took my hand and tugged me down the path toward a wooden archway. Music thumped in the distance. I couldn't identify the song, but it had an old, vicious beat like something from before even my dad's time.

"What're you doing?" Happy sputtered. "You never come into camp."

Rafe frowned when Happy caught up to us. "You're on lookout."

A few of the big oaks on this side of the fence had platforms built into the highest branches.

"I just reassigned myself. Now I'm on the welcoming committee." Grinning, Happy hooked an arm through mine.

"We're not staying," Rafe said roughly. "We're just here to collect the guard."

I studied the archway. "Why don't you have a gate?"

"Why would we?" Happy asked.

"What if a feral gets in?" I scanned the area but saw only trees and a few rustic wooden buildings.

He shrugged. "What's it going to do — bite us? We're already infected."

"What if it tries to eat you?"

"Oh, you mean Gabe," Happy said and glanced at Rafe.

"Gabe?" I echoed.

"Gabe Varones. The guy infected with Komodo," Happy went on. "He's pretty territorial. Just don't go stomping around his gorge, and he probably won't bother you."

Probably? Gabe had sure as heck bothered Boone! A fact that Rafe was weirdly keeping to himself. I shot him a questioning look, but he just shook his head slightly in return. Fine. I wouldn't say a word. Though maybe if the manimals knew that lizard-dude *ate* Boone, they'd add a gate.

"You're not from Heartland," Happy said, eyeing me.

"No," I admitted, but didn't offer him any further explanation. "What was this place?"

"A summer camp. It's a real sweet setup. We're on a peninsula with lake on three sides," he said proudly.

I glanced down at the uneven ground, where broken glass, garbage, and hundreds of spent shell casings were scattered in the dirt. Not exactly what I expected to find on the grounds of a summer camp, but okay.

"There's electricity?" I asked Happy.

"A couple of solar generators," he said. "But we don't use 'em much, 'cept for music. Keeps us pumped."

But not pumped enough to pick up all the garbage. Rafe pulled me toward a large rustic building with a loading dock off the back, where a fresh deer carcass lay on a workbench, waiting to be butchered. Flies buzzed around the blood that pooled on the cement as dead doe eyes stared back at me. My stomach curled in on itself.

"There're fifty cabins, an infirmary, and a dining hall." Happy hooked a thumb at the large building as we approached, its wood siding worn with what looked like a century's worth of weather. "Plenty of room. You know, in case you want to stay."

"She doesn't," Rafe said sharply. "She's human, remember? Why would she stay here, when she can go anywhere?"

Happy's expression turned sulky. "I was just saying."

"It was a nice offer," I assured him before shooting Rafe a dirty look.

"Yeah, real nice," he mocked. "'Come live with a bunch of freaks who were stupid enough to get themselves infected.'"

Happy stopped short to glare at Rafe. "You're infected."

"Yep. I'm just as stupid and freaky as the rest of you."

"Jerk," Happy muttered, and stalked back the way we came, looking anything but happy.

"If the Olympics ever add victim blaming as a sport," I said, "you'll get the gold."

"Gold's not good for much around here. I'd rather get an Uzi," he said, completely unrepentant.

When a bloodcurdling yell rose from the other side of the dining hall, I jerked to a stop, heart racing.

"Welcome to camp." Rafe led me past a row of animal skins stretched on frames and up several rotting steps to the dining hall's covered porch.

Meat hung from porch beams in long strips, scenting the air with blood. One step closer and I realized the meat strips were actually skinned snakes. Pest control? Food? I couldn't think of a single reason why I'd want to know. I pursed my lips and stepped around the splatters of blood, though they were hard to spot, considering the entire porch was coated in a mixture of sludge and dead leaves. I followed Rafe to the front of the porch, where he took a seat on top of a picnic table.

The dining hall was one of many buildings that circled a giant field, where some sort of game was going on. One that involved running after, tackling, and then flinging a given player out of the giant circle that had been painted onto the grass. Male, female, big, small, didn't matter. All the players were tossed with equal disregard. And everyone was coated in mud — players and spectators alike. Rafe had said that Echo was an all-manimal camp, but it hadn't prepared me for seeing so many in one place. Some of them only had a few physical markers, while others were quite mutated. All of them looked dangerous — even the children, a few no more than toddlers, who were shouting encouragement from the circle's perimeter.

"It's called Take the Teddy." Rafe spoke loudly to be heard over the yelling and the music that blasted from a speaker a few yards away from us on the porch. Pre-exodus music, on some old format that didn't require a computer.

Rafe pointed to a black-furred man running for a telephone pole at the center of the enormous circle. He clutched a soggy object in one hand. He hurled it at the bucket sitting on top of the pole and missed. Clearly the bucket had been nailed into place because it didn't so much as wobble when the man slammed into the pole with two players on his back. The teddy bear he'd thrown lay forgotten in the grass. A bunch of the other players carried the furred man to the edge of the circle and flung him into the crowd. Even though he took down several spectators, the crowd roared with laughter and threw out insults.

"No one can touch the teddy until the runner is dealt with," Rafe explained.

Dealt with indeed. The furred man picked himself up and, to my surprise, pounced right back into the game.

"And then a player can only grab the teddy if one of their team members helped fling the runner."

"How many people are on a team?" I asked as a player snatched up the toy and threw it to another player.

"Three."

I did a quick count. "So there are ten teams out there."

"Probably less. Lots of randos join in the tossing just for the fun of it. Fling her!" he shouted along with the rest of the crowd.

"I can barely hold myself back," I muttered.

A tall woman with spotted skin and fuzzy pointed ears leapt onto the porch, skipping the rotten wooden steps entirely. The sides of her head were shaved, and the mohawk of remaining hair was woven into a long French braid. The better to show off her ears? Her tattered T-shirt was only splattered with mud, not coated, indicating that she'd been at the back of the crowd.

She grinned at Rafe. "You came for dinner! This is a first."

"Nah," he said. "I'm looking for the human that came in earlier. A line guard."

The woman gestured toward a squat little building on the other side of the field, at the tip of the peninsula. "Infirmary," she said, though her attention had moved to me.

"Is he hurt?" I asked while wondering how I was going to cut through the game. Going around the spectators would be difficult since they were spread out as far as the lake on either side of the peninsula. And as much as I hated to admit it — even to myself — I didn't want to squeeze through this crowd. My brain knew that I couldn't breathe in the Ferae virus, but my nervous system didn't want to take any chances.

"No," she told me. "He's waiting for Aaron to wake up now that his fever's broken."

My heart leapt. "Aaron is here?"

"Came in at dawn," she said, and sent Rafe a sidelong look.

He snorted. "I had nothing to do with it."

"Of course not," she said with a smirk. "We all know you're just out for yourself."

"Glad that's clear," he replied.

"Is Aaron okay?" I asked the woman.

"He's got a major adjustment ahead of him," she said, studying me as if checking that my question was sincere. "But he's young. He'll do fine." Her piercing dark eyes cataloged every detail of my appearance.

I looked down at myself. I was cut, covered in dirt, and soaked in sweat. Six months ago, I would've taken myself to an emergency room to get decontaminated. Now I just longed for a shower.

"Are you newly infected?" she asked, as if that would be no big deal.

"No," Rafe answered for me. "Pure human. She came with the guard. I'm trying to pair 'em up again."

His meaning was so clear that even the spotted woman

caught on. She shot him a curious look. "So in addition to being a hunter and a hack, you're hiring out as a yenta?"

"Sure. Whatever that means," he said distractedly as a cheer went up from the field. Rafe got to his feet, his gaze fixed on a giant man with uneven horns twisting up from his misshapen head. Infected with . . . goat maybe? He lumbered over to the dog pile of muddy, bloody players and began tossing them aside like he was digging into a Cracker Jack box to get to the prize.

"Lane, this is Little One," Rafe said with a wave of introduction to the woman, though he never took his eyes off the goat-man, who was still throwing players aside.

When the man reached the player at the bottom of the pile, he hauled her to her feet, pointed at the bucket atop the pole, and hoisted up her arm. My mouth dropped open as I recognized Deepnita under all that mud. Cheers rang out around the field, though there were a few boos too. Before Deepnita had even lowered her arm, half the crowd peeled off and stampeded toward the dining hall. Toward us.

"Guess I don't need to ring the dinner bell," Little One observed.

I pulled up my feet and knelt on the picnic table as manimals infected with dozens of different Ferae strains swept up the porch stairs and plowed into the dining hall. The rotten floorboards should have collapsed under the abuse. I heard a shout from the field and glanced over just as Deepnita went down again, slammed back into the muck by a jubilant Neve. A shrieking Mahari piled on top of them.

So. While I was being chased by a giant lizard-dude, they were playing Take the Teddy.

My flash of resentment flamed out one second later as I recalled that Mahari had spent the past two weeks in an eerie basement lab — never mind that the three of them had spent years in a cage and had just lost Charmaine. They deserved every moment of happiness they could scrounge up.

When the goat-man joined in the fun and hefted Mahari into the air, hands high on her waist, she turned into a yowling, spitting cat. He put her down and snatched his hands back, but not before she'd put bloody tracks down his forearms with her claws. His lips parted with surprise as he stared at his torn skin. My body tensed for the blow that was sure to come. My hands tingled as the moment stretched out, and then the guy threw back his head and . . . laughed. Mahari didn't share his amusement and neatly knocked away his hand when he reached out to clap her on the back.

Rafe made a noise of disgust. "Proving that 'randy as a goat' isn't just a saying."

"Leave him alone," Little One snapped. "He's been miserable since Charity turned last summer."

"Be right back," Rafe said, and leapt off the porch.

"Where are you going?" I called after him.

He glanced back, but his eyes were on Little One. "Feed her," he said.

"I don't take orders anymore," she replied without offense. "Not since I left Heartland."

He grinned, unrepentant. "You'll feed her. She's like you. Always trying to be nice."

"Jerk," she huffed as he continued across the field without a backward glance.

"You don't have to feed me," I said as I climbed off the picnic table. My legs trembled a little, but that was a good thing. My muscles were revving up, in case I needed to run for my life.

"I'm going in to dinner anyway," Little One said. "May as well bring you along."

"Because it's convenient, not because he told you to," I couldn't help but tease.

She smiled, revealing a line of sharp little teeth. "Of course."

"Who makes sure there's enough food for everyone?"

She shrugged. "The only meal we plan is dinner, but no one goes hungry. There are plenty of fish in the lake, and the kids love to fish. They go out every morning and grill lunch over the fire drums that we keep burning. Also, the woods are full of game — pureblood animals and mongrels. Doesn't matter to us if our meat is infected with Ferae before it hits the grill."

"But there's no leader?"

"Nope. We had enough of that back at Heartland. Boone has that place laced up tight — we were so worried about slacking off that we never had time to question the things he told us."

Not anymore . . .

She glanced at the goat-man in the field, who was still grinning at an unimpressed Mahari. "What does Rafe want with Glenfiddich?"

"I don't know." Maybe to pass on the info that lizard-dude had killed Boone. "Is . . . Glenfiddich," I stumbled over his name, "from the Heartland Compound?"

When she nodded, I asked, "Isn't that a kind of whiskey?"

One of my dad's clients had given him a bottle on top of the exorbitant finder's fee. Little had I known at the time that my dad had earned every penny acquiring a Magritte titled *Time Transfixed* from the Art Institute of Chicago.

"When a person arrives at Echo, we tell them to pick a new name to go along with their new identity as a manimal. We encourage them to name themselves after something worth living for. We need those daily reminders — especially in the beginning."

"What does Little One remind you of?"

"Lost children," she said softly. "The little ones who've been chased out of their compounds and need to be found before it's too late."

"Oh," I said as my heart swelled inside my chest. "That is worth living for."

She smiled her sharp-toothed smile. "I think so."

"So not everyone is from Heartland?"

"A lot of us are." She beckoned me toward the entrance to the dining hall. "But not all. When someone gets banished from their compound, they tend to come looking for Camp Echo. The hacks spread the word about us and how we'll take in anyone who wants to join — though not all of them can handle camp life."

She pulled open the screen door and waved me in as if proving a point.

I was apparently one of those who wouldn't be able to handle it. The level of noise alone set my teeth on edge. But on top of that, half the people stayed on their feet as they ate — though there were plenty of empty seats at the round tables — the better to dodge the flying food. Someone shouted for a drumstick, and five were hurtled at him from all directions. Not in an aggressive way. Evidently, throwing food was just another way to pass it. Not surprisingly, the wood plank floors were carpeted in bones and garbage. My boots squelched with every step.

Too few wall torches fought to light the dark interior. Inhuman faces peered out from the shadows. Some flashed eerie, distinctly nonhuman smiles. A man infected with baboon caught me staring and snapped his fangs at me. "The better to eat you with, my pretty." His guffaws echoed off the dining hall's wood-paneled walls.

"Vengeance," Little One shouted over the din, "save us two seats."

Someone thought vengeance was worth living for? I wondered with a shiver.

Little One held out a metal plate and pointed to the side of the room where the boisterous manimals were gathered. "Chow counter. Load up your plate."

"Where's the end of the line?" I asked.

She barked out a laugh. "Line? What're you — civilized? Get over there, shove your way in, and take your share. Better yet, take more than your share."

"Uh, okay, thanks." Thanks to the orphans, I'd gotten used to being jostled, but still, a crowd of manimals represented my own personal gauntlet.

Little One gave me a friendly shove toward the service window that opened onto the kitchen. I shot her a dirty look over my shoulder, but she just laughed again. I slipped through a break in the milling bodies to find a wide counter laden with hot food, which included a platter of roasted snakes. Unasked question answered! Other options included fried catfish with whiskers and barely seared steaks. I remembered my dad's warning: Even if you're desperate for food, never eat red meat in the Feral Zone — it might have come from an infected mammal. Since I didn't eat meat of any kind, I rounded the group to get to the far end of the counter, where I found a selection of eggs and roasted vegetables. I piled my tray with two potatoes, one hard-boiled egg, and a lump of green stuff, which might have been boiled spinach or maybe grass.

I joined Little One at a big round table.

Her steak overflowed the edges of the plate onto the food-crusted table. She pulled out the chair next to hers, and I slid onto it gratefully.

She looked at my plate and said, "Ah, yes. Sometimes I forget we have gardens, for the veggie lovers among us."

The kid in the next seat leaned toward me and inhaled deeply. "She's human," he announced with disgust.

Every person at our table, other tables, and milling nearby turned to stare at me.

"What's she doing here?" hissed a man with mottled orange skin on the other side of Little One. His black fedora hid much of his face because it sat so low on his head. He had no ears to keep his hat in place, only holes where his ears had once been.

"She's with Rafe," Little One said in a voice loud enough to be heard by all. Her clipped tone implied that was the only answer they were going to get, and to my shock, that seemed to be all they needed.

Most of the manimals turned back to their dinner plates, but then I noticed their gazes intermittently flashing my way. They were still watching me, but doing it on the sly now, which spiked my anxiety. Or maybe my nerves were snapping because the bumpy orange-skinned man clenched and unclenched his fists as if fighting for control.

"Oh," Little One said with mock curiosity. "You don't think we owe him, Vengeance?"

Snatching up his plate, Vengeance got to his feet. "We do. But that doesn't mean I have to sit here and lose my appetite." With a last glare at me, he strode off. Several of the others at our table rose and followed him. On his way out, the kid sent me a perfect imitation of Vengeance's glare.

As long as no one bit me, I wasn't going to take their hostility personally. After all, humans had banished them from their homes, and then there was the Titan wall, which had turned the West into one big gated community. Besides, my anxiety was losing ground to my curiosity; I wanted to hear more about Rafe and what the camp owed him. But before I could ask Little One, a hunched man in a hooded raincoat shuffled over to our table.

"Is Rafe here?" he rasped.

"He's in camp," Little One told the elderly man. "But not in the dining hall. You got a problem with him, Cohiba?" she asked.

He swung his head back and forth as if his neck was unable to twist. As he returned to his own table, I had to hold in a gasp. He had long spines poking through the back of his raincoat.

"Cohiba?" I asked softly.

"It's some kind of fancy cigar."

I nodded. It hit me then that he was the oldest person I'd seen in camp so far. The oldest by decades. "Most of the people here are really young. How come?"

"Ferae is a hard disease, physically and mentally," Little One explained. "Hard to watch your body change every day. Hard to know that someday you'll lose your mind. A lot of the older people can't handle it and opt for a fast way out. Others can't get past the grief of leaving family behind — husbands, wives, children, and all their friends. They know they can't go back; they'd just get driven off again, so they give up. Stop eating, stop taking care of themselves. They opt for a slow way out. Those of us who are left, we know we're going to go feral someday — probably sooner than later — so we cram as much life as we can into the time we have left."

"What happens when, uh . . . when someone turns?"

Little One shrugged. "You mean, aside from the snarling and drooling? We keep a logbook in the office" — she pointed at a door to the right of the kitchen — "where we write down who joins us, what strain they're infected with, and how they want us to handle it when they turn. Some people can't bring themselves to plan ahead, and that's fine. Others want to be locked up or shot, and we try to oblige . . . within reason."

Her matter-of-fact tone sent a chill over me, but I could understand why it was necessary. She couldn't lose it every time a manimal turned feral in camp. How long had she been infected? I wondered, but it felt rude to ask.

Little One twisted in her seat to watch the screen door, and a moment later it opened. Manimal senses were unnerving.

Glenfiddich lumbered into the hall with Rafe one step behind.

"All right already. I won't listen to them," Glenfiddich grouched as they approached our table. "No one here is looking for trouble."

Uh-oh. Rafe must have told him about Mahari. I was glad to have missed that exchange. Scratches on Glenfiddich's arms oozed blood, which freaked me out beyond belief, even with the big round table between him and me.

"What're you talking about?" Rafe scoffed. "Everyone here is always looking for trouble. When they can't find it, they start it. I'm telling you, the pride will be a match to your drum of oil. Kick 'em out now. And bandage up those scratches and quit bleeding all over the place, will you?" It was as if he'd read my anxiety level without even looking at me.

The old porcupine-man, Cohiba, pushed himself to his feet. "The boy wants to see you," he called to Rafe.

Ignoring him, Rafe jogged up two steps onto a dais at the front of the room. "Hey!" he shouted, and the hall fell silent. "I need a rifle. If anyone has one they want to trade, talk to me. Also, Boone is dead," he said like it was no big deal. The announcement was met with stunned silence.

Rafe started for the edge of the dais, when Glenfiddich stopped him with a loud "How?"

"Gabe ate him."

There were a few gasps but far more grunts of acceptance.

"He was outside the compound," Rafe went on. "Far from where he shoulda been. I don't know what that means for you all."

"Squat," Little One called out, and several others voiced their agreement. "Nothing's going to change in Heartland. Zeke and Habib will carry on."

"Boone kept us safe," a girl infected with bear protested.

"Boone was a liar," Glenfiddich countered.

"What did he lie about?" I asked Little One in a low voice.

Glenfiddich heard me. "Us," he said roughly. "Do we look dead to you?"

"Uh . . . no," I murmured.

"He wants to thank you," Cohiba told Rafe as he stepped down from the dais.

I pushed to my feet. "Do you mean Aaron?"

"I mean the boy who was too fevered to walk but somehow managed to make his way here. Like all the others." Cohiba smiled at Rafe, who scowled in return.

"You don't know what you're talking about, old man."

Cohiba just beamed brighter. "Thanks to you."

With a hiss of disgust, Rafe spun on his heel and left the dining hall, letting the screen door slap closed behind him.

· TWENTY-THREE ·

I ran after Rafe, potato in hand. Though the sun had set, in the purple twilight I could see that he was heading for the infirmary. Halfway across the field, I heard someone call my name. It was Everson, rising from his seat beside a giant bonfire on the beach. He walked toward me quickly, his relief at seeing me blatant. We met on the periphery of the bonfire and exchanged a tight hug.

"I'm glad you're all right," I said breathlessly.

"I was going out of my mind," he said. He scanned me from head to toe. "Are you okay? Boone — he didn't — didn't hurt you?" he said awkwardly.

"No," I told him. "I'm okay."

"We tried to find you," Everson told me. "But the pride lost you at the stream. We leveraged a fallen tree across the ravine, but they couldn't catch your scent on the other side. We were going to head out again in the morning to look for you."

"I found Rafe. He's going to see Aaron now."

"So he's not feral." Everson lifted his chin toward Rafe, who had just pulled open the infirmary door.

"He acted feral to keep the pride away." I spotted the lionesses collecting wood on the other side of the bonfire. They were still covered in mud and didn't seem to mind at all, going by their laughter. "He said they've been stirring up trouble, rounding up gangs of angry manimals and attacking human compounds — and maybe even Moline."

"I believe it. They make their own rules." There was a note in his voice I hadn't heard before when talking about them — grudging admiration. In fact, I was surprised that he was at the bonfire at all, surrounded by manimals. I wanted to ask him about it, but I wasn't sure how to bring it up.

Everson looked over his shoulder at the manimals gathered around the fire. "I have to say" — he cleared his throat as if it was difficult to get the words out — "that I was wrong about some things, and you were right."

I rocked back on my heels, floored by the tone of his voice. He actually sounded *humble*.

"Uh-huh," I said.

"Being here with these . . . people . . . I've changed my mind about the way we've been conducting the research. I'm going to talk to Dr. Solis. I think he'll listen. We need to change our protocols so that we're working strictly with volunteers. They'll stay at the lab as guests — as patients. Not as test subjects . . . in cages." He winced on the last word.

Wow. As harrowing as this trip had been, something good had come out of it. If Everson hadn't come into the zone with me . . . hadn't spent time with the manimals as equals, he would never have changed his mind about them.

"Go ahead," he said, his voice sounding raw. "Rub it in. I deserve it."

"Nah," I said, feeling a swell of admiration for him. "It's more effective if you do it yourself."

He snorted and then glanced toward the infirmary. "Did you get a blood sample from him?"

And with that, the warmth in my chest snuffed out, leaving me feeling cold and hollow. "He wouldn't let me. He broke the vial."

"What?" Everson demanded, and then paused, his wide shoulders shifting. "Why?"

"He said it'll be worse for the manimals, if the guards are vaccinated. There'll be nothing to keep them from storming into the zone and killing everyone who isn't one hundred percent human."

"The vaccine isn't just for the guards," Everson said angrily.

"Yeah, but he has a point. The vaccine could be a nasty political tool in the wrong hands." I didn't say his mother's hands, but going by Everson's sigh, he'd gotten the message. "And here's the weird part: Rafe won't take the cure, and he won't tell me why."

Everson thought about it. "Maybe he'll tell me."

"Why would he tell you and not me?" I asked, genuinely perplexed. "Because you're a guy?"

"Because he doesn't have to worry about me getting upset."

Who wouldn't be? Rafe was choosing the disease over the cure. "How's Aaron?" I asked, not caring that it was such a conspicuous change of subject.

"He's just getting over the fever," Everson said. "When I left him, he was sleeping. Rafe brought him here and left him at the gate. Apparently he does that a lot but won't admit it. He usually scares newly infected people into running in this direction. He's got a heck of a reputation around here. And would you believe, it's all good. He leaves them supplies, including freshly killed deer."

Everson might have been baffled by Rafe's actions, but I wasn't. Flashes of memory rose in my mind: Rafe telling Cosmo a bedtime story; holding Cosmo as he died; Rafe charging Chorda to protect me, though he had to know he had no chance of winning that fight. I already knew his shallow and self-serving persona was a cover for the more compassionate parts of his personality.

"But he doesn't stick around long enough for anyone to thank him," Everson went on. "And when anyone tries, he says it wasn't him."

"Why?"

Everson shrugged. "No idea. He never struck me as the modest type."

Rafe wasn't. But for some reason, he didn't want credit or thanks for helping the manimals. Maybe he didn't feel like he deserved it after years of mocking them. There it was again, the idea that Rafe felt he didn't deserve something.

"Anyway, stay here," Everson said. "I'll try talking to him." He strode off toward the infirmary.

Deepnita saw me and gestured for me to join them by the bonfire. "Glad you found your way here," she said as I took a seat on a log next to her. Neve came crashing up from the beach and hugged me hard around the neck from behind, almost pulling me off the log and making us both laugh. Mahari followed more slowly with an armload of wood she dropped next to the fire. She raised a hand toward me in greeting. Was I hallucinating in the flickering firelight, or did she actually smile at me?

The warmth of the fire felt amazing, and as I looked around at the manimals gathered in pairs and small groups around the fire, I felt myself relaxing, maybe for the first time since my dad and I had come over the wall. A few bottles made their way around the circle. Cohiba was sitting on a stump, his hood pulled back to reveal the spines protruding from his scalp, telling a story that had Glenfiddich and a few others laughing. Happy strummed a guitar while a girl around my age sang a love song in a wavering voice. Lounging near the fire, Little One purred loudly as an older woman with a wolfish face unbraided and combed her hair. A young boy and girl with black claws and white streaks in their wiry black hair picked up twigs from the ground and ran to throw them into the roaring fire, screeching when it got too hot.

"Not too close, now!" the older woman called to the kids. The little girl ran to her and hugged her, and I saw joy and sorrow battling in the woman's expression.

They were all just people. Friends and makeshift families living hard, playing hard, knowing that tomorrow might be the day their sanity — or that of a partner, a friend, a child — slipped away. I suddenly missed my dad and wished there was some way to get a message to him that I was okay.

Cohiba offered me a bottle, and I passed it on to Deepnita before pulling out my dial and pushing record.

A few minutes later, I headed to the infirmary to see how Aaron was doing.

As I approached the building, I heard raised voices. I stopped in the shadows around the corner and spotted Everson and Rafe outside, a solar lantern on the ground between them.

"What is your problem?" Everson demanded. "I can't believe you would make the whole human race suffer."

So much for the magic of guy talk.

Rafe said, "I'm wondering what happened to the version of you I saw in Chicago, the smart one who knew it was a bad idea to break me out of the zoo."

"You're still pissed about that?"

"No, I'm serious. You made the right call then. So why would you bring Lane here?"

"What are you talking about?"

"She was safe in the West. Even safe on Arsenal. Why bring her here?"

"You think I could've stopped her?" Everson scoffed.

"You could've trumped up some charge and sent her back over the wall."

"She can't go back."

"Why not?"

Everson told him about the viral video, and Rafe blew out his breath loudly, shaking his head.

"One of the things you and I actually agreed on was that keeping her human was the most important thing."

Everson looked shocked. "It's not my place to stop her from doing what she thinks is right."

"Then you make it your place," Rafe snapped. "You're the guy she should be with."

"No, actually, I'm not. Yeah, I was into her when we first met, but — we're too different."

We were. And after he'd lied to me and I'd seen him treat manimals like they didn't deserve basic human rights, we were still repairing our friendship. Forget anything romantic.

"Lane and I will only ever be friends," Everson went on. "Even if you get your sorry self killed or choose insanity over the only cure we've got."

Rafe tensed. "What are you talking about?"

"Figure it out. Maybe try using brainpower instead of testosterone."

"Huh." The corners of Rafe's mouth twitched up into a grin. "I'll bet that works like a charm with girls. Tossing out big words like that. It's giving *me* tingles."

Everson threw up his hands. "Screw this. I have to go. I need to figure out how to find another person infected with tiger who's willing to give a blood sample. Should be a snap." Turning on his heel, he stalked off.

I flattened myself against the side of the building as he came around the corner, on his way back toward the bonfire. When I peered around the corner again, I saw that Rafe's grin had fallen away, replaced by a look of steely determination as he picked up the lantern and opened the door to the infirmary. Rafe was so skilled at driving people away, I wondered if he could stop doing it even if he wanted to.

Once Rafe had gone inside, I slipped in after him as quietly as I could and tucked myself into a corner in the shadowy entryway. The room contained three sturdy cots covered in crisp white sheets. The scuffed hardwood floor was swept clean, and a tray of steel instruments gleamed in the corner. I couldn't believe how clean it was in here compared to the rest of the camp.

Aaron sat propped up on pillows in one of the cots, his face smooth — unmarked. How did that square with what I saw last night . . . Rafe rearing up and slashing Aaron? I now knew that Rafe didn't have claws, so he must have been holding a knife — using it to cut the gag off Aaron. And I'd nearly put a bullet in him . . .

Rafe dropped onto the cot next to Aaron's. Neither gave

any sign that they'd heard me come in, though Rafe probably knew from my scent. I checked that my dial was still recording.

"Did you squeeze out all of it under your lip?" he asked Aaron. The flattened yellow tube lay on the small table next to the bed.

When Aaron nodded and ran his tongue under his upper lip, I felt something within me tear and then break. Hope. Rafe had just given it away — his dose, his second chance. For months, I'd worried about him, and I came so far and risked so much to find him . . . to save him. But Rafe didn't want to be saved. He wanted to self-destruct and smile and joke while doing it. Someday, I'd admire him for giving Aaron his dose of the cure. But today, now, I wanted to kick him in the gut and yell and cry and hold him — all at once. Like that was something new. "Why'd I have to take it?" Aaron asked. "I don't feel sick anymore."

"It'll keep the fever from coming back," Rafe told him.

"But I'm infected now," Aaron pointed out.

Rafe shrugged. "Maybe. Maybe not. We'll get one of those test strips and find out."

Aaron's face lost all its color. "I told you, that . . . that thing bit me."

"You arguing with me?"

"No!" Aaron swung his legs over the bed and stared out the window at the bonfire blazing in the distance. "I thought they were all dead," he whispered.

Just as everyone at Heartland now thought he was dead.

"Yeah, Boone lied to you," Rafe said. "Far as I know, only Habib and Zeke know the truth."

A few things clicked into place in my mind, among them: Rafe was really good at knowing who was full of crap. Boone had been as full of it as anyone I'd ever met.

"Why don't they go back to Heartland?" Aaron asked.

"Because the whole compound sang 'em off. Told them they're dead — that it's time to move on. They're not welcome anymore."

"We sing to keep the ghosts away."

"Yeah. Them." He hooked a thumb at the window and the camp beyond. "Get it? The infected are the ghosts. And everyone at Heartland buys into it. The infected think they're being noble, not going back. They tell themselves it's better for their families this way. Less worry, less heartache, if they're plain old dead and gone."

"My mom wouldn't feel that way," Aaron said with the utmost conviction. "Did Boone lie to her?"

"Yep," Rafe said. "They even burned your body at dawn."

Aaron jammed his feet into his beat-up sneakers. "I have to tell her I'm alive."

My heart hurt for Aaron and for his mom. I thought of my own mother, who I still missed every day. I thought of my dad. I hoped he was all right. Maybe Moline had settled down since the lionesses had been out of circulation. I sent a mental message through the woods and ravines and up the river: *I'm okay, Dad! I'm okay.*

"You can't," Rafe said firmly. "If you get anywhere near Heartland, a sniper will pick you off before you reach the gate. Boone's dead, but things aren't going to change."

Aaron's head shot up, eyes wide. I remembered Boone's dying screams now with a more detached sense of horror.

Because maybe there had been some justice in what had happened to him.

"Zeke and Habib will keep up the lie," Rafe went on. "Saying it's for the good of the compound. You live here now, in Echo, so you might as well make the best of it."

Aaron turned toward the door but then paused.

"Go on," Rafe urged. "You might even remember a few of them."

Still Aaron hesitated. "Are they different? I mean, the way they act."

"Only one way to find out." Rafe sent me a sidelong glance, proving he'd known I was there all along. "Go on."

When the door closed behind Aaron, I moved into the center of the room. "You gave him your dose." The words slipped out of me. Clumsy, broken sounds.

"It's only fair," he said with a shrug. "It's my fault he got infected. People from Heartland . . . They don't leave the compound except in groups and armed. Then Aaron and his friends started daring one another to go farther. Alone. Morons. Gabe eats animals mostly. Mammals. Nothing humans will touch. So he's not taking food from anyone. He's just living his life. I'd never seen him go after a person."

"He's feral."

"Yeah. But if people would just leave him alone —" He stopped himself and shook his head with disgust. "I'm the moron. Someone was going to cross his path sooner or later. If it had only been Boone or his hunters, I wouldn't have cared. But Aaron's just a kid. A stupid kid."

"You've killed ferals before," I said. I shuddered

inwardly, remembering the moment I'd come upon Rafe beating Chorda with a crowbar. "Why not Gabe?"

Rafe stepped close enough that I could feel his body heat. "You sure you want to know?"

I drew a slow breath, my stomach buzzing with nerves, and nodded.

"It's easier to just show you." He signaled for me to follow him, and we slipped out of the infirmary.

· TWENTY-FOUR ·

Rafe led me down a well-worn path along the lake, past several of the rustic camp cabins. A howl fractured the night as we approached a decrepit-looking barn. Inside, it was even darker, and the air stank of dust, horses, and rotting hay. Debris from the barn's roof littered the floor, and moonlight shafted through the gaps, but it was the four large animal cages that had me stumbling.

The square cages were about seven feet tall, six feet wide, and one was occupied. A man with long, matted hair paced the length of his cage and back, snarling and agitated. Probably infected with wolf or maybe husky. He wore only sweatpants and looked like he was in serious need of a bath. He sniffed loudly as we neared but otherwise ignored us.

"He's feral?" I asked Rafe in the barest whisper.

"Yep," Rafe replied, not bothering to lower his voice. "This is Scribe. He turned a year ago."

I inhaled sharply when Scribe swung his vicious gaze onto us and snarled, showing off sharp fangs. Anger twisted his features. His wide cheekbones jutted more than was normal for a human, and his nose was flatter; however, it was the sheen of saliva coating his mouth that sent a chill skipping down my spine.

"Has he been in that cage since he turned?" I asked softly.

"Longer," Rafe said like it was no big deal. "He went in a couple of months before he went feral. He felt himself slipping and figured it'd be easier on everyone if he was already locked up."

"That's . . . that's —"

"Practical," Rafe suggested.

"Sad," I whispered.

Scribe threw back his head and howled. The sound was terrifying and yet haunting too.

"Can't you at least leave a light in here?"

Rafe shook his head. "Bright light makes him feel exposed. Makes him worse. The ones infected with predator like keeping to the shadows."

"Oh." I waited for my hands to die on me, go numb, but it didn't happen. Instead of my usual panic, I felt only sad and sorry for him.

Suddenly Scribe leapt at us as if rebounding off a trampoline, only to slam into the cage bars. He shoved out an arm, fingers scrabbling to make up the distance between us. I wasn't even close to being within grabbing range, and yet I backed up several steps.

"Why'd you bring me here?" I asked Rafe. "What does he have to do with Gabe?"

"Come on." Rafe turned to go. "We're riling him up."

We left the barn and walked the path along the lake. It was a cool, clear night. The lake lapped at the shore, and loons called across the moonlit water. We could hear the music and laughter from the bonfire.

"My mom lived in that cage for two years," Rafe said softly.

My heart clenched. "Your mother was feral?"

"Yeah. And living here. In that exact cage. And I had no idea. Eventually she stopped eating. A lot of them do. Deep down, under all the crazy, they know they're never going to get out, so what's the point?"

Now I understood why he hadn't told Hagen or anyone else about his parents.

"I was born at the Heartland Compound," he said.

I nodded, and Rafe looked surprised. "Boone told me," I said.

"Gabe was my sister's husband, my brother-in-law."

What? It was my turn to be shocked. I was so shocked my legs stopped moving.

"He was a good guy. Good to her. Good to me."

"Oh no." It sounded so lame, so pointless, but I felt sick from the effort of saying it, of feeling it. I knew what had happened to Rafe's sister: Her husband had gone feral and had killed her while Rafe hid under the bed. And now the perpetrator of that horrific crime, Gabe — someone Rafe had once loved and depended on — had become that lizard thing. I studied Rafe's face. The moonlight exaggerated the hollows in his cheeks and the black outlines of his eyes, making him look profoundly sad, haunted even.

I veered off the path to lean up against the siding of the nearest cabin.

Rafe stood in front of me, just out of reach, with his hands in his pockets. "Until I was seven, I lived at Heartland with my parents and my sister, Sophie, who was a lot older than me, born before the plague. Our dad died when I was really young, of pneumonia — I barely remember him. One day our mom went outside the compound fence to collect herbs to use in medicines. She never came back. Sophie and I thought she was dead — 'cause that's what Boone told us. He said she was attacked by a feral and died. We even sang her off. She got to hear her own kids sing a pretty song, telling her to get lost and never come back. Boone said the crying we heard outside the fence, that was her ghost. She didn't stay long. Probably thought we'd be better off without an infected mother. But he shouldn't have decided for her. For us. We didn't even get to say good-bye."

"Rafe, no! I'm so sorry." I didn't know what I would have done if I hadn't been able to say good-bye to my mom before she died, if I didn't have the images and footage of her to remember her by. I took a step toward him. I wanted to hug him, but he held up his hands defensively.

"Your mother's name, you found it in the logbook here?" I asked.

Rafe nodded. "She lived here for years before going feral. Years we could've been with her. Boone took that from me and Sophie . . . and my mom." He waved back toward the bonfire. "He took it from all of them. A lot of them have families at Heartland who think they're dead. So yeah, when I found out my mom had been living here for years and died alone in a cage, I started to watch for him — Boone. I was going to slice him open, but then —"

"You couldn't."

His laugh was ugly. "No, then I realized I'd be letting him off too easy. He needed to see what it was like to live apart from his family. To have them think he was dead. So I bit him." He snarled the words. "'Cause I'm worse than a feral. People like Scribe" — he gestured toward the barn — "can't help it. They're driven to bite. But me, I *chose* to. And it changed nothing. I'm still furious that I lost those years with my mom."

A flash of how it felt to have my mom's arms around me. How cold the world felt when she was gone from it. I knew that fury, that bitterness, that bottomless grief. Again I wanted to touch him, to comfort him — and in that moment I wanted his comfort too. But as if reading the impulse in my muscles, he took a step away from me. As if he didn't deserve to be comforted.

"And on top of it," he went on, "now I know I'm worse than the monsters I used to hunt."

"You didn't infect Boone. The virus wasn't in your saliva yet."

"Doesn't matter. I tried to. 'Cause that's who I am."

"You can't define yourself by one stupid, angry action. You saved Aaron's life." *You saved my life.* "You brought him here — and all those other infected people. And if you come to Arsenal with me and take the cure, you'll be able to keep on helping people. Because *that's* who you are."

He shook his head. "I have to put Gabe down. If I'd done it years ago like I should've, Aaron would still be living at Heartland with his mom," he said bitterly.

"Why can't someone else put him down?"

"I owe it to him. He didn't want to end up this way." Rafe hesitated and looked away.

"What?" I said.

"She promised him — he made Sophie promise —"

Promise me, Lane.

"What? What did she promise him?" I asked hoarsely.

"That she would put him down when he turned."

Just like Hagen and her daughter, Delilah. Rafe had told Everson and me that when Delilah got infected, Hagen knew she couldn't put Delilah down herself, so she'd asked Rafe to do it. And Rafe, burning with fever, had forced me to make that same awful promise. How many times had this same scenario played out on this side of the wall — loved ones making heartbreaking promises they hoped they'd never have to keep?

"And after Sophie died," Rafe said, "I knew I had to keep that promise for her. But every time I have him in my sights . . . I can't do it. Even now." He held out his hands and examined them in the moonlight, as if looking for signs that his mutation was progressing.

I finally understood why my promise had seemed so important to him. I wondered if, after surviving the first stage of infection in Chicago, he'd come back to Heartland in part to finally fulfill Sophie's promise to Gabe.

"When I first started hunting ferals, I could still see the human in them, and it was hard. Killing them made me hard. But not when it came to Gabe. Even after what he did to my sister, I couldn't pull the trigger. It's stupid. I know that thing's not him — not the guy who loved Sophie and looked out for me." He looked up at me again. His mouth tightened. "But he's the only family I have left."

"You have us — me and my dad. He's like a father to you."

"A mentor, not a father."

"I saw that mural you painted in the prison. My dad and two kids — you and me."

"I don't think of Mack as a dad, and I don't think of you as a sister."

The look he gave me made my skin warm. If I was being honest with myself, I didn't think of him as a brother either.

Rafe looked away. "I used to think: *Maybe those Titan docs will come up with a cure. Why should I kill him when he still might have a shot at coming back?* But that was just a story I was telling myself. Gabe's been too far gone for too long. I've just got to do it."

He looked heartbroken but determined.

"Okay," I said. "When do we leave?"

"Thanks. But Gabe's not your problem."

"Yes, he is." At Rafe's skeptical look, the words burst out of me. "I feel like . . ." *Like you're mine.* "Like I'm part of your story, and you're part of mine." When Rafe shrugged like that was a given, I felt bold enough to add, "You've always been my favorite character."

"Yeah," he said, again unsurprised. "I'm me. And Mack tells good stories," he allowed.

"I'm trying to say that I care what happens to you."

"Don't. You don't have to feel bad about anything."

"That's not why —"

"You want to know what's going to happen to me?" He pointed toward the barn — toward Scribe. "You just saw it."

I sighed in frustration. Why did he keep insisting that he was doomed to die insane and alone? "Come back to the base with me and you can take the cure."

"Sure. Go back with the stiff, and I'll catch up with you."

I could tell by the flat look in his eyes that Rafe had no intention of coming to the base.

"Don't tell me what to do," I said. "Besides, killing Gabe won't be enough. Those hunters are going to blame you for Boone's death. They'll come after you unless we can prove the

Komodo-man is real. We need to bring them his body, and then maybe they'll leave you alone. I promised I'd come back and find you, to give you the cure or to" — I could barely choke out the words — "put you down if you'd gone feral. And I was so happy to find out that you hadn't gone feral —"

"I thought you'd send a hunter, not come yourself," he said with disgust. "I never should have asked for that promise. Forget it, okay? We're good. We're clear. Enough people around here hate me. One of them will put me down sooner or later. You don't have to keep that promise. I release you."

He started to turn away from me, but I lunged forward and caught him by the shirt.

"I don't want to be released," I said. "I want you to stop lying to me about what's really going on with you."

Rafe's expression darkened, and with a growl in his throat, he stepped toward me until he had me backed up against the cabin. He put his hands on either side of my head and leaned in close, his eyes glinting in the dim light. I wanted to be a lioness, but my heart was beating like a rabbit's.

"You want to know the truth, Lane? Every day I think about what I did. What I didn't do. I cut you. Left you alone in a chimpa warren. I shouldn't have even let you step outside that house by yourself —"

I'd gone outside alone to pee. I cleared my tightening throat. "You couldn't have stopped that one."

"Wrong. You want to hear the ways we could have done that different? Because I swear I've thought of them all."

His voice had gotten hoarse. I watched his lips to make sure I was hearing his words right — words that felt like a warm wave washing through me, taking away my fear.

His hand drifted to my face to cup my cheek. "But you don't have to worry about that ever again. When I'm with you, I'll keep you safe. You can count on it."

He dropped his hand and stepped back, never breaking eye contact. His promise, his intensity, sent a shudder through me. But it wasn't from fear. It was from something much, much hotter. I stepped closer and put my hands on his chest, wanting his kiss more than anything, but his eyes widened and he froze.

"No, Lane."

"You haven't been infected that long. It doesn't get into the saliva until close to the end."

"You think I'm going to chance that with you?"

His eyes were glowing in the darkness, but now they were beautiful to me, like precious gems.

"Okay," I said heavily. "Then let's go kill the dragon."

"Think again, silky. You're staying right here, even if I have to tie you up and leave you in this cabin," he said, eyes narrowed as if he was actually considering it.

"Try it," I dared. "I'd love to wrestle with you. You'll have to get really close to get a rope on me, and I'm sure I can get a kiss in somehow."

He hauled back several paces. "That's not funny."

Actually his horrified expression was kind of funny. But then his look became pained.

"Lane —"

"Oh, give up," I said, cutting him off. "I can either go with you, or I can follow you. Isn't it just easier to take me along?" I gave him my most winning smile. He scowled in return.

Rafe and I joined the crowd at the bonfire long enough for Rafe to get a rifle from Cohiba and to find out from Little One which cabins were empty. I told Everson that Rafe and I would be leaving at dawn to find Gabe and put him down.

"Well, that's the worst idea I've heard in a while," he said, running his hand over his buzz cut. "And I've heard some bad ideas lately." No doubt he had, spending so much time with the lionesses.

"We'll meet you back here," I said, "and we'll all go to Arsenal together to get the cure."

"Why don't we all go find Gabe together as well?" Everson said. "I think we'll all be safer if we stick together."

His logic seemed airtight, and I was too tired to argue. He said he'd talk to the lionesses, and we agreed to meet at the gateway at dawn. I didn't say anything to Rafe. If Everson had learned to get along with the lionesses, maybe Rafe could too.

As Rafe and I walked together toward our cabin, I worked up the nerve to slip my hand into his and smiled inwardly when he didn't shake me off.

"Why do people call you Wraith?" I asked.

"You like it?"

"It was your idea?"

"Cool, right?" His eyes danced with amusement. "I almost went with Wrath, but who has the energy to live up to that?"

I went light-headed at the sound of his laughter, the feeling of laughing with him. And yet, there was so much more I wanted to know. "What happened after you left me in the zoo?"

"I don't remember much," he admitted with a shrug. "The fever came on fast. Then Dromo found me. He and some of the other waiters tackled me and then tied me to a bed until my fever broke."

"Dromo was a butler," I corrected. I hadn't liked the ginger-haired man infected with ram, who'd been the queen's toady — not at first. Later, I realized Dromo played the part of officious servant in order to survive the chaos that was Chorda's court. I wasn't surprised now to hear that he'd helped Rafe.

"Were the manimals able to overthrow the handlers?" I asked.

Rafe nodded. "I stayed for a while. They've got a good setup going. But I didn't drag you out here, to the last empty cabin in camp, to talk about Chicago."

"What?"

Suddenly, my brain and body were fully awake, and not just because the night had turned chilly. I stole a sidelong look at him as we walked along the path. He caught it, of course, and pulled me in close to his side. We paused at the door to the cabin, and when he turned to me, the electricity between us seemed almost visible, like tiny sparks in the darkness.

"Come on, silky. Let's turn in," he coaxed, mockingly seductive.

I laughed nervously. Could he tell with his supersenses that I was blushing? I hurried ahead of him up the rotting steps of cabin 21.

The cabin had built-in bunks with crunchy foam mattresses and thin wool blankets. I winced to think how old the mattresses were and what microorganisms lived inside them. But I was bone-tired, and an old mattress was better than the floor.

Rafe toed off his boots and came to stand in front of me, his hands in his pockets, his eyes glowing in the dark. And there it was again, that electricity between us, short-circuiting my ability to think.

"Which bunk do you want?" he asked, casual once more. But I was through backtracking.

"Whichever one you're in," I said.

His eyes widened at my boldness, and I felt an exhilarating flash of victory. I climbed into the bottom bunk and scooted close to the wall to make room for him. I spread out the blanket, and he lay down under it, facing me. We locked eyes, and I reached out and touched his stomach, his rib cage. His muscles tensed as if he might leap away at any moment. His eyes searched my face, and then he groaned and reached for me, sliding his hand under my shirt and over the curve of my waist. I sucked in a breath at the contact, and he shuddered as if answering me.

"Silky," he murmured. "That's your manimal name. Not that you'll ever need one."

"I want to kiss you."

"We can't." He sounded gutted. "I shouldn't even be this close to you."

"But it's just right . . ." I whispered, snuggling in close to him, and he tightened his hold on me, and we slept.

What must have been hours later, I woke alone in the dark to the sound of gunfire.

· TWENTY-FIVE ·

"Rafe!" I lurched out of the bunk, slung my backpack over my shoulders, and stumbled out of the cabin. It was still pitch-black outside, hours before daylight. I didn't see Rafe anywhere. He couldn't have left the camp without me. He wouldn't. Would he?

The shots were coming from somewhere near the front of the property. I sidled along the cabins toward the dining hall, where I found Everson loading his rifle.

"What's happening?"

"The patrol's here!"

"What do they want?"

"Rafe," he said grimly.

"He's gone," I said. "He left while I was sleeping."

"Typical," Everson said. "But now I'm kind of glad he did."

I nodded, my throat tight with emotion. I followed Everson to the fence, staying clear of the open archway. Light shafted between the slats — flashlights or gun sights. Why didn't the line guards just come in, with no gate to stop them? Then it occurred to me: They were afraid of infection.

Everson glanced up at the tree stand on our side of the archway, where Mahari, Deepnita, and Neve crouched among the budding branches.

"Attack them," Everson snapped at them, "and we're done!"

With a snarl, Mahari jumped down from the platform to face him. "They're attacking us."

I climbed the slats nailed to the trunk and hauled myself onto the tree stand to try to see what was going on outside the fence. Deepnita, Neve, and I watched as a guard wearing night-vision goggles motioned to his team to spread out. Moving quickly, they set up a series of boxes along the fence.

Captain Hyrax motioned to the guards and then put on padded headphones. The others did the same as the guard next to Hyrax fiddled with a small handheld device. On Hyrax's nod, the guard flipped a switch, and a high-frequency whine cut through the night. I clamped my hands to my ears while Deepnita and Neve writhed and yowled on the platform next to me. Howls erupted from all over the campground, some tortured, some angry. Just as abruptly, the sound cut out. The howling took longer to fade.

Hyrax smiled at the manimals' distress. "Bring Rafe out, and it stops," he shouted. "Fail to bring him, we power up the flamethrowers and burn down this garbage dump."

The three of us scrambled down from the platform and huddled with Everson and Mahari.

"How did they find us?" I asked.

"Best guess, one of us is carrying a tracking chip. Could be tucked into a jacket."

"Or implanted in Mahari," I snapped.

Her glowing eyes narrowed. "What?"

I wasn't about to tell her that in the West, most pet owners implanted tracking chips in their beloved animals these days.

Everson frowned but didn't discount my theory.

"I told you to let us take Rafe's blood," Mahari said to Everson. "Then we'd already be on our way to Arsenal, and I wouldn't have to kill these humans."

Deepnita and Neve nodded. Wait, when had Mahari and Everson discussed the lionesses taking Rafe's blood? And what else had they been talking about behind my back? It was a good thing they hadn't tried. I didn't want to picture what a showdown between Rafe and the pride would look like.

"I saw a place in the fence where we can slip outside and pounce from behind," Deepnita said. "Their first mistake is thinking they've got the upper hand."

"Show me where," Mahari said.

Neve bounced up and down. "Yay! We get to pounce!"

"I don't pounce, but I can attack in my own way," Happy said, holding up a crossbow. He and the other manimals had begun to gather around us.

"Me too," Little One said.

"I'm in," said Vengeance, his mottled skin glistening in the dark.

"Are the children someplace safe?" I asked Little One.

She nodded grimly. "Kindness is with them in the storm cellar, but they're scared."

"Nobody's pouncing. Or attacking," Everson said, and everyone turned toward him. He stepped up to Mahari until they stood toe to toe, chest to chest. She jutted out a hip, all casual nonchalance, but I could feel the tension crackling between them.

"You're not doing this," he said.

"You have a better plan, human?" Mahari asked, acid dripping from her voice, and a murmur rose from the manimals.

"They have machine guns and flamethrowers," Everson countered. "And you have *claws*."

"Oh, no, we have much more than that," she purred. "We're walking, talking weapons. Bioweapons. One bucket of our blood dumped from on high, and I guarantee they'll scatter."

"Yeah," Everson agreed. "They'll scatter . . . and then pull out the grenade launchers."

"Back off," she ordered the others. "I need to make this guard see sense."

They backed off fast.

"Without Wraith's blood," Mahari hissed at Everson, "we have no bargaining chip to trade for the cure." She tilted her head up until she was nose to nose with him. "You really think we're going to back down from this fight? We have nothing to lose . . . except our minds."

Something occurred to me in a flash. "Wait!" I said. "We do have another bargaining chip!"

Everson and Mahari turned to me in tandem. I stared intently at Everson. "Hyrax knows you're here, right? He has to."

Realization dawned in Everson's eyes. "Lane," he said with a warning in his voice.

"Back at the lab, you said you were just trying to help. So help."

Everson groaned. His shoulders sagged.

"What are you guys talking about?" Neve asked, looking from Everson's face to mine and back again. "Do we still get to pounce?"

"How can he help?" Mahari demanded.

"I'm your bargaining chip. You'll take me hostage and exchange me for the cure," Everson said.

"They won't make that deal," Mahari snapped. "You're one guard among hundreds."

"Not to my mother."

"Your mother?"

"Ilsa Prejean. She owns it all — the wall, the patrol, the lab — it's all hers."

"That's why they call you the prince!" Mahari said with a gasp, and then a slow grin spread over her black lips.

Everson was not intimidated — or amused. "Don't ever call me that."

"The other guards used to joke about locking you in with me," Mahari went on in a purr. "One even promised to free me if I took a bite out of you. I would've done it if I'd ever gotten the chance. Not that I trusted him to keep his end of the bargain — I just liked the idea of you turning into one of us. I like it even better now that I know you're Ilsa Prejean's son."

Everson eyed her. "You say my mother's name like you know her."

"Yes, we're old friends. We used to have little chats. Just her and me."

"Chats?" he scoffed.

"Her on a screen," Mahari went on. "Me in a cage."

"About what?" he demanded.

"The zone. About what's out there and how to kill it."

My heart sped up. "And you told her?"

Mahari cut me an exasperated look. "I told her exactly how I'd disembowel her the first chance I got." She held up splayed claws.

"Perfect!" I pulled out Spurling's dial. "Stay just like that."

Everson swung to me. "How is that perfect?"

"Your mother already knows she's a bloodthirsty beast." I glanced at Mahari. "No offense."

Mahari grinned. "None taken."

"She's a threat," I explained quickly. "A very, very dangerous threat."

The crease between Everson's brows deepened. "To who?"

"You." I beckoned to Neve. "Still ready to pounce?"

She bounced in place. "On him?" She pointed at Everson.

"No," Mahari snapped.

"Yes," I said. A split second after I hit record, Neve took him down.

As Everson shoved and shouted at her to get off, Deepnita dropped to her knees by his shoulders, tossed his gun aside, and caught hold of his hands. With a laugh, Neve scrambled back to straddle his thighs, pinning them down with her considerable weight. Another guy might have enjoyed wrestling with a pair of wild, beautiful women, but Everson looked furious as he fought to throw them off. And he almost succeeded. But then Mahari dropped onto his chest and took the breath right out of him. Literally.

I recorded it all, sweat sliming my skin because it looked all too real. Certainly Everson was acquiring very real bruises. I hissed in a breath when Mahari tore open his shirt with her claws and then raked them down his chest — hard enough to leave red welts, but light enough not to draw blood.

With a jerk of my hand, I got Deepnita to pull him into a sitting position. Mahari slid down to settle on his lap. She leaned back into Neve's embrace as I edged closer, trying to get the best angle. Neve rested her chin on Mahari's shoulder, fangs bared, looking dangerously unhinged. When she snarled at him, my nerves jerked taut. Was she so caught up in the moment she'd forgotten it was an act? I jabbed a finger at Everson, directing him to speak. Coughing and sputtering, he struggled to catch his breath.

"Captain Hyrax," he finally rasped. "Take the guards and go. If you attack the camp, they'll infect me. The only way they'll free me is if you bring them a hundred doses of the antigen and a hundred blood tests. Only Bear Lake can make the drop. Please pass this on to my mother. If she doesn't give them the cure, they'll infect me. Without it, they've got nothing to lose."

I climbed into the tree stand and located Captain Hyrax among the guards. Then I projected the video in 3-D outside the fence where he would see it. I played it twice, and the second time he held up his lapel mic, letting someone else hear the threat. Then he had a heated conversation via radio with, I assumed, Chairman Prejean.

Hyrax approached the archway and shouted, "The terms have been received and accepted."

A low cheer went up below me inside the compound.

Outside the fence, Hyrax made a circular motion with his hand above his head. "Withdraw!" he shouted. "I repeat, we are withdrawing, people!"

The line guards fell into formation and moved back into the dark forest. I wondered where their hovercopters were and hoped it was nowhere near where Rafe was going. Where I was going.

I climbed down from the tree and found Everson.

"Hyrax came all this way for two things," I said. "You and Rafe's blood. He can't touch you, so what're the chances he's going after Rafe right now? I have to find him. I have to warn him the guards are close," I said. "And then I'm going to Heartland Compound and showing them the footage I shot here. They need to know that their family members are still alive. I need to tell them. To *show* them." I held up the dial. "So they can help their loved ones if the patrol comes back."

"Right," Everson said. "'Cause footage of infected people worked so well in the West. You know what the reaction was? Terror. Not 'How can we help?' but 'Hire more guards.'"

"I have to try," I snapped. "These people don't have the luxury of time."

Everson crossed his arms over his chest. "Fine," he said reluctantly. "But I'm going with you."

"I'm going too," someone said from behind me.

I turned around. It was Aaron.

"Aaron, no," I said. "It's too dangerous. And you've been sick."

"I feel fine, strong," he said. He showed no signs of infection. If he took a Ferae test now, I wondered if it would come back negative, as Rafe had suggested.

"With Boone gone," Aaron said, "they might listen to us. I think they'll come. Besides, I know how to get into the compound without the lookouts seeing us. I know who to talk to."

Everson and I exchanged a look — it would be crazy to turn Aaron down.

"Okay," Everson said. "We'll go to Gabe's territory first and find Rafe. Then we'll backtrack to Heartland."

"That'll take too long. I'll find Rafe." I pushed the dial into Everson's hand. "You go to Heartland and show them what's on here."

Everson gave me a look, and I thought he was going to argue with me, but then he nodded curtly and pocketed the dial. "All right. We'll hike together to just outside Heartland, near the place where we camped. Can you find Gabe's territory from there?"

I nodded and hoped it was true. I took off my backpack and dug around in it until I found my compass, which I hooked to a belt loop. Someone behind me touched my shoulder. It was Little One.

"Good luck," she said. Then she held out a pistol in a holster and two loaded magazines. "Here," she said. "It's an extra. In case you need more than luck." She hugged me.

My hands shook as I pushed one of the magazines into the gun and threaded my belt through the holster. I stowed the extra magazine in my backpack.

Everson turned to Mahari. "Set a twenty-four-hour watch," he said. "I don't think Hyrax will come back — the stakes are too high — but plan an evacuation just in case. And brainstorm ideas for defense against the sonic weapon they used. That could be devastating."

"You'd better be careful, guard," Mahari hissed. "If anything happens to you, we lose everything."

· TWENTY-SIX ·

When Everson, Aaron, and I set out, the woods were utterly black, and mist had begun to blanket the forest floor. Everson, in the lead, carried a glow stick, but we couldn't risk any more light, with all the ferals prowling around at night. Every so often, we heard rustling in the brush nearby, and once, we heard the truncated scream of a rabbit. Twice something howled, making the hair on the back of my neck stand on end.

Everson gave me a glow stick of my own hours later, when we reached the point where our paths would part. By then, the sun was up, and I tucked the light into my backpack and hoped that I wouldn't need it, that by nightfall we would all be back at Echo.

I started the solo part of my hike, checking my compass often, and soon I located the path that Boone and I had taken. Up the cliff and through the woods, until I reached the ravine. The ropes still dangled from the tree on the other side, but Boone had gotten across somehow, and I had to find the crossing. I stuck close to the edge and headed toward the source of the snowmelt. The tallest peaks. I hoped Gabe would stay on his side of the ravine until I got there.

I tasted blood and realized I'd been biting the inside of my cheek. No surprise. I was close to losing the lock I had on my fear. I couldn't believe I was looking for Gabe rather than looking for ways to avoid him for the rest of my life. But wherever he was, that's where I would find Rafe, so all I could do was put my blinders on and plunge forward.

From the top of the ridge, I spotted a narrow section of the ravine where a fallen tree lay across it — maybe the tree Everson and the pride had put there when they were looking for me. That's where I crossed, inch by inch on my hands and knees, not looking down.

I didn't find Rafe until late afternoon when I climbed a pine tree to mask my scent and get a lay of the land. I spotted him in the distance, creeping through the foliage at the edge of a steep drop-off. He paused to extend the back handle of his gun and click it into place. Had he spotted Gabe with his tiger-enhanced vision, or was he just waiting for Gabe to show up? I started to shimmy down the tree, planning to circle back so I could come up behind him. Alerting him to my presence from this distance might also alert Gabe, and I figured Rafe would catch my scent before I reached him.

Suddenly Rafe's head whipped to the left, and a split second later, he roared and spasmed so hard he fell over. Line guards swarmed out of the woods to surround him. One was holding a Taser.

"No!" I screamed, scrambling the rest of the way down the tree and crashing through the brush toward them.

By the time I reached the spot where Rafe had been standing, the guards had bound his hands and feet and were carrying him away at a quick pace through the trees and down the rocky slope out of sight.

I sprinted to catch up with them, shouting, "Just take his blood! You don't need *him*!"

I was gaining on them, pebbles cascading down the slope under my feet. They were headed for the two hover-copters in the clearing below. Halfway down the slope, Captain Hyrax stepped from behind a pine, between the guards and me, talking into his radio. "Asset acquired," he said.

"Why are you taking him?" I shouted at him as the guards threw Rafe's inert body into one of the copters. "You only need a blood sample!"

As I tried to run past Hyrax, his hand shot out and caught my arm and spun me around.

"*You.*" He said it as though it were a curse word. He tightened his grip. "Where's Cruz? What did those infected animals do to him?"

"Nothing. He's fine."

Hyrax unholstered his sidearm, and my panic spiked. "I'm tempted to put a bullet in you right here," he said, "for no other reason than you've been a thorn in my side since you set foot on my base."

Hyrax's radio beeped. "Captain, sir," a voice said. "We've got the blood sample. What should we do with him?"

Hyrax paused and then said into his radio, "Leave him. Get your shots in now. Departure in five."

I pulled against his grip. "What do you mean, 'Get your shots in'?"

Hyrax snorted. "He'll be lucky if they leave him alive."

I craned my neck to get a glimpse of the hovercopter and watched as the guards pulled Rafe out, still bound, and threw him to the ground. One kicked him, hard, with an ugly laughter. Another drew back and sent his fist into Rafe's face. A crazy feeling was building in me, making me feel seriously feral. But then something rustled the bushes at the top of the ridge, in the direction Rafe had been aiming his rifle. When a foul smell rode in on the breeze, I reared against Hyrax's grip. "It's coming. Let me go!"

"You think I'm stupid?" Hyrax shoved the gun's muzzle into my gut. "You think —"

With a low rumble, Gabe rose out of the brush. Hyrax wheeled around, dropping my arm as Gabe smashed through the foliage and ran for us, faster than I'd ever seen anything move. I scrambled backward, without turning, without taking my eyes from the horror unfolding. Jaws wide and dripping, Gabe leapt for Hyrax. The gun blasted, but wildly, as Gabe slashed into Hyrax's midsection with his six-inch claws. Screaming, Hyrax fell back, the Komodo-man locked on top of him, a blur of claws and serrated teeth.

Shouting erupted inside the second hovercopter, and guards spilled out. I ran toward them — toward Rafe — while they raced toward the horrible scene. The guards from the first 'copter joined them, leaving Rafe motionless on the ground.

"Run!" I screamed as I passed through them, but they didn't listen.

I skittered to a stop at Rafe's side. Some ignorant guard had slapped a piece of duct tape over his beautiful mouth, probably to keep him from biting. His eyes were closed, and there were purple-red marks on his cheek, jaw, and eye.

"Rafe," I said, pulling the tape from his mouth, "you have to wake up. We have to go." I patted his waist, looking for one of his knives to cut through the zip ties that bound his wrists and ankles. His eyes opened a crack, showcasing the golden starbursts at their centers. He smiled crookedly up at me.

"Just can't get enough, huh?" he rasped.

"Shh. Gabe's coming."

I heard yelling, a flurry of gunshots, and one guard and then another scream. Boots pounded through the brush and down the bluff as several guards finally took my advice. When my fingertips brushed Rafe's knife, I snatched it from its sheath. Clumsy with adrenaline, I sawed desperately at the zip tie on his wrists when the stench of rancid meat overwhelmed me. Gagging, I pushed the knife into Rafe's hand and looked into his eyes for what I hoped was not the last time.

"Run," he hissed, his gaze hard. "Now."

"Planning on it," I said and then heaved him under the hovercopter as Gabe crashed through the trees into the clearing.

"Lane, no!" Rafe shouted.

"Gabe!" I yelled while shuffling sideways, away from Rafe. When Gabe's bloodshot eyes started tracking me, I whirled and ran for the fallen tree, unholstering my pistol as I went. The ground trembled under Gabe's weight as he pounded after me. I wouldn't glance back. I couldn't. If I saw his insane face behind me, his drool-coated teeth, my brain would melt. So I ran with total abandon, whipping around trees and scrambling over boulders, pausing only long enough to hear something crashing through the woods behind me — too large to be a guard. I launched forward, boot landing on a loose rock, and barely caught myself. I didn't fall, but my ankle twisted under me, bringing instant agony.

A hiss cut the air . . .

I glanced back long enough to see a dark shape bearing down on me. I steadied my hand and got off three shots, but there was no change in Gabe's pace. I took off again, closing in on the ravine, eyes burning from the stabbing pain in my ankle. *Faster*, my brain urged, but I was nowhere near the fallen tree. I almost jumped blind, but then I saw what was beneath me: rapids, ten feet down.

"Lane, jump!" a voice shouted. Little One stood ahead of me on the other side of the ravine, waving both arms.

"Jump!"

Was she insane?

Gabe in all his gory glory came loping out of the dark woods. Dead skin peeling in strips off muscle-packed arms, claws extended from fingertips. Ragged bits of flesh and hair hung from his teeth. When my gaze met his, those starved, feral eyes of his gave me the jolt I needed and I jumped.

· TWENTY-SEVEN ·

I fell, hurtling through the air, eyes shut, crying out as I hit the frigid water. My lungs screamed for air. My frozen legs kicked. I sucked in a gasping breath at the surface. Water surged into my nose, bringing me a shot of clarity. Back to myself.

Blinking against the spray, I zoomed past trees and rocks. I screamed as my fingers scrabbled across the steep sides of the ravine, barely keeping my head above the surface. Growing dizzy and sick as the currents spun me around and around. My stomach lurched. When I heaved, water flooded my mouth, choking me.

A boulder loomed. Instead of parting to the sides, the stream rushed straight for it. Would I bash against it? End up pinned there forever by the rushing water? At the last second, the current tossed me to the left. And suddenly the stream seemed to smooth out before me, and I was simply adrift.

A howl ricocheted off the rock walls, and I glanced back in time to see Gabe the lizard-man fly past the boulder. He had followed me into the ravine and was caught up in the current as well! He tumbled along behind me, mottled skin glistening, gulping in water with every bob. At that moment, he spotted me and thrashed about as if trying to catch up.

Even half-drowned, he hunted me, his ravenous gaze intent, jaws snapping.

The water quickened again, propelling us both along, but I could swear he was moving faster. Gaining on me. Gasping and choking, I threw myself backward in the water, but somehow he lunged at me, claws extended, his horrible, foul mouth open to bite —

Then a gunshot echoed like a cannon blast in the ravine. Gabe fell back, away from me, and one of his pale eyes exploded with blood. And then another shot, on the heels of the first, and Gabe's other eye disappeared, and his body writhed for a few seconds and then went limp. Tendrils of his blood swirled away on the current. His body, floating now, continued to ride the current beside me.

I struggled to look up toward the edge of the ravine in the direction of the shots. There was a figure there, silhouetted against the darkening sky. A figure I would have recognized anywhere. How had Rafe freed himself so quickly? He'd had a driving reason, that's how. He'd needed to fulfill his sister's promise to Gabe. And he had. And he'd saved me from getting infected or eaten alive in the process.

He jogged along the edge of the ravine, keeping pace with me while yelling something. I couldn't catch a single word between the rush of the stream and water slapping at my ears. Rafe stabbed a finger downstream and then jogged back into the woods.

I kicked against the current, bobbing above the froth long enough to see the stream widening up ahead and then . . . Terror shot through me as I fell into the spray once more, but it was too late to unsee it. The water dropping away in the distance — into nothing. Into a waterfall! And I was crashing and splashing right for it. In minutes, I'd be swept over those rocks.

Kicking frantically, I tried to surge above the surface and stay there. I came up fast on a large branch whipping against the current where it had lodged between some rocks. I grabbed on, tearing my palms as it dragged through my grip, but the waterlogged branch bent under my weight and splintered.

Exhausted and battered, I thrashed around, desperately searching for something, anything, to grab hold of. But then another voice rose above the rush of the water. Shouts echoed off the rock, seeming to come from all around me. I flung myself upward over and over, searching the ledge that ran along the right side of the ravine. In flashes, I spotted figures there, and on the left side too! All waving and shouting and arranged like they were playing tug-of-war with a rope strung between them — hanging inches above the water.

Just then the current whipped me around backward. Thrashing against it, I tried to turn back before I missed the rope. I would only have seconds to find it. I swept out my deadened arms but felt nothing. I swept them out again and felt it but couldn't catch hold. Couldn't — I had it! Hooked it with an elbow even though my flesh was so battered and numb I could barely hold on. With a cry, I clung with numb hands to my lifeline, bobbing like a cork. Gabe's body hit the rope just after I caught it and made it jerk in my hands.

Instantly, the group on the left side of the ravine released their end of the rope, and Gabe's body, freed, disappeared over the falls a moment later. The current caught me again, whipping me toward the drop-off as the rope's slack played out. I held on as best I could as my rescuers hauled me toward the steep side of the ravine. Looking up, I could see now that it was the recon group from Camp Echo — Happy and Little One and Vengeance and a couple of other manimals — and Rafe.

They hauled me up the side of the ravine, and when I finally flopped onto the ledge above the rapids, everyone cheered, including the group on the opposite bank.

Rafe and Little One crouched beside me as I huffed in breaths through clenched teeth. Rafe had a broad smile on his beat-up face — I'd never seen him smile that way — and when I sat up and then tried to get to my feet, he put his arms around me and held me tightly to keep me seated.

"Relax, silky," he said into my ear. "Enough heroics for one day."

I shook uncontrollably. Each breath was agony. My ankle screamed, and my palm throbbed. I tried to smile, but my teeth were chattering too violently.

Vengeance took something from his pack and gave it to Happy, and he and Rafe wrapped a foil thermal blanket around me. Then Rafe gently squeezed the water from my ponytail and pulled the hood of the foil blanket over my head. He sat down behind me, and I leaned back against his chest as he put his arms around me. The warmth of his body gradually sank into me, and my trembling calmed.

On the other side of the ravine, I saw Everson and Aaron and others who looked human — they must have come from Heartland. I gave a grateful, if weak, wave, and they cheered again.

"We're coming over!" Everson shouted, and Happy gave him two thumbs up.

"What are you guys doing here?" I asked Little One in amazement.

"We decided to trail the guards all the way to their 'copters," Little One said. "We figured if they started back for Echo, we could easily outpace them and warn the others."

"We were in the woods with you," Vengeance said, pushing back his fedora, "watching the 'copters and waiting for Rafe to take the Komodo out. So we saw what went down. Lucky for us, the group from Heartland showed up across the way. Otherwise we were going to send Happy down on the rope to try to fish you out."

"How did you get the rope across?" I asked.

Happy beamed. "That was my idea. I tied a rock to the cut end and threw it across."

"Thank you." I reached out and grasped his long, strong fingers. "Thank you all."

I stared toward the waterfall where Gabe had gone over. My stomach curled in on itself when I thought of how close he'd come to biting me. I turned to look at Rafe, fumbling for the words to thank him.

"Nice shot," I said finally.

He wasn't smiling anymore. In fact, his face was completely still, his eyes carefully blank, as though he'd pulled on a mask.

"Not sure why you'd do something so stupid," he said, and I flinched.

Really? After what we'd both gone through today? Then it occurred to me that I'd scared him badly by drawing Gabe away from the hovercopter.

I tamped down my own defensive anger. "If I was down and hurt," I said, "what would you have done? The same thing." An image flashed in my mind — Rafe, in the cage at the Lincoln Park Zoo, slamming into Chorda to keep him from ripping out my heart.

"Why'd you save my life back in Chicago?" I asked.

He stared at me, his face still expressionless.

"Tell me," I pressed, not breaking eye contact with him, not caring that others were listening. With effort, I got onto my knees, put a hand on each of his hard thighs, and leaned toward him on my trembling arms. "Please."

My insistence shifted something in him. His mouth relaxed, and his eyes lost that flat look I'd come to dread. A warm light came into them, as if he was recognizing me in a crowd. "You know why," he said.

I gave him a shaky smile. "Uh-huh. Same reason I did it. Same reason I'm here." I leaned in until our foreheads touched.

Just then Everson and Aaron and the group from Heartland arrived on our side of the ravine, having crossed at the tree farther upstream.

Everson crouched to examine my injuries.

"No cuts," he announced after peeling off my flak jacket.

Rafe hoisted my jacket with one finger. "I guess we can thank the line patrol for something."

"Did any of the lizard's blood get on you or near you in the water?" Everson asked.

I shook my head.

"I wouldn't have let that happen," Rafe said from behind me.

"Yeah, well, some things are out of our control." Everson lifted my foot and turned it from side to side and prodded my swollen purple ankle. "It's not broken," he said. "But you can't put any weight on it for a while." He squinted up at Rafe. "Find something she can use as a crutch."

"Yes, sir," Rafe said mockingly, but he rose and headed into the woods.

Everson made a makeshift splint for me out of sticks and cord, and Rafe brought me a couple of tall thick branches I could use for support on the hike back to Camp Echo.

"Your turn," Everson said to Rafe. "What happened?"

"What can I say? A couple of guards got me in a compromising position."

Rafe allowed Everson to check the injuries on his face. Then he hitched up his shirt on the left side, and I gasped at the storm-dark bruises where the guard had kicked him. When Everson felt along his ribs, Rafe winced.

"They're not broken," Everson pronounced. "But this bruising is bad, so don't get any bright ideas about carrying Lane back to Camp Echo. One of them could be cracked, and it could break and puncture a lung, if you're not careful."

Rafe shot Everson a belligerent look as he pulled his shirt down.

Everson helped me to my feet, and I squeezed his hands. "I'm double-timing it back to Camp Echo," he said. "It'll mean trouble for Mahari — and for all them — if the patrol comes back and I'm not there."

Rafe's expression turned sly. "So you and Mahari, huh?" He held up his fist for a bump.

What?

Everson literally looked down his nose at Rafe, ignoring the raised fist. "What are you talking about?"

Rafe smirked. "When I was leaving Echo last night, I saw the lionesses sleeping next to the fire, but there were only two of them. Where, I wondered, was Mahari? I couldn't believe she'd fall for Glenfiddich's lame come-ons. Then I caught wind of you two tucked up together in cabin five. Don't worry, I didn't get close enough to hear anything."

All the manimals and humans gathered with us on the ridge were, of course, listening, and someone chuckled.

Everson's cheek twitched as he fought to keep his irritation in check. "You can wipe that look off your face. She's the only person who annoys me more than you."

Rafe held up his hands in mock surrender. "Whoa, you're further gone than I thought."

"Bite me."

"Hah. Look at that. Now you're trying to change for her. That's sweet." Rafe waved him off. "But I gotta turn you down. You'd make a lousy tiger."

Everson actually laughed at that.

My initial surprise about him and Mahari faded quickly. Everson's change of heart toward her and the others just proved that I'd been on the right track when I uploaded my video, even if that version was too scary. Hopefully this version would heal the rift. I still had to do interviews with the healthy people living in Moline for Director Spurling, but that didn't have to be the only footage I gave her. The people in the West needed to see the manimals up close — hear about their lives. Who can resist a story filled with struggle and heartbreak and love? Who could remain indifferent?

I smiled at Everson. "If you don't leave, he's just going to keep talking."

"Right," Everson said, pulling on his backpack and zipping his jacket against the chilly evening air. "Take your time getting back to camp," he ordered. "Go slow on that ankle."

Vengeance approached us. "Happy and I are going with you. We wouldn't want to lose our hostage to a feral."

Everson nodded, and the three of them set off along the ravine.

The rest of us followed more slowly and found a place in the forest to camp for the night. As we were gathering wood for a fire, we spotted the hovercopters rising above the treetops in the dark sky, on their way back to Arsenal. The surviving guards had apparently returned to the scene and gathered their dead. Rafe and I exchanged a look.

"That means your blood's on the way to Dr. Solis," I said.

"I wonder how long we've got before the patrol tries to take back the East."

I shivered thinking about what Hyrax had said about feral eradication. Moline, so close to Arsenal, would surely be one of their first targets. "I need to warn my dad and the others."

"Yeah," Rafe agreed. "But you've got some time. They won't hit Moline till they've got more than one squad of vaccinated guards."

He was right. Dr. Solis couldn't develop the vaccine overnight. I settled by the fire and tried to will my muscles to relax.

The bonfire burned hot and bright as the people from Heartland shared bread and jerky and dried fruit with the manimals from Camp Echo. I ate one of my last three protein bars, which was miraculously dry in its foil wrapper. Rafe went off in the dark to gather what belongings he had squirreled away in the caves, which included a sleeping bag and an extra shirt that he gave me to wear while my own shirts, jacket, and backpack dried next to the fire.

We slept on the sleeping bag, under the foil blanket, his arm resting protectively across my stomach. I fell asleep immediately, to the sound of Rafe's breath like waves lapping near my ear. I dreamed that I was running from Gabe, crashing through bushes and leaping over logs, but it was so dark I couldn't see more than a few feet ahead of me. Too late, I felt the gravel at the edge off the ravine, too late to stop, and I fell headlong toward the water, starting awake with a gasp.

Rafe's hand gripped my rib cage. "Shh," he murmured. "You're safe."

· TWENTY-EIGHT ·

When I opened my eyes again, it was dawn, and Rafe was already awake, his aqua eyes gleaming in the weak light. Mist had formed in the woods overnight, and the trees around us gradually became visible as we lay there in the cocoon of our shared warmth, talking quietly about how soon we could get to Moline. It would take days of hard hiking. We planned to go back to Camp Echo with the others and wait for my ankle and Rafe's ribs to heal. Everson had said that could take weeks, but I wasn't going to wait that long. Not when I was already stocking up serious anxiety about what would happen to my dad and the rest of the community in Moline once the patrol was deployed in the Feral Zone. Everson would be going back to Arsenal soon. He would warn them. Using his influence with his mother, he might even be able to stop it from happening. For now, I had to believe that was possible. Otherwise my sense of helplessness would push me into hiking north on crutches.

And then there was the issue of Rafe and the cure and how, once Bearly dropped it off, I would find a way to persuade him to take it.

For me, the trek back to Camp Echo was painful and slow. I was silent much of the way, teeth clenched, while our traveling companions caught up excitedly and discussed ways to reunite the two communities.

For a few miles, Aaron and his mother, Carmen, walked with me and Rafe, Carmen with her arm slung over Aaron's shoulders.

"Thank you," was the first thing she said to us, "for returning my son to me."

"You're welcome," I said. "But he was never really lost."

"I wouldn't be here if it weren't for you," Aaron told Rafe.

"Sure, you would. Lane wouldn't have let anything happen to you," Rafe assured him.

As we walked, Rafe asked them questions about life inside Heartland, wondering how it had changed since he'd lived there. Turned out it hadn't changed much at all.

"You probably don't remember me," Carmen said. "You were little when you left, but I was friends with Sophie."

Rafe shook his head. "Sorry, no."

"Sophie and I were about the same age. We used to get into trouble together. My parents didn't know how to handle teenage rebellion. At all. But your mom, she was great. I can't tell you how many times she talked us out of some crazy scheme to get out of Heartland and somehow get past the Titan wall and see civilization for ourselves."

"What else do you remember about my mom?" he asked, and Carmen told him how she appeared mild-mannered but had a wicked sense of humor.

I thought of Rafe having been needlessly separated from his mother for all those years, and my heart ached. He'd been only seven years old when he lost her, and I wondered if most of his memories of her had slipped away over time.

I could still conjure up the way my own mom smelled, like honey. And that memory, more than the digital photos and film clips I had of her, was the most precious to me because I had no idea how long it would last.

We reached Camp Echo that afternoon, and a cry went up from inside the fence as we neared the archway. A moment later, our group was engulfed by jubilant manimals, and there was much screeching, yowling, and crying.

Carmen approached us and handed me my dial, which I had completely forgotten about. The green light was on — meaning it was recording. She smiled at my surprise. "I was only ten when the plague hit, and back then smart phones were rectangular, but I never forgot how to work one." She gestured to the manimals and humans hugging and crying and talking all around us. "I thought this was worth recording."

"Definitely," I said. "Thank you." I slipped the chain around my neck and continued to record the happy chaos.

Tomorrow, Bearly would return in the hovercopter with the antigen. Once it was distributed, hopefully she'd fly me, Rafe, and Everson back up the river. Part of me couldn't wait to get back to Arsenal to see my dad and the orphans. However, another part wanted time to freeze.

That night, between Rafe's bruised ribs and my sprained ankle, we weren't able to sleep together on the narrow bunk — not comfortably, anyway. So he stayed with me under the wool blanket until I was warm and drowsy and then he climbed up to the top bunk, and we talked softly until I fell asleep — a routine that I knew, and Rafe knew, wasn't going to fly under my dad's watch.

The next morning, I limped around Echo's haphazard chicken enclosure, collecting eggs, when I heard a commotion near the archway. Some of the manimals were gathered there, and others were running in that direction from their cabins, from the playing field, from the river. I came out of the coop as Little One loped by.

"What's going on?" I called.

"A hovercopter just landed outside the fence," she said, shooting me a flash of her sharp smile.

I hobbled over to join the growing crowd, and after a few minutes, Everson came through the archway carrying a blue plastic medical crate. Mahari followed him with another. Everson set down the crate and held up his hands, and everyone fell silent.

"We have the antigen," he said. "Enough for everyone here who wants it."

The air exploded with ferocious cheering, and with a grin, Everson threw back his head and whooped right along with them.

All day my brain had been whirring constantly, searching for the right way to talk to Rafe about the cure. He'd been so subdued since we'd come back, and the truth was that I was afraid to ask what was on his mind.

Rafe appeared then, in the archway behind the crowd, a deer carcass slung across his shoulders. So much for taking care of his bruised ribs. He disappeared behind the dining hall, where there was a butchering area, and then he joined me among the manimals and their family members. A thrill went through me when he entwined his fingers with mine as if it was the most natural thing in the world.

"We got it," I said. "The cure."

He nodded.

It was now or never. I lifted his hand and drew his arm around my shoulders. I pressed myself to his side. "What would a certain girl have to say to convince a certain guy — using the term loosely — to take it?"

His eyes glinted. "She doesn't have to say anything. She already convinced him without words."

"I — I did?" I stammered. "When?"

"Quiet, everyone," Everson called out, and the crowd fell silent. Every last person hung on his words until he was finished explaining exactly how to take the cure and how soon it would be effective.

"You need to understand that we've given this antigen to other manimals under test conditions and had success, but we still don't know its long-term effects. If you take it, you take it at your own risk."

A murmur rose up from the crowd. Then Glenfiddich climbed several rungs up the tree ladder and shouted, "What's risk to us? We live with it every minute of every day, always asking, 'Will I go feral tonight? Tomorrow?' At least with this risk comes hope. I say that's a risk worth taking."

The crowd erupted into cheers again.

"It should be fully effective sometime next week," Everson said. "At that time, take a blood test to check your viral load. It should read zero. I'll stay in camp for the rest of the day to make sure no one has a bad reaction to the drug. It hasn't happened yet, but I'd rather stick around to be sure."

Everson pried the top off the crate to reveal dozens upon

dozens of yellow tubes. As Mahari began to pass them out, Everson glanced at me. "I forgot, Bearly said she needs to talk to you."

I nodded but didn't move. I wasn't going anywhere until I saw Rafe take the antigen with my own eyes.

Everson offered Rafe a tube. When he took it and unscrewed the cap, my jaw fell open.

"You're really going to take it?" I asked.

"I am."

"Good," Everson said, and clapped him on the back. "I didn't want to have to come back to the zone to put you down."

Rafe snorted. "Like you could get within a mile of me."

Everson just smiled and headed off to help those who needed it, leaving us alone.

I squinted at Rafe, trying to gauge his mood. "When did you decide to take it?"

He pulled me close and spoke against my hair. "Remember how I bragged about what a great hunter I've become since getting infected?"

I nodded, trying to concentrate on what he was saying. Being this close to him was messing with my brain's ability to process information.

"I was thinking about something you said, about how Boone snuck up on me. And so did the patrol when I was looking for Gabe. See, I thought it was the animal in me, keeping me alive, but it's not. It's you. Yeah, you saved my life out there." He lifted his chin toward the fence. "But you also give me a reason to stay alive. I didn't think I deserved to, not after all the things I've done and the people I've hurt. But then you shoved me under that hovercopter . . . and I

got it. This feeling that I'd do anything to keep you safe —
you feel that about me. I don't deserve it. I know that."

I opened my mouth to object, but he laid a finger across
my lips.

"But I'm going to try to, okay?" he said quietly. "I'm
going to try."

"Okay," I whispered, and then watched him squeeze the
tube of antigen under his upper lip. After a couple of minutes, I asked, "Do you feel anything?"

"Yeah. The need to kiss you without worrying that I'll
infect you," he said, sounding completely serious. "I don't
want to be the one who turns you into an animal, silky."

I grinned. "You sure about that?"

He fell back a step, surprise evident in every line of his
body. "You don't get to say things like that for at least a
week."

"Okay," I said cheerfully.

"I mean it."

"I know." I backed off and turned. "I'm going to go see
what Bearly wants," I said over my shoulder.

I found Bearly outside the fence.

"Lane," she said, nodding a curt greeting. She looked
down at my leg but didn't comment on my limp. "Thought
you should know that Chairman Prejean kicked the orphans
off Arsenal."

"No!"

"She wasn't happy that you took Ev with you into
the zone."

"He took himself."

"She doesn't see it that way. She said you put her kid at
risk, so she was returning the favor," Bearly said with faint

disgust. "Don't worry. I got the river patrol to take 'em to Moline. They're with your dad."

I felt light-headed with relief. My dad was used to living with all sorts of strays. He never cared how many I brought home as long as I took care of them. He wouldn't mind having the orphans underfoot. Of course, Hagen was living with him now, but somehow I didn't think she'd mind either.

"Thank you," I told Bearly. "But if the chairman finds out you —"

"What was I gonna do, leave 'em alone out there?" she said with a shrug.

"Well, thanks," I said again, and then I asked, "Has the executive order taken effect yet? The one that gives Chairman Prejean free rein?"

Bearly's expression remained inscrutable. "Yeah, and Congress immediately tripled Titan's budget. The hovercopters are stacked up over Arsenal waiting to drop new recruits in the river." Her mouth softened when she saw my stricken expression. "But the order's been frozen," she said. "A veterans group is challenging it in federal court, so it's frozen until the judge rules."

"Listen, I know you're coming back tonight to get Everson . . . Is there any way you could drop me and Rafe off in Moline?" I said his name quickly, hoping it would slide right past her.

"You and *Rafe*?" she said, her astonishment clear on her face. "You've got to be kidding me," she huffed. "No self-respecting line guard would let that thief aboard a Titan hovercopter unless he was dead or on his way to a jail cell on Arsenal."

"Are you one of those self-respecting line guards?" I asked.

She narrowed her dark eyes at me, but after a beat, she sighed heavily. "Fine. But we're leaving as soon as Ev is done in camp."

"Thank you!"

It was a strange day, for sure, even for a place that could have appeared in the dictionary as an illustration of the word. The manimals celebrated the cure for most of it until around dinnertime, when some of them snapped awake into the reality that they had been living in squalor. Living as if it was their last day on earth had had its advantages: no rules, no schedules, no thoughts of the future. But now that they felt they'd gotten their humanity back, some of them looked around the garbage-strewn common areas as if seeing them for the first time and put together a clean-up crew. Others thought security was the most important issue, especially with relatives visiting from Heartland, and began working on a gate for the archway. They didn't want to chance any ferals breaking into camp and endangering their loved ones.

No one had a bad reaction to the antigen, so Rafe and I packed our stuff before sunset and met Everson inside the archway. Deep breathing wasn't helping my strung-out nerves, so I welcomed the distraction when the lionesses hugged me good-bye in turn. As worried as I was about what would happen once the line guards were vaccinated against Ferae, I knew the pride would survive any fight that came their way.

"Take care, little sister," Deepnita said, amusement in her amber eyes.

"You're my favorite girl human," Neve told me in all seriousness. And then she hugged me hard, purring against my hair. After a long, tight minute, I tried to wiggle loose politely, but in the end, Deepnita had to help me extricate myself from Neve's loving embrace.

"You missed your chance to join us." Mahari said with a slow, indulgent curve of her lips. "And now it's too late."

"I don't need the virus to be a lioness," I said, returning her smile.

"And you." Mahari lifted her chin at Rafe. "There may be no love between us, but there is respect."

Rafe raised a mocking fist. "Go, felines."

Everson reached for Mahari's hand, but she was quick to snatch it away.

"I'll meet you at Arsenal in a few days," he told her, and then looked past her to the other two lionesses. "Be safe."

"You're going to Arsenal?" I asked them.

"On foot," Deepnita said firmly.

"No more boats," Neve added with a shudder. "And nothing that goes up in the sky."

"They're going to work with me to distribute the antigen throughout the zone," Everson explained.

Mahari bared her fangs at him. "So he says. More likely he'll get back to his human world and forget we ever existed. We'll be like a dream to him."

"Best he's ever had," Rafe murmured.

"Not going to happen," Everson assured her. He stood inches from Mahari, looking deeply into her eyes as she glared back at him, and then she shivered. The movement was so slight I blinked, thinking I'd strained my eyes.

"We should keep you as a hostage," she hissed, though she'd dialed back the scary. "Then they'd have to bring us more of the cure."

Everson cupped her face with one hand. "I will get you all the antigen you want, cat-girl." His thumb stroked her bottom lip. "I promise."

"I'd be a fool to trust you." She pressed an accusing finger into his chest. *"Human."*

He dropped his mouth to her ear and spoke two soft words that made her snort, though her lips curved into a faint smile. The hand she'd jabbed him with now curled into the fabric of his shirt, and she drew him closer.

"Smooth," Rafe murmured.

Neve clapped when they kissed, while Deepnita merely yawned.

"What did he say?" I whispered to Rafe. Yes, I was being nosy, but I was the only one here besides Everson with pathetic human ears.

Rafe slid an arm around my waist and pulled me back against the warmth of his body. "He said he's *her* human."

My smile was as wide as Neve's; I was even tempted to clap too.

When Everson released Mahari, she was breathless. "Sure you don't want to come with us in the 'copter?" he asked. "There's plenty of room."

"Nooo!" Neve backed off fast, followed closely by Deepnita, shaking her head.

"I'd pass if I could," Rafe admitted.

"We'll be there in three days," Mahari said, putting a hand to Everson's scarred cheek. "And you better be waiting."

The hum of a hovercopter dropped precisely through the trees on the other side of the fence. We waited a moment, making sure that it was the only one, and then we went out through the archway to meet it. As Bearly turned off the blades and shed her headset, I pulled Everson aside.

"I probably won't get the chance later," I said, "so I'll say it now. Thank you for coming with me. Thank you for everything."

A fleeting smile crossed his lips. "Good things are going to happen because of you."

"Because of you too," I replied.

I shared his hope about what might happen next. When people in the West saw the manimals living their desperate lives, when they saw Aaron taking the antigen, and when they saw families reunited with their infected loved ones, everyone would have to agree that ending the quarantine was the right thing to do. Wouldn't they?

Bearly emerged from the cockpit and helped Everson and Mahari load the medical equipment. Rafe, however, hung back, pack in hand, eyeing the hovercopter and Bearly with active dislike. I joined him and knocked my shoulder into his. "Don't worry. She's a good pilot."

"She's squirrelly," he countered in a low tone. "And I don't mean infected with squirrel."

She returned his glare, completely unfazed.

I shrugged. "She doesn't like you. None of the guards do."

"It's more than that," he muttered. "She's hiding something."

I opened my mouth to protest but then shut it. From what I'd seen, Rafe's crap detector was infallible. Unfortunately his doubts about her stirred up the panic I'd been pressing down for days. We had to get back to Moline — now. We had to warn my dad and Hagen that the line patrol was on the verge of invading the Feral Zone. My ankle, while improved, was still swollen and bruised. It would take days of painful hiking to get back there on foot. My best option was hitching a ride with Bearly, no matter the risk.

"She helped the orphans," I reminded Rafe. "She got them to Moline after Everson's mother kicked them off the base. She went behind Chairman Prejean's back to do it."

"She could've made that up to get you to trust her. Point is, that pilot is hiding something. Might have nothing to do with us, I don't know. But we're trusting her to take us upriver and I don't want our trip to end in a jail cell. You've been around her. What's your gut say — friend or foe?"

The weight of that decision flattened me. "My gut says . . . friend. But that might be wishful thinking. I thought Chorda was —"

"We'll go with your gut," Rafe said — no hesitation at all. "Besides, we don't have a choice if we want to get to Moline this week."

Rafe was already carrying a rifle in a holster slung across his back, but now he checked his knife holsters — all four of them — and then produced a handgun and shoulder holster from his pack. I dug out the pistol Little One had given me, snapped in a cartridge, and threaded the holster through my belt. "When we land," he said, "stick close."

Just then Neve appeared, shrugging out of the body armor jacket she'd peeled off the guard on the riverbank, which now seemed like ages ago. She offered the jacket to Rafe. "Take it," she insisted, and pointed at me. "So you match."

The reasoning was pure Neve. But I had a feeling that she'd overheard us — from twenty yards away — and knew we were nervous about flying to Moline with Bearly.

"Besides," Neve went on as she pulled the strap of Rafe's

holster off his shoulder, "you need it more than me. I'm faster and stronger."

"True," Rafe said, brows raised. To his credit, he didn't let his gaze stray from her face.

As she pulled off his old jacket, her golden eyes moved over his lean muscular form, and a warning siren sounded in my brain. Maybe he was still human enough for her to want as a pet.

Just as a sick feeling began to pool in my gut, Rafe met my eyes over her shoulder and winked. And like that, the bad feeling evaporated. I even laughed when she forced his arm into the sleeve of the body armor like she was dressing a doll.

"Easy there," he protested as she moved to the other sleeve. "I'm infected with tiger, not snake."

I left them to it and headed over to put my pack in the hovercopter.

"Any news on Dr. Solis's progress on the vaccine?" Everson asked Bearly.

"He's testing it now, but he thinks it'll work. The chairman's counting on it. She's scheduled a vaccination date for every base on the Mississippi, spacing them months apart. You know, in case there are side effects," Bearly drawled. "Guess which base is up first . . . in three days."

Everson fell back a step, alarm evident in every line of his body. "Why isn't Dr. Solis testing it on mammals first?"

"Guards are mammals," she deadpanned, though there was no missing the anger under her words.

"She can't make you take it," I said, breaking into their conversation.

"Most of the guards want to take it." Bearly's lips twisted with disgust. "They're itching to cross the bridge and 'clear out the zone.'"

"Right." Rafe sauntered over while zipping up his new patrol-issue armor. "Like the virus is the only thing over here that can hurt 'em." He smoothed the jacket into place and grinned. "Matches my stripes."

· TWENTY-NINE ·

The sun was just beginning to set when Moline came into view. My heart swelled in my chest. I couldn't wait to see my dad. And the orphans. And maybe at some point get a bath. Rafe would probably want one too considering he seemed to be slick with sweat. He hadn't so much as glanced outside since takeoff. His gaze was fixed on his hands, white knuckled and clamped on the seat's edge.

"Almost there," I assured him, and got a curt nod in return.

Bearly navigated the hovercopter between the crumbling buildings that were heaped with vines and punctured by trees and then slowed three blocks from the compound gate. She hovered over what must have been a small park twenty years ago. Now the overflowing vegetation had washed out the surrounding streets and drowned the nearby buildings.

"Take us in closer," Everson shouted above the whir of the blades.

With a shake of her head, Bearly aimed the 'copter's spotlight at a wide patch of unbroken asphalt at the edge of the park.

Everson dismissed her suggestion with a jerk of his head. "You don't have to land. Just get low enough that they —"

Bearly set the hovercopter down with a teeth-jarring thump exactly where she'd indicated. She pulled off her headset. "They can walk from here," she announced, and glanced over her shoulder at me. "Right?"

I nodded, despite my unease.

"A hack would've taken us door to door," Rafe said, throwing off his seat belt. "And made sure we got past the gate. But we can take it from here." He scrambled through the hovercopter's open side, only to stumble on shaky legs. He popped back up with a glare that dared us to laugh.

No one did.

Bearly wasn't even looking at him. She swung her gaze from the overgrown park to the nearest buildings and back again before turning off the engine. Probably wondering, like I was, if mongrels were watching us from the ravaged storefronts and rusted vehicles that lined what was left of the street.

I climbed out of the 'copter in silence. Beyond this island of asphalt, the road vanished, broken apart by waist-high grasses and other scrub. The compound was only a small part of what had once been Moline, sectioned off with a wall of crushed cars, stacked five high. Since my last visit, the gate had been fortified with patchwork sheets of corrugated metal and sliding doors from freight cars. "Rando grups" wouldn't be ramming their way into the compound now.

"Ev," Bearly said, sounding agitated as Everson threw open the cockpit door and jumped down. "My orders are to take you back to base."

He unholstered his rifle. "I'm going to walk them to the gate."

We waded into the prairie grass, but after a few yards, Rafe backpedaled several steps. "Smells wrong."

"Wrong how?" Everson asked, scanning the area.

"Like boot polish. Like the base . . ." He hauled me around, shoving me back toward the hovercopter, hissing, "Run."

And I did, my ankle screaming with every pounding step.

Our sudden dash triggered something behind us. Suddenly Everson barked out a curse and then yelled, "Stop there!"

Us?

I glanced back as Rafe steered me under the hovercopter's tail. Everson stood tall in the grass, his back to us, his rifle trained off to the left. One block down, the buildings were crawling with line guards — rounding corners and clambering through shopwindows — nearly invisible with blackened faces and gray body armor.

"Lane," Rafe growled.

I tore my eyes from the ruined ambush and caught up, putting the hovercopter between me and the oncoming guards. Rafe motioned toward a side street and then took off in a hunkered jog with me on his heels. We plowed through milkweed and brambles and stumbled over hidden chunks of concrete. Somehow my pistol was in my hand, though I didn't remember taking it from its holster. I flipped off the safety.

Everson shouted from beyond the hovercopter and I braced for a gunshot, but it never came. Of course he wouldn't fire on fellow guards, but his threatening stance had bought us some time.

"Fan out," another voice yelled. "Find them."

Rafe ducked around an overturned dumpster. Ignoring the pain shooting up my shin, I pivoted after him into what was once an alley, now blocked off by rusting cars and mountains of rubble. Without pausing, Rafe plunged through the crack in a partially collapsed wall, trusting that I'd follow. And I did, in body anyway. In mind, I wanted no part of this.

Nothing about the ancient department store seemed safe — not the buckling ceiling, not the dim interior that looked like a war zone complete with scattered bodies of fallen mannequins. The farther in we went, the darker the gloom. I paused by a shattered counter.

Without glancing back or breaking stride, Rafe beckoned me to follow. Glass crunched under his boots as he disappeared down a dusty aisle. Still I hesitated. Shadows pulsed in my peripheral vision, only to melt into the surrounding darkness when I turned my head. How did I want to die? Cave-in, mongrel attack, or bullet?

Rafe didn't give me time to mull it over. "Lane," he urged from somewhere off to my right. And yet, it was the shouted order from the street outside that got me moving again. The guards were closing in.

I hurried through the maze of pillars and empty clothing racks, overwhelmed by the dirt and the silence. Looters had picked the place clean. Not surprising since the store was just blocks from the compound. I found Rafe in what was once the shoe department. Thin beams of sunlight filtered in through a bank of windows, now open to the elements and curtained in dead ivy. Rafe peered through the vines, backed off, and held up two fingers. So, two guards. Right outside.

I followed him through drifts of dead leaves and high-stepped over fallen shoe racks like a recruit navigating a ropes course. When we plunged deeper into the store, where the shadows shifted with liquid grace like shades in Hades, I had to ask it: "Do you have a plan?"

He shot back a "Please" with a lift of an eyebrow.

I slowed in silent protest. I trusted him but hated being left in the dark — figuratively and literally. Especially literally. He might be able to see down these dark aisles with his night vision, but I had to rely on my imagination to fill in the details. And I did *not* like what my brain was conjuring.

"Drain tunnel," he said under his breath, though not low enough to hide his exasperation. "A block from here. It's a back door into the compound."

I nodded my thanks and exhaled a little tension. A plan made this situation bearable. A plan kept any faint clicking sounds from seeming ominous . . . at least until Rafe stopped short.

"Don't talk. Don't move," he hissed while doing both. He backpedaled into me, forcing me into reverse. "It's a nest."

Nest? Broken glass and lumps of moldering fabric coated the floor. Nothing looked like a . . . A hunched figure sidled in and out of the shadows beyond us. My guts sloshed and my fingers spasmed across Rafe's body armor but couldn't catch hold.

"What . . ." The word hissed out as faint as air from a bike tire.

"Adders," he whispered back.

As in snakes?

Since when did snakes come hip high? I made a slow-motion pivot, poised to sprint back the way we'd come, but another dark shape crossed behind us — slinking and glistening like freshly poured tar . . . on legs. I stifled a scream by huffing hard through my nose.

Then the clicking came from all around us — closer, louder. Claws on tile. The sound crawled into my ears, down my throat, and into my heart. I remembered I had a pistol, went to raise it, and saw that I already held it in front of me. I tried to take aim but caught only glimpses of the creatures — a glint of eyes on the right, the blur of a thick sinewy body on the left — then nothing.

"They're herding us." This time Rafe didn't bother to keep his voice low.

"Snakes don't herd people," I protested without taking my eyes from the weaving shadows.

"They do when they're mostly wolf." Rafe swiveled in place, his pupils wide and shining with reflected light, as he peered into the darkness.

I followed the trajectory of his stare to a wolf-sized creature slinking along the top of a high display cabinet. Only it wasn't a wolf. It was a nightmare. Shiny reptilian skin — gray with black markings — and a flat triangular head. I clapped a second hand to my pistol to keep it from shaking right out of my grip.

"Don't shoot," Rafe ordered, thrusting my gun down. "The noise'll bring the guards."

"But —"

The mongrel above us made a sound more hiss than growl that ended with a hacking bark. The noise excited the others, and phlegmy barking broke out around us as the circle of glinting green eyes tightened. Rafe flipped his rifle around to use as a club just as the closest mongrel reared up on its hind legs and swayed, its black serpent fangs glistening in dead white gums. Before Rafe could bash in its head, I squeezed my gun's trigger. Three bullets tore into the mongrel's scaled chest, knocking it backward into the writhing mass of its brethren.

Rafe glanced back, lips pursed like I'd just spoiled his fun.

"I'd rather deal with guards," I said in a tone that dared him to argue.

With a sigh and a "Fine," he flipped his rifle back around and let loose an arc of bullets. The rest of the nest scattered, yipping as they darted down aisles and leapt over displays, tails lashing like snakes. The explosion of noise left my ears ringing.

"Let's get out of here." Rafe hooked my elbow and sprinted toward the frozen escalator, its steps piled with debris.

I hauled back. "You're heading deeper into the store."

His brows hiked. "You know this place?"

"That's the escalator," I explained — which meant exactly nothing to him. "They're in the center — Never mind." I turned him around. "Just put your back to it and go. Any direction. We'll hit an exit."

On a nod, he took off, angling away from the way we'd come. We fled past spinning chairs and toppled cosmetic displays, toward what had been double glass doors but was now a gaping exit fringed with dead vines. Freedom. One last counter to go, when — beams of light blinded us. Helmet beams. Show over.

Three guards blocked our exit, assault rifles raised. "Drop your weapons," ordered the woman in front.

I looked past their faceplates and saw who was on point. Bearly. My anger surged — anger at myself. Why had I trusted her?

She locked hard eyes on me and repeated, "Weapons down."

I drew a few breaths against the tightness in my chest and let my fury smother my fear. "You set us up?"

She didn't even have the grace to look guilty. "Now."

There was nothing to do. At this close range, their bullets would rip through our body armor. We set our guns on the mud-smeared floor.

"I say we waste him right here," sneered the pimple-faced guy on Bearly's right. "Who's going to know?"

"I will, for one," Rafe deadpanned.

Bearly shot the guard a lethal dose of side eye. "We have our orders."

The third guard held her stance, making it clear that she had no dog in this fight.

"Grup's breaking for the river," the guy said with mock alarm. He hiked up his rifle, shifting from a gut shot to Rafe's head. "Gotta secure the line."

I went cold. Instantly. Mind and body. "We're nowhere near the river."

"Do it," Bearly bit out, "and I'll drag your broken body to the brig myself. Got me?"

The guy glared at Rafe for a long moment before giving Bearly the barest nod.

They picked up our weapons then and, at gunpoint, escorted us back out into the purple haze of twilight, through the prairie grass to the broken asphalt. Everson knelt near the hovercopter with his hands zip-tied behind his back.

"Are you okay?" I called.

He nodded. "You?"

I was a long way from okay but sent back a sturdy "Yeah." Then I noticed that the guards standing next to him were nursing injuries — a bloody nose and a split lip — which brightened my mood. I smirked at them just for kicks. I was already swaying on a tightrope of trouble; a potshot of smug couldn't make our situation much worse.

Bearly and her cohorts herded us to a spot near Everson. Then Bearly headed back toward the hovercopter, and the other two joined the rest of the guards on the far side of the road, facing us. An unbroken line of gray riot gear.

I leaned into Rafe. "Titan hovercopters are armored." I couldn't hear my own words over my thundering heart, but he caught them and nodded.

"Run for it," he added in a rasp. "First chance we get."

I edged back a step, clearing the path to the hovercopter's open side. He needed to take the lead because my lower leg now throbbed with a pain so intense, I felt crippled — mentally and physically. But then the grind of an engine wiped all thought from my brain. After spending over a week in the zone where motors didn't exist, this one sounded so out of place it came off eerie. And then, when the vehicle rounded the parked hovercopter, eerie morphed into outright alarming. A white RV jounced along the broken street toward us. Chairman Ilsa Prejean's RV.

Not possible. No way she'd come here, into the zone, risking germs and infection . . . unless . . . unless she'd been vaccinated against Ferae. Which meant that Bearly had been lying about that too. She was probably vaccinated herself, along with all the guards in this strike team.

The RV lurched to a stop just behind Everson. As he twisted around to see it, the side door hissed open and two black-clad line guards emerged, followed by the chairman herself, wrapped in a level-four protective suit. She peered out of the face shield on her helmet like a seasick sailor viewing the world through a porthole.

"And people call *me* a freak," Rafe muttered.

"Everson," she cried through the speaker in her helmet, which both amplified and hollowed out her voice. "Are you all right?" She pushed past her elite guards to get to him, her gloved hand outstretched. Only his cold stare stopped her from completing that caress. She rocked back a step and seemed to collect herself, then turned a glare on the guards behind him. "Free his hands."

They hauled Everson to his feet and slashed the zip tie from his wrists, but he never took his eyes off his mother. His expression was one of contained emotion, his jaw tight with it. "Guess the vaccine works . . . if you're here, mixing it up with the infected."

"We can talk about it back at the base," she said, her tone conciliatory. She waved an airy hand toward the van. "Vincent is waiting inside with a dose for you."

"I'll get in the van, Chairman," Everson said, turning the word *chairman* into an insult, "after Lane and Rafe are inside the compound." His tone was cool, but the scars on his cheeks stood out white against an angry flush.

She took in his resolve and then sent a strained smile my way. "You must be so pleased with yourself, Lane. You convinced my son to follow you again. Into the zone, into danger without a thought, like a lovesick puppy."

Everson snorted while I shook my head and said, "It's not like that."

"I told her to choose him," Rafe said, his tone dripping with commiseration. "Look at him. A total prince. But she wouldn't listen." He slid an arm around my waist and tugged me close.

The chairman's lips thinned into a tight seam. "Of course. Any girl would choose you over my son. He's the Titan heir and you're . . . what? An infected thief."

Rafe gave a blithe shrug. "I've got a few other skills too."

"Lane and I are just friends, Mom." Everson rubbed his wrists where the zip tie had cut into his flesh, and then a corner of his mouth lifted. "But there is someone I'd follow anywhere."

She eyed him warily. "Who?"

"You know her actually, from the maze. You used to have chats with her."

The chairman's expression contorted with revulsion. "That — that lion creature?"

"She prefers 'queen of the jungle,'" Everson said, sounding amused.

Not exactly a smart thing to say to his mother, but Everson's fury had gotten the better of him. And now we could all hear the chairman heaving behind her face shield as she tried to keep her head from exploding. Rafe nudged me, and we edged toward the hovercopter, even though Bearly sat in the pilot seat, talking into a radio. Probably giving the base a full report of the goings-on.

"You're lying," the chairman croaked.

"I'm not," Everson said. "Mahari is cured of Ferae. She's not infectious, and that's all that matters. I don't care what her DNA looks like. And you better get over it too 'cause, who knows, maybe someday your grandchildren will have claws and tails."

The chairman made a sputtering sound as if she was about to gurgle up blood. "Get him in the van," she ordered her guards, her voice high and thin, and they half pushed, half carried Everson into the RV. The whole vehicle shook with the effort of shoving him through the door.

Now it was just Rafe and me and the chairman — and fourteen line guards with assault rifles. Maybe Chairman Prejean had come into the zone for just one reason — to retrieve Everson and get him vaccinated before he got infected. Maybe she didn't care that I'd threatened national security with my video and that Rafe had caused the line patrol no end of trouble and expense. And if I could just remember to breathe, then maybe I could convince myself of these things.

The chairman stared at the van long after the side door banged shut, arms folded across her middle. A protective gesture on top of a protective suit. When she finally turned back to us, her expression, behind the porthole, was wiped of all emotion. "Now," she said lightly. "What to do with you?"

"You don't have to do anything with us." I stepped hard on my fear so I could concentrate. "I'll live in Moline and look after the orphans. And Rafe will go back to Camp Echo, far from here."

Beside me, Rafe stiffened. He had to know that I was lying to her . . . right? I stole a glance at him, but his attention was on the line of guards — or maybe blocks past them, on the compound gate, which was still shut and locked. "Stall," he said, so softly I wasn't sure I'd heard him right.

"I'm afraid that's not possible, Lane." The chairman gestured to the leader of the strike team, her protective suit crinkling with every move. "You see, no one in the West can ever learn that an antigen exists. And, unfortunately, keeping secrets doesn't seem to be your strong suit."

A door slammed shut in my chest. Would she have the scientists stop making it? "Why can't they know about the cure?"

"It's not a cure," she corrected. "These creatures, these infected humans" — she nodded toward Rafe, who seemed to accept the label in stride — "they're polluted at a genetic level. Dr. Solis may have found a way to clear the virus, but he can't repair their corrupted DNA."

"But they can't infect anyone," I protested. "They're not a threat to public health."

"Wrong." Her gaze narrowed on me. "If we say the manimals are cured and let them rejoin society, their potential for contagion becomes even greater."

"How?" I demanded. Beside me, Rafe gave the barest nod. Encouraging me . . . to stall.

"It's not the wall that keeps people away from abominations like him." She eyed Rafe, her loathing on full display. "It's the risk of infection. Eliminate the virus and you eliminate the need for a quarantine. Do you really want people carrying animal DNA mixing in with the healthy population? Integration will lead to marriages, children . . . Children who will inherit corrupted DNA. Can you even imagine what the human race would look like in three generations? Four? Unrecognizable, that's what." She inhaled deeply as if to calm herself and glanced toward the RV, clearly wishing she could escape into its sterile confines.

I felt as pinched and pale as she looked. There was so much in what she'd just said that I couldn't easily pull it

apart. Rafe shifted his weight from one foot to the other —
an impatient bounce. Right. Stall.

"I get it," I said just as the chairman was turning away.
"I do. You're already a villain in the history books . . .
Mother of the plague and all."

That got her attention. She swung back, eyes pinned to
me. Only me.

I put on a sympathetic face. "I can see why you wouldn't
want to be the person who ends the human race as we know it."

She jerked toward the line of guards. "Who's in charge
of this squad?"

As a burly, dark-eyed man strode forward, Rafe nudged
me toward the hovercopter.

"Name?" the chairman demanded.

"Guardsman Bhatt."

He cut his eyes to me, and I froze, certain he'd noticed
our retreat, but then my stomach curdled. He was the guard
who'd bullied Jia the night I'd come to Arsenal. And going
by the ugly twist of his lips, he hadn't forgotten that encoun-
ter either. Somehow I breathed out a smile, despite my
apprehension, which made the tendons in his neck pop out.
Straining to bite back words? Good.

"As soon as I'm on my way back to base," the chairman
told him, "take care of them."

As in kill them?! She couldn't mean it. She couldn't. But
then, the line guards killed people all the time — infected
people and quarantine breakers. I was neither and Rafe
was cured. That should matter. But already my vision was
tunneling as the image of a fetch played on the multiplex in
my mind — a fetch at the foot of the wall, facing a firing
squad.

Just as Bhatt parted his lips to respond, Rafe cut in sharply, "Hear that?"

Lines of cold fury bracketed Bhatt's mouth at the interruption, but then he whipped toward the overgrown park. I heard it then as well — snapping twigs, the crack of a branch. I squinted, trying to make out what moved in the shadows between the scraggly pines.

"What is it?" the chairman demanded.

"Could be wildlife." Bhatt spoke in a low voice. "Or . . . we've got company."

The rustling grew louder, now coming from several places within the park. On a gesture from Bhatt, the guards fanned out, forming a line between us and whatever lurked on the far side of the clearing.

"Chairman," he said abruptly, "you should wait in the van until we know what we're dealing with."

On a nod, the chairman edged back, a hand pressed to her throat, only to pause when the distant pine trees shivered and shook out their needles.

All at once, shouts and snarls erupted across the park as shadowy figures burst through the trees, dozens of them. They raced headlong into the tall prairie grass, thrashing paths from every direction, their mutated features twisted with hate. Ferals? Manimals? Impossible to tell from this distance. Virus driven or not, they bared jagged teeth and sharp claws, roaring as they raced across the park.

Racing for us.

· THIRTY ·

"Wait for my order," Bhatt yelled to the guards, who stood between us and the oncoming horde.

The snarls, punctuated by roars, hiked in volume as the infected people thrashed paths through the prairie grass. They converged halfway across the park to form one long line — one pounding wave — heading for us. And yet, my fingers didn't prickle, my head didn't ache, and I wasn't paralyzed with fear. Yes, every pulse point in my body beat loud and fast but on high alert. If these people were feral, I wouldn't freeze up.

"Wait . . ." Bhatt repeated softly, fist raised. The guards held their positions, eyes to their gun scopes.

I glanced at Rafe. Did he know the attackers? Beyond him, between the broken asphalt and crumbling buildings, the tall grass shimmied in a dozen places. I held my breath and touched Rafe's hand, prompting him to follow my gaze. The guards, however, remained focused on the attackers in front of us.

"Come on," Bhatt coaxed. "Don't chicken out now."

Hearing his frustration, I turned to see that the attacking manimals had stopped halfway across the park. When they dropped into the prairie grass, Bhatt snorted. "You're not getting away that easy."

An elbow knocked my arm as someone nudged between me and Rafe and kept going. More followed until a stream of silent people rushed between us like the incoming tide past pilings. They emerged from the undergrowth at the edges of the old road, humans and manimals, moving swiftly en masse toward the line of guards. A second later, I lost Rafe as the crowd swept me along with them — only they were armed and I wasn't. They carried everything from knives and guns to pitchforks. A string of chaotic thoughts raced through my mind as I recognized several of them from my one visit to Moline. Was my dad here?

Chairman Prejean backed away with a muted cry and then broke for the van, but something large sailed out from nowhere — a rusty car door — and crashed a foot in front of her. It would've hit her dead on if she hadn't tripped at the last second and fallen flat on her helmet-face.

Bhatt glanced back then, but it was too late. Sid, the Moline gatekeeper who was infected with boar, was already in position behind him, shotgun muzzle pressed to the chink between Bhatt's helmet and flak jacket. Bhatt stiffened at the cold kiss of metal. And then the tidal wave of Moline residents crashed over the line of guards, roaring and pounding as mercilessly as any tsunami.

When shots rang out, my desperation reached fever pitch. My dad had to be somewhere in the melee with his bad leg. He wouldn't have — there! Helping the chairman to her feet with a firm grip on her elbow. Then I lost sight of them in the crowd.

"Lane!" Rafe reached for me between the surge of bodies and snagged my hand.

We wove through the mob, breaking for the hovercopter,

when Everson threw open the van's side door. We veered for him as he stepped down.

"My mother?" he asked.

"With my dad," I said, looking around for them.

The fight seemed to have ended before it even got started. The residents of Moline, human and manimal, had the guards down on their knees in an awkward row, their weapons confiscated. More shocking than that, Chairman Prejean's helmet had been wrenched from her protective suit and she stood near the hovercopter, bald-headed and blinking as if blinded by sunlight, though the evening was well upon us.

"Over there." I pointed her out.

Everson followed my gesture, and his jaw went slack. "She's out in the open without a mask," he murmured. "She never . . . ever —"

"I don't think the mayor gave her a choice," Rafe observed.

I swung my attention to the woman guarding Chairman Prejean. It was dad's girlfriend, Hagen! Her dark curls danced in the wind as she propped a hiking boot on the hood of a dilapidated car and rested her crossbow on her thigh. I smiled despite the undercurrent of tension surrounding us.

When a guard groaned over his dislocated arm and another begged for a bandage, Everson tore his eyes from his mother and scanned the crowd. "I don't see any serious injuries."

"There was no fight," I pointed out. "The guards were outnumbered twenty to one."

"And looking the wrong way," Rafe added with a chuckle. "I can't believe they fell for that."

I turned to him. "Did you know they'd come out for us?"

He snapped to attention, eyes on Sid. "All I know is that pork chop over there still has my gun." He stalked after the group of manimals headed back into the compound.

Everson pushed open the RV's side door. Even with all its slick, washable surfaces, the van's interior resembled an elegant living room. Dr. Solis seemed out of place, sitting at the chairman's desk, bent over a microscope. "This is remarkable, Ev," he said without looking up.

"Yeah," Everson agreed. "But you're going to have to study it later. There are a couple of banged-up guards out here who could use some attention."

Dr. Solis lifted his eye from the microscope with obvious reluctance. "Of course," he said, and then rose, looking more alert than I'd ever seen him.

He grabbed a medical kit off the top of a sturdy blue crate — a crate like the one Bearly had delivered to Camp Echo. Was that crate also filled with tubes of the antigen? Only one way to find out.

Dr. Solis stepped out of the RV. "Are you in one piece?" he asked me.

I nodded and then caught Everson's arm before he could head off with the doctor. "You said your mom's RV has Web access."

"It does."

"Can I post something?" I lifted my dial out from under my shirt and watched his features tense. "She doesn't want anyone to know about the antigen. Your mother. She's trying to —"

"Yes," Everson interrupted with a wave toward the open door.

I hesitated. "You're in the footage . . ."

"Great. More fan mail," he said with a resigned huff. "Fine. But this time I'm keeping the care packages." His expression turned serious then. "Look, I don't know what's happening here . . ." He swept a hand toward his mother and the kneeling guards. "I don't know if this is the beginning of the end or if it's nothing. But, Lane, if it is just a glitch in the status quo and you post another video, you'll top the Biohaz most wanted list."

He was right. Absolutely right. But I couldn't think past the emotions burning in my gut. "People need to know there's a cure. If they could stop being so afraid of the world beyond the wall — even if just for a minute — they'd see there's nothing to be afraid of. Not anymore."

"Okay," he said roughly. "I followed you into the zone . . . Twice. I've got your back on this too. Go."

I hurried into the RV and locked the door behind me. I crouched by the blue crate and cracked the lid. Sure enough, it was filled to the brim with tubes of the antigen. Not enough for all the manimals in Moline, but then, maybe some of them wouldn't want to take an untested drug. A problem to solve later. Right now, I had my own risk to take, because this time, I wasn't going to post my video anonymously in a hit-and-run job. This time, I was going on record.

I settled on top of the crate and scrolled through my footage from the last couple of days: the basement maze with its desolate and crazed occupants; Mahari's rescue and Everson's kiss, which woke her from her Lulled slumber; Rafe giving Aaron his dose of the cure in the Camp Echo infirmary; and the reunion, which went from the waterfall back to Camp Echo. I deleted Everson's hostage message because that had been staged, and I wanted to be able to stand by every second of my account — even under oath.

I wasn't a fighter like Rafe. Or a rebel leader like Mahari. I couldn't create a cure like Dr. Solis and Everson. But I could bear witness to what was happening around me, and that wasn't nothing.

I held the dial at arm's length in front of my face, pushed record, and spoke directly to the small round screen.

"My name is Delaney Park McEvoy and this is my second video about the world beyond the wall. I swear that everything you're about to see really happened and that all the people are real — the infected and the uninfected. You might not believe it, but that's because the West is the ultimate gated community. We stay comfortable and safe while ignoring the people who are suffering on the other side of the gate. Or, in our case, *wall*. Those people might look strange to you — inhuman — and, if you only go by DNA, some of them are technically inhuman. But that doesn't mean they lack humanity." I paused just long enough to catch my breath. "But don't believe me. Watch the video. Judge for yourself. I live here now, on the wild side of the wall, because I've fallen in love with the Feral Zone. I hope you will too."

After recording the introduction, it was nothing to transfer my footage onto the chairman's tablet and post it to the same social media site as my first video.

By the time I stepped out of the RV, the manimals were herding the guards into the compound while Everson hunkered before a Moline resident, gently manipulating her wrist. Dr. Solis tossed him a rolled bandage from several patients down, all with what looked like minor injuries. I waved to Hagen and she beckoned me over.

Chairman Prejean kept a gloved hand cupped over her nose and mouth as she spoke. "Exactly what do you hope to gain from this?" Her glare remained on Hagen as I joined them. "I have guards on *sixty* bases along this river. Do you think they don't know where I am? I suggest you release us right now or the entire line patrol will descend on your compound like —"

"A plague?" Hagen asked coolly. "Lady, we survived the first one you caused. We'll survive whatever else you cook up."

"She's not going to be cooking up much of anything." My dad limped past the nose of the hovercopter, swinging his cane like he didn't need it.

I rushed over and threw my arms around him. Up close he wasn't the civilized art dealer he'd once been — his khakis were rumpled, and he'd grown a beard. No doubt I looked rougher too.

"You okay?" he hugged me back and asked.

I nodded and then realized he wasn't alone. Bearly stood several feet away, an assault rifle cradled in her arms. I drew back, trying to tug my dad with me, but he just smiled.

"This is Special Agent Johnson," he told us. "She reports to Director Spurling. Always has."

Chairman Prejean stiffened as if touched by a live wire while I gaped. Had Everson known about Bearly's side gig?

"Nice to meet you, Bear Lake," Hagen said as she slung her crossbow onto her back. "Jia's told us all about you. Now, if you three have this in hand, I'm going to check on our people. Though," she added with a smirk for the chairman, "yours are the ones looking worse for the wear." As she strolled past me, she smiled. "Hey, Delaney Park. It's good to see you."

"How did you know the guards were going to ambush us?" I asked. "How did you even know we were coming to Moline?"

"The orphans told us," she said.

"How did the orphans know?"

"Bearly told them," my dad said.

"Don't worry, hon, we'll get you caught up later," Hagen assured me, and hooked a thumb over her shoulder. "After that gets sorted."

She left me struggling to make sense of things. Chairman Prejean, however, had regained her composure.

"It doesn't matter if Guardsman Johnson has been spying for Biohaz," she informed my father as if Bearly wasn't standing right there. "Taryn Spurling has no authority on this side of the wall."

"Had," my dad replied.

"Excuse me?" The chairman's tone was the vocal equivalent of freezer burn.

"You *had* sixty bases along the river." My dad pursed his lips as if reluctant to deliver the news, though his eyes promised ice-cold vengeance. Even though he'd agreed to fetch the missing strains for Titan, he still hated Ilsa Prejean for corrupting the biosphere on a whim. "According to Special Agent Johnson," he went on, "the federal government is repossessing the Titan bases . . . and canceling your contract."

"Spurling doesn't have the power to cancel Titan's contract," the chairman sputtered.

"No," Bearly agreed as she unclipped handcuffs from her belt. "But the State Department does — and has, since the line patrol is under investigation for using unnecessary and excessive deadly force in the field. And for withholding information about a potential cure from the Department of Biohazard Defense. Nine of your former employees — guards and scientists — are set to testify in front of a federal grand jury this week. And you" — Bearly pried the chairman's hand from her face — "are under arrest for ordering the unjustified execution of a civilian."

As Bearly snapped on the cuffs, Chairman Prejean choked and coughed like she'd just sucked in a lungful of poisonous gas.

"Sorry that got so close, Lane," Bearly said over the noise. "I knew the guards were a threat. I figured they might shoot Rafe on sight . . . But I never thought she'd order an execution in the field."

"What?" The word burst out of my dad.

The chairman stopped gagging long enough to bleat, "Everson," when Bearly propelled her forward.

"Bearly, hold up," Everson called as he jogged toward us. "Where are you taking her?" He might as well have been covered in steel plating for all the emotion he was showing.

"To the Department of Biohazard Defense," she informed him. "In the 'copter."

"Everson . . ." his mother said again as sweat dripped into her eyes — a consequence of over-plucked brows.

Everson spared her a glance and then addressed Bearly. "I'd like to go with you." At her nod, he swung to me. "Let me get my mother settled in the 'copter," he said as Bearly led her off. "Don't leave, okay? I need to tell you something." Without waiting for my answer, he caught up with Bearly.

"Told you I'd find her," a familiar voice called out from behind me.

I pivoted to see Rafe leading several small figures through

the compound's open gate. Jia, Dusty, Sage, Tasha, Trader, Rose, and Fixit broke into a run, stampeding toward me, screaming, "Lane!" And when they had me surrounded, they did the unthinkable — they threw their arms around any part of me they could grab and hugged me so hard, they dragged me down into a warm writhing pile of bodies. I'd never felt so at home.

I came up for air in time to see my dad draw Rafe into a hug. I hoped he would take the news well — the news of how close Rafe and I had become. After releasing him, my dad clapped a hand to his shoulder and they continued to talk quietly. Rafe nodded at something my dad said and lifted his shirt to reveal the dark markings on his ribs.

Jia sprang to her feet, her eyes fixed on stripes along Rafe's torso. Gesturing wildly, she shouted, "The tiger-man!"

The other orphans crowded around her, their eyes widening as they took in the faint stripes on Rafe's face, the gold coronas around his pupils. Sage and Tasha began to growl.

Rafe glanced over and let out a wildcat snarl that must have sent every animal within a quarter mile scurrying for cover. The orphans flinched backward as one but then stood their ground, growling, baring their teeth, curling their fingers into make-believe claws. My dad just laughed while leaning on his cane.

"All right," I said, stepping between them. "Enough. He's a friend. So, try to act human."

"Tell *him* to act human!" Trader protested.

"Listen, you guys, I have a mission for you." I beckoned them into a huddle. "If you think you're up for it . . ."

That was met with a chorus of assurances. I gave a covert

nod toward the RV and whispered, "There's a blue crate in there, on the floor — filled with little, yellow tubes."

Rafe's attention snapped to me even though he and my dad were standing several yards away. Guess the antigen hadn't messed with his new, improved hearing. When he questioned me with a lift of his brows, I nodded and then went on with my instructions: "Get the crate and bring it to me, okay? I —" let the rest of my sentence roll off. The orphans were already bounding across the broken asphalt like a pack of puppies.

As Rafe gave my dad a quick rundown on the antigen, I closed the distance between us. My dad turned to me, his expression one of wary excitement. "And it works?"

"Seems to. But they don't know for how long."

"Vincent," my dad called to Dr. Solis, who was crouched next to a man infected with bat.

The doctor looked up to reply but then spotted several orphans dragging the blue crate out the van. He rose swiftly. "Oh, no, children. No!"

More orphans scrambled out, clasping things that had nothing to do with their mission — including the microscope. Like a swan protecting its nest, Dr. Solis dashed for the RV, shooing off the orphans. My dad limped after him, using his cane for once.

The orphans faltered in their getaway when the hovercopter's head beams snapped on and Everson hopped out. Dr. Solis took the moment to reclaim the crate, letting the kids run off with the rest of their plunder.

Everson held up a finger to let Bearly know he'd be right back and then headed for us. Rafe and I met him halfway.

"You're flying back to base?" Rafe asked.

"Over the wall," Everson told him. "As soon as we touch down, Bearly's going to perp walk my mother into Biohaz. I can't let her face that alone."

"No, you can't," Rafe said firmly. "Whatever she's done, she's still your mom."

I wanted to say something comforting, but there was no bright side to his mother's arrest. Instead, I asked, "What did you need to tell me?"

Behind us, the hovercopter's blades whirred to life and the headlights strobed. Everson responded with an over-the-shoulder wave but kept his eyes locked on me. "You're not going to believe this. It's crazy. Before giving me the vaccine, Solis tested my blood to make sure I wasn't already infected . . . I wasn't. But it turns out, I don't need the vaccine."

My mind shook out the puzzle pieces, looking for corners and edges. "What does that mean?"

"I have antibodies in my blood," Everson said like he still couldn't believe it.

"Crazy," Rafe intoned. "Now, how 'bout a recap in English?"

"Antibodies to *Ferae*," Everson explained, though the extra clue didn't help me any more than Rafe. Everson tried again, "Like what we see in the blood of cured manimals. Lane, you probably won't need the vaccine either," he said, looking pointedly at Rafe. "If Dr. Solis is right . . . the antibodies are passed through a manimal's saliva, one who's taken the antigen."

With that, the puzzle pieces snapped into place. "You're saying immunity can be passed with a kiss?" I asked with a gasp.

Everson held up a cautioning hand. "We'll have to

confirm the results with more testing first. But the implications are —"

"Like something out of a fairy tale!"

"That's not how I'd put it, but sure," he allowed.

"The orphans are going to love it," I said with a clap, and then laughed when Rafe wrinkled his brow, looking adorably confused. "The wild boy all grown up," I explained. "Traveling through the zone, giving out magic kisses that protect people from Ferae. You were born to star in bedtime stories."

"So were you," he replied, and didn't even turn it into something dirty.

Looking into his eyes, I guessed that, like me, he was thinking of the picture he'd painted on the prison wall in Joliet of a little girl and boy holding hands. Me and him. An illustration for one of my father's stories. Our story.

"Uh . . . yeah," Everson said, looking between us. "Getting back to the science part, if that result is consistent, then it just got a whole lot easier to vaccinate the people living in compounds."

"Just so we're clear . . ." Rafe directed a finger at him. "I'm not hiking all over the zone, giving out magic kisses."

"Ev," Bearly shouted from inside the hovercopter. "Let's go!"

"Coming," he yelled back.

"Wait! What happens if your mother gets convicted?" I asked in a rush. "To the patrol — to Titan?" Everson glanced back, cheeks flushed, though his expression was steely. "It means Titan is mine. She said she's signing everything over to me as soon as we land."

"Whoa," Rafe and I whispered in unison.

Everson shook hands with Rafe and gave me a tight hug. Close to my ear, he said, "Thanks again."

"For what?"

"For being a bad influence. Right now, I'd be giving a lab tour if it weren't for you."

As the hovercopter lifted into the darkening sky, the orphans surrounded me once again. Rafe and Dr. Solis carried the blue crate into the compound while my dad held the gate, but the kids and I didn't follow them. Not yet. We watched the 'copter arc toward the looming shadow across the river. When the blinking lights finally disappeared past the wall, Jia slipped her hand into mine and we walked toward the open gate together.

"You know the chairman-lady with the plastic face and no hair?" Jia asked.

I nodded, trying not to smile at her description.

"She's mad at you. That's why she kicked us off base."

I shrugged. Chairman Prejean was now the least of my worries. "It's better here anyway, don't you think?" I said.

"I do!" Dusty said, catching up to us. "They've got secret passageways and tunnels and everything!"

"I'm still thinking about it," Jia announced, and I squeezed her hand.

"You let me know what you decide," I said, and she nodded.

As we strolled through the gate under Sid's narrow-eyed gaze, the orphans pressed close to me, heads ducked. I couldn't blame them. Thrusting out his sharp tusks and tapping a semi-hoofed foot, Sid was doing his best to seem intimidating, though we were matched in height. I smiled at him. "Hey, Sid. How've you been?"

"You're moving too slow," he snapped, sounding officious until his voice cracked and his words ended on a squeal, which he tried to cover by jangling his giant key ring. "This gate gets locked at sundown, girly, and doesn't open again till dawn. No exceptions! Especially not for a friend of Rafe's."

"He took his gun back, huh?" I asked, trying to sound sympathetic.

He slammed the dead bolt home, twisted three keys into three different locks, and then trotted off, grumbling under his breath the whole time.

"Good night, Sid," I called after him, and then steered the kids toward the brick building near the river's edge, where my dad and Hagen lived. As we navigated the narrow street single file, the orphans relaxed and got their swagger back. Maybe someday the slightest hint of a threat wouldn't throw them into high alert, but we weren't there yet. "Who wants to hear a story?" I asked.

"About the tiger-man?" Tasha asked as we crossed the town square at the center of the compound. People lounged in rocking chairs along the boardwalk that edged the square, laughing and retelling the events of the day. They waved as we passed.

I returned their greetings and then answered Tasha, "Nope. This story is about a dragon-man."

"Did the brave little girl kill him?" Rose asked.

Sage pushed between the others, trying to get closer to me. "Or the wild boy?"

"Nope," I said, warming to the task. "This time it took the whole compound, including the infected people who'd been driven out . . . humans and manimals, all working together."

· THIRTY-ONE ·

What a difference a week made. The manimals gathered around me in the town square had all tested clear for the virus. I had to believe that Rafe would too, but I didn't know for sure. Not yet.

He'd left Moline the night we'd arrived to take twenty tubes of the antigen to Chicago. He was worried about Dromo, who'd been infected for years. Rafe wanted to get him the antigen as soon as possible. My dad said it would take about twenty hours to get to Chicago on a bike and twenty hours back. Rafe had been gone six days. I got that he'd have to spend a couple of days tracking down his friends, but hopefully he was on his way back to me now.

The sun had just disappeared behind the wall when my dad pushed open the double doors of the old brick building that was our home. Well, the second floor was home, anyway. The gutted first floor was something else entirely.

"Thank you for coming out to celebrate this momentous occasion with us," my dad said, booming like a ringmaster, and then he dropped the act with a laugh. "But you're too early. The sun just set."

"Come on, Mack," a voice in the crowd cajoled. "It's dark enough."

"You won't get the full effect," my dad protested. "Come back later."

"Please, Mack," a woman called. "I'm letting the kids stay up just to see it."

Two little voices echoed, "Please!"

"I think you're outnumbered, hon," Hagen called from the doorway. Like the other buildings in the town center, ours had the look of a lush ruin with its crumbling mortar and vine-draped facade.

"Oh, all right," my dad relented. That got him a smattering of applause, so he bowed. He was in his element here, which explained why he kept coming back to the zone all those years even with the stakes so high.

As for me, I might never get totally comfortable with the Wild West feel of Moline or hearing the howls and chittering of ferals at night, and sometimes I did long for a sparkling-white bathroom where the hot water never ran out . . . But still, this was home.

"You sure, Mack?" Hagen teased. "We can send everybody away and wait for the perfect moment."

"Go ahead." Dad waved her on. "Flip the switch."

With a chuckle, Hagen disappeared into the building and, a moment later, those of us gathered outside gasped in unison. Above the double doors, the words "Mack's Place" strobed to life for the first time ever — in neon cursive, no less. A hack found the sign on one of his trips into the zone and sold it to my dad for a month's worth of meals. And it was worth every crumb!

Applause broke out, followed by whistles and whinnies and roars. I clapped and cheered along with my neighbors but then scanned the edges of the square for a familiar head of light-brown hair. If Rafe wasn't back by tomorrow, I'd officially start worrying. Even if he couldn't get infected twice, there were so many ways to die in the zone. Maybe he —

This.

This was why my dad had kept me in the dark about his life as a fetch. To keep me from imagining the worst every time he ventured east. Worrying wouldn't bring Rafe back any faster and it wouldn't keep him safe. I might as well get to work, welcoming people to Mack's, our newly electrified social club. It was the first of its kind in the Feral Zone . . . at least, as far as we knew.

Inside, the century-old building had been stripped to its bones — exposed brick, old timber, and metal pipes. Hagen had turned the front section into a casual dining area with comfy chairs clustered around low tables, all scavenged from abandoned buildings. A three-sided bar made from reclaimed window shutters took up the center of the space, and behind that was the so-called casino — really just a roulette wheel, craps table, and a smattering of card tables. The whole building could fit into a corner of the Moline train station, which functioned as the compound's town hall, marketplace, and cafeteria all rolled into one. But, because our social club was smaller, it made for a cozy alternative to the racket of the station.

My dad went to check on the kitchen staff as they prepped for a busy night. Jia, Trader, and Sage pivoted on their barstools, thin legs dangling, as they pestered the bartender for glasses of carbonated water. They'd all been adopted by Moline families, yet the kids liked working as food runners and table bussers. They liked the hubbub and music and how my dad paid them in meals.

"Ev's here!" Jia yelled at my elbow and leapt from her stool. She flew through the open door and into the center square, where a jeep pulled up with Everson behind the wheel, Bearly at his side, and two more line guards in back. He'd come every evening since the night the lionesses arrived at the compound on foot.

"Hey, punk." Everson climbed out of the jeep and swung Jia up for a hug. He hardly had time to set her back on her feet before a certain lioness charged past me and ran straight into his arms.

Mahari slid her golden-furred arms around his neck, looking as fierce as ever in a red halter dress that hugged her curves. As they locked lips, Jia dipped a hand into Everson's pocket.

"Bearly!" I shouted as she swung out the jeep.

She twisted to follow my frantic pointing to Jia, who'd slipped behind the wheel. Bearly dove across the seats just as the jeep's engine roared to life. She knocked Jia's right hand off the gearshift while prying the key fob from her left.

Watching Bearly wrestle with a determined orphan was funny, but not as funny as the leaping exit made by the two backseat guards. They hit the ground and skittered away from the rocking vehicle. The guard on the left looked so alarmed that — my laugh fizzled in my throat and I blinked, certain my eyes had it wrong. I stumbled toward the line guard with the satiny dark skin and springing curls. Anna! Here. On the wrong side of the wall.

"Annapolis Brown," I cried and dashed for her.

She bounced with excitement. "Surprise!"

And then we were screaming and hugging in front of the club's open windows. The people inside turned in their seats to stare at us and then, threat assessed, returned to their conversations. I pulled back to gape at her gray fatigues. "I can't believe you're a line guard."

"I'm not," she said with a laugh.

"She's a peace offering," the other guard informed me as she rounded the jeep. On closer inspection, she wasn't a line guard either, despite the head-to-toe body armor. Director Spurling gave a small shrug and added, "Or a hostess gift. Take your pick."

Hopefully that meant she wasn't here to arrest me for posting another video.

"I'm here for the whole week," Anna explained. "On Arsenal. As her intern." She tipped her head toward Spurling.

"Why are you here?" I asked Spurling.

Before she could answer, my dad limped outside. He took in our little group with interest. "You made it across the river, Director Spurling."

Guess her line guard attire hadn't fooled him. "Did you come to talk about your census idea?" I asked.

She nodded. "Among other things."

Everson spoke up then while keeping one arm draped around Mahari's waist. "Director Spurling worked with the State Department to renegotiate Titan's contract. We'll still secure the quarantine line, but without the bloodshed, and we'll oversee relief missions."

I turned a stunned look on him. "Relief missions?"

"Distributing the antigen throughout the zone. Pro bono," he added casually — like the for-free part should go without saying. As it should.

Mahari shook off Everson's one-armed embrace and glared. "You think we're going to let line guards take over the zone? Think again, human."

Everson shot Spurling a sidelong look. "Told you."

"You did," she agreed and turned to Mahari. "And that is why the president signed an executive order yesterday, making the Feral Zone a US territory. You'll need to set up a governing body for the zone as a whole and appoint someone to act as a liaison with the West. That way your people can coordinate the relief missions with Titan."

Everson held out a hand to Mahari. "Know anyone who'd make a good ambassador?" he asked.

She entwined her fingers with his. "Ambassador is a step down from queen," she informed him.

"True," he agreed, tugging her close. "But you'll get to negotiate with officials from the West and scare the spit out of them — all for the good of the zone."

Mahari's eyes gleamed. "I'd like that," she purred.

His lips twitched. "I figured."

The two of them strolled away then, before I could ask Everson how his mother was doing. The stress of her arrest and exposure to the outdoors pushed her germaphobia to a delusional level. In custody, Chairman Prejean had a complete mental breakdown and got carted off to a psychiatric facility — a place she wouldn't be leaving anytime soon. According to Everson, she'd been judged too "mentally unfit" to stand trial.

Spurling told Anna to take a break while she toured the compound with my dad, so we settled into a corner of the dining area and caught up. But Anna was having a hard time staying focused — not that I blamed her. Watching her flinch and suppress gasps over the manimals in the club reminded me how shocked I'd been when I'd first arrived in Moline. My dad's stories hadn't prepared me for the sight of a real live chimpacabra any more than my video had prepared Anna for Sid playing the piano in the corner or the waiter infected with badger. Some things you just had to see for yourself.

Now she was staring past me toward the open door, lips parted. "Oh my," she drawled.

The atmosphere in the room changed, became charged, and without turning I knew Rafe had finally made it home. I twisted in my seat and there he was, leaning against the doorjamb, his eyes shockingly blue in the dim light. Even bluer: the stick that hung on a cord around his neck. A Ferae test like those that everyone in the Chicago court had been forced to wear, putting their health status on full display. A red test stick meant the person had Ferae. Electric blue meant —

"You tested clear!" I gasped and got to my feet, only then realizing that a small part of me had believed he might be the one person resistant to the antigen.

"Yep." He dropped his duffle by the bar and strolled closer. "And not a single side effect."

If Rafe was cured, then his ban on kissing had just reached its expiration date. Meaning, we could. Finally. All I had to do was throw myself into his arms and press my mouth to his. And I would . . . if I was a lioness and not standing in the middle of Mack's Place with dozens of witnesses, including Anna. He was the wild boy who lived in a castle, right out of my bedtime stories. Our first kiss should be special. Of course, looking the way he did and living on his own in the zone for so many years, Rafe had probably kissed dozens of girls. A kiss would be nothing to him. Just a prelude to —

"Silky," he called softly as if coaxing me down from a tree. "Where'd you go?"

"N-nowhere," I stammered. "I just —"

"It's not a trick," he said, lifting the blue test stick. "If that's what you're thinking, I don't blame you. First time we met, I was stealing medicine off Arsenal. You've seen me lie, and I'm guessing you know I'll scam, cheat, and fight dirty if it'll buy me another day on this earth. But you also gotta know, I'll never lie to you. It's the real deal, I swear." He let the test stick fall from his fingers. "But I took a blood test too. That's even more accurate, right?"

I nodded quickly, eyes prickling.

"Then there you go. Science doesn't lie." He held out his arms as if offering himself up for inspection — just like he'd done the day we met on Arsenal. "I'm as good as new."

"No," I said softly. "You're better."

"I knew he'd be fun," said a voice from behind us. We turned to find Director Spurling watching us, a corner of her mouth quirked up. "I was rooting for you," she told Rafe.

"Thanks," he said and then frowned. "Who're you?"

"This is Director Spurling from the Department of Biohazard Defense." As I made the introduction, Anna popped up so fast, I had to laugh. "And this is my best friend —"

"Anna," Rafe said, surprising Anna and me. He smirked. "I remember everything you say, silky. And a few things you don't say — with words, at least." His attention slid past me to where my dad stood, not smiling. Rafe shifted, suddenly uncomfortable. "Hey, Mack."

"Did you see?" I asked quickly, pointing to the blue stick dangling against Rafe's chest. "He's cured."

"Functionally cured," my dad corrected, using the language that Everson had drummed into our heads last night when he'd announced that all the manimals in Moline had tested clear for Ferae.

"So, Lane," Spurling cut in, "have I mentioned that your second video, like the first, went viral?"

"It did?" I asked warily.

"Yes. But this one seems to have done what it was supposed to. It humanized the people living over here. All of them."

"Really?" A smile pulled at my lips. "That's wonderful."

"The girl who ended the quarantine . . ." Rafe said with amazement, then turned to my father. "How'd you know?"

My dad took my hand and squeezed it. "I had a feeling," he said. "And if not you, then someone in your generation was going to find a way out of this mess. I'm proud it was you."

"Let's not get ahead of ourselves," Spurling cut in. "Until we treat the sick, vaccinate the well, and contain the diseased animals, the quarantine will stay in place, and it's going to be harder than ever to maintain. Now that people know the zone isn't one giant graveyard, they'll want to start searching for their missing relatives — as in, right now. They're not going to wait for the quarantine to lift. And since no one thinks it's a good idea to pump more money into the line patrol, I proposed that we legalize fetching."

"How will that stop people from trying to break quarantine?" I asked. If I learned that my mom was still alive and living across the river, nothing would stop me from trying to find her. The answer came to me then. "Instead of fetching things left behind, you'll fetch people."

"Just their names and locations for now," Spurling said. "If the government offers a legal way to get the information they want, people will take it. And that, Delaney, is what I came to ask your father: if he'd consider a job as a government-sanctioned fetch."

I turned to my dad. "And you said . . ."

"That my fetching days are behind me," he said ruefully, tapping his leg with his cane. "But I did say that I know two people who might be interested in running the operation from this side of the wall."

He looked from me to Rafe, and I remembered that sense of awe I felt seeing Aaron and Carmen reunited — especially knowing that I'd helped make it happen.

"How're you going to pay us?" Rafe asked Director Spurling.

"You figure that out," she told us, "and tell me your price tomorrow."

"You're coming back to Moline?" I asked.

"Come to Arsenal," she instructed. "I'll be staying there for awhile to oversee its transition to a government facility — lab and all."

Everson stepped into the club then. After greeting Rafe and congratulating him on his blue test stick, he turned to Director Spurling. "It's getting dark, Director. We should head back to base . . . unless you want to spend the night in Moline," he added hopefully.

She cut him a look. "Not tonight, Mr. Cruz. Find Bearly and start the jeep."

As Anna and I hugged good-bye, she whispered, "I want a boy with tiger blood."

Over her shoulder, I saw Rafe smirk. Next time I met up with Anna, I'd tell her about manimal supersenses. I waved as she headed out the door with Everson.

Spurling was right behind them when she glanced back. "I'll see you two tomorrow?"

Rafe and I met eyes and smiled in agreement. "You will," I told her.

"I've never had a partner before," Rafe commented as we watched her go. Without thinking, we found each other's hands, only to drop them again when my dad gave us a questioning look from behind his wire-rimmed glasses.

"We — uh —" I said, my cheeks growing hot. "We're together."

Beside me, Rafe seemed to brace for my dad's reaction, which ended up being no more than an unconcerned nod.

Rafe frowned. "What? You predicted this too?"

"Let's just say, I'm not surprised," my dad said as his eyes lit with laughter.

He had only himself to blame since he'd been telling each of us about the other through stories for years. "We're going to go check out your new sign now that's it's getting dark," I told him.

Taking up Rafe's hand once more, I led him toward the stairs.

"The sign's outside," my dad called after us. "Where're you going?"

"The roof," I said over my shoulder. "For a bird's-eye view."

Two staircases later, Rafe and I stepped onto the flat expanse of the club's roof. Someday, Hagen hoped to turn it into a rooftop garden, but for now it offered a view of the river and not much else. I propped open the door with a cinder block to buy myself a minute as my eyes adjusted to the darkness. Rafe, with the advantage of night vision, strolled toward the parapet, navigating around rain barrels and solar generators. He put a boot on the edge and leaned over. "Cool sign."

I joined him, more amazed at the glowing island in the middle of the river. From here, the lights on Arsenal made the base look like a summer carnival, while on the far bank, the Titan wall disappeared in the darkness. Maybe someday it would disappear for good.

"So how will it work?" Rafe asked, turning to me. "The client gives us a name and the last place their relative was seen and we go looking for him? You know the chances of finding those people are zero to zilch." His grin flashed white in the darkness. "I'm all in."

Of course he'd throw himself into the business of fetching people wholeheartedly. He knew what was at stake. He knew how quickly time slipped away from the infected and how a single day could mean the difference between sane and feral. Rafe also knew what it felt like to learn that a loved one had been alive all along and that knowledge had been kept from you. Of course he wanted to reunite family members.

"I think we should work backward," I said, hugging myself against the cool night air. "Visit as many compounds as we can and get the names of everyone living in the area and where they're originally from. That'll give us a master list to work off."

Rafe's hand came up, cradling my chin. His fingers warm on my skin. "We? You can be the contact person. You don't have to leave Moline."

"I want to explore the zone with you." I kept my tone low-key even though I was excited at the idea of venturing into uncharted territory and of spending the time with him. "We're partners. I'll have your back."

"No, silky," Rafe said, pulling me in close. "You have all of me."

His fingers tightened and suddenly he was kissing me. Soft and slow at first, lips barely touching, as if to give me the chance to change my mind. Moonlight bounced off his eyes and made them flash hollow-green as they stared into my own, checking my reaction. The intensity of his look and the warmth pouring off him sent a wave of fire through me. I wanted more. Needed more.

I rolled onto my toes, pushed my fingers through his hair, raking his scalp with my nails, and took our kiss from sweet to serious. Rafe froze, and then his arms tightened and he molded me to him. We fit with stunning perfection. Inhaling his scent — sweat and pine and woodsmoke — I finally got it. I got why people loved old-fashioned kissing, despite the germs. Our bodies defied the boundaries of science and flowed together like two rivers joining.

Rafe drew back and brushed a finger across my lips. "What are you smiling at?"

"I'm smiling?"

"You are."

"Well," I said, conceding, "I guess because as far as happily-ever-afters go, I lucked out."

"You're not about to say 'the end,' are you?" he teased. "Because it isn't. Not for us."

"Not even close," I agreed.

· ACKNOWLEDGMENTS ·

It's finally done. Whew, and then some. I don't know why it took me so long to finish this particular book. Not that I've ever been a fast writer. I'm a backtracker and an overthinker and, for the first time, a worrier. I got frozen while writing this one and I can't explain why. I just did. And that is why I'm so very grateful to the people who cheered me on even as I kept tripping myself up.

Here is an incomplete list of those I'd like to thank:

My brilliant agent, Josh Adams, with a shout-out to his business partner and wife, the fabulous Tracey Schatvet Adams. You took me on when I was an unknown quantity and have given me support and sage advice every step of the way. Thank you!

Next, the silver lining to having taken so long to write *Undaunted* is that I got to work with two amazing editors: Nick Eliopulos and Orlando Dos Reis. Thank you both for your encouraging words and spot-on story notes. Specifically, I thank Nick for helping me figure out how to launch the story in an exciting way (hopefully!) and Orlando for making my manuscript shine and for "strengthening the connective narrative tissue between Books 1 and 2." (Loved the concept and your notes that helped me accomplish it.)

Everyone at Scholastic, you do such an amazing job of getting books into young readers' hands and I'm grateful for it both personally and for society at large. Your efforts make the world a better place. It's an honor to work with you all. Plus, extra thanks to Christopher Stengel for designing my books — all of them. Seeing his gorgeous cover design for the first time is always one of my favorite moments of the publishing process.

My critique partners, Joanna Volavka and Debbie Kraus, who gave me invaluable feedback on *Undaunted*. Extra love to Debbie for seeing me through four books now, being a dear friend, and never pulling her punches when giving notes. I couldn't be more grateful.

Merle Reskin for her unwavering support and friendship and for the use of the charmed Thatchitty Cottage. My muse loves it there.

The Ragdale Foundation, which to me equals a productive writing retreat and the best summer camp ever, even though all four of my residencies occurred in the dead of winter. No matter the time of year, Ragdale is a magical place. While there, I always get lots written and get to know artists of all stripes, all against a background of idyllic prairie.

My husband, Bob, who inspires me by continuing to wrangle with creative work even when he's feeling the most stuck and for being all I could ever want in a partner. I'm buoyed every day, knowing that he's in my corner.

Declan, Vivienne, and Connor, who are the lights of my life, my beloved beta readers, and the reason I started writing for tweens and teens.

My dad, Cornelius Moynihan — Connie, to his friends — who didn't live to see me finish *Undaunted* but never doubted that I would. He read early drafts of all my books, methodically corrected my grammar, and excitedly discussed all the sci-fi elements in my work. Not surprising. He was a renowned scientist after all and the big geek who got me hooked on the genre at a really young age. I miss you, Dad. So very much.

Finally, my readers. Thank you from the bottom of my heart for waiting for *Undaunted* and just for being readers in general. Between us, you're my very favorite sort of people.

· ABOUT THE AUTHOR ·

Kat Falls lives with her husband and three children in Evanston, Illinois, where she teaches screenwriting at Northwestern University. She is the author of *Dark Life*, *Rip Tide*, and *Inhuman*. Follow her online at katfalls.com.